Growing up near the beach, **Annie West** spent lots of time observing tall, burnished lifeguards—early research! Now she spends her days fantasising about gorgeous men and their love-lives. Annie has been a reader all her life. She also loves travel, long walks, good company and great food. You can contact her at annie@annie-west.com or via PO Box 1041, Warners Bay, NSW 2282, Australia.

Joss Wood loves books and travelling—especially to the wild places of Southern Africa and, well… anywhere! She's a wife, mum to two teenagers, and slave to two cats. After a career in local economic development she now writes full-time. Joss is a member of Romance Writers of America and Romance Writers of South Africa.

THE KING'S BRIDE BY ARRANGEMENT

ANNIE WEST

HOW TO UNDO THE PROUD BILLIONAIRE

JOSS WOOD

MILLS & BOON

First Published in Great Britain 2020
by Mills & Boon, an imprint of HarperCollins*Publishers*
1 London Bridge Street, London, SE1 9GF

The King's Bride by Arrangement © 2020 Annie West

How to Undo the Proud Billionaire © 2020 Joss Wood

ISBN: 978-0-263-28228-3

MIX
Paper from
responsible sources
FSC® C007454

This book is produced from independently certified FSC™ paper
to ensure responsible forest management.
For more information visit www.harpercollins.co.uk/green.

Printed and bound in Spain
by CPI, Barcelona

THE KING'S BRIDE BY ARRANGEMENT

ANNIE WEST

This book is for all the people who read *Revelations of a Secret Princess* and asked if King Paul would get his own story.

Thank you for your enthusiasm!

I had a wonderful time writing this. I hope you enjoy it as much as I did.

CHAPTER ONE

'PRINCESS EVA OF TARENTIA.'

The chamberlain projected his voice across the glittering crowd that filled the ballroom's gilded antechamber.

Heads turned, keen eyes sizing her up, from her brown hair, piled high, past the sapphire drop earrings to the ball gown of royal blue.

Eva felt their stares, as she always did, like hundreds of tiny pinpricks. But at twenty-four she'd learned to accept the public's interest. She no longer shrank from the limelight as she had when young.

Besides, there was only one person here whose opinion she cared about.

There he was, chatting to a blonde in silver sequins. At the chamberlain's words, he looked up to where she stood on the staircase above the throng. His mouth lifted in a smile.

Eva's heart tripped a beat then hammered faster. She felt the pulse high in her throat.

Even from this distance Paul did that to her. She was too far away to feel the full impact of those stunning indigo eyes but his smile always unravelled her. From the day at fifteen when she'd first seen him, thundering down the polo field, so athletic, so handsome and so *nice*. After the match her brother Leo, who'd been on the opposing team, had introduced them and Eva had been instantly smitten.

Because the then Prince Paul of St Ancilla hadn't thought it uncool to talk to his acquaintance's little sister. He hadn't seemed to notice her braces or the lingering spots that had erupted thanks to her monthly cycle. He'd been kind and friendly even when she'd been tongue-tied.

Eva had been in love with him ever since.

She moved down the staircase with practised grace, keeping her chin high. Woe betide any princess who couldn't descend a grand staircase without looking at her feet. Even in a full-length dress and high heels.

She reached the floor and pinned on her social smile for the St Ancillan Prime Minister, who enquired if she'd had a good journey. As the flight from Tarentia in northern Europe to the Mediterranean Island of St Ancilla wasn't long, the question was a formality. Yet Eva felt herself relax. After four years of regular visits to St Ancilla, she and the Prime Minister were well acquainted.

'Here's His Majesty now.' The Prime Minister turned and inclined his head in a bow.

Instantly Eva's smile solidified, the muscles in her cheeks stretching taut as she fought the urge to grin up into Paul's face. The inevitable rush of excitement she felt around him always undermined her and she strove not to reveal her feelings. It was never a problem with anyone else but around Paul it was a constant worry.

Because she felt so much while he felt so little.

Her heart beat an urgent tattoo and moisture glazed the back of her neck as he neared. She angled her head up to meet his gaze. Eva's breath released in a sigh of resignation as she met those amazing dark-blue eyes.

What had she expected? That absence would make the heart grow fonder? That in the months since they'd last seen each other he'd realised what a treasure she was?

That he'd developed feelings for her?

Or, impossibly, that she'd read the eager heat of desire in his face?

Deep inside, disappointment stirred.

Paul's easy smile was the same one he gave the Prime Minister. The same one he'd worn when he'd tilted his head to listen to the blonde siren in shimmery silver.

The blonde who'd defied royal protocol and stood so close to the King it was a wonder a discreet bodyguard hadn't hauled her away. Eva had noticed and had to repress a spike of unreasonable jealousy.

'Princess Eva. You look as delightful as ever.' Paul's deep voice tugged at her vulnerable heart.

He took her hand and lifted it to his mouth, and Eva fought to stop her expression betraying her. Her forehead twitched and the corners of her mouth compressed with the effort not to grin with delight.

As it was, she hoped Paul couldn't see the way her nipples hardened into needy peaks just because he touched her.

He was everything a king should be. Hard working, decent, dedicated and caring of his people. She loved all those things about him. But, even after knowing him for nine years, it was the angle of his high-cut cheekbones, the handsome line of jaw and nose and his vibrant aura of energetic, virile maleness that got to her every time. Even the way his coal-black hair had a tendency to flop over his forehead turned her insides to mush.

Reluctantly Eva tugged her hand from his, too conscious that a tiny change in his grip would reveal the too-rapid flutter of her pulse at her wrist.

She caught a glimpse of something in his eyes. Annoyance? Surprise? But of course it was gone in an instant. Royals were trained to conceal rather than reveal emotions.

It was tempting to wonder if he was disappointed at her withdrawal. But she was a pragmatist, despite her romantic feelings for him. She forced herself to face the truth. Paul might be surprised at her withdrawal but not saddened.

'Thank you, Your Majesty.' Meticulously, she used his title, as protocol demanded of their first meeting in six months. She sank to the polished floor in a deep curtsey.

'Paul, please.'

'Thank you, Paul.'

Protocol also decreed that, given their circumstances, she could address him by his first name in public, with his permission.

She bit down hard on the impulse to gush that he looked terrific himself.

The dress uniform of black, navy and gold showcased his tall, upright figure. He should have looked distant and untouchable in his regalia but instead he was mouth-wateringly attractive. Her fingers tingled with the desire to reach out and touch him. To follow the line of those wide shoulders and down across his powerful chest.

Paul didn't hold out his hand to help her rise. Why should he when she'd just tugged away from him? Yet Eva noted the fact, just as she noted the hint of a frown marring his brow.

A little shiver of premonition scrolled down her spine.

Now she stood before him, she realised his smile looked pinched. It certainly didn't reach his eyes.

'You had a good flight, despite the delay?'

What was that note in his voice? Not censure, not annoyance, but definitely something strained.

Once more Eva experienced that inching shiver of disquiet. This time it felt like a chill cascading down her vertebrae.

'Yes, it was fine.' She'd only just arrived in time to change and meet him here at the ball rather than in private. 'A mechanical problem held us up on the tarmac. But the flight itself was uneventful.'

Paul nodded. 'You're safely here. That's the main thing.'

Yet, reading his expression, Eva felt something else was going on. Something she didn't yet understand.

Not that she expected him to confide in her. They didn't have that sort of relationship, no matter how much she wished they did.

'Shall we?' He lifted one hand and, after a moment's hesitation in which she marshalled all her resources to appear cool, Eva put her hand on his.

Instantly heat rushed through her bloodstream from the point of contact and spread all through her body.

The one mercy was that Eva didn't blush. Paul and all the people around them had no idea of her body's hectic response to his touch.

He turned and they walked together across the room. The throng of guests parted to make way, men bowing and women curtseying. Eva noticed more than one woman followed Paul's progress with longing in their eyes.

Before them a pair of gigantic gilded doors was flung open onto the ballroom. The blaze of light from rows of chandeliers, reflected in a wall of mirrors, dazzled. But, as she'd been trained to do, Eva entered the room with head held high, conscious of the swell of the crowd following them.

Paul led her to a point dead-centre under the biggest and brightest of the chandeliers. They stopped on the ornate star that marked the middle of the exquisite, heritage-listed parquetry floor.

Under the brilliant light she read lines bracketing his mouth that hadn't been there six months ago. And around his eyes was a look of tension.

Impulsively, Eva squeezed his hand. 'Paul, are you—?'

'The ball will be opened,' boomed the chamberlain, 'by His Majesty King Paul of Ancilla and his fiancée, Princess Eva of Tarentia.'

Applause filled the room as every eye focused on them.

For once Eva didn't care. She leaned closer to the man before her, sure now that something was amiss.

'What is it?' she whispered. 'Something's wrong.'

For an instant his eyes widened, as if in surprise that she'd noticed, then his mouth curled up in a crooked smile that didn't look in the least amused. 'Not now, Eva. Not here. Later.'

Then King Paul, the man she'd been betrothed to for four long years, clasped her hand in his and curled his other arm around her back. Heat shimmered everywhere he touched and Eva froze, fighting hard not to respond.

For a second longer they stood, toe to toe, gazes locked, separated by the precise distance decreed by royal decorum. Then, as the music swelled, Paul swept her into a waltz with the superb grace of a natural athlete and all the warmth of an automaton.

Paul danced the last dance of the night with Karen Villiers, head of the new software company he'd lured to set up headquarters in the capital city's business park. Lured with tax incentives designed to make St Ancilla an appealing long-term investment prospect.

Right now, though, it seemed it wasn't St Ancilla that she saw as appealing. It was him.

Keeping a smile on his face, Paul put a little distance between himself and Karen's sinuously seductive body. A curvaceous blonde, she was very attractive. He hadn't missed how her minimalist silver dress showed off her spectacular body.

But he wasn't in the market for a girlfriend. Not even a dalliance, especially under the glare of public attention.

He wasn't free. He had a fiancée! Here, at the ball.

The thought of Eva tightened the iron bands clamping his skull and the dull pounding in his temples intensified.

It had been a long day, a long month, and the day was far from over. He couldn't allow it to end without talking to his fiancée. No matter how little he relished the prospect.

There'd been a moment, as he'd looked up and seen her at the head of the staircase, when he'd been glad she was here. Not because it meant that at last they could have the interview he'd been dreading but because it was good to see her.

The feeling hadn't lasted.

Eva being here meant unpalatable duty, even if it was for the best.

Then there was the way she'd reacted to him or, more precisely, not reacted. As usual. In her teens she'd been shy but engaging, and everything he'd heard about her from Leo and others indicated she was warm and generous. But in adulthood—with Paul, at least—it was another story.

To others she was charming and gracious, but with him cool and distant. To the extent that he'd wondered why she'd agreed to their engagement. Except he knew the answer to that. It had been arranged by their parents and she'd been left little choice.

It rankled that she didn't care for him. That she'd never have chosen him for herself.

No wonder she held herself aloof. Never unfriendly, but guarded. Distant.

Unlike the woman leaning too close in his arms.

For a moment Paul wondered what it would be like to accept the implicit invitation in Karen Villiers's wide eyes and sultry body. And instantly stifled the thought.

Honour dictated there would be no other women while he was betrothed. Even if he and his fiancée had never got more intimate than him kissing her hand.

Fire shot to Paul's belly as the effects of four years of celibacy made themselves felt.

That was one thing that would change after tonight.

Was it any wonder he felt on edge? He was torn between

the almost impossible demands of St Ancilla, and the need
to preserve an illusion that all was well here, while keeping
a lid on natural masculine desires. After four years of con-
tinuous strain he felt perilously close to the breaking point.

As the music reached its closing bars his gaze sought
Eva. There she was, dancing with the famous film director
who was here checking out locations for his next movie.
Paul's staff had labelled him difficult yet the guy was laughing at something Eva had said.

A dart of something sharp pierced Paul's chest as he
saw Eva's answering smile. It transformed her composed
features into something altogether different.

'So, Your Majesty,' said a throaty feminine voice. 'I
thought I'd end the night at the new night club everyone's
talking about. Is there a chance I'll see you there?'

He looked into Karen Villiers's face and read the invitation in her saucy smile. Not just to a night club but to
something far more intimate.

'I'm afraid not. I have further commitments tonight.'

Once more his gaze turned towards his fiancée, still
deep in conversation with her dance partner, even though
the music had ceased. Paul's brow twitched. What did she
find so fascinating about a man so famously self-absorbed?
Her slim frame was tilted towards him as if she drank in
his every word.

'Ah, of course. I'd forgotten Princess Eva is here now.'

Paul turned his attention back to the woman before him.
Did she really think he'd lope off to a rendezvous with her,
leaving his fiancée in the palace? Or that he'd been available for an affair until the Princess had arrived, as if out
of sight was out of mind?

Suddenly Ms Villiers's sex appeal dimmed.

Eva might not care for him much but they understood
each other and had grown up with the same values, the
same sense of dedication to duty.

He supposed it was remarkable in his case, given the example of his appalling father. Yet maybe it was because of him that Paul had leaned the other way, choosing integrity over dishonesty. Plus, there had been the influence of his mother and tutors, all determined to make him the sort of ruler his father had never been.

Paul realised he was scowling and rearranged his features into a smile. 'It's kind of you to invite me. I hope you enjoy yourself. Now, if you'll excuse me, I must go.'

It took an inordinate amount of time for the ballroom to empty. Finally he was alone with his fiancée.

Eva stood, as still as one of the statues on the wide terrace outside. Only her eyes, an unremarkable smudge of colour between grey and blue, hinted that she wasn't as sanguine as she appeared.

Paul recalled her surprising hint of concern before the ball and wondered if she'd guessed his discomfort. That would be a first. They'd never been close enough to share secrets or develop a sense of intimacy.

He drew a slow breath. He wasn't looking forward to this.

'Do you fancy a nightcap, Eva? It's been a long evening, but we need to talk.'

Did he imagine that she drew in a sharp breath? Certainly her breasts rose high beneath the shimmery fabric of her royal blue ball gown.

'Thank you. I'd like that.'

She turned and walked with him, nodding to the members of staff waiting outside the ballroom ready to come in and restore it to its usual pristine splendour. She paused before the chamberlain and the chief housekeeper, congratulating them on the success of the event and the staff's efforts tonight.

It was the sort of thing Paul usually did. And it proved how easily Eva fitted into his world. On the face of it she made the perfect partner. He had no doubt that she'd support her husband in every way she could, sharing the burdens of royalty with grace and goodwill.

His gaze snagged on the pale shoulder bared by her dress and the sweep of her slender neck up to her neat chin. Standing beside her, he was aware of her suddenly as a desirable woman rather than a life partner in a dynastic marriage neither of them had asked for.

Then she turned, caught him watching, and the remnants of her smile died.

One thing was clear. Eva didn't desire him. Sometimes he wondered if she even approved of him. Did she think he was tarred with the same brush as his dead father? Bitterness coated Paul's tongue at the thought of his old man, repugnant in so many ways and still the source of most of Paul's problems.

But he was being unfair to Eva. His fiancée might be cool and self-contained but she'd never been disapproving or disagreeable. Simply distant.

Paul gestured for her to precede him into the King's study. It had changed since his father's day, devoid now of the massive gilded desk and rows of unopened books. In their place was a modern desk, filing cabinets, framed maps of the country and a couple of comfortable lounges, which was where he led her.

'What will you have?' he asked as he un-stoppered a single malt.

'Whisky would be good, thanks. With a touch of soda.'

Paul shot a startled look at his betrothed. 'Whisky?' The most he'd ever seen her drink was a glass of wine over dinner.

Eva shrugged and once more his attention was drawn to the expanse of pearly skin left uncovered by the gown that sat off her shoulders. It wasn't revealing in the way Karen

Villiers's dress had been—blatantly provocative—yet Paul felt a tangled thread of desire snarl in his belly.

Tonight Eva's air of untouchability was tempered by something else. Something deeply feminine and alluring.

As for untouchable, he recalled the feel of her in his arms, poised and regal, yet disturbingly warm and unquestionably feminine.

Four years of celibacy...

That must be the reason.

Abruptly he turned and poured two whiskies. Large ones.

Dutch courage?

He told himself this would be straightforward. Yet he had to tread carefully so as not to turn a perfectly sensible idea into a diplomatic nightmare.

'Please,' he gestured to the leather sofas, 'have a seat.'

With one last unreadable look his way, Eva subsided in a wave of royal-blue silk. The colour suited her, he decided as he leaned forward, passing her drink.

As ever she took it carefully, her fingers never touching his.

Paul jerked upright, teeth clenching. As if he needed a reminder that he wasn't her personal choice of husband! She might not say it out loud but her body language made it abundantly clear.

How on earth did she expect to get through their wedding night? By closing her eyes and thinking of her duty as a Tarentian princess?

He swung away and stalked to the window. Floodlights illuminated the perimeter of the palace gardens in the distance. A far cry from when his father had been King and they'd spent a fortune lighting up all the ornate gardens throughout the night, wasting precious energy.

'Paul? What is it? You said you'd explain. Is everything... Are you all right?'

He spun on his heel, surprised by the note of concern in Eva's voice. Or had he imagined it?

'I'm fine.' He lifted the tumbler of whisky and swallowed, letting the fiery warmth burn its way down. 'But I have something important to discuss.'

Now it came to the moment, this was more difficult than he'd anticipated, though he was doing the right thing.

It struck him how weary he was of always doing the right thing. Of the onerous treadmill on which he ran, juggling the demands of his nation, his family and his father's creditors. For four years he'd done his best, achieved things he'd never believed possible, snatching success from the jaws of disaster. His father, dead from a massive stroke less than six months after his abdication, hadn't lived with the consequences of his actions. Nor had his mother returned to St Ancilla to support her son. Instead she lived a life of genteel retirement in Paris.

'I'm listening.' Eva was ramrod-straight, the glass cupped in her hands.

Because she feared what he might say? Yet it was Eva who'd benefit from what he must do, Paul who would pay the consequences.

He hefted a deep breath, looked down at the drink in his hands then up at his betrothed.

'I'm releasing you from our engagement, Eva. It's over.'

CHAPTER TWO

'OVER?' EVA STARED up at Paul, disbelieving her ears. Surely he didn't mean what it sounded like?

Yet the determined thrust of his chin and the tight grip of his fingers around the crystal tumbler mocked her desperate hopes. He looked like a man facing an unpalatable duty.

'You're jilting me?'

Unbelievable to discover her voice still worked. Her throat constricted and her lungs hurt. She couldn't seem to drag in enough air. Yet somehow she managed to sound utterly calm. It was as if she was listening to some other woman.

'That's a very emotional word, Eva. I'm not *abandoning* you. Just giving you your freedom.'

Her heart battered so hard against her ribs, it was a wonder he couldn't hear it.

But he looked too caught up in his own thoughts to read her emotions. His expression was severe, drawn tight with tension, disapproval or hauteur. She didn't know which. Maybe all three.

Because she'd dared to question him? That wasn't like Paul.

Eva stared up into that familiar face and felt as if the world had turned inside out.

Her fiancé was considerate and, when it came to his obligations, utterly reliable. Wasn't their engagement an obligation? He certainly didn't love her. The arrangement had been concocted for dynastic reasons but surely that meant it was even harder to break? He was a stickler for doing the right thing.

Yet Paul's expression was implacable.

She looked up at him and was torn between dismay and that old, familiar melting sensation. Because he was as heartbreakingly handsome as ever with his strongly defined features and tall, well-built frame. His dress uniform drew attention to straight shoulders and long, powerful legs, and the dark blue might have been designed to highlight his indigo eyes. Even his black hair, rumpled since he'd dragged his fingers through it, was attractive.

'Eva? Say something.'

She blinked and felt something stir inside. Something other than shock and dismay. A niggle of...anger?

'You want a response when you haven't even told me what's going on?' She stared straight back at him. 'You owe me an explanation first.'

He was lifting his glass to his mouth and stilled, arrested mid-movement.

What? Did he expect her to sit here meekly and agree to whatever he decreed? That wasn't the man she knew.

Or did he think her a complete door mat? It was true that around him she felt self-conscious, so wary of betraying her feelings that she accepted without question the arrangements made for her visits to St Ancilla. She thought that made her a good guest. It didn't mean she was a pushover.

Eva lifted her drink and downed half of it in one swallow.

She rarely drank and struggled to contain a cough as raw fire hit the back of her throat then trickled down. Seconds later warmth exploded within, counteracting the glacial chill that had crept through her inch by crackling inch at his announcement.

'I apologise.' He rubbed the back of his neck in a rare show of discomfort. 'I meant to talk with you and sort this out before the ball. But you were delayed.'

Eva felt her eyes bulge. 'What was your plan? To send me packing back to Tarentia before the ball?'

A hint of dull colour streaked across those high cheekbones.

'Of course not.' He drew himself up, the picture of frowning indignation. 'I just thought that the sooner we sorted out this situation the better, for you especially.' He shook his head. 'I thought you'd be pleased.'

Pleased!

But, of course, he had no idea how she felt about him.

She'd spent her journey to St Ancilla rehearsing how she'd persuade him that it was time to set a date for their long-delayed wedding.

While he'd been planning to sever their connection.

The irony of it made her cringe.

Suddenly Eva could no longer meet his probing gaze. She looked down to where she cradled the finely cut crystal. Colours winked as her hands trembled and the glass caught the light, a contrast to the deep blue lustre of her new gown.

It struck Eva that her dress was the same colour as Paul's eyes. Had she subconsciously chosen it for that very reason?

Her breath hitched so hard, the bodice of her strapless gown felt too tight.

Was she really so pathetic?

Grimly she took another swallow of whisky, enjoying the shocking blast of alcohol, as if it could burn away her feelings for him. Because they made her weak.

But no amount of spirits could eradicate her feelings. Something like despair hit and she slumped back in her seat.

'Why don't you just explain what's going on?'

* * *

Paul watched her warily. For the first time in years he could see the ripple of Eva's emotions just below the surface of her composure.

Yet she was still an enigma. Still unreadable. Except that now he sensed far more than her usual cool acceptance. Something stronger motivated his fiancée.

That look she'd sent him when she'd demanded an explanation! It had had all the hauteur of his father at his most uppity. And, far from appearing chilly or remote, those brilliant eyes had seared him. He'd almost swear that stare had left scorch marks.

Now, though, Eva seemed to have deflated. Her shoulders hunched in a way that aroused his protective instincts. Which was crazy. He was doing this for her.

'I know you don't want to marry me, Eva. I've known it almost from the first.'

That yanked her gaze up from her glass.

How had he ever thought her eyes a dull sort of colour? They shone with a silvery light he'd never noticed before.

'Go on,' she urged.

Paul raised his glass to his mouth, found it empty and stood.

'I'll have another too, please.' Eva extended her arm, watching him with a look that on anyone else he'd categorise as challenging. When he reached out and took her glass their fingers brushed. Did he imagine her flicker of reaction? A tiny shiver?

He turned away to get their drinks, forcing his thoughts back to the issue under discussion rather than imagining Eva responding to his touch.

'You were going to explain.' Her voice gave nothing away. She might have spoken of the weather in those same polished tones.

'I thought you'd be happy,' he murmured as he topped

up their drinks and turned, only to halt abruptly as he took in the sight of her.

He couldn't describe how she looked different, yet she did. More vibrant. More arresting.

He'd seen her wearing a ball gown before so it wasn't the spill of rich blue silk pooling around her feet, or the slope of pale flesh rising from it that made him stare. She wore gems but that wasn't new. Nor was the perfect posture. It was something around her eyes and her mouth, and even about the way her breasts pressed high against the confines of her bodice. There was challenge in that brilliant stare and something more. Something almost haunted.

Could it be...*hurt*?

His chest tightened. His brows angled down in a frown as he tried to puzzle out what Eva felt.

'Happy that after a four-year betrothal you want to set me aside like an outdated fashion accessory?' Eva lifted one eyebrow in an expression he'd never seen her wear.

Okay. Not hurt then. *Angry.*

Paul leaned across and held out her glass. Once more their fingers brushed. She didn't seem to notice but he did. A spark of something like electricity tingled through his hand and up his arm. His breath stilled as he frowned down at her.

'What?' She looked up at him. 'You didn't expect me to mind?'

He shook his head and sank onto the lounge opposite her, carefully placing his glass on a side table while he sought the right words. This interview had morphed from just difficult to difficult and surprising. He needed his wits about him.

'Have you fallen in love? Is that it?' Her words whipped his gaze back to her. They snapped out, sharp and precise with an undercurrent rich in disapproval. 'Perhaps with Ms Villiers?'

'No and no.' Paul shook his head.

When would he have time to fall in love? He was too busy propping up a kingdom, working sixteen-hour days most of the time.

'Are you sure? The pair of you seemed very close tonight.'

In another woman he'd have read that tone as jealousy. But this was Eva, the woman who if anything shrank from his touch, and who'd turned away the only time he'd tried to kiss her.

'I'm King. You know a love match doesn't enter into it.'

Especially a king grappling with such financial problems. Maybe his younger brothers, currently studying overseas, might one day have the freedom to marry where they chose.

Eva sipped her drink, regarding him thoughtfully, her mouth no longer prim as usual but almost pouting, the contours of her lips glistening in the lamplight. Something stirred low in Paul's belly.

'Your sister married for love.'

'Caro is different. You know she rarely even lived at court.'

Yet that hadn't saved her from their father's machinations. His plans to marry her off to a rich banker had been the least of his crimes against her. Fortunately, she'd finally found her lost daughter and happiness with Jake Maynard. Together they'd faced down the old King and had stood by Paul when he'd ascended the throne. Now he counted his half-sister and her husband as two of his closest friends, even if they lived on the other side of the world. As far as he knew, Caro was the only member of the St Ancillan royal family to marry for love, not duty.

'So you're not in love.' Eva's tone expressed doubt. 'Then why end our engagement?'

Once more Paul heard a hint of something in her voice

that might have been hurt. Except that glittering stare looked more annoyed than anything.

'For your sake, Eva.'

'Mine? It doesn't feel like it from where I'm sitting.'

Paul raked his hand through his hair then leaned forward, resting his elbows on his thighs. This conversation hadn't gone the way he'd planned. He was used to taking charge, to persuading or occasionally ordering others into acting in his country's best interests. He sweet-talked investors and handled difficult negotiations as a matter of course. But tonight, confronted with Eva, who seemed suddenly not like the Eva he knew, he'd inadvertently relinquished control.

'It's simple.' He held her gaze and watched her glass stop on the way to those lush lips. 'I know you didn't have a choice in this engagement. That you don't want to marry me. I want to give you your freedom. I don't want an unwilling wife.'

She said nothing, just looked down at her glass with a puckered brow, as if surprised to see it in her hand.

It wasn't the response he'd expected.

'Eva?'

She looked up and for a moment he read confusion in her stormy eyes. Then she looked down again at the tumbler, raised it and took a long swallow. This time she barely shuddered at the strong liquor.

'Why now? Why not refuse four years ago?'

'Because I didn't know initially how little you wanted this match. And…' He paused, the result of a lifetime's training in keeping unpalatable truths hidden. 'Soon after our engagement was announced, I discovered my father had already squandered the portion of your dowry that was transferred on our betrothal. I wasn't in a position to pay it back.'

Did she stiffen? The gems at her ears caught the light as they swayed.

'Ah. So we *are* speaking plainly.'

'I thought that's what you wanted.'

Not if it means you dumping me.

Eva bit her bottom lip rather than blurt out that home truth.

She didn't know if she should feel proud or pathetic that she had to ask. 'So you don't need my dowry any more?'

That made him sit straighter. His shoulders drew back like a soldier on parade.

What? Had she insulted him? He was the one who wanted plain speaking.

'Public funds are still tight in St Ancilla. But that's not the key issue.'

'Isn't it?'

She recalled her father's fury when he'd discovered, too late, the enormous ocean of debt the previous King of St Ancilla had run up. It was a secret known only to a select few. The two monarchs had earlier concocted a dynastic betrothal between Eva and Paul. It had come as a shock when King Hugo had abdicated soon after and retired to a distant island. A nastier shock when Eva's father had learned Hugo had been secretly forced to abdicate, then had been banished, the alternative being to have stood trial on multiple counts of fraud, theft and embezzlement of public funds.

Eva's father had wanted to cancel her engagement on the spot, but had been persuaded to let it stand rather than court unwanted media speculation. The portion of her dowry given to St Ancilla on her betrothal was long gone and she knew Paul fought to save his country from bankruptcy and scandal. From what her father had said, it would take years to make good the money stolen by King Hugo.

Even so, she'd wanted the marriage. She'd persuaded her

parents to allow a long engagement, ostensibly because she and Paul were young, and so she could complete her university studies. Her parents hoped that after all this time she'd agree to end the engagement. It would surprise no one, they said, if she and Paul had grown apart over four years. That, of course, was code for the fact that there would be minimal public scandal now. Yet Eva's plan was still to marry the one man she'd ever loved. Hoping that one day he'd come to care for her the way she cared for him.

Tonight's bombshell threatened that dream.

Once more Paul forked his fingers through his hair in a gesture of frustration.

'The financial situation is getting better. Slowly.' He shook his head. 'You don't need to hear the details, Eva. The fact is I don't want your money. It would be wrong. I intend to pay back every penny.'

'You're not very like your father, are you?' She'd never liked King Hugo, an overbearing, arrogant man, far too easy to anger.

Paul's mouth curled up in a tight smile. 'Thank you. I can't think of a better compliment.'

'You're honourable.'

His dark eyebrows twitched together. 'Why doesn't that sound like a positive when you say it?'

She blinked and let her eyes widen. 'I can't imagine. It's one of the things I like about you.'

'You do? I didn't think you liked me at all.'

'You think I'd promise to marry a man I don't even like?' He really did think her a door mat!

He shrugged those lovely broad shoulders but Eva kept her eyes on his. 'My father was a master in the art of coercion and bullying. I thought…'

'That mine is too?' She shook her head. 'He's proud and stiff-necked but he's no bully.'

It was only when Eva had shyly admitted to her parents

that she wanted to marry the Crown Prince of St Ancilla that the betrothal had gone ahead.

Her mistake, apparently, had been not telling Paul himself. Because she feared he'd read her true feelings and be scared off by a clinging wife. Because he'd never been interested in her romantically. From what she'd heard and observed as a teenager, his taste ran to well-endowed blondes. Since their engagement, there'd mercifully been no gossip about him with any woman other than her.

She drew a fortifying breath. 'My parents never forced my hand, Paul. I was content to marry you. I still am.'

'Content?' His mouth twisted in a grimace but even now he was the most attractive man she'd ever known.

'Happy, then. I'm happy to marry you.'

'You don't give the impression of a woman who wants to marry me.'

A spark ignited deep inside. Deep where she hid her feelings behind a façade of calm composure.

'What do you want, Paul? A fiancée who bats her eyelashes at you and follows you around like an orphaned puppy panting for attention?'

Eva feared she'd come close to that in her teenage years, using any excuse to trap him into conversation, wishing he'd see her, just once, as a desirable woman instead of someone he had to be polite to.

'Of course not!'

'Good.' Her chin tilted up. 'Because I don't recall you being particularly lover-like either.' Except that one time when he'd tried to kiss her. But, even she, as close to a complete innocent as you could get, had realised his heart wasn't in it. He'd thought it expected of him, but there'd been no real enthusiasm.

Even now, years later, that hurt.

Maybe, after all, she should cut her losses. Walk away

from Paul and hope, one day, to find another man who'd
make her heart beat faster.

Except she couldn't. Not while she loved him. The
thought of turning her back on him carved an aching hollow right through her middle.

She was trapped by her feelings. Not by public expectations or the legal documents binding them.

'Eva? Are you all right?'

It was the first time Paul had spoken to her like that,
his voice gentle and…concerned. As if he really did care
about her feelings, not about doing the honourable thing.

She blinked and discovered her eyes were too moist.
Hastily she looked down at the glass in her hand, the amber
liquid swirling in the bottom.

'Well, if we're going to be honest, I'm not sure. Why end
the engagement now? If there's someone else, or if you've
taken me in dislike—'

'Of course I haven't taken you in dislike. You're everything I could look for in a royal bride.'

But not in a wife.

There was a difference and, innocent though she might
be when it came to sex, Eva was quick to understand it. A
royal bride would fulfil her regal duties, something Eva had
been trained to do from birth. But a wife…a wife would
share his whole life, his love, his dreams…

'And there's no one else.' He paused, his features taut.
'But it's been four years since our engagement. Time to
release you. You and your family didn't know the mess St
Ancilla was in when you agreed to marry me.'

He laughed, a bitter, grating sound that made him sound
a decade older. It reinforced what she'd seen for herself, how
the burden of the last four years had made him stronger
and tougher than the glamorous young man she'd first met.
'*I* didn't know, for that matter. It's not fair to tie you to me
and hold you to your promise. You were only twenty when

we got engaged, after all, and your father wanted you to finish your degree before we married. If we separate now, people will assume we've simply drifted apart. This way you won't be dogged by scandal.'

Eva was hurt and angry. Her pride was battered, and her self-esteem, for putting herself in this position. For cleaving to a man who patently didn't want to be tied to her. Even so, her heart turned over at his words. He didn't love her but he wanted what he believed was best for her. Even though parting ways would deny him the rest of the fortune she'd bring into the marriage.

He was noble. Self-sacrificing. Determined to set her free.

Eva didn't know in this moment whether she loved Paul of St Ancilla or hated him.

Because he'd never looked and really seen *her*. The woman behind the royal façade. The woman eating her heart out for him.

She downed the last of her drink in a defiant gulp and shot to her feet, buoyed by a sudden upswing of rebellious energy.

'Eva? What's wrong?' He stood before her, his brow creasing in a frown, and now his concern was like a match thrown on petrol.

That he had to ask showed how little he understood her.

It was on the tip of her tongue to lay it all out for him. Her feelings…how she'd pined for him for nine long years. How her schoolgirl crush had morphed into something stronger and deeper. Her determination to stand by his side, no matter how difficult the challenges they faced, to be the perfect supportive Queen through thick and thin. Her love for him.

But he wouldn't thank her. He would just be horrified.

And she'd regret it when he looked at her with pity in those stunning blue eyes.

'It's been a very long day,' she said through a throat that seemed lined with jagged glass. 'Can we continue this tomorrow?'

'It would be better to sort it out now.' He paused, his gaze probing, as if seeing the chinks in her armour. Eva stood straighter, willing the tumbling whirl of emotions back behind her tattered veneer of composure.

Finally, Paul nodded, though she read his reluctance. 'But if you're tired we can talk in the morning.'

Was it imagination or did she hear relief mixed with his impatience?

'I'll have my secretary arrange a time.'

'Of course you will.'

Because this was business. Not love.

He'd schedule a meeting and they'd sit on opposite sides of his desk while he told her again that he didn't want her.

Eva's mouth trembled as a great, welling surge of despair rose. She battened it down and swung away in a swirl of royal blue before her control slipped. 'Till tomorrow, then.'

Eva stripped off her ball gown and placed it on a hanger. Despite her fizzing temper, and the cloud of gloom around her, she'd no more think of dropping her clothes on the floor than she'd walk naked in public. Responsibility was ingrained. Royal standards had been drilled into her. From being gracious to others, standing patiently for hours in interminably long public gatherings, down to looking after the exquisite clothes she was lucky enough to wear.

Even if the sight of this gown, the same colour as her fiancé's eyes, made her want to fling it across the room and stomp on it.

It was no good. She couldn't find calm.

Because, somewhere between Paul's announcement that he was setting her free and her escaping to her room, her heart had broken.

Hands on hips, Eva bent double, her lungs cramping at the sudden shaft of pain shearing through her chest.

Surely it should make some sound—all her dreams shattering?

Yet there was only silence, unless she counted the raw grating of her laboured breaths. Even the ripping ache behind her ribs was deathly silent.

Summoning her strength, she stood straight, to be confronted by the sight of herself in the full-length mirror. Her hair was still piled high and sapphire earrings caught the light. Yet in a nude strapless bra and panties, and equally nude stockings, she didn't look royal. Or special. Or in any way likely to capture Paul's interest.

From her mid-brown hair and indeterminate-coloured eyes to her average body, she was completely ordinary.

She sucked in a deep breath and her breasts swelled against her bra. Even then they succeeded only in looking average. Not bounteous. She knew he liked bounteous. The way he'd smiled down at Karen Villiers tonight—she of the perfectly sculpted body and pert, prominent breasts— hadn't been anything like the way he looked at her, his fiancée.

Ex-fiancée by morning.

Another breath-stealing cramp hit her and she had to concentrate on breathing through the pain.

Numbly, she pondered how a broken heart could be so painful. This wasn't just sorrow. This was physical as well as mental and emotional.

Because she'd never suffered and then got over puppy love. Because when her friends had been going through the thrills and pangs of teen crushes she'd had none. She'd been the last of them to discover romance, and when she had, at fifteen, her feelings for Paul had taken permanent root.

Look where that had got her.

She *was* no better than a door mat. Too terrified of rejection to reveal her feelings to her fiancé and now it was too late.

Eva tilted her head, surveying her reflection. She might be ordinary but she wasn't a troll. Some men would think her attractive.

Wouldn't they?

She wrapped her arms around herself, hugging in the welling hurt, refusing to let the tears prickling her eyes gather and fall.

Somewhere out there was a man who'd appreciate her for herself. Not for the value of her dowry, or to strengthen dynastic links or to avoid a scandal. Her lip curled. That was what Paul was afraid of—stirring too much press attention that might lead to someone discovering the real reason his father had abdicated. That was why he'd waited four whole years to jilt her. Four years in which she'd spun fruitless fantasies of happy-ever-after.

Eva swung away, heart hammering. She wouldn't think of Paul. Tomorrow he'd end their engagement and she'd still love him. The thought threatened to swallow her whole.

Perhaps it was the two glasses of whisky she'd had on top of earlier champagne. Or simply that she'd reached the limit of her endurance. But abruptly Eva was overwhelmed by the need to prove she wasn't just a princess but a woman.

A desirable woman.

Pride, ego, self-respect and years of patiently waiting for Paul to notice her fused into fierce determination.

To be herself. To unwind. Not to worry about appearances or protocol. To laugh when she wanted to, talk with whomever she wanted. To go dancing, flirt with a handsome man. To live a little. To feel attractive and appreciated.

Just a few hours incognito. How could it hurt?

CHAPTER THREE

'SORRY TO BOTHER you so late, sir, but I thought you'd prefer to know. Princess Eva has gone out.'

'Out?' Paul looked at the time. Two a.m. Where would
she go at this time? Never in her years of visiting St Ancilla
had she made an unscheduled excursion. She'd followed
the timetable devised by his staff. 'You're sure?'

Stupid question. His Head of Security would never make
mistakes like that.

'Absolutely. She left via a back entrance and headed
into the old town. One of my men is following at a discreet distance.'

Paul's grip on the phone tightened. The man's voice was
so carefully neutral, it boded bad news. He'd been employed
at the palace during King Hugo's reign and had learned discretion in the face of royals behaving badly.

Paul wanted to protest that Eva wasn't like that. There'd
be no late-night gambling, drunkenness or temper displays.
She'd probably just gone for a walk.

At two in the morning? When she had the whole of the
palace gardens to walk in?

He remembered how she'd been an hour ago. The ripple of suppressed emotion…the look in her eyes that had
haunted him since. Hurt or anger. He still couldn't cata-
logue it. Then her abrupt departure, leaving him to the
knowledge he hadn't handled their interview well.

It wasn't a feeling he was used to. Usually he dealt with important matters far more smoothly.

But she'd been unexpectedly prickly. Not relieved, as he'd expected. Or biddable.

'Where is she?'

'At a night club.'

Paul frowned. A night club?

He couldn't imagine Eva clubbing. She seemed so... sedate. No, that made her sound priggish. It was just that he couldn't imagine her drinking and dancing in some badly lit venue to the throb of mind-numbingly loud music. Or cosying up to a stranger in the *faux* intimacy of near-darkness.

A sour taste filled his mouth.

'Is she alone?'

'Not at the moment.' His Head of Security's voice became absolutely toneless and something nasty skittered down Paul's spine. His belly clenched hard and his fingers tightened on the phone.

He opened his mouth to ask if she was with a man then shut it.

Of course she wasn't. Eva was the soul of discretion and, moreover, his fiancée.

Till tomorrow, a sly voice whispered in his ear. *From tomorrow you and she will be as good as strangers. She'll have no obligation to you nor you to her.*

Paul's mouth firmed. She was his responsibility. Not just because of their engagement. Or because she was a guest in his country and home, though both those factors were important.

What weighed most was the glimpse of hurt he'd seen shadow her eyes tonight. The unfamiliar slump of her shoulders, later banished by an almost fiercely regal bearing that he'd sensed hid more than tiredness.

He'd taken the easy route, though, hadn't he? He hadn't

forced her to stay so they could sort out the tangle of their relationship. He'd known she was upset but it had been easier to let her go and hope she'd have her emotions under control by morning.

Guilt bit at his gut.

Whatever was happening, he knew Eva well enough to understand tonight's excursion wasn't typical. Had it been prompted by their conversation?

'Give me the location and have a car waiting for me at the north entrance.'

Fifteen minutes later, Paul parked the anonymous vehicle in a side street.

He'd refused a security escort but knew somewhere behind him there'd be a minder or two discreetly melding into the night. It wasn't unheard of for royals to escape for a couple of hours' private partying. At such times security staff kept their distance.

Paul's plan was to find Eva and bring her back to the palace.

She had a perfect right to party but the idea of her doing so without him, possibly prey to the advances of predatory guys, disturbed him.

He loped down the cobble-stoned street towards the night club, mouth tightening at the coincidence that this was the same place Karen Villiers had invited him to. Fervently he hoped she was no longer on the premises.

Quickening his step, he was crossing a narrow lane on the way to the main entrance when a woman's voice stopped him.

'I said, let *go* of me!' Gasping as if from effort, higher pitched than normal, the voice was still familiar.

Eva.

Paul swung round and hurried towards the sound. The lane was dark, illuminated only by a feeble bulb near a metal door—the night club's back entrance, he assumed.

He could see movement, a jumble of figures and a flash of light. There was a hiss of breath and a curse.

In that moment's bright light, he saw enough. There were people milling near the club's back door but another couple caught his attention. A woman had her back to the wall, straining away from a man boxing her in who pawed at her short skirt, lifting it up her thigh.

As Paul broke into a run he saw the woman jerk one knee up and the man hunch, cursing. There was just enough light to make out the woman's horrified features.

Eva.

Nausea filled Paul, and an unholy rage.

He reached them as the guy straightened, filling the air with a stream of ugly curses.

Ignoring the bystanders in the doorway, Paul grabbed the man by the shoulder and spun him round.

It all happened so fast, Eva had trouble taking it in. A minute ago she'd been fending off her companion's suddenly groping hands. She'd been stunned by how he'd morphed from debonair, amusing company to mauling octopus, his lips wet on her neck and cheek when she tried to avoid his kisses.

He hadn't taken rejection well, ignoring her first polite request that he step back. Instead he'd used his size and weight to pin her to the wall and try to lift her skirt, his other hand groping at her breast.

That was when fear had kicked in. But her desperate knee to his groin had only slowed him. Her hackles had risen in terror at what he'd said then, and the raw fury in his voice, but before he could follow through on his threats he was wrenched away.

To her right came the sound of breaking glass and the alley was plunged into darkness.

She was aware of raised voices near the club's exit but

kept her eyes on the heaving figures before her. All she could discern was two men and the sound of fighting. Grunts, thuds and at one point a crunching that turned her stomach.

Then a man's voice whispered in her ear. 'Palace security, Your Highness. You need to leave now.' A hand at her elbow urged her to move away from the club.

She shook her head, trying to make out what was happening in front of her.

'We can't go. He might need help.' They couldn't abandon the man who'd rescued her.

The reply was so soft, she had to strain to hear it. 'His Majesty has things in hand. He'll join us in a moment.'

His Majesty? Did he mean Paul?

'This way, please.' She was propelled, half-carried, to the end of the alley and round the corner.

Shocked and out of breath, Eva finally gathered her thoughts and found enough purchase on the slippery cobbles to slow their progress.

'No. I refuse to go until I know he's okay.' She yanked her arm free of the bodyguard's hold, but only, she knew, because of who she was, not because she'd managed to break his grip. 'We can't just leave him. What if he's injured?'

The man opened his mouth as if to argue then stopped, turning to face the way they'd come.

Finally, over the pounding of her pulse in her ears, Eva made out the sound of footsteps approaching. She turned.

There was Paul, striding towards them. In the dim light he looked different. Bigger, somehow, and broader in a dark sweater and trousers instead of the dress uniform he'd worn earlier tonight. His hair was rumpled, falling forward across his brow, and she thought she saw a smear of something across his cheek.

'Why haven't you already gone?' He addressed the

bodyguard rather than her. 'The Princess needs to be away from here.'

'The lady was concerned about you, Your Majesty.'

'Really?' Paul turned to her, his expression unreadable in the darkness.

'Really,' she said when she found her voice. 'You could have been hurt.'

'So could you.' His voice sliced like a honed blade through butter. 'Didn't you think of that?'

Eva stared up at him. She'd never heard her fiancé angry. If anything she'd have called him even-tempered. Yet now it sounded as if he spoke through gritted teeth. Even in the gloom she saw the way his dark eyebrows angled down in a disapproving V.

Was he angry with *her*?

She hadn't created that scene back there.

Abruptly she shivered, her hands rubbing her bare arms as the night air blanketed her. But the chill in her bones wasn't because of the weather.

'If I might suggest, Your Majesty.' The bodyguard spoke. 'If you take the Princess away, I'll tidy up here.'

Tidy up? What did that entail?

She had to ask. 'How is he? Fabrice?'

'Fabrice?' Paul shifted closer to her.

'The man you fought.'

'You're worried about the man who assaulted you?'

No. I'm worried about what you'll face if he's badly injured.

The last thing Paul needed was a scandal when every action in his reign had been directed to protecting St Ancilla from the revelation of his father's iniquities. That would lead to loss of confidence in the country and its financial system.

'If he needs a hospital—'

'Hardly. He's just a little bruised.'

Eva squinted up at her fiancé, hearing unmistakeable satisfaction in his voice. Had he *enjoyed* the fight? The idea was out of step with everything she knew of him.

'Okay.' Paul nodded to the security guy. 'Go and do what needs to be done.'

'Yes, sir. And my apologies for not intervening earlier. It wasn't obvious initially that the Princess would welcome intervention. When I realised the situation, I was delayed by onlookers.'

'I understand. I'll look after the Princess.'

Another shiver rippled through Eva. Because the man had thought she'd wanted to be groped. And because of Paul's harsh tone. As if she were some chore, an unwanted obligation.

But that was exactly what she was. Paul had just stopped pretending otherwise.

'What's so funny?'

Eva blinked and realised she'd given a huff of bitter laughter. She looked past him. They were alone now, their companion already disappearing round the corner to the lane at the back of the night club.

'Nothing.' She tilted her head higher, meeting Paul's gaze full-on. 'Absolutely nothing.'

As nights went, this was an utter disaster. The worst of her life. Rejected by the man she loved. Taken in by a charming stranger who'd offered to walk her to a taxi rank when she'd decided the night-club visit was a mistake. Groped and savagely threatened. And now, if she read the crackling atmosphere right, she'd infuriated the man who'd rescued her.

Tough. He infuriated her.

She turned away and marched down the street.

'Where are you going?'

'Back to the palace. If the police need me to make a statement, your man can direct them there.'

'There'll be no need for that.'

She tossed a look over her shoulder and found Paul right behind her, so close he could have curled his arm around her if he'd wanted. But of course he didn't want, did he? A rising tide of bitterness engulfed her.

'Why? Are you going to get your staff to paper over the incident, like your father would have done?' She stumbled to a halt, fear sucking in her breath. 'He's not going to be dumped somewhere, is he?'

Eva didn't know the full details of King Hugo's crimes but she knew he'd ruthlessly used his security services to make problems disappear. He'd had Princess Caro's infant daughter stolen from her at birth because he'd refused to acknowledge an illegitimate grandchild. Eva had been shocked when her then future sister-in-law had confided that secret, but pleased she'd trusted her with it. Especially as the story had a happy ending, Caro finally reuniting with the child she'd once believed stillborn.

'Dumped?' Paul stared down at her. 'What do you think's going on? He works for the royal family, not the Mafia.'

'Then how do you know the police won't get involved?'

He angled his head as if to view her better. 'Because I assume you don't want to press charges and face the publicity that would bring. Your Fabrice sure won't. He'll thank his lucky stars he's not locked up. Unless you *do* want the police involved?'

Eva considered it for a whole three seconds. 'No, I don't.' She cringed at the thought of reliving those horrible moments for the authorities. Of what had happened becoming fodder for the press.

What she wanted was to go back to her suite and take a long, hot shower.

'Good. Come this way.' Paul didn't touch her but ges-

tured to a car parked up ahead, its lights blinking as he unlocked it with a remote control.

Eva didn't want to go with Paul. Didn't want to sit in
that confined space with him of all people while her nerves
were so jangled and her flesh crawled at the too-real memory of that man's hands on her. Especially as Paul seemed
to blame her for what had happened.

'Eva?'

She glanced at those imposing shoulders, then at the solidity of that strong jaw. Why had she never thought of it
as stubborn before?

She was tempted to keep on walking. To say she needed
to clear her head rather than subject herself to his frowning fury. But she wasn't that stupid. She'd been gullible,
trusting a stranger after such a short acquaintance, but the
thought of walking down these deserted streets back to
the palace...

Eva marched to where Paul stood holding the car door
open. Her high heels clicked smartly on the cobbles. She
kept her chin up, clutching her small shoulder bag to her
side, and got into the passenger seat without once brushing against him or meeting his eyes.

Paul seethed, the satisfaction he'd got from downing the
man who'd dared touch her already fading.

Her precious Fabrice.

He hadn't believed his ears when Eva had asked how he
was. The man had assaulted her and yet she was concerned
about him. It had been there in her voice.

Had she known him before tonight?

Was there something between them?

Paul had assumed they were virtual strangers but...

'If you take your hand away I'll shut the door.' Her voice
came crisply but otherwise uninflected from inside the car.

Belatedly Paul stirred, realising he was making her a

target for curious eyes with the door open and the car's interior light on. He stepped away and closed the door gently, concealing the roiling anger inside him.

No one had ever made him so furious. Except his late, unlamented father. But then King Hugo had been monstrous—narcissistic, venal and with a wrathful temper that had scorched anyone who disobeyed him.

Was it any wonder Paul had made it his life's work to contain his temper? To ensure he was as unlike his father as possible?

He shook his head and stalked round the car. Sliding inside, he shut his door and started the engine, plunging them into darkness.

But not soon enough to blot out the image of Eva's long, pale legs stretching out beside him from under that short dress.

Why hadn't he known she had legs like that? Legs that dragged a man's eyes down then up again even when his thoughts were still half with the guy he'd left sprawling in the alley. When she'd walked down the street, chin up and hips swinging... No, not walked. Sashayed. Her rump twitching, hips swaying and those legs...

Stifling a growl of frustration in the back of his throat, he reached for his seat belt and eased the car into gear.

'Buckle up.'

But of course she already had. Princess Eva of Tarentia always followed the rules. Her grasp of court etiquette was second to none, her willingness to do what was expected of her one of the reasons she'd been put forward as a royal bride.

Except when she didn't do what was expected. Like tonight.

Another thing he'd only just discovered. The fact that the woman who was still his fiancée was a rule breaker, skiving off to a night club notorious as a venue for discreet hook-ups wearing a dress that barely covered the essentials.

Then, when some chancer had tried to take advantage, had she thanked him, Paul, for rescuing her? No, she'd worried about the man who'd tried to undress her in an alleyway, all but accusing Paul of wrongdoing.

The car shot forward with a growl and the squeal of rubber on wet stone, forcing him to focus on his driving.

The way things had gone so far, he just needed to smash the car to round off a terrific evening.

Her voice cut through his turbulent thoughts. 'Are you all right?'

'I'm fine.' Belatedly he recalled she'd been concerned for him earlier. Or so she'd said. Had she been more worried about how Fabrice emerged from the encounter with Paul's fists?

'You're not acting like you are.'

Paul clenched his teeth, easing his foot off the accelerator. 'Perhaps I'm just tired. It was late when I came out to rescue you.'

Which wasn't strictly true. It had been late but he'd been wide awake, working his way through reams of paperwork. He hadn't bothered going to bed because his conversation with Eva had left him unsettled and discomfited. He wasn't used to his carefully laid plans being upended.

His mouth twisted grimly.

All these years he and so many royal advisors had considered Eva the perfect, conformable, *comfortable* royal spouse. None of them had realised her hidden, troublesome depths.

He shot her a sideways glance, caught sight of gleaming pale flesh in the darkness and registered the now-familiar grab and twist of desire low in his belly, and even lower, in his groin.

Even the sight of all that lustrous hair disturbed him. It

was loose down her back and around her shoulders, and slightly dishevelled.

He couldn't help but wonder if that was how she looked in bed.

Sultry, delicious and rumpled.

He sucked in a sharp breath, trying and failing to banish the thought.

There was something subtly decadent about the sight of her hair loose, almost to her waist. It caught him on the raw that she'd worn it like that for a stranger but not for him.

Before tonight he'd felt sorry for his fiancée, trapped in a betrothal she patently didn't want. He'd worked hard not to take that personally, and had almost succeeded.

Tonight Eva had upset the tenuous balance of their relationship. Instead of sensibly agreeing to separate, she'd refused his plan. She hadn't precisely objected, but she'd tossed a spanner in the works with her announcement that she was content to marry him.

Content!

Had she any idea what an affront that was? What an insult to a man who, even allowing for the pull of his royal title, always had his fair share of female interest?

He might have inherited a kingdom that was a financial basket-case but Paul wasn't used to being dismissed so easily by any woman. He'd spent the last four years fending off females, only too eager to offer him solace and support while his fiancée was away, because he took his betrothal vow seriously.

His jaw worked and pain radiated from his grinding molars as he thought of the efforts he'd gone to for Eva. And did she appreciate them?

'This isn't the way to the palace.' Her voice came out of the darkness, drawing him back to the present.

Paul inhaled a slow breath and forced the negative thoughts to slide away. He refused to pile his frustrations

one on top of the other, or to blame them all on Eva. He
wasn't his father. He'd work through their difficulties and
find a reasonable solution, not rage about them, lashing
out indiscriminately.

'No. We passed the turn a few streets ago.'

In his peripheral vision he caught the pale oval of her
face turning towards him.

'Where are we going?'

'Somewhere where we can talk without interruption.'

Because, whether Eva liked it or not, there were things
they needed to sort out. Now. Tonight.

Their engagement. The potential fallout from tonight's
escapade. And the unexpected zap of electric awareness
between them that undercut everything he'd told himself
about a lack of attraction.

He was torn between two competing impulses. To berate Eva for putting herself at the mercy of a stranger. Or
pull over to the side of the road and kiss the mouth he'd
discovered was anything but prim when she forgot to hold
it taut. A mouth as lush and inviting as any he'd known.

Another spasm of pain circled his jaw.

One thing was certain. Tonight was a test of his control
in ways he'd never expected.

CHAPTER FOUR

THE CAR PULLED up in a world of thick shadows. Tall trees lined either side of the road and they'd left the city lights far behind.

As Paul swept to a halt at the end of a long, gravelled drive, sensor lights switched on to reveal a quaint building, several storeys high, and built in a style that harked back to a previous era.

Eva blinked. It looked like some fanciful, snow-white sugar decoration. There were huge, rounded windows surrounded by whimsical plaster-work decorations, an enormous double front door, what looked like a free-form glass conservatory at one end, and at the other a tower, complete with a blue tulip-shaped dome that belonged in an illustration of some fantasy kingdom.

Her breath caught as she made out peacocks, butterflies and…was that a pair of lobsters in the intricate work beneath one window? Surely not.

'What is this place?'

Paul was already opening his door but paused. 'Welcome to the royal hunting lodge. Built by an ancestor who loved Art Nouveau.'

Eva shook her head. 'Those aren't…lobsters, are they?' She pointed to the elaborate decoration below one window.

'They are. If you're interested, you'll also find crabs, swordfish and tortoises, along with dozens of bird species. My ancestor fancied himself as a naturalist. When he wasn't shooting the local fauna, that is.'

Amusement tinged Paul's voice and, as they sat taking in the sheer exuberance of the building before them, Eva felt a moment's bond. As if they were still friends, or at least had a common purpose.

Then, abruptly he got out, slamming the door behind him, leaving her to the sound of the engine ticking in the thickening silence.

Reluctantly Eva opened her door just before Paul got to it and swung her legs out. For a second she had the impression he was about to say something as he stood looking down at her. But his mouth turned into a thin line and he merely waited till she was out to lock the door and lead the way to the building.

'We won't be disturbed here,' he murmured as he turned on more lights and ushered her inside.

She should have known this wouldn't be like the old hunting lodges in Tarentia—closed-in spaces full of dark wood and mounted hunting trophies. The walls of the two-storey entrance foyer gleamed a soft shell-pink and a staircase, embellished with decorative iron-work that looked like butterflies in flight, curved up to the next floor.

'It's charming.'

'And costly to maintain. Unfortunately, there's a heritage listing on the building so it can't be bulldozed.'

Her head swung round at the bitterness in Paul's voice. It wasn't something she'd heard from him before, though he carried a massive burden of responsibility, rebuilding his nation's wealth after his father's excesses.

First anger, now bitterness. What other surprises did he have for her?

He shrugged and his expression turned rueful. 'Don't worry, I'd never do it. I'm actually quite fond of the place.

It's where I used to escape when...' He shook his head. 'Never mind. Come this way.'

He moved past the stairs, towards the back of the building, leaving Eva to wonder who or what he'd had to escape.

It didn't take a genius to work out it was most likely his father. But this was the first time Paul had come close to revealing any of the difficulties he'd faced as King Hugo's son. Everything Eva knew of the old King, she'd heard in confidence from her parents or from Princess Caro on a previous visit. Paul had said once he preferred not to dwell on the past but look to the future.

Because the past was so awful or because, as far as she could tell, he spent most of his time working to secure the future of his country?

'Coming, Eva?'

He stood in the shadows of the corridor, looking back over his shoulder. It struck her once more that tonight, in these casual clothes, he seemed like a stranger. Someone she barely knew.

Trepidation licked through her like a cold flame. She shrugged off the sensation and followed him.

They ended up in the kitchen. White and blue tiles and acres of scrubbed wood. It was cavernous but surprisingly cosy.

Eva had had a wrap when she'd gone to the night club but had lost it somewhere along the way. She looked down at the bare legs revealed by her higher than usual hemline and her mouth twisted. No wonder she'd felt chilled. Partly it was reaction to tonight's events and partly that she never went out wearing so little.

Maybe Paul thought the same. She looked up to find him staring at her legs from the far end of the bench where he was making hot drinks.

His stare made her want to tug her hemline down but she resisted it. There was nothing particularly skimpy about what she wore, especially compared with what she'd seen at the night club. When she stood the hem went halfway down her thighs. It was just when she sat…

'Are you warm enough?' His voice hit a gravel note.

'I'm fine.'

His gaze skated her shoulders, bare but for thin straps of satin.

Heat churned in her middle, embarrassment rising. There was no way Paul could know this wasn't actually a dress but a custom-made slip. It had been designed to be worn under a sheer chiffon dress that floated all the way to her knees like most of her other outfits. Worn separately, it looked like a plain but well-cut dress, perfect for dancing. She'd convinced herself the dark anthracite grey was sophisticated enough for a night out.

Because it had been her only choice.

When she'd looked for something to wear dancing, she'd found nothing suitable. Everything was too formal or conservative. Not frumpy, for she'd been taught to dress with elegance and care, but she had nothing *young* or *fun* in her wardrobe.

It was a sad statement about her life that at twenty-four she had nothing to wear for a night on the town.

Some night it had been.

Her fingers clenched and she pressed her knees together as she relived the heavy touch of grasping hands on her body, that hot breath on her face, the smell of wine and the slightly sour aftershave that had vied with the taste of panic on her tongue.

'Here.' It was Paul, holding out a steaming mug.

Eva blinked up, read his brooding expression and quickly focused on taking the drink without touching him.

That frown made her feel about six years old, caught in some misdemeanour.

Whereas she'd done nothing wrong.

She took a seat at the table, watched him take the seat opposite and raised her drink to her lips.

'Hot chocolate?' She'd thought he was making her coffee.

'Sugar's good for shock.' He paused. 'I'm assuming what happened was a shock?'

Eva slammed the mug down on the table as she swallowed the wrong way and began to choke. When the coughing finished, she glared at him.

'It was a complete surprise. He offered to take me to a taxi rank. I didn't expect or want...' She shook her head, her throat constricting.

'Then you shouldn't have headed into a deserted, dark alley with a stranger.' Paul's voice was brutally hard.

He was right. She'd been naïve, but the pounding music, and sense of melancholy that had surrounded her since Paul had dropped his bombshell, had made her regret her decision to go to the club almost as soon as she'd arrived. Eva had been desperate to leave. She'd forced herself to stay for a couple of dances, as if needing to prove something to herself, though she didn't know what. When her dance partner had commiserated over her burgeoning headache and said he knew where there'd be a taxi waiting, it had seemed a good idea.

'It wasn't deserted. There were other people going out that way.'

'And that makes it okay?'

Once more Eva discovered the back of her eyes prickling with hot tears. She hated that Paul could make her feel so...so...

She shoved her chair back and shot to her feet.

Angry.

That was how he made her feel.

Angry at herself for being duped and for not taking bet-

ter precautions. But angry with Paul, too, for continually
needling her.

Eva refused to let him make her feel small. She'd already
felt that way tonight. Small, weak, vulnerable and incredibly scared as she'd realised, in a moment's abrupt horror,
how much she was at a stranger's mercy. How vast was the
difference in physical power between them.

Despite the self-defence classes she'd so proudly taken,
she'd felt at a loss. As if she couldn't believe this was happening to *her*.

A lifetime's training in good manners had had her asking more than once that he let her go, instead of taking action instantly. Her brain had taken for ever to catch up with
the fact she was being groped against her will and needed
to *do* something. Even when she'd kneed him it had only
stopped him temporarily and she'd been too frozen to the
spot to escape back into the club, watching in horror as he
regrouped.

All this shot through her mind in a flash, while her anger
bubbled from simmering to boiling point.

'I don't appreciate your attitude, Paul.'

There was no need for him to grind her down into the
dirt with his disapproval. She already felt as if she'd been
dragged through it tonight.

'*My* attitude?' He rocketed to his feet, palms planted on
the table. 'I'm the one who saved you, remember?'

His words cut through her indignation. What would have
happened if he hadn't been there?

Eva stared down at the red marks on one of his hands,
a graze, a reminder that he'd put himself between her and
her attacker. Her stomach churned.

'Thank you.' The words came out stiffly, her vocal cords
constricted and her chest tight as a drum, making it hard
to catch her breath. 'I don't remember if I thanked you before. I appreciate what you did.'

She surveyed him for signs of injury but saw none. He'd wiped off the mark she'd seen on his face before she could determine what it was.

Paul shrugged then lowered those wide shoulders a fraction. 'You're welcome.'

Yet the silence that followed bristled.

Eva swallowed again but it was no good. The words on her tongue insisted on spilling out.

'What, exactly, is your problem? You're not...' She waved one hand in a vague gesture. 'You're different.'

'*I'm* different? What about you? Haring off like that and—'

Her hackles rose again. 'I wasn't aware I had to get your permission before leaving the palace.'

Tonight her world had shattered. Her hopes and plans as well as her heart. Was it surprising she hadn't meekly toddled off to bed?

'Now you're being ridiculous. You know it wasn't a matter of permission.' He shoved his hands deep into his trouser pockets, the movement emphasising the breadth of his chest and the solidity of his thighs. His clenched jaw was the epitome of angry masculinity.

Her body responded eagerly to all that raw virility. The quickening in her blood and a clenching between her thighs felt like the ultimate betrayal.

Ridiculous, was she?

Her nostrils flared and she gathered herself up to her full height. 'If it's not about permission then what?'

'You're my fiancée, Eva. Don't you think I care for your well being?'

She blinked, stunned by his blind disregard for the truth.

Heat thrummed through her, indignation rising at his selective memory. For seconds she grappled with the dictates that had become second nature after a lifetime of royal obedience. To behave graciously. To smooth over ruffled feelings and restore harmony.

But she couldn't do it. Not tonight. Not after what had happened. She couldn't obediently agree and pretend she'd done something wrong. She'd spent four years holding back, pretending and hiding her feelings. That stopped now.

Eva took a step towards him, hands fisted at her sides, her shoulders back and her spine straight. Coolly, with all the hauteur seven centuries of royal breeding could conjure, she lifted her chin.

'First, I'm not your fiancée, Paul. You're dumping me, remember?'

Scowling, he opened his mouth to reply, but she was too quick, speaking as she closed the distance between them. 'Second, even if I were your fiancée, I have a right to go out to a public venue if I want.'

'I'm not disputing that, Eva—'

'In fact, if I'd chosen to visit every night club and bar in the city, that would still have been my choice, not yours.'

She swallowed, her throat scratchy. 'I admit I made a mistake. Following Fabrice outside wasn't a wise decision, though I thought, given the fact there were others around, it would be safe.'

'That's just where—'

'*But*,' she forged on, unwilling to allow argument, 'what I really can't stand is the fact that you blame *me* for being attacked. As if I should have *known* what he intended. As if I didn't have a right to feel safe in your capital. As if...' she paused and dragged air into lungs that had stopped working '...finding fault with the victim is easier than blaming a man who thinks he has a right to assault a woman just because he fancies her.'

Paul's scowl had vanished and his piercing blue eyes were wide with what looked like shock.

'I've got news for you, Paul.' Her finger jabbed his ster-

num, his chest just as immoveable as it looked. 'It's attitudes like yours that make this world unsafe for innocent
women and girls. As if men can't be responsible for their actions around them. I'd thought better of you. I never thought
you'd resort to victim-shaming.'

Her vocal cords closed around her last words but Eva
stood firm, her eyes locked on his.

Hell and damnation!

Paul raked his hand back through his hair as he met Eva's
fierce stare. Her eyes blazed with seething, silvery fire that
made her look like a disdainful goddess.

He went to speak then shook his head. She was right.
Her scorn burned him all over.

His mouth dried as he went back through their conversations. No wonder she'd thought he was blaming her, when
all the time the real target of his ferocity was the man in
the alley. And himself.

Paul should have done a better job of protecting her. He
knew their earlier, abortive conversation had some part to
play in her decision to go off alone tonight. But he'd taken
his anger and frustration out on her.

Dragging his hands from his pockets, he spread them
wide. 'I'm sorry, Eva. You're right. I made it sound like this
is all your fault. I apologise.

That militant sparkle still flashed in her gaze but she
drew a deep breath, as if relaxing a little.

A tiny part of him wondered what had happened to the
woman whose thoughts and emotions he couldn't read.
That Eva had disappeared completely.

But mainly he was consumed with shame. The last thing
she needed was someone berating her after what had happened.

'I got a fright and lashed out. It's no excuse, I know.'

'*You* got a fright?' She sounded disbelieving.

Her jabbing finger dropped from his chest and, weirdly, he missed the connection. The feel of her touching him. Because the contact had been reassuring. He still couldn't banish the thought of what might have happened to her if he hadn't arrived when he had.

Nausea twisted his gut and the skin across his neck and shoulders prickled as it drew tight. He'd heard what her attacker had promised in retribution for her defensive knee to the groin. He only hoped that, since he'd spoken Ancillan, and coarse slang at that, Eva hadn't understood.

Paul's blood had run cold at the threat to her.

He couldn't recall ever feeling as furious as he had tonight. Even facing the full extent of his father's appalling legacy. Then he'd been angry, but it had been nothing like the red mist that had filled his vision as that loser had pawed Eva.

Something had snapped. He'd wanted to break her attacker's hands.

'I was petrified,' he admitted. 'At what might have happened if I hadn't reached you in time.'

Her eyes widened and the martial light left her gaze.

'It would have been nasty,' she admitted slowly. 'But I'd have screamed, and there were others nearby. Someone would have helped.'

Paul said nothing. He couldn't be so sanguine about her chances. But saying so might amplify any fear she felt after tonight's events.

'What?' Her brow puckered, as if she read his churning thoughts.

He shook his head. 'I still feel guilty. I should have protected you better.'

Logic decreed that was impossible, since she'd abandoned his protection to go clubbing alone, yet it was true. Eva and he were connected.

Her chin jerked up. 'I'm not your responsibility any more, remember?'

It amazed him that she'd ever fooled the world, and him in particular, that she was cool to the point of remoteness. He could almost hear the crack and sizzle of her temper.

It was…invigorating.

'I can't help it, Eva. Like it or not, there's a link between us.'

He waited for her to berate him but instead her mouth crimped in a way he'd never seen before. Her chin crumpled and when she lifted her hand to brush her long hair back off her shoulder he saw it shake.

'Eva?' He stepped nearer, so they stood toe to toe. A faint waft of scent teased him, something light and floral. Inviting.

He captured her wrist. Her pulse raced and fine tremors vibrated under his touch. His concern notched up. Maybe her attacker had hurt her worse than Paul had thought. Or perhaps she was coming down from the adrenaline overload as shock set in.

'What can I do?' He bent his head, trying to catch her eye, but she'd dropped her gaze to somewhere near his chin.

She dragged in a shuddery breath. 'Don't be nice to me.'

He frowned, trying to fathom what was going on. 'You'd rather I was angry with you?'

This time her lips curved in a wobbly approximation of a smile that made pain pierce his chest. She was hurting, and he discovered he hated that.

She shook her head and he watched, fascinated, as her long hair slipped over her shoulders. Earlier, in the gloom, he'd thought it seductive. Now it threatened to distract him totally. He wanted to reach out and…

'Come and sit down. Drink your hot chocolate. You'll feel better.'

She lifted her chin and met his eyes, just for a moment.

He couldn't read her expression now. It reminded him of when they'd been together at the palace, talking about ending their betrothal.

She looked away. 'Thanks, but I don't want hot chocolate.'

Paul curved his other hand round her upper arm, her skin like cool silk.

'You're shaking.'

She shrugged. 'It will pass.'

Not good enough. Paul was used to taking action. Making things happen. Fixing problems.

'There must be something I can do. Something that would help.'

Another half-smile, this time unmistakeably wry.

'What?'

'It's nothing.'

Paul frowned. If there was one thing he'd learned tonight, it was that Eva could be forthright when she wanted to be. Why wasn't she now?

Releasing her wrist, he curled his finger under her chin, lifting it so he could hold her gaze.

His breath stalled as he saw how forlorn she looked.

His other hand stroked up her arm to her bare shoulder and back down to grasp her hand.

'It will be all right, Eva. Truly. It's over now.'

Her tiny huff of amusement was unexpected. 'Yes. You're right. It's over.'

But, though her posture was as perfect as ever and her stare direct, he wasn't fooled. It wasn't just the fact that she still trembled. It was the expression in her eyes.

'Eva. Tell me what I can do to help.'

For a long moment he thought she wasn't going to say anything. Then he heard, 'Kiss me. I want you to kiss me.'

CHAPTER FIVE

PAUL STARED AT her as if no woman had ever wanted to kiss him before. His eyebrows lifted from their deep V of concern and his eyes widened.

At least he looked stunned rather than sorry for her. That was an improvement.

When he'd been kind, Eva's heart had twisted. She'd had a tough night in so many ways and sympathy would only crack her veneer of calm. She'd feared she might slip up and reveal her feelings for him.

And when he'd said there was a link between them… She hadn't known whether to laugh or cry.

She'd been the one to recognise that link years ago. To treasure it and dream of a future built on it. Paul had been completely oblivious.

If he'd felt that link tonight…

No, it was just that he felt some responsibility since, in the eyes of the world, they were to be married.

'Eva? What are you saying?'

Her lips firmed as she fought despair with anger.

'You heard me, Paul.'

She wasn't going to say it again. Even though it was true. The one thing that at this moment would make her feel better was Paul's lips on hers, blotting out tonight's bitter regrets and searing hurt. Giving her the solace of his caress.

His frown was back, deeper than ever. His hand beneath

her chin moved to her shoulder. To hold her at a distance or to deliver a paternal pat of solace? As if she didn't know her own mind.

He'd asked what she wanted and she'd told him.

Abruptly, gloriously, she didn't care what he thought. Only that this was the last chance she'd ever have to kiss the man she'd adored since she'd been fifteen. The man who'd cracked her heart wide open and didn't even know it.

Tomorrow—later this morning—she'd say goodbye to him for ever. For now, they were alone, and she still wanted so much more than he'd ever give her.

Instinct told her to grab this opportunity for just a moment's solace, and that was what she did. One hand settled on that hard, straight shoulder. The other curled around the back of his neck, learning the texture of hot skin and soft hair. She rose on her toes and pulled his head down.

Paul stared down into the face of a woman he didn't know. Felt her hands on him, surprisingly strong, and stopping her didn't enter his brain.

Curiosity buzzed, stronger than surprise.

And something more than curiosity. Something that made his heart leap in his chest as soft lips settled against his.

That mouth. How had he not recognised that mouth for what it was? Pure seduction.

Her lips brushed his, making his breath still and his grip on her waist tighten.

He couldn't even recall reaching for Eva. But now he couldn't imagine relinquishing his hold. Her waist was narrow but he felt the sensual curve that led to the flare of her hips. Even the slippery satin of her dress—the dress that had taunted him from the moment he'd seen her in it—felt like an invitation.

She was so alluringly feminine. Delicious curves. Decadently inviting lips. A body that stretched seductively up against his, her breasts cushioning him in a way that bent his self-control out of shape.

From the first touch of her hand at his neck he'd gone rigid. The caress of her lips on his sent bolts of searing tension straight to his groin.

Once more she kissed him, a light caress that hinted at passion but was more tease than anything. Then, as his fingers tightened around her middle, she gasped and finally her tongue flicked out to trace his lips.

Instantly Paul took the lead. Because tantalising caresses simply weren't enough. She'd woken the need he'd kept stringently under control for four long years. That, and his curiosity to know this new, unexpected Eva, dragged him straight into temptation.

Once he tasted her, there was no going back.

Sweet and distinctive like wild honey from the mountains. No other woman tasted like Eva. Then there was the tiny little humming sound that came from the back of her throat and sounded like approval and invitation.

He opened his mouth and sucked in her tongue.

Paul felt her jolt of surprise, wondered at it then forgot about it as he concentrated on the sensations of her tongue in his mouth and the quiver of her body against him.

His hands were possessive. He wanted to haul her close, but he had enough control not to. Not after her experience tonight.

Yet she *was* flush against him, not because he'd dragged her there but because she'd closed the space between them.

His eyes closed at the sinuous movement of her soft body against his, igniting molten fire in his groin. He tried to ignore it, but that left his brain free to concentrate on their kiss.

Eva's tongue curled around his then drew back. He followed, plunging into sweet heat, needing more. Was that a heartbeat's hesitation? No, he'd imagined it. If anything her hands clung tighter than before, fingers digging into him as she tilted her head and sucked him deeper with a desperation that matched his own.

He shuddered at the fierce wave of pleasure cresting within him. His hands tightened at her waist and his body canted forward, bending her back, striving to absorb the flavour of her, the piercingly arousing perfection of Eva in his arms offering so much.

Eva, the woman he'd thought he'd known.

He'd known nothing.

Tonight was a revelation. Not just of her but of his own feelings. He'd imagined what he felt for her was simply duty. But when put to the test he discovered nothing about his relationship with Eva was what it seemed. *She* wasn't what she seemed.

She only had to pout those pretty lips and flash those bright eyes and he wanted everything.

Paul's guard slipped completely when he heard it again, and felt it too—that humming vibration of approval that came from Eva's mouth and trembled across his tongue. It was a lover's invitation.

How was he supposed to resist? That tiny sound alone was enough to test even a man trained in self-denial from years of celibacy.

Her thighs shifted restlessly against his, her body tantalising as she moved, cushioning his hardening erection against her belly.

The force of his arousal stunned him. It was so instantaneous, so complete. So unbelievable after years of implacable control. In the past he'd ground down any inclination for sex with long hours of work, achieving the impossible, because it was his duty to save his nation and he refused to countenance failure.

But now, with Eva supple and seductive in his arms, he

couldn't focus on duty. Even the simple dictates of his conscience, telling him not to take advantage of a woman who was suffering from shock, seemed beyond him.

Her hands palmed his cheeks then his shoulders to settle splayed on his chest, where his heart hammered. He felt her touch like a brand, a scorching incentive to take more.

Finally, with a last burst of determination, he lifted his head. But the action was a hollow victory because he ached for her with every cell of his being. He didn't want to do the right thing. He wanted to kiss Eva. He wanted to delight in her eager body and passionate kisses and...

'Don't stop!'

Paul gritted his teeth and closed his eyes, blotting out the beguiling sight of her wide eyes, now more blue than grey, beseeching him.

As if she wanted exactly what he wanted.

What he couldn't allow himself to take.

'Eva.' His voice was unrecognisable, a strained rumble, as if it came from some distant chasm far below the earth's surface. He tried again, opening his eyes to meet her gaze, ignoring the jolt of response that hit him like an unseen blow as their gazes locked. 'Eva, we can't do this. You're not thinking—'

'Don't you *dare* try to tell me I don't know what I want!'

Anger made her eyes glitter but, instead of withdrawing, she stayed pressed against him.

She'd never looked so magnificent.

Inevitably his admiration made itself known in the most obvious way. An expression he couldn't identify crossed her features as his erection stirred against her.

'I wouldn't dream of it.' Especially when he didn't want to stop either. Yet Paul couldn't shake the conviction that he needed to protect her, even from himself. 'But you've had a shock and it would be wrong to take advantage of that. You're not yourself.'

Her nostrils flared and her mouth turned down in the corners in a way that should have made her look unattractive but instead turned into the sexiest, sultriest pout he'd ever seen.

The throb of need that pulsed through his body almost undid him.

'Because you don't really want me. You just feel sorry for me.'

Paul couldn't contain the crack of laugher that escaped his lips. 'You know I want you. I can't disguise that.'

How much more obvious could it be, with his erection hard against her and his control hanging by a thread? He didn't yet have the power to pull away.

On that thought, he finally managed to do what he should have done earlier. He stepped back, coming up against the huge kitchen table that filled the centre of the room.

Eva moved a split second later, following him. Her luscious body blanketed his, fraying his tattered determination. He was trying to do the decent thing but she made it tough.

'Eva…' Her name turned into a sigh as she grabbed one of his hands and put it to her breast. Convulsively his fingers closed on satin and warm, rounded flesh. Her eyes darkened as he squeezed. Her gaze turned the hazy blue of the sea at dawn.

She was killing him.

Then his eyes rolled back in his head as she cupped his erection with her other hand. His breath hissed and his body turned to stone. All except that throbbing, eager part of him that surged harder against her touch.

'Kiss me, Paul. Please.'

Her lips were against his, inviting him. The perfect swell of her breast was in his hand and the possessive clasp of her fingers around him obliterated all thought.

Paul kissed her. Hard.

It wasn't enough. He wanted all her sweetness. He wanted…

Dazed, he let himself savour the heady prospect of her giving him exactly what he wanted—relief from the tangle of frustrated longing, thwarted passion and the inhibiting voice of his conscience that told him to move away.

This was just a moment's fantasy, not reality.

Yet he exhaled with relief and something close to despair as Eva tugged his zip down and slid her fingers inside his trousers to hold him, her soft hand against hard, needy flesh.

Lightning seared his blackened vision, strobe lights of white-hot energy that arced and whirled as Eva tested his length, then squeezed.

Air expelled from his lungs in a guttural rush. There was a thrumming in his ears as he tried to collect his scattered control.

He'd be strong again in a second. When he had time to regroup. Except now, somehow, he held both her breasts in his hands, testing their weight, revelling in the graze of her pebbled nipples. Barely, he resisted the need to strip away the flimsy satin dress so he could feast on her ripeness.

Then she was undoing his belt with her other hand.

It was exactly what he wanted and everything he shouldn't.

He opened his mouth to stop her when Eva's mouth collided with his again. The movement was clumsy, almost desperate, but so beautiful that he felt himself sink back into the bliss of the moment.

Paul's whole body trembled. He relinquished her breasts, wrapping one arm round her and using the other to push back her long hair that had fallen forward, caressing his cheek.

It was incredibly soft, impossibly decadent, that long

skein of silk that somehow wrapped itself around his fingers, just as she wrapped her fingers around him, stroking, teasing.

He had to let her go. Make her release him too.

But then, before he could act, there it was, thundering towards him like a freight train racing down a mountain. Paul felt the building pressure, the torture of a body grown too taut and hard to contain itself. The careering rush of pleasure.

He just had enough time to read Eva's wide-eyed look of elation, and cover the head of his erection with his hand, before he convulsed, helpless, against the sudden, raw rush of ecstasy.

Eva was stunned.

How could a man be magnificently powerful and at the same time so vulnerable?

The sight of Paul lost in the throes of climax, the feel of him jerkily pulsing in her hand, was the most exciting thing she'd known.

Watching his big shoulders judder, seeing him fling his head back, the tendons in his throat standing proud, made him seem not weak but incredibly strong.

Despite the fact he was at her mercy.

The knowledge floored her.

No, this wasn't about knowledge, it was about the visceral feeling, the love, compassion and deep sense of connection.

How she loved the feel of him, satin-soft yet impossibly hard, beneath her hand. The feel of him shuddering with pleasure at her touch.

Hers. Not someone else's but hers. *She'd* done that. Brought sexual fulfilment to the man she loved.

Pinpricks of delight exploded through her.

Even when he bowed his head and nudged her hand

aside, those great, racking shudders easing to small tremors, she was dumbstruck by the power she'd unleashed.

She'd had no idea it could be like this. So intense, so exciting. Because of course theory was no substitute for reality. Her knowledge of sex, apart from a few pretty innocent kisses, was all theoretical.

Even the heavy musk scent in the air and the sound of Paul's laboured breaths were something completely new.

New and exhilarating. Though she still felt that edgy, needy sensation between her thighs, making her shift her weight to ease it.

She sighed, trying to ignore her own needs. Instead she took in the dull flush of colour across Paul's high cheek bones, the heavy-lidded look from glittering eyes that spoke of sensuality and satisfaction.

A shiver ripped through her and headed straight to her sex. Everything inside her softened.

Watching Paul come, *feeling* his potent explosion, was the single most exciting moment of her life.

He turned away, cleaning himself up, and Eva supposed she should do the same. Her hand was sticky. But she stayed where she was, her brain whirring on overdrive, her body revved. Because she loved how she'd affected him.

Just for a short time, he'd been *hers*.

Their kiss had been everything she'd hoped for. Passionate, beautiful and definitely mutual. Her heart had soared. Yet she'd feared it wouldn't last. She'd known Paul would pull away, because she was the fiancée he no longer wanted. And she'd been right, though he'd couched his rejection in terms of looking after her, not wanting to take advantage.

Take advantage! Was that what *she'd* done? Shoving her hand in his trousers?

Even now she could barely believe she'd done that. It was so out of character.

Because all her life she'd conformed, agreed, been polite and never pushed for what she wanted. Except when her parents had asked if she wanted to marry Paul of St Ancilla and she'd said yes.

But all those years of polite waiting, of doing the right thing, being gracious and amenable, hadn't got her what she wanted. Because Paul had never wanted her, Eva. Just a royal princess who'd do her royal duty and, as a bonus, bring her fortune with her.

Something had snapped in her tonight. Maybe because of the danger she'd been in at the hands of a stranger. Or maybe because Paul had snarked at her, as if she'd been to blame.

Whatever the cause, Eva had finally had enough. She was about to lose him. That knowledge had spurred her on to kiss him, touch him, as she'd previously only dreamed of. To snatch at least a moment for herself.

It had been glorious.

But now it was over.

She heard the sound of his zip, saw the straight set of his shoulders as he turned on a tap, his back still to her. Paul hadn't looked at her once since that gleaming, sexually charged stare that had pierced straight to her womb.

Just thinking of it, another tremor raked her from head to toe. Once more it ended at that sensitive place between her legs.

Paul turned and she braced herself for rejection.

His face was unreadable, his features tight, the curve of his cheek and the angle of his jaw pronounced. He looked more handsome than ever and even more unattainable.

Eva's heart dropped.

His mouth twisted up in a grimace that reinforced her fears. 'I'm sorry, Eva.'

'Sorry?' she parroted. She should be the one apologising. She'd been the one to force him to kiss her, to touch him.

He closed the space between them with a couple of strides and she found herself pressed up against the table.

'I lost control.' His brow furrowed into a scowl.

'I know.' And it had been glorious, but she didn't say that. 'You didn't…enjoy it?'

Now she was confused. Surely that powerful climax told its own story?

The scowl eased a little and the curl of his lip looked a fraction softer. 'Of course I enjoyed it. But I shouldn't have. I don't know what came over me. One touch.' His voice lowered to a mutter. 'One touch and I was done for.' He shook his head. 'I showed all the finesse and self-control of a teenager.'

Eva tilted her head, trying to gauge whether it was embarrassment or genuine regret behind his words.

'What's the problem? That you came so fast or that it was me that made you?'

Her eyes widened a little as the words shot from her mouth, for this was the sort of straight talking she never engaged in. She raised her chin too. She wasn't ashamed of what she'd done.

Unless Paul saw it as some sort of assault. The idea made her flesh crawl. Had she been so wrapped up in her own desire she'd misunderstood his protests? How unwilling had he been?

His crooked smile eased her fears. 'I'm a big boy, Eva. If I hadn't wanted your touch, I'd have fended you off.'

So he'd *wanted* her touch.

The constriction that had hampered her last few breaths eased.

'I'm not usually so gauche.' Another shake of his head. 'But it's been a long time since a woman touched me.'

'It has?' She'd imagined that with his looks and charm he'd have a bevy of women waiting to provide comfort to the lonely Prince who saw so little of his fiancée.

Paul's gaze caught hers. 'Of course. We've been engaged for four years. I exchanged promises with you and I take my word seriously.'

Eva had thought by now she'd withstood every shock the night could possibly have in store. She was wrong. She stared up at him, eyes bulging.

'You mean…?' She shook her head, then paused to shove her hair back from her face when it obscured her vision. 'You've been celibate all this time?'

It seemed impossible. Paul abstaining from sexual pleasure because of her.

'I made a promise to be loyal to you as my bride-to-be. I don't break my promises.'

Eva couldn't tell if that was pride, hauteur or disapproval stiffening his tall form.

'I take it you didn't feel the same?' His tone was austere. 'I suppose you wouldn't. We're only together a couple of times a year.'

'That wasn't my choice.' Her hands slid to her hips. 'I offered to visit more often but you said no.' That still rankled. During the first year of their engagement, she'd only seen him twice!

'Only because I've been very busy. I didn't have time to entertain you on a social visit.'

Eva drew a deep breath and counted to ten. 'Maybe I don't need entertaining. Maybe I wanted to support you.'

It was clear from Paul's stunned stare that the thought had never occurred to him. Which was typical of their non-relationship, wasn't it?

Suddenly Eva was tired of all this. The false relationship, the tiptoeing around the truth. It was over and that was that.

Even her breaking heart and the ache of rejection could wait till tomorrow. For now, she just wanted to escape. There was no reason to stay for a post mortem on their engagement. Or to rehash tonight's events.

She turned towards the door, already forming words of farewell. Except long fingers wrapped around her arm, stopping her.

Immediate heat flashed through her. Excitement. Need.

Eva hated that she couldn't prevent her reaction to him. But it was time to face facts. Whatever they'd shared was over.

Yet when she tried to free her arm Paul captured her other arm too, his long fingers gentle but implacable.

'Where do you think you're going?' His voice dropped an octave, rumbling across her skin on an unfamiliar note that made her insides clench.

Eva looked up but didn't meet those keen eyes. 'Tonight has been a disaster. It's time we went our separate ways, don't you think?'

'You've got to be kidding. We've barely started.'

Stunned as much by Paul's unmistakably suggestive tone as by his words, she met his gaze. And couldn't look away. His expression made her hot inside. Hotter than she already was.

He released one arm and lifted his hand to her face, long fingers sliding gently across her cheek to her mouth, his thumb capturing her bottom lip and pressing till she opened for him. Instantly, without her consciously planning it, her tongue slipped out to lick him, drawing the taste of him— hot, salty male—into her mouth.

Those dark blue eyes flared and his mouth rucked up in an approving smile.

'No, I don't believe we're anywhere near finished.'

For the second time in one night she looked into the face of a man with sex on his mind. But this wasn't a stranger who dismayed or disgusted her. The roaring rush of blood in her ears and the catapulting thump of her heart were all about excitement.

Paul's head lowered, slowly enough that she could turn

away if she wanted. Instead Eva tilted her chin higher, meeting his lips with hers.

Eva was struck by how familiar it felt. The shape of Paul's mouth on hers, the taste and scent of him, something fresh like pine trees and the outdoors. The wonderful warmth of his body against hers, his embrace enfolding her.

It didn't even matter that this was simply sex, not love. If this was all she'd have of Paul before they parted, she'd take it gladly.

She slid her hands up his broad chest to link around the back of his neck, the ends of her fingers tunnelling through his hair. Surprising how intimate that felt, given how she'd touched him earlier.

A chuckle bubbled inside her, but died when powerful hands palmed her buttocks and lifted her off the floor. Her eyes snapped open and for a moment she lost herself in his indigo gaze.

He moved and then she was sitting on the table with Paul standing wedged between her thighs.

Heat squirmed through her, making her shift on the scrubbed surface.

'What...?'

But then he was kissing her again, tenderly, thoroughly, learning her and what she liked. It seemed she liked everything, from the gentle bite of his teeth on her bottom lip that made her nipples tingle, to the languorously slow kisses that made her melt inside.

Her eyelids were heavy and her body fluid with pleasure when she registered his hands on her legs. Their kiss didn't falter as her hem crept up her thighs and his hand slid down to cup wet silk.

Eva moaned into his mouth, her hips tilting needily.

Another caress, another circle of her hips, and the hunger for fulfilment grew. Was this how Paul had felt when she'd caressed him, at first tentatively, then with determination?

There was nothing tentative about Paul's touch. He knew exactly what he was doing. Looping an arm around her waist, he lifted her off the table just enough to drag her silk underwear down. Then he backed away from her, rolling her panties down her bare legs.

And still their lips were locked, his tongue stroking hers, then delving rhythmically into her mouth in a way that made her even more restless.

Finally, he touched her again between the legs. A slow, sliding caress through damp folds that nearly had her jumping off the table.

Eva moaned against his mouth then stopped as he pulled away. Appalled, she met his knowing gaze. Was he going to stop? He couldn't, surely? Not when he made her feel…

'Patience, Eva.' He lifted her hand to his mouth, but instead of a courtly kiss to the back of her hand he held her gaze and licked her from the inside of her wrist, across her palm and right to the end of her fingers, drawing them into his mouth and sucking.

A dart of fire shot from her nipples to her womb, exploding in shuddering waves. Her internal muscles clenched and her breath hissed in sharply.

Looking into that proud, determined face, Eva realised she didn't know Paul as well as she'd imagined. This flagrant carnality was a side of him she'd never suspected when she'd imagined his kisses and, yes, sex. She'd known being with him would be wonderful because she loved him. But the earthy appreciation in his expression as he looked down her body to where his fingers teased was something she hadn't expected.

Eva felt she should be shocked. Instead she was incredibly aroused.

And he knew. It was there in the triumphant look he gave her from under those straight black eyebrows.

She opened her mouth to say something but words

eluded her. Then he was gone, sinking to his knees before her. One hard yank dragged her right to the edge of the table and then, while she watched in disbelief, he leaned in to kiss her.

It was like watching a film in slow motion. Each frame froze as she struggled to take in what she was seeing. Then, with the touch of his mouth on her most sensitive skin, the film sped up to match her racketing pulse.

Eva stared, trying to connect the sight of Paul between her legs and the exquisitely arousing sensations as he used his tongue and lips to pleasure her.

It didn't take much. She was ready for him, so on edge. What he made her feel was wondrous, so exactly what she needed, that soon she teetered on the brink of losing herself.

It was the sight of Paul looking up that did it. The expression of satisfaction in his gaze as it met hers, as if the pair of them shared a delicious secret, that sent her over the edge.

Fingers clamped on the table, legs spread wide by his shoulders, Eva tossed her head back and screamed as ecstasy took her.

It went on and on, writhing through her, a pleasure so intense it came close to pain, except that this made her feel as if she'd shot to heaven.

Eyes closed, all she could do was cling on and ride out the waves of powerful sensation. Till somehow it wasn't wood that she clutched but Paul, his shoulders hard beneath her clenching fingers, his arms tight around her, his voice rough but reassuring in her ear.

Foggily, Eva wondered if it was possible she'd died and gone to paradise. Then she gave up trying to think and slumped into his strong arms.

CHAPTER SIX

EVA FITTED HIS hold perfectly. Strange that he hadn't considered that before. Even when they'd danced at various balls he hadn't realised how good she'd feel against him.

He'd been aware of her femininity, of course. You couldn't waltz with a woman like Eva and not be drawn to her. But in the past he'd been busy trying to find a way through her reserve, frustrated at her aloofness. Sometimes, when her conversation had consisted of platitudes and she'd barely met his eyes, he'd focused his mind instead on the most pressing of the nation's debts and his plans to reduce them.

Now she had his full attention.

She'd had it since she'd swept into the ball, head high and with a light in her eyes he'd never seen before.

There was so much about Eva he'd never seen or suspected before.

Her fiery anger.

Her obstinacy.

Her passion.

Her ability to take him from zero to a blistering climax in what felt like seconds.

His belly clenched and heat eddied deep inside. Paul was torn between shame at how he'd come apart so easily and the burning need to have her touch him again.

As for the sight of her losing herself with such abandon, the scent and wild honey taste of her…

He hefted her higher in his arms and strode from the kitchen towards the tower's spiral staircase. He knew every step of the way but was glad of the low-level sensor lighting that sprang up on the steps. He didn't want to stumble with Eva in his embrace.

She turned her face into his neck, but gave no other sign of being awake.

Paul smiled. Her orgasm had left her soft as a sleepy kitten against him. It made a change from the defiant, obstinate woman who'd made her appearance tonight. And from the coolly distant fiancée who'd visited St Ancilla for years.

He was determined to discover which of them was the real Eva.

As he strode higher he quickly reviewed practicalities. They needed time alone and here at the lodge they'd have privacy, more so than at the palace.

Key staff knew where he was. The car had a tracker and he'd used handprint security to enter the house, at the same time remotely locking the gates. Staff could contact him in an emergency. No doubt there was a guard on duty now in the discreet security building near the front gate.

But, with any luck, no one would need him for the next twenty-four hours. He'd kept a full day free of appointments, knowing that his plans to end the engagement would mean he'd need to be available to discuss the details with Eva. To agree on how and when they'd announce the news of their separation.

Now, with her hair tickling his chin, her delicious body in his embrace and the scent of sex and spring flowers tantalising his nostrils, the end of their betrothal was the last thing on his mind.

For years Paul had stifled his libido as best he could,

working to the point of exhaustion. He hadn't fully succeeded but he hadn't given in to its urges.

Tonight he had. Spectacularly.

And the most intriguing thing was that, despite his clumsiness, his ego-bruising gaucheness at coming the way he had, the last half-hour with Eva had rivalled any sex he could recall.

He reached the top of the stairs and shouldered his way into the suite he kept for himself, a round room with windows on three sides and an *en suite* bathroom. No lights were on here, but the curtains at one window were open and he had no trouble finding his way.

Moments later he lowered Eva onto the bed. She stretched, turning her head into the pillow and arching her back. It was an instinctive, sensual movement and it dragged the tension in his belly up another notch.

He liked having Eva in his bed, her hair spilling like a dark cloud around her pale shoulders. Her legs bare and her toes curling.

Paul recalled the thud as her high heels had dropped unheeded to the kitchen floor as she screamed her release, and the skin across his neck and shoulders prickled.

Reaching back, he grabbed his lightweight sweater at the neck and hauled it over his head, tossing it onto a nearby chair. He looked forward to having Eva in his arms again, skin to skin.

The thought sent a luxurious shiver through him as he bent to rifle the bedside table, hoping to find… Yes, he was in luck. There at the back of the drawer was a box of condoms. He opened it, dropping its contents onto the top of the table.

'What are you doing?' There it was again, that husky note he'd heard in Eva's voice for the first time tonight. It rasped across the tight skin of his belly, sending another surge of heat to his groin.

She lay on her side and had raised herself on one elbow. Even in the gloom he appreciated the feminine allure of her silhouette, the deepened dip to her waist and the sweet curve up to her hips.

Paul's throat dried. 'Making sure we have protection.'

In this light he didn't see her move but he'd swear she stiffened.

'Aren't you taking a lot for granted?'

But, when her gaze turned from the table to him, he heard her indrawn breath as she surveyed his bare torso.

Paul wasn't vain but he knew his wide-shouldered frame, kept trim by his love of sport, drew female attention. Now, as he felt Eva's gaze track from his ribs to his belt, he bit back a smile.

He sat beside her, one hand planted on the bed beyond her hip.

'What, you were going to take your pleasure from me then just walk away?'

She shifted, wriggling up the bed towards the pillows. In the process he felt the brush of her legs and inhaled again the heady scent of warm woman and sex. His trousers tightened against his groin but he didn't move.

'You've already...taken *your* pleasure.'

Was that embarrassment he heard? Surely not from the woman who'd thrust her hand into his pants!

He shuddered at the memory of her soft palm sliding along his length, her fingers encircling him. She'd been a little clumsy but that had only added to the piquancy, proof that she was too eager for finesse.

Paul laughed, the sound rusty with barely suppressed desire. 'That was just a start, Eva.' He had plans for the rest of the night and they didn't include sleep. 'When a man's fiancée shows she's eager for sex—'

'I'm not your fiancée.'

Paul refused to touch that one. He had more pressing things on his mind than another argument.

He lifted his hand to trail his fingers down her satin-clad thigh. 'But you want me, don't you, lover?'

Her breath hissed in and he felt her tremble. Yet he made himself stop, his fingertips barely touching the place where satin met smooth, enticing flesh. It was surprising how difficult it was not to caress her. Once he'd touched her and tasted her, he wanted so much more.

'You want to have sex?'

Once more he found her tone difficult to read. That almost sounded like doubt in her voice. As if he'd left any doubts about his desire for her!

'Absolutely.' He swallowed hard. 'I suspect we'll be phenomenal together.'

When still she said nothing, Paul frowned and made himself lift his hand away.

After what they'd done downstairs it seemed impossible but perhaps, after all, he'd read Eva wrong and she didn't want...

A slim hand grabbed his and settled it palm-down on her bare thigh.

Paul's heart leapt high in his throat, the throb in his groin pulsing even harder.

He splayed his fingers, sliding them round her silky skin, and she shifted, parting her legs a little to give him better access.

Doubt vanished in a flash, replaced by excitement.

Eva's heartbeat quickened as Paul caressed her leg in long, deliberate strokes. They were as easy and regular as waves rippling in to shore, but with each slide of his hand her pulse pounded harder and she became more aware of that aching spot between her thighs.

He reached down to circle her ankles and calves, pausing to massage her soles, and a blissful sigh escaped. She tried to tell herself it was because she'd worn high heels for hours but even a woman as innocent as she knew the difference between relaxation and arousal.

By the time Paul worked his way back up her other leg to the hem of her dress, she was twitching and eager for so much more.

'I want to see all of you, Eva.' His low voice burred across her skin as he pushed the material up her thighs in slow, breath-stealing increments.

It was what she wanted. Yet the thought of lying naked before him, like some carnal offering, made her supremely uneasy. She'd never been naked for any man. She wanted Paul, wanted to be possessed by him, but, despite what they'd just done to each other, shyness rose in a baffling wave.

How could she be shy after that scene in the kitchen?

Yet it was true. More, she feared revealing her inexperience. This was her only chance to make love with Paul. She was under no illusions that sex would alter his decision to call off their wedding. She'd take tonight gladly, though, and give him no reason to back off.

'You first.' Her tight vocal cords turned the words into a throaty command instead of a tentative suggestion.

Paul didn't seem to mind. He shrugged, those wide shoulders rising. She caught the white gleam of his smile. 'If you like.'

He half-turned from her and she clamped her mouth shut over an instinctive protest at the loss of contact. It took only seconds for him to remove his shoes and socks, then he was standing by the bed, shucking the rest of his clothes off, and Eva's eyes rounded at the sight of him.

Even in the half-light he was magnificent. Tall, lean but powerful across the chest, with a flat abdomen, narrow hips and long, muscled legs. His erection stood out proud and ready for her and Eva squeezed her thighs together as moist heat drenched her.

'Would you like to put the condom on me?' He picked up a packet from the table and tore it open.

Eva swallowed, torn between excitement and horror. She did want to, but if she fumbled too much he might guess she'd never done this before. It was a wonder he hadn't already. Down in the kitchen she'd acted on instinct rather than experience. Presumably he'd been too aroused to notice.

Four years of celibacy, he'd said. That must explain it. No wonder he'd been so responsive to her touch.

Her heart dipped. Paul's eager reaction hadn't been to *her* specifically. He'd been primed by abstinence to respond to a woman's caresses.

Even so, Eva wanted this. Wanted him. This was her one opportunity for intimacy with the man she still, despite everything, loved.

So much for pride. But pride was a cold bed-fellow. She craved the warmth of his loving, even if it was only a travesty of the emotional response she needed from him.

Whatever the reason, Paul wanted *her*. She couldn't refuse him or herself.

'No. I want to watch you do it.' Her voice was a rough croak but he didn't seem to mind.

Paul laughed. 'Do you, indeed? Well, it's probably better. I don't want to disgrace myself again like I did downstairs. This time I intend to last long enough to satisfy you.'

Eva's indrawn breath was fire and molten metal as her brain provided a picture of him doing just that.

Then he was on the bed, knees straddling her legs.

'Sit up, sweetheart.'

Eva's silly heart somersaulted at the casual endearment. Part of her brain screamed she was a fool. The other part urged her on.

She raised herself so Paul could reach behind to her zip. Slowly he peeled the narrow straps down her arms. Then gently, almost reverently, he undid her bra.

Any hesitation she felt about baring her breasts died as he leaned in and kissed her, murmuring how beautiful she was as he cupped her with his big, warm hands.

Heat shot through her, another arrowing dart of fire, and then she was on her back, lifting her hips as he dragged her dress down and away. Their knees bumped and she didn't know quite what to do with her hands. But none of that detracted from the shivery delight of Paul's hands on her, his mouth caressing hers, and that possessive-sounding growl as he palmed her bare hips.

Finally, they were naked. He turned her towards him so they lay on their sides, facing each other. Then he pulled back and looked down, grinning.

'You're exquisite.'

It was on the tip of her tongue to refute it, knowing he didn't mean it, but then his fingertips touched her nipple in the most delicate touch and her breath fractured.

When he touched her like that she *felt* different. Special. She imagined his eyes glowed with a light she hadn't seen before, even though common sense said she couldn't really read his expression. She tried to tell herself it was simply lust but her aching heart wanted to believe it was because at last Paul saw the woman she really was.

The harping voice of caution was silenced by the sheer magic of this moment with Paul.

His caresses as he skimmed her body brought fire in their wake, and when he bent to kiss her breast, then suck her nipple, Eva arched into him, a lightning bolt of desire ripping through her.

She was panting when finally, after exploring her thoroughly with his hands and mouth, he rolled on top of her. Eva was bombarded with sensation. The weight of him, pressing her down onto the bed. He was taller and broader than her. It might have felt suffocating but instead she welcomed it, wrapping her arms around him. His skin was smooth as silk, swelling intriguingly over lean muscle and bone. His hairy legs tickled hers and the hair on his chest abraded her breasts so deliciously, her breath caught.

'You like that?' He settled more firmly between her legs, and that was new too, the feel of her thighs cradling his hot, hard body.

Eva nodded, her throat constricted. She didn't want to talk.

'What else do you like?' He propped himself on his elbows above her, his patient stillness as he waited for her response warring with the sexual promise implicit in his preternaturally still frame.

Eva didn't want to wait. She wanted him to deliver what his body promised.

'You, just you.'

She lifted her feet, hooking her ankles around the back of his thighs, feeling him sink deeper against her, his erection stiff and long. Almost daunting, but she refused to think that way. Instead Eva lifted her hands to the back of his head, driving her fingers through his thick hair, cupping his skull, pulling him down. 'I want you inside me. Now.'

Finally, he succumbed to her tugging and lowered his mouth to hers.

Once again she felt it. Not just the sharp tug of desire but the overwhelming tenderness of love. That it was all on her side no longer mattered. She wanted Paul so badly. He would be her first lover. That would be something wonderful, even though they were destined to go their separate ways tomorrow. At least she'd have the memory of tonight to take with her.

Paul's kiss was surprisingly tender. She felt a tremor of tension running through him and the heavy press of his erection. Eva sensed he was suppressing his own urgency for her benefit.

Then his hand slipped between them, his fingers arrowing straight to the achy, wet place between her thighs that throbbed with such need.

His head lifted and he smiled. A secret, intimate smile that tugged at her heart strings.

Then she had no time to think about anything but the extraordinary feeling of Paul pushing against her, into her, so full and heavy and...

Her breath fractured on a searing slash of pain. She stiffened all over at the sharp sting that went on and on. For some reason she hadn't expected it, assuming that years of riding and other exercise would have removed the physical proof of her virginity.

Paul froze. 'Eva?'

She watched his shoulders rise away from her as he pulled back.

Instantly she tightened the grip of her legs around him and grabbed at him, sinking her fingers in the taut flesh of his buttocks, pulling him close so that he sank deep inside.

Tears pricked the backs of her eyes at that final flash of pain, and she arched up. Eva rested her forehead against his hard collarbone, inhaling his reassuringly familiar, outdoorsy scent as she gasped for air.

The world stilled. She heard the thrum of her pulse in her ears and felt it pound through her whole body.

His hand stroked her head, making her long hair slide around her shoulders.

'Oh, Eva.' His deep voice was a caress in itself. 'It'll be all right soon.'

Finally, trembling, she sank back against the pillows. Above her she made out the wide line of Paul's shoulders against the darkness, and the glint of his eyes.

'Are you okay?'

Eva nodded. 'Fine.' She almost was. She just felt…disoriented, adjusting to the unaccustomed weight of him. The fullness that she'd somehow never expected but which now made perfect sense.

Cautiously, she breathed deep. Her muscles relaxed a little more. Again his fingers brushed her hair back, then lingered to caress her cheek, lips and throat. By the time he lifted his hand she was arching up, eager for that hand on her breast. He obliged, gently squeezing there, and a little sizzle of excitement shot through her.

'You should have told me.'

Eva didn't want to talk about it. She just wanted this, him. Them. For now, her body had relaxed, and this no longer felt like an impossible burden but a potent promise of pleasure.

'Shh.' She put her fingers to his mouth, tracing those beautifully sculpted lips. Something rose inside her. The familiar welling of love and with it the need for him.

Raking her fingers through his hair, she drew his head down, lifting her other hand up to clutch his shoulder.

Then, everything changed as Paul began to move slowly, cautiously, but even so she felt the phenomenal power of them together. Her untried body responded with a tentative tilt of the hips that made him sink deeper, touching a spot that sent sheet lightning blasting through her.

There was a hiss of breath and Eva realised it came from Paul. She was so wrapped up in wonder at new sensations as they moved together, still slowly, but with increasing confidence. They were like two halves of a whole, melding then almost separating, only to join again in a way that made even the orgasm he'd given her seem insignificant.

Because now they were one, sharing the same ripples of delight, so closely joined it seemed impossible they'd ever again be two separate people.

Eva's heart ached with the beauty of it. She revelled in

the husky, velvet undertone of Paul's deep voice, so deep now she barely heard it, but rather felt it like an approving rumble shuddering through her.

His hands were gentle, his mouth on hers deliciously languorous, enticing her to open wide and share all that she was. Meanwhile that honed, lean, powerful body moved with her, drawing her away from everything she'd known and up into the starlit night.

She wanted to sigh at the beauty of it but the tempo of their coupling quickened and she had no breath to spare. Little explosions of excitement began to prickle her body, from her scalp to her soles and everywhere in between.

Her toes curled and she locked him close, hanging on as their rhythm disintegrated into a pounding, desperate rush.

'Eva!' Her name on his lips sounded beautiful.

But she had no time to concentrate on that as he bit down on the sensitive spot where her shoulder curved up to her neck, and a shot of electric energy tore through her. Paul's hand slid between them, unerringly locating that sensitive nub and pressing hard as he powered hard and fast into her, again and again and again.

It was too much, even though she didn't want it ever to end. Eva felt the flex of his powerful thighs against hers, his glutes bunch hard and a vibration begin in his body and end in hers.

The shaft of pleasure from their joining was so intense, so profound, it obliterated all else.

She heard a shout of triumph, felt heat consume her and then she was lost in a whirl of ecstasy.

When a lifetime later she floated back to earth to find herself sprawled across Paul's damp, heaving chest, she couldn't stop the smile that curved her lips.

That had been the single most wonderful experience of her life.

She and Paul together… Hadn't she known they were made for each other?

Eva lay where she was, her ear pressed to his chest, inhaling the rich, spicy scent of him. Slowly her breathing evened out and her racketing pulse returned to something like normal, but her arms and legs remained boneless. Never mind. She didn't ever want to move.

Except slowly, finally, her brain began to work. To register more than the aftermath of intoxicating pleasure.

That was when her skin began to chill.

Not just her skin, but her blood too.

For, held in Paul's loose embrace, plastered to his magnificent body, her own still humming with the joy he'd given her, she realised the huge mistake she'd made.

She'd loved him since she was fifteen. Had been overwhelmed by hurt and dismay when he'd told her he didn't want her in his life. But instead of walking away with her head up she'd proved just how desperate she was for him. She'd come on to him *even though he didn't want her.*

He might have called out her name as he'd climaxed but he'd only come to bed with her because he'd been primed for sex. Any woman would have done. And this way he hadn't broken his promise to be faithful to his fiancée.

Tonight had changed her life. Yet for Paul it had simply been a convenient and welcome release from celibacy.

That wasn't the worst, though.

Her breath backed up in her lungs.

No, worse by far was the realisation she'd only increased the burden she bore.

Loving Paul from afar had been bad enough. But now she'd had a taste of glory. He'd opened her eyes to a world she'd never known. A world not just of sexual delight but of profound joy. She'd been lucky enough to know the wondrous rapture of sharing herself body and soul with the man she loved.

It was a gift some people never knew. She supposed she should be grateful.

But this gift came at an unbearable cost. It would make leaving, never to see him again, so much more difficult than she'd believed possible even a few short hours before. Because she knew now what she'd be missing.

Eva stared dry-eyed across the room and wished with her whole heart that she'd never laid eyes on Paul of St Ancilla.

CHAPTER SEVEN

SHE WAS STILL asleep when he came back from the bathroom.

As they'd lain entwined in each other's arms, he'd spoken her name and brushed the hair gently from her cheek, but she hadn't responded.

Paul had been almost certain she was awake. She'd held herself so still.

He'd opened his mouth to quiz her then shut it again. He had so many questions, but perhaps this wasn't the time, no matter that his curiosity was insatiable.

How she'd come to be a virgin at twenty-four.

Why tonight she'd suddenly let him past that rigid wall of reserve.

Whether she regretted what they'd done.

He'd drawn in a slow breath and remained silent. No, he was happy to wait for her answer on that one.

Soon after her body had softened against him, her breathing slowing, and he'd known she was indeed sleeping.

He'd waited a little then had gone to dispose of the condom. Now, back in the bed, he lay close enough to feel her warmth, but didn't touch her.

Because if he did there'd be precious little thinking done. Sex with Eva had been phenomenal. He tried to tell himself it was because he'd abstained for so long. It was true he felt a strange, muted triumph at being Eva's first lover, but until now he'd sought experienced partners. If she'd said she was inexperienced, he wouldn't have touched her.

Yeah, right. You'd never have been able to resist. Just looking at her in that short dress drove you to the brink.

A shudder passed through his sated body as he recalled Eva in that slinky dress. He felt a tightening in his groin. A feather of arousal skimmed his spine as she shifted beside him and he inhaled her delectable scent: hot, sexy woman with an intriguing hint of spring flowers.

Even her long hair, almost waist-length, was seductive. The way she looked with it down around her shoulders, her pert breasts peeping out from beneath the silky curtain. The feel of it caressing his flesh as he moved against her.

Gritting his teeth, Paul rolled away and stared towards the window. Already dawn was coming. He saw the first glow of morning.

It was far too soon. He needed to think, and fast. Because dealing with Eva had just got incredibly complicated.

He'd planned to give her her freedom. Except she didn't seem to want it. Now, if he was truthful, letting her walk away held precious little appeal. The way they'd been together...

He drew a slow breath and tried to concentrate. Not on sex. Not on the physical presence of the woman in bed with him. But on what to do now their relationship had exploded into something completely unrecognisable.

Eva had always been an enigma, apparently docile and always agreeable but never allowing any degree of intimacy. Until tonight. She'd been anything but docile. She'd proceeded to blow the back right off his skull with her sexy mouth and eager hands, reducing him to slavering desperation. Not once but twice.

And she'd been a virgin!

How much more dangerous would she be with a bit more experience?

Paul shuddered and tried to tell himself it was in dismay, not anticipation.

Despite his agitated thoughts, a mighty yawn cracked his jaw as a second night without sleep caught up with him.

The night before the ball he'd pulled an all-nighter, recalibrating the plans his advisers and his brother-in-law, Jake—a financial guru—had devised to keep St Ancilla afloat.

Years of hard work, refinancing and ruthless expenditure-cutting meant the economy hadn't collapsed on itself after King Hugo's depredations. But it was still a close thing. Made particularly difficult as the full extent of those debts, which Paul had personally shouldered, wasn't publicly known. The monarchy was the mainstay of the small kingdom and he had no intention of allowing public confidence to unravel. The good news was that, after coming close to bankruptcy, things were finally turning around.

Paul sighed and closed his eyes for a moment. Just a moment, while he pondered this latest challenge in an already demanding kingship. How to deal with his feisty, surprising fiancée.

Eva smiled and stretched. She felt oh, so warm and cosy. This was the softest bed she'd slept in and she was only too happy to sink into it, not wanting to stir.

Strange. Normally she was a morning person, awake early and full of energy. But not now. She could stay here for ever. She'd never felt so good.

Except for that curious sensation between her legs and…

Her eyelids snapped open. She found herself staring at bright sky through a canopy of spring leaves. She frowned. This wasn't her bedroom. It looked as if she was in a tree house or…

Movement behind her cut off her thoughts.

Heat, searing but delicious, right up against her body.

The slide of muscled, hairy legs behind her thighs. A callused palm grazing across her hip to settle at her naked waist, a powerful arm roping her to the man behind her.

Paul!

The hunting lodge.

Their naked bodies moving together. Climaxing as one.

Eva shut her eyes, trying to regroup from the onslaught of memories. But remembering didn't help. It merely heightened her panic.

Her heart thumped so high against her ribs, it felt as if it were trying to escape through her throat.

But it wasn't merely panic she felt, was it? She made no attempt to pull away from him.

'You're awake.' Before last night she'd had no notion Paul could sound like this. Like a lazy lion growling out his satisfaction.

Except, as his rod slid up against her buttocks, hard and powerful, she knew he was anything but lazy, and nowhere near satisfied.

A strange little jiggle set up inside her. A dancing, twisting sensation that felt far too much like eagerness. Because she'd learned last night how very, very good it was when Paul's voice grazed that particular low note across her skin. Almost as good as the feel of him deep inside her or—memory hit with a shudder of delight—kneeling before her, caressing her with his mouth.

Eva opened her lips to speak but whatever she'd been about to say disintegrated on a sigh as he cupped her breast, his hard fingers exquisitely gentle.

'You like that.' Another rumble of that deep voice. This time she felt the words as puffs of hot air stirring the hair at her nape. He leaned in and nuzzled her there, his muscled chest at her back.

'So do you.'

His erection felt huge. Had she really accommodated all

that last night? A shivery feeling began at what she guessed was her womb then radiated through her whole body.

'You're right. I do.' His teeth grazed her neck and Eva arched back, like a bow strung tight, breast pushing into his palm, backside rubbing against his erection. It was totally instinctive, unplanned, and part of her despaired that she had so little resistance. Until she heard Paul's guttural murmur against her skin, felt his matching thrust against her and knew she wasn't the only one acting on pure instinct.

'I want you, Eva.'

His voice had the roughened richness of whisky and it did terrible things to her brain. Even so, she had just enough sense of self-preservation left to remember that sex with Paul was no good for her. No matter how good it felt.

She swallowed, about to tell him she wasn't interested, when his palm left her breast and arrowed down over her belly, straight to the core of her. His hand settled there as if it belonged, sliding against dampness, easily insinuating to the very spot where...

Her view of leaves and sunlight blurred as her body jerked against his touch.

He kissed her shoulder. 'Hold that thought.' Then, before she could respond, he was gone. She heard the rustle of foil behind her and realised he was getting a condom.

Now was the time to move. To think with her brain, not her body, and get up.

She'd actually put her hand on the mattress, about to lever herself off the bed, when he spoke behind her. 'You're not sore? I've never been with a virgin. I don't want to hurt you.'

Eva paused, her heart squeezing. She told herself it made no difference that Paul was concerned about her. That he wasn't totally driven by his own carnal needs.

Yet it did make a difference.

'Eva? You *are* okay, aren't you?' He was close again,

capturing some of her hair and drawing it aside to reveal one side of her face and a shoulder.

There it was again. Concern. Caring. Her well being mattered to him.

Yeah, because when he washes his hands of you he doesn't want any excuse to feel bad.

Strangely, the bitter thought didn't overwhelm her. Instead it made her feel stronger.

At least she knew exactly what she meant to him. She wasn't his possession, or his responsibility. She was an independent woman and could choose as she wished, do what she wished.

Sternly, she banished the voice that told her being intimate with Paul would only make things harder to bear later. She'd worry about later when it came. After all, the damage was already done. Why not do what he did and enjoy the moment?

'Of course I'm okay. I'm not a porcelain doll.'

Even so, for the longest time he didn't move. She felt him watching her, staring at her profile, as if searching for some sign that she wasn't okay at all.

Briefly, the thought entered her head that she should turn to him and tell him how she felt. That, at least, would solve the issue of keeping her distance from him so as to avoid more hurt. Because hearing a declaration of love would be guaranteed to cool his ardour. But, perversely, Eva didn't want him to pull back. Her need for him was stronger, not weaker.

Even her anger at him for not reciprocating her feelings only served to fuel her need.

So, instead of turning her head to look up at the man peering over her shoulder, Eva arched her back again so her buttocks pushed against hard male flesh and she heard his rough intake of breath.

Triumph filled her. In this at least she had power. She

felt it thrum through her as his hand clutched convulsively at her hip and his body slid against hers.

Tentatively she wriggled her hips, as if getting more comfortable on the bed, and was rewarded with something that sounded like a groan.

'Unless you're not up to it,' she purred, gaze focused on the flickering leaves beyond the window. 'I'll understand if you feel too tired.'

Paul growled something under his breath. Something gruff and low. Then his hand moved from her hip to other, far more sensitive places and Eva lost any interest in talking.

This time their coupling was so easy, it amazed her. Not only was there no pain but it seemed so simple, so right, even that first thrust stole her breath. The perfection of them moving together, finding their rhythm, dazzled her.

Paul was still behind her when she felt his climax begin. She stared blindly in the direction of the tree tops outside. Yet in her mind's eye it was Paul she saw, his strong throat arching as he shouted his release, his eyes glittering like dark sapphires.

A sob broke from her throat, her heart aching. He was the man for her, the only one she'd ever wanted. That thought and the ache it brought died as with one final surge he drew her down into rapturous pleasure.

Eva's orgasm was drawn out, lingering and potent. She had no doubt what made it so amazing was the fact she shared it with the man she loved. That was the definition of bliss.

Finally, they lay together, quaking yet boneless. As the rapture faded, she felt a tear track across her cheek.

She didn't raise a hand to wipe it away. She didn't have the energy. And Paul wouldn't notice. He lay spooned behind her, his face buried in her hair.

Well, what was one tear? She'd permit herself that single sign of weakness. After this there'd be no leeway. She couldn't afford any slip-ups that might betray her true feelings.

She'd be dry-eyed and completely controlled when they separated.

It was late when Paul finally roused again. He peered out at the lowering sky and steady drizzle and wondered how long he'd slept.

Two nights with little sleep had caught up with him. And a couple of stupendous climaxes. He yawned and tried to focus. He hadn't meant to sleep again. Even in this grey light he could tell the day was well advanced.

He turned his head to see if Eva was awake, only to discover the bed empty.

He shot up, heart thumping.

One thing he'd learned last night was never again to take Eva for granted. Far from being predictable, she'd turned his world on its head in less than a day.

A second later he was on his feet, prowling the room. There were his clothes, flung anyhow across the floor. But not Eva's.

Paul swung his head round, peering into corners, but found nothing. Not a trace of her. The open door to the bathroom showed she wasn't there.

His gut clenched in a way that told its own story. Concern, annoyance and something like fear brewed deep inside.

Where had she gone? They needed to talk, now more than ever. Important issues were in the balance. Besides, he realised, raking his hand across his scalp, he needed to make sure she was okay.

Inevitably his gaze trailed back to the bed and the small but telling spot on the rumpled sheet. A reminder, as if he needed it, that he hadn't merely taken a lover last night.

He'd deflowered a virgin. While Eva had seemed fine earlier this morning—more than fine, in fact—he couldn't kick the concern weighing on him. She'd been as enthusiastic as him for morning sex but was she now regretting it?

Where was she?

The woman he'd once thought he knew had changed. There was no saying what she'd do or where she was. Maybe she'd gone, leaving him behind as she'd done last night, heading off alone and unprotected for that nightclub.

The thought made his hackles rise and every protective instinct kick in.

A second later he was taking the stairs two at a time.

He found her in the kitchen, barefoot and wearing the short, satiny dress that clung to her curves.

Paul swallowed and stopped in the doorway.

She stood at the coffee machine. It was a large commercial-grade one but she looked as at home as she did gracing a royal ball.

Her hair was up, but not in its usual, almost severe style. It was bunched up loose and low, looking as if one quick tug would make it tumble free.

Paul had instant recall of the texture of those long tresses against his skin. He'd never made love to a woman with hair like Eva's. Hadn't realised how incredibly alluring those long swathes of silk could be.

He drew a sharp breath, pungent with the aroma of fresh coffee and the lingering scent of Eva.

Hell! They needed to have a serious discussion, and here he was, imagining her naked in bed with him. Or not even naked. Memory hammered into him of Eva on that huge, scrubbed wooden table, her thighs warm around him, her head flung back and breasts thrusting forward as she rode out the orgasm he'd given her. So beautiful. So...

'Paul!'

She swung round, a cup in her hand, and was staring at him as if she'd never seen him.

If he'd hoped for a smile or any sort of welcome he was doomed to disappointment. His lover—his *lover*. Satisfaction stirred at the thought—was frowning as if wondering why he was here.

Pushing back his shoulders, Paul sauntered into the kitchen, the old flagstones smooth beneath his feet.

'That smells amazing. Can you make me some too?'

For a moment she didn't speak, just stared at him with wide eyes the colour of the wintry sky outside.

And hello to you too.

It had been a long time since Paul had done a morning-after but he recalled them being a whole lot more affectionate than this. Eva looked at him as if he were something conjured from a nightmare.

Except… Her gaze skittered from his, down, a long way down, then up again, slowly. The tip of her tongue caught at the corner of her mouth and her nostrils flared as she breathed deep.

When she met his eyes again, she looked a little dazed. Or was that masculine ego talking? He almost forgave her for that initial horrified look.

He covered the rest of the space between them to stand a breath away from her. She smelt like coffee and that distinctive green floral scent of hers. And the memory of rapture.

A frisson of arousal shuddered through him and he contemplated deferring chitchat for something more satisfying.

'Of course.' Her voice was crisp, at odds with the expression on her face. 'I'll make it while you get dressed.' Her gaze dropped as far as his shoulders then quickly rose.

'That's okay. I'll wait for it. Besides, we have things to discuss.'

Because those furtive glances gave the lie to her tone. She might want to pretend nothing had happened between them but Paul refused to let her retreat again, acting as if they were no more than polite strangers. He'd stop her from re-erecting those barriers if he had to stand here, naked, for the next hour.

She swallowed, and abruptly she didn't look distant but vulnerable.

'I'd prefer it if you were dressed.' Her breath was a barely audible sigh. 'You're too distracting like that.'

'Good.' He leaned down and brushed her lips with his, then lingered as he tasted her. His hand lifted to her cheek, his knuckles sliding down soft flesh.

'Careful!' She jerked back. 'I don't want to spill coffee on you. Really, you should get dressed.'

Her gaze left his face and focused on his groin where, even after their earlier, vigorous activity, his burgeoning interest was evident.

Paul's mouth curved. That was better. Eva looked anything but distant now. Her eyes were round and her lips parted. She looked adorable.

'On one condition.' Her head jerked up and their gazes meshed. 'That when I come back downstairs you stop trying to put up barriers between us. We need to talk frankly with each other, Eva. No holding back. No pretending last night didn't happen. Okay?'

She hesitated then nodded. 'Okay.'

Paul turned and strode to the door, giving Eva a perfect view of his muscled back and taut glutes. Even after last night's intimacies, she was stunned by the sight of him naked.

It was a sight she was pretty sure she'd carry for the rest of her days.

Eva put her coffee down with a hand that trembled and turned on the tap, putting her wrists under the flow of cool running water, then lifting them to her cheeks. Heat had bloomed inside the instant he'd appeared stark naked and overwhelmingly, stunningly gorgeous.

Paul didn't fight fair. Standing there looking like...like...

She shook her head and gave up trying to think of a word. When she'd turned round and seen him in the doorway, her brain had emptied. When she'd recovered it was to the realisation that making love to him had indeed left her more vulnerable than ever before.

He'd been semi-erect again, and she'd been torn between fascination and horror at the messages her traitorous body sent to her brain. To forget pride and common sense, and the fact that he didn't want her long term, and offer herself to him again. Even though she needed to break her ties to him, not make them stronger.

She closed her eyes, trying and failing to banish the image of that powerful body and potently attractive grin.

He was incredibly sexy, yet it wasn't just that. Her hormones responded predictably to the picture he presented, all virile male, but she'd noticed something more than invitation in his expression. He was concerned about her.

Eva firmed her lips. The last thing she needed was for him to come over all honourable and worried about the fact she'd been a virgin. She might long for him with all her heart but last night had seen a shift in her. Better, she realised now, to move on than stay with a man who'd never reciprocate her feelings.

Straightening from the sink, she took out another cup and turned to the coffee machine.

They'd have the discussion he wanted.

She'd agree to end the engagement, stay while they sorted out a suitable press release then return home.

And do what?

Stunned, she stood frozen as revelation sank into her.

She'd thought for so long that she was destined to be Queen of St Ancilla. Even the university degree she'd completed hadn't been done with the aim of securing herself a job. Her job was supposed to be supporting Paul and the people of St Ancilla. She'd been trained from birth to be a royal, to serve a nation. As a teenager she'd thought of a career, but after her betrothal had thought that that was impossible.

Now it wasn't only possible. It was vital.

What would she do with her life? She couldn't see herself returning to Tarentia to live in her parents' shadow for ever.

She had to start thinking of the future. A future away from St Ancilla, though she'd come to love the place. A future where she worked at something other than being royal.

Eva clutched at the kitchen bench, for a moment overwhelmed by the enormous changes she faced.

But this was a positive. She could build a career and be independent, not tied to the royal court, always living up to impossibly high expectations.

She just had to decide what that future would be. Hopefully something fulfilling. Something where she could make a difference.

Footsteps descending the staircase cut through her thoughts and she moved to the coffee machine. It was easier to focus on making a perfect espresso than grapple with the issue of her future. There'd be plenty of time once she left here. An endless lifetime ahead without Paul.

Don't think like that.

Think of this as an opportunity. Think about the freedom to work at something you enjoy. The freedom and independence.

Her nape prickled. Paul had arrived. Her body always told her when he was looking at her.

Straightening her shoulders, she practised a nonchalant smile. All she had to do was agree on how they were going to break the news of their split and she could leave.

She ignored the cramping pain through her middle.

'Here.' She turned, that small smile pinned to her face. 'Just the way you like it.'

She held out his coffee but Paul ignored it. Slowly he looked up from his phone. His brow was crunched in a scowl that drew his eyebrows close. Deep lines cut around his mouth and his jaw looked as if it was carved of granite.

'Paul? What is it?' Her heart leapt. 'Bad news?'

Belatedly he reached out and took the cup, only to place it on the table beside him.

He pulled a chair from the table for her. 'You'd better sit down.'

He must have read her sudden fear for he shook his head and his mouth curved ever so slightly. 'Don't worry. It's not bad news from Tarentia. Your family is fine.'

His eyes cut to his phone. 'But we have a problem.'

CHAPTER EIGHT

EVA WATCHED PAUL take the chair next to hers. 'Tell me.'

His dark-blue eyes bored into hers. There was nothing lover-like about his gaze now. Though there was concern. 'Last night. That scene behind the night club.' His mouth hooked down at the corners. 'It's all over social media and the press.'

'I don't understand.' But that was just her brain rejecting his words. Looking into his grim features, Eva understood this was all too real.

'You were right about others being in the vicinity when you went out the back door. Someone had a phone and used it to snap a photo.'

'Of you fighting?'

Eva recalled Fabrice's hot breath and grasping hands. His heavy weight against her. His violent snarl as he'd promised retribution for that knee to the groin. She'd been so thankful when Paul had ripped him off her. She wasn't a fan of violence but in the circumstances she could feel nothing but gratitude and relief that he'd intervened. But a shot of the king brawling in a back alley would be a PR nightmare, even though he'd been saving her.

Paul shook his head. 'No. The photo is of you and him up against the wall.'

Bile rose at the thought. It was bad enough to live with the vivid recollection, to feel that phantom clutch of greedy hands and the slide of those wet lips. But to have others *see* what had happened…

Eva's shoulders hunched as she pulled her arms in tight against her body. She felt grubby, tainted. It did little good to say *she'd* done nothing wrong. That it was Fabrice who should feel shame. But, despite logic, something deeper and more primitive scoured through her. She didn't want to hear this. Even more, she didn't want everyone else to know about it.

'So the press are reporting the attack.' She told herself it would be a nine-day wonder. That after the initial flurry of interest it would be forgotten.

'Not exactly.'

She looked up sharply and didn't like the expression she saw on Paul's face. Anger but something else she couldn't name. 'What?'

'There's only one photo and it's of *you*. You and…'

'Fabrice,' she said through clenched teeth. Was that even his real name?

'Fabrice.' He leaned back in his seat, as if getting more comfortable, except every line of his rigid body spoke of tension. 'The story splashed everywhere is that you were making out with him willingly. That, far from wanting me to interrupt, you were planning to go off with him to…'

Something jammed high up in Eva's chest as if someone had stuck a knife between her ribs, catching her lungs in the process so she couldn't breathe.

Finally, she forced out the words. 'Say it.'

Serious eyes held hers and now the expression she read there was overwhelmingly of sympathy.

'To have sex. Apparently you were on the prowl, looking for a one-night stand, until I came and butted in. The stories about what happened next are sketchy, presumably because there aren't photos. In some versions there was a fight. In others I simply grabbed you and marched you back to the palace.'

Pain banded Eva's torso. Breathing actually hurt.

How could that be, when she knew full well the media's ability to turn the most innocent glance into something totally different? The press spun stories out of air, inventing feuds, rivalries, love stories and so much more. Not that she'd been a particular victim.

But this... Turning the most shocking, frightening experience of her life into salacious gossip for the masses... She pressed her hand to her stomach, clamping her lips shut as nausea hit.

'Here.' Eventually she heard Paul's voice, soft near her ear. He wrapped her hand round a glass. Eva looked down and saw she held a half-full glass of water, its surface rippling as her hand shook.

'Thanks.' She sipped it, forcing the liquid down her constricted throat. That gave her something to focus on other than the raging whirl of emotions inside.

Putting down the glass, she held out her hand for his phone. 'Show me.'

Hers was still in the small bag she'd taken with her last night and the battery was flat.

'I don't think you really—'

'No, I'm sure I don't want to see what they say.' Determined, she held his gaze. 'But I need to. Please.'

Reluctantly, he placed in on her palm. Her fingers closed round it tentatively, as if it might bite. Her mouth curled in a bitter smile. It was too late to worry about getting hurt. The damage was done.

Even so, the next five minutes were a test of her endurance. Her stomach curdled as she read the stories and speculation about her. When she saw the photo, her stomach cramped so hard she thought she'd vomit.

From this angle you couldn't tell the embrace was forced.

It was obvious he'd kissed her and the position of his grop- ing hand at her breast was revoltingly clear.

Her hand was up against his shoulder. Eva recalled shov- ing with all her might. But that could look as though she'd clung for support.

The shot was taken from one side. Fabrice's face was un- clear but the side of Eva's face was in focus, including one of the distinctive sapphire earrings she'd worn to the ball that night. And, if there'd been any doubt about her identity, the engagement ring Paul had given her was there for all to see. A pear-shaped blue diamond. It was truly distinctive.

A shudder passed through her then she gave the phone back to him and got up, collecting both his coffee cup and hers.

'Where are you going?' Instantly Paul was beside her.

Did he think she was going to storm off?

And do what? Track down Fabrice, whose surname she didn't even know, and force him to admit what had hap- pened?

Complain to the press?

Rant on social media?

Eva breathed deep and tipped the cold coffee out of the untouched cups.

'To make us fresh coffee.' She didn't need the caffeine. She already had so much adrenaline storming through her bloodstream, she'd be wired for the rest of the day. But it gave her something to do.

'I'm sorry about this, Eva.'

'It's not your fault.' She sent him a sideways glance, not- ing the harsh set of his steely jaw.

'It is. I should have thought about photos. But all I could focus on was making you safe and getting you away from there.'

Eva concentrated on measuring the ground coffee. 'And I'm grateful.'

She couldn't let herself dwell on how she felt right now. Or on the temptation to seek comfort in his arms.

From the corner of her eye she saw him rake his hand through his hair. The gesture pulled his thin sweater taut across his chest and her breath snagged. Not in distress but appreciation.

Her emotions were all over the place. If Paul turned to her now, took her hand and whispered seduction in her ear, she'd follow him back up the stairs to that round tower-room and let his loving push all this grimy gossip from her mind.

He didn't.

Of course he didn't.

'We'll deal with this, Eva. Don't fret.'

She shot him a stunned glance, then realised she shouldn't be surprised. Paul had a protective streak a mile wide and a well-honed sense of responsibility.

But Eva was no longer his responsibility.

'You don't need to get involved. I'll handle it once I'm gone.'

'Gone?'

She frowned, her thoughts on what she had to do next.

Eva handed him his tiny cup and picked up her own, sniffing the rich aroma, telling herself she'd feel stronger once she'd drunk it.

'Once I'm in Tarentia. We're no longer engaged, remember?'

For a second he stood motionless, regarding her. Then he lifted the cup and drank, not even grimacing as he swallowed the scalding hot coffee.

He half-turned to put his cup down then faced her again, the picture of assured, powerful male. To her dismay, Eva really did feel tempted to lean against that broad shoulder and let him take charge.

'You're upset, and that seems to have affected your memory. Fortunately, I have perfect recall. I raised the possibility of breaking our engagement and you didn't like the idea. We agreed to discuss it today.'

'Okay, we'll discuss it now.' She sipped her coffee, willing the warm liquid to make her feel stronger. 'I agree that we should end the engagement. It's sensible for us to split up.'

A half-smile hooked up the corner of Paul's mouth. Despite the sick feeling lurking in her stomach, his smile sent delicious warmth cascading through her. As if they were still upstairs in bed and the only thing on their minds was sex.

'I disagree.'

'You what? It was your idea!' She felt her eyes round as she stared up at him. She'd never seen Paul look quite so...immoveable. But then she'd never taken an opposing position to him before. Until last night.

Eva took in his widened stance, crossed arms and a glint in his eyes that signalled his intention to be very obstinate indeed.

'Now, more than ever, we need to stick together.' He spoke softly but his voice hit a low register that gave his words gravitas. As if his decision was best and there could be no reasonable argument.

Eva shook her head at his stubbornness. She took a sip of coffee, searching for the words she needed to end this once and for all.

'You can't afford the scandal, Paul. I know you've worked hard to put on a good front for the public. That you want to avoid anyone digging too deep into the royal family's doings because they might uncover your father's crimes. It makes sense to end this now, before the media storm gets worse.'

If Paul had looked obstinate and half-amused before, that expression vanished as he frowned.

'You think *that's* what motivates me? Fear of scandal?'

Eva's brow puckered. That was what her father had said and it made sense, given what she'd heard about King Hugo's involvement in fraud and outright theft from the public purse.

'There are reasons I preferred that the press didn't run with the full details of my father's crimes at the time. St Ancilla's finances were seriously compromised. A fortune in investment funds was squandered on the turn of a roulette wheel, money that should have gone into social development projects. Meanwhile, more public funds were syphoned off to cronies.'

A tic started up in the vein at his temple, something she'd never seen before.

'Since then we've worked hard to refinance, attract additional investors and begin, slowly, to make good the losses. Because if the bare facts had been known earlier it would have caused such loss of confidence, the nation itself might have been in peril.' He drew a breath that made that broad chest rise.

'For major investors and many of our citizens, the royal family *is* St Ancilla. That's why the full details haven't yet become public. So we could keep afloat long enough to be viable again.'

'I'm not accusing you of anything.' He had too much integrity. She knew he wasn't tainted by his father's activities.

Paul shook his head and his dark hair flopped down across his forehead, making Eva's fingers twitch with the urge to reach out and brush it back. It made him look less daunting and even sexier, despite the simmering indignation in his eyes. Instead she moved to put her cup down.

'But you think I'm running scared of negative publicity.' His stare bored into hers and heat drilled through her.

'I don't give a damn about protecting my father's reputation. I only want to make good what he and his cronies

took. We've had a team of forensic accountants and inves-
tigators tracking money and preparing briefs of evidence
that will go to court soon. It's taken years of complex in-
vestigations to get the necessary evidence.' He shrugged.
'And I'm not saying we're out of the woods yet, financially,
but things are better than they were.'

'I had no idea.'

'Why should you? We don't discuss financial matters.'

*We don't discuss anything important. We don't have that
kind of relationship.*

Or, they hadn't. It felt as if last night had changed that.

Paul spread his hands in a gesture that invited trust.
'If you think for a second I'd abandon you now when you
need me, just to avoid bad publicity, then you don't know
me at all.'

'It sounds,' she said slowly, thinking things through,
'that bad publicity is going to hit your family when the
court cases start anyway.'

He shrugged. 'So be it. Crimes were committed and have
to be dealt with. Sweeping it under the carpet isn't a long-
term option. As for the publicity, it's nothing I can't handle.
My siblings aren't even in the country and my mother is
retired from public life, living in France.'

So the decks were cleared. The one who'd face the media
storm would be Paul. He had it all worked out.

Something about his expression gave Eva pause, her
mind ticking over.

Had this been a factor in him wanting to end their engagement? He'd said he wanted to make good the dowry
money his father had already spent. Had he also planned
to ensure Eva wouldn't be caught up in negative publicity
around the St Ancillan royal family?

She opened her mouth to ask then shut it again. Maybe
he simply didn't want to marry her. Didn't like her enough

to spend the rest of his life with her. She felt bruised enough without making him say that to her face.

Eva shrugged. 'I applaud what you're doing, Paul. I'm impressed.' Doubly so because, despite his talk of an international team, she guessed he was the one driving the process. A man who'd inherited the crown in his early twenties and who'd had to manage incredibly difficult challenges, learning as he went. He had enough to contend with.

'But you don't need this.'

'No buts, Eva. We're in this together. The worst, the absolute worst, thing we could do right now is end our engagement. People would think it confirmed the stories being circulated about you.'

'What if I say I don't care what people say? Bad publicity isn't the end of the world.'

Paul reached out and took her hand. Funny, she hadn't realised she was cold till she felt his warm fingers enfold hers. She didn't even try to tug free. His touch was so comforting.

'I'd say you haven't thought through how bad it can be. That one photo can taint you for ever.'

His words shafted ice through her. Eva knew she could face what she had to, but it wouldn't be pleasant. The idea of one incident being misinterpreted and haunting her for the rest of her days made her nauseous.

'We stick together, Eva. We don't give the story any oxygen. It's the only way. Surely you see that?'

Still she hesitated. Instinct told her that, if she was going to break this engagement, the sooner the better. Her emotions were tangled enough already.

She shook her head. 'It's not up to us. The story will run, no matter what we do.'

His hand tightened on hers. 'But it will run its course faster if you stay here in St Ancilla, at my side. If we're seen spending time together, enjoying each other's company.'

'You mean, if you're seen to trust me.'

'Exactly.' His expression grew more serious. 'Please, Eva, let me do this for you.'

Eva sighed, her breath shuddering out as the fight finally left her.

She didn't have a heavy schedule in Tarentia. She'd finished studying, had thought she'd be busy the next few months preparing for their wedding. A chill enveloped her.

She told herself this was the sensible option. But secretly she wondered if the real reason she wavered was because part of her still hadn't got the message about cutting her ties with Paul.

He stood so near, she inhaled that reassuring scent of pine trees and the outdoors. And his touch, the feel of his fingers wrapped casually around her hand, evoked memories of other more intimate touches.

'Eva?' He bent closer, snagging her attention.

Expelling her breath in a sigh of acceptance, she inclined her head. 'On two conditions.'

One black eyebrow arched high. 'Go on.'

'That this is time-limited.' Stupidly, she felt her throat close on the last word, as if her subconscious didn't want her to make the break from him.

'Fair enough. We'll review the situation in a couple of months.'

Eva frowned. 'One.'

'Not long enough. Two minimum.' He read her expression. 'If we separate too soon, it will have been for nothing. How about we regroup in six weeks and assess how things are? But in that time you stay here in St Ancilla.'

She hesitated. 'Surely me staying here all that time will just raise false expectations?'

'The whole point is for us to be seen as a caring couple, finally free to spend time together now you've finished your studies. What happens later...' he shrugged '...well, that's for later. The point is to show what happened hasn't affected my feelings. That I trust your integrity.'

He was railroading her. Yet what were her options? She shrank from returning home with her tail between her legs, knowing her parents' media advisers would be lumbered with responsibility for fixing this.

Again she told herself the publicity was no big deal. Yet in Tarentia it would be. As far as the public was concerned, she was a bit of a goody two-shoes. Always proper, never putting a foot out of line. Last night's adventure would be fodder for press gossip for a long time to come, and the dissolution of her engagement on top of that… No, she couldn't embarrass her family that way.

'Okay. Agreed.'

Light blazed in his eyes. Triumph or approval?

'Excellent. And the other condition?'

'We handle the media my way.'

CHAPTER NINE

PAUL HAD TO hand it to Eva—she didn't shirk. For a moment yesterday when she'd spoken of handling the media her way he'd wondered if she meant hiding from the press and hoping the negative stories would all go away.

Which was totally ludicrous, if you knew Eva. And he was beginning to know Eva.

In some ways he still had so much to learn about her. In others, he knew Eva very well indeed. The surreptitious thought crept up on him, threatening to unravel his composure as he relived the sweet sound of her climaxing, and the feel of her moving against him. Her movements had been eager, if a little inept, till she'd found her rhythm, and all the more arousing for that.

He concentrated on marshalling his features into a sympathetic expression as he turned from the journalists in front of him to the woman speaking beside him.

Definitely better to look sympathetic than like he was lusting after her. Which he was.

Not just now but ever since she'd kissed him in the kitchen and shattered the sexual barriers between them.

Or maybe earlier. That night, as she'd flounced down the stairs to the ball looking remote and superior and at the same time too sexy for his equanimity.

He yanked his attention back to what Eva was saying. That women had the right to be unmolested, at night as well as in daylight. That dancing with a man didn't confer sexual rights. That, in hindsight, she'd think twice about accepting at face value a stranger's offer of assistance in locating a taxi. But wasn't that a sad state of affairs?

Pride swelled as he listened. She'd been right to do this herself rather than leave the PR specialists to craft a press release. Eva had a naturalness, a charming approachability, that drew her listeners in and made her moments of gravity all the more profound.

She'd be such an asset at his side long-term. How had he not realised?

But then the only time they'd faced the press together had been on the occasion of their betrothal, each nervous, each aware that the match had been engineered not because of personal preference but for dynastic reasons.

He looked back now and wondered why he'd let her obvious discomfort colour his view of her. He'd been uncomfortable too. His attempt to kiss her had been clumsy and ill-timed. No wonder she'd pulled away.

Not like her kisses now.

Heat brewed deep in his belly.

'And your thoughts, Your Majesty?' He turned to meet the inquisitive stare of a local reporter.

Paul reached out his hand and took Eva's, threading his fingers through hers.

'Frankly, I feel ashamed that this should happen in St Ancilla. Naturally, at a personal level, my fiancée's distress weighs on me. It's also drawn my attention to the danger any woman can face at any time from predatory men. It's something we're all aware of but too often we—that is, men—forget because we think it doesn't affect us personally.'

Slim fingers squeezed his and warmth shot through him. Not the heat of arousal like before, but something altogether different, yet just as potent. He liked it.

'It does affect us,' he continued. 'Unless we *want* a society where our neighbours, colleagues, sisters, wives and fiancées are potentially under threat.'

'So what do you suggest we do?' asked a man in the second row. 'Are you advocating violence? It's been reported that you brawled with the man.'

Paul felt as much as heard the hush fall across the small crowd of journalists. Eva's hand tightened around his. In warning?

He turned towards her and saw she once again wore what he now thought of as her public face. Her expression was serene, but he knew her well enough now to understand the slightly up-tilted angle of her jaw and the silvery glitter in her eyes. This session was tougher than she was letting on and she was upset, or perhaps worried about where this was leading.

Did she fear charges might be laid against him?

Paul turned back to his questioner. 'I'm not advocating violence. I'm suggesting we all think carefully about our behaviour. About the words and actions we, as a society, want to model for our children, or let pass as acceptable. We should call out bad behaviour rather than pretend that sexist or aggressive comments and actions are a bit of a joke. And of course we should each do our bit to help others feel safe.'

'By beating up transgressors?'

Paul met the journalist's stare. 'I had in mind more positive actions, like group car-pooling after an evening out. Or walking friends home.'

'But you—'

'As for my actions the other night, it's true I intervened. The man sexually assaulted my fiancée and was threatening more violence. I pulled him away from her and when he swung at me, yes, I punched him.'

That was a shortened version of events. The guy hadn't given up quickly and Paul hadn't been in a forgiving mood.

'If the man in question wants to come forward and lay charges against me for defending Princess Eva, I'd welcome that. I'm sure the police will be very interested in interviewing him about the events of that evening. It appears likely he was using a false name, which has hampered attempts to find him.'

He turned to Eva beside him. 'For my part, I don't regret what I did. I just wish I'd been there sooner.'

Eva and Paul left the room while palace staff ushered the journalists out of the palace. Paul still held her hand as he led the way silently away from the public reception rooms and she didn't object. His touch was supportive, understanding, and it helped.

The worst was over.

Hopefully.

She breathed a deep sigh as some of the tension fell away from her stiff shoulders.

Relief filled her, laced with a shot of self-disgust. What had happened to her had been nothing compared with the sexual violence suffered by many other women. It seemed almost self-indulgent to feel so undone, reliving the experience.

'Are you all right?' Paul led her into his study and to a big, leather-upholstered lounge. He drew her down to sit beside him.

'Of course. Don't I look it?'

His mouth quirked in a semi-smile that tugged at her heartstrings. 'You look beautiful, elegant and just a little ruffled.' Then, seeing her dismay, he added, 'No, don't worry. No one else would notice.'

Because he understood her so well he could see what she tried to hide? It was a disturbing idea. As was her reaction to being called beautiful. For too long, she'd craved his interest and approval.

'You did brilliantly, Eva. Reporting of the incident will take a new direction now. One you don't have to worry about.'

She nodded. 'I hope you're right. They seemed to accept the truth, even though a couple of them obviously preferred the original story.'

He shrugged. 'Because it's more scandalous, and scandal sells.'

Eva thought of the report from Paul's security staff. That in the melee, as the security officer had tried to reach her that night, he'd knocked against someone whose phone had dropped and smashed. She didn't ask if that was accidental, just felt relieved there weren't even more photos of the scene.

'Something else is bothering you.'

It wasn't a question but a statement. His perspicacity was scary. For so long she'd prided herself on keeping her emotions hidden from him. If he continued to read her so well, what other things would he uncover?

'Eva?'

She withdrew her hand from his, wondering if it was something about the physical connection that helped him understand her thoughts.

'It's nothing.'

Paul's steady gaze told her he didn't believe it.

She shrugged. 'Just that I feel a bit of a fraud. All this talk about sexual assault when, really, it could have been so much worse.'

'Would you feel better if he'd raped you?'

'Of course not! It's just that, compared with what other women experience… All this fuss is just because I'm newsworthy.' Her stomach gave a nauseating little twist.

He watched her for so long, she wondered what he was thinking.

'You're right. The public attention is because of who you are. But what he did was wrong. A man who thinks he can force himself on a woman is wrong, whether he managed to rape you or grope you or kiss you when you were unwilling.' He paused. 'But, if it's nagging at you, maybe you need to see this as a chance for positive action.'

'Like you did, talking about changing attitudes and behaviour?' His words had resonated. She'd admired him, not because he'd deflected attention from her, but because she could see he meant every word.

'Why not? As you say, you have the public profile to draw media attention. You could capitalise on that. Use the opportunity to focus public discussion towards change. Every bit helps.'

Slowly, she nodded. 'It's a good idea.' And it would give her something to keep her occupied. Her enforced six-week stay in St Ancilla, longer than any previous visit, stretched ahead without any real plans.

'And Eva?' She met Paul's eyes again and felt a throb of energy pulse through her. 'It *was* sexual assault, and it was inexcusable.'

There it was again, that flash of heat that she'd seen in his eyes when he'd turned to her at the press conference and said he didn't regret fighting her assailant. That he wished he'd got there sooner.

Eva guessed the journalists would take that to mean he wished he'd been there in time to prevent the assault, and she knew that was true. But she also knew, at a primal, bone-deep level, that Paul wished he'd had more time alone with her assailant to make him regret what he'd done.

The realisation should shock her. The civilised woman she was shied from the idea.

But at a deep-seated, not at all civilised level Eva felt jubilation. And excitement. Not at the idea of violence, but because Paul really cared about her. There was no mistaking the emotion in that searing gaze. This wasn't protectiveness because of an arranged betrothal or for the sake of public appearance. This was something primal.

A shiver raced through her, then another, tightening her flesh and making her nipples bud.

For a second, then another, she luxuriated in what felt like possessiveness. The sort of possessiveness a man felt for his mate.

Then common sense intervened and she tore her gaze away.

She'd had an emotionally draining morning and it had affected her judgement. She was imagining things. Paul didn't regard her as *his*, except in the most temporary way. He'd have done the same for any woman.

For the next month and a half, she had to act the loving fiancée and not read the impossible into Paul's actions when he kept up the same masquerade. Because soon they'd go their separate ways.

Her resolve was tested that very day when he announced they were dining out. Not at a royal function, where she'd be busy making small talk with official guests, but at a private dinner for two.

It would be the first time they'd been alone since they'd left the hunting lodge, except for that brief half-hour following their press conference. For no sooner had they returned to the palace than everyone wanted Paul's attention.

How he'd carved out time for a private dinner, she didn't know. But, despite her nerves at being alone with him again, she was grateful. The St Ancillan palace was comfortable, and the staff eager to please, but it wasn't like being in her own home where she had responsibilities to keep her busy.

Besides, no matter how often she reminded herself their brief period of sexual intimacy must end, she missed him.

They'd had less than twelve hours alone together at the lodge, yet it felt as if everything had changed.

Everything Eva felt for him was intensified. She told herself the idea of a woman fixating on the man who'd taken her virginity was outdated. The trouble was this was no passing sexual obsession. It was just another facet of the love she felt.

The love she had to find a way to conquer.

Even so, she dressed for their dinner date with even more care than when she'd prepared for the royal ball.

She hadn't missed Paul's appreciation of her hair. It had fascinated him when she'd worn it loose. If he hadn't been staring at it he'd been touching it, caressing it with long, slow strokes or wrapping his fists in it, as if to hold her close as they'd crested the wave of rapture together.

Her heart gave a little blip and she decided on impulse to leave her hair loose which she never did for any royal function. Even if they were no longer to be lovers, it didn't mean she could resist the chance to look her best for him.

To show him what he'd miss when he eventually gave her up.

Eva grimaced. Since when had she become petty?

But having the man she loved look at her appreciatively was a temptation too great to be ignored. She brushed her hair till it shone then secured it back on one side with a pearl clip.

Her dress was new, by a designer she'd met on her last visit here. Of pearl-grey chiffon over grey silk, it was embroidered in graduating shades of pink. The colours might be subdued but it fitted like a dream. Its flirty, floaty skirt made her feel good and the colour did wonders for her nondescript eyes.

Nevertheless, Eva wasn't prepared for the blatant admiration in Paul's expression as he met her in the palace entry hall.

'You look ravishing.' His voice burred to that gravelly baritone note that undid something inside her and, when he lifted her hand to his lips and kissed it, that sensation of being undone intensified. She had to stiffen her legs, stand taller in her pale-grey sling-backs and focus on smiling.

His exaggerated response would be for the benefit of the footman waiting near the front door, and any other staff in the vicinity.

'Thank you. You look pretty good yourself.'

In black trousers, a dark jacket that moulded his straight shoulders and a crisp shirt of palest blue, he looked good enough to eat.

Heat washed her belly as an image filled her head. Of her returning Paul's favour and doing to him what he'd done for her the other night at that big kitchen table.

Lust shuddered through her and she had to fight not to jump as he reached out and tucked her arm through his, leading the way outside.

Suddenly it didn't seem such a good idea, wearing her pretty dress, with her hair down and a new shade of lipstick she thought made her mouth look appealing. She'd have been better off in a sombre suit. At least that would remind her that the night wouldn't end with them sharing a bed.

Because she couldn't afford sexual intimacy again if she was going to keep her sanity when the time came to walk away from this engagement.

As for the sideways glance Paul gave her as they descended the steps to his car, that pierced every protective barrier. It was going to take all her determination to keep her distance.

Half an hour later, seated at a discreet table for two on a balcony that hung out over the sea, Eva didn't know whether to laugh or cry. The scene looked like something from a photo shoot of the world's most romantic getaways.

Being here with Paul came heart-achingly close to a parody of what she really wanted from him. Wanted but could never have.

He cared for her, wanted to protect her, had enjoyed sex with her, but he didn't love her. And if he didn't now the chances were he never would.

The sea glimmered below them, indigo shot with the bright colours of the dying sun. Their view down the coast was unparalleled and the restaurant balcony was deserted but for them. Fragrant wisteria spilled down nearby columns, its perfume mingling with sea spice and Paul's warm, outdoorsy scent to create something intoxicating.

Or maybe that was the effect of Paul's dark gaze.

Instead of electric lighting, a myriad of candles in glass holders created an intimate atmosphere.

As for Paul, he looked… No. No more superlatives. She was in deep enough as it was.

'We've never done this before,' she blurted.

His mouth hooked up in a slow smile. If she hadn't known this date was for show, it would have made her wayward heart hammer even faster than it already did.

'No. That was a definite oversight.'

But totally understandable. Because until now their engagement had been driven by duty and court protocol. Now it was something different. Personal because they'd made it so, yet not a real romance.

The thought dimmed some of the evening's radiance but she countered it with a bright smile.

'So, an unexpected benefit, eh?'

'I hope you'll enjoy it.' His smile reached out to her, as if he really had nothing on his mind but her.

Eva turned to look past him, but realised they were sheltered from view of the diners inside. And, if paparazzi wanted to try to photograph them, they'd have to take a boat off the coast. But then it only took one talkative waiter to spread news of their mood over dinner.

As if conjured by her thoughts, a waiter arrived bearing a platter of appetisers.

When he'd gone, Eva leaned forward, voice low. 'Great choice of venue. We really look like a courting couple out for a romantic interlude.' Hopefully saying it out loud would remind her this was a pretence.

Paul's expression changed. She couldn't define how, just a sense of stillness, almost of wariness.

'You think so?' He reached out and lifted her hand, putting it to his lips, sending a little quake of longing through her. 'I aim to please.'

Yet now she'd swear she read something like annoyance in his features. It didn't make sense.

'There's no need to kiss my hand,' she murmured. Yet she didn't withdraw. Heaven help her, despite her resolve, breaking physical contact was too tough.

'But you never know,' he said against her knuckles, 'when another staff member might appear. We need to put on a good show.'

Grimly Eva realised there was no need at all for her to act. Being alone with Paul in this beautiful setting, having him focus all his attention on her, elicited the responses she'd tried to hide from him for years. The breathless excitement, hammering heart and dazzled stare.

Eva looked different. Or maybe he just saw things he hadn't noticed in the past. The soft flush of colour high across her cheeks. The invitation of her slightly parted lips. Those tantalising eyes now silver, now misty blue, enticing him.

He closed his hand around hers and placed it on the linen table cloth.

'I'm glad you approve. I've never been here before.' His

secretary had said it was the most romantic restaurant in St Ancilla, and Paul had deemed that perfect, because he wanted to reinforce to any interested watchers that they were genuinely romantically involved.

Except now, sitting here with Eva—so alluring—inhaling the gentle drift of hyacinth scent from her warm skin... A tremor raced through him straight to his groin because these days he only had to look at her to want her. His chest felt over-full as he felt her hand shake in his.

Her vulnerability evoked protective instincts. And possessive ones. That had to be the reason he had trouble focusing on anything but her.

'I have a request.' His voice came out with a curiously raspy edge.

She tilted her head in question, her long hair falling over one shoulder. Paul remembered how it had felt against his bare skin. Soft as silk yet a hundred times more erotic.

He cleared his throat. 'Don't wear your hair down in public.'

'Sorry?' She sat straighter, indignation in that speaking stare.

He felt his mouth curve in an appreciative smile. This was something new. To be attracted to a woman even when she looked annoyed....

Paul leaned in, forcing himself not to lift his other hand to caress her. 'Your hair is incredibly sexy. When I see it down, I have this recurring fantasy about dragging your clothes off and doing things with you that I haven't been able to for a whole day. It's too tempting. Too distracting.' He paused, watching her eyes grow wide. 'Besides, it's unfair on all those other men who will never get the chance to—'

'I get the idea!'

Eva didn't exactly blush but she looked adorably ruffled and Paul wished he hadn't had the brainwave of bringing her here for dinner. An intimate meal in his private apartments would have been so much more comfortable.

And convenient.

But his first consideration was Eva and the need to scotch the speculation about her supposedly wild private life. He'd seen how hurt she'd been by that. He intended to have her by his side as much as possible, giving no one cause to think he had any doubts about her loyalty or her character.

'Paul, we need to talk.' Her gaze flicked past him to the wine waiter returning with drinks.

A few minutes later when they were alone, she said in answer to his question, 'No, not here. It's not private. I'll tell you later.' Then she changed the subject, leaving him curious.

Reluctantly, sensing the subject she deferred was important, he told her about his upcoming schedule and some of the events he thought she might get involved in. His intention was to draw her more into the royal commitments in St Ancilla. It would help rehabilitate her in the eyes of any doubters and, frankly, he'd be grateful for her assistance.

It was fascinating watching her sift through the information he gave her, quickly assessing areas where she could contribute. She was intelligent and had a good appreciation of the work involved even in those events which sounded, to the uninitiated, like mere ceremonial occasions.

Another plus for the dynastic marriage that had been arranged between them. The marriage he'd planned to avoid.

Interesting how that didn't seem such a good idea now.

Eva was born and bred to this work, as was he.

Luckily it seemed her father wasn't the ogre his had been. Failing to live up to King Hugo's expectations had, more often than not, ended with a severe thrashing as well as more devious penalties designed to instil obedience. Was it any wonder Paul had encouraged his younger brothers to go to school out of the country, well away from their father's reach?

The evening passed quickly. He was surprised to discover how late it was when finally he signalled for the bill. From discussing the royal schedule, they'd moved onto his social reform agenda and were soon debating the pros and cons of a number of initiatives.

Paul enjoyed the way Eva was ready to listen to a contrary view and to argue her case. In fact, he intended to refer a couple of initiatives she mentioned to the appropriate staff for further investigation.

All in all, it had been a productive evening. Their dinner out would be reported on and read about by those hungry for signs of a royal split. Eva herself looked so much more relaxed than she had this morning after the press conference.

And now...

He smiled as he helped her into the car then walked around to the driver's seat. Now they had the rest of the night to themselves.

It was only that thought, the promise of Eva's sweet body in his bed later, that had got him through the hours of sitting with her unable to do more than touch her hand.

It had been a revelation, watching her face change as she'd spoken enthusiastically about a project, queried some detail or, occasionally, complimented him on an achievement. Paul hadn't thought himself a vain man but Eva's praise, and the light of approval in her wide eyes, had done crazy things to his ego and his self-control.

He got into the car, strapped on his belt and started the ignition.

'Now, tell me. What was it you couldn't say at the restaurant?' He let out the clutch and the car purred down the long driveway.

Paul looked forward to hearing Eva purr exactly like that, arching under his touch and rubbing herself needily against him. Tonight there'd only be time to do a few of the things he'd been imagining ever since they'd left the seclusion of the hunting lodge. But that would be a start.

Heat stoked deep in his belly and his smile widened. Soon...

'This charade,' she began, then stopped. 'Our engagement.'

'Yes?' Paul's neck prickled. Something in her voice warned him he wasn't going to like this.

'We're going to review the situation in six weeks and decide on the best time to announce we're splitting, right?'

Paul felt an instant protest rise on his tongue and frowned. Six weeks was far too soon to be sure Eva's reputation wasn't damaged. And to put an end to the passionate encounters they'd only just begun.

'Right,' he said slowly.

It was what they'd agreed. No need to say that he was already sure six weeks wouldn't be enough. It had been a tough couple of days for Eva and there was no point getting into an argument about it now. He'd prove to her in the coming month and a half that their engagement should last longer. In fact, all things considered, he was tempted to suggest...

'So I'm only in St Ancilla for a short time before I move on with my life.'

Paul's frown deepened. He didn't like the finality of the picture she was painting. He opened his mouth to respond but she was already speaking.

'In the circumstances, it's better if we don't repeat what happened the other night.' Paul's hands tightened on the wheel and the car veered towards the centre line before he dragged it back. 'We need to keep this as simple and straightforward as possible. I don't want sex with you, Paul. Not tonight. Not ever again.'

CHAPTER TEN

OF COURSE HE tried to change her mind. But once more Eva showed that obstinate streak he'd discovered just a couple of days before.

Nothing he said made a difference. And, as she refused to continue their discussion somewhere private when they returned to the palace, Paul wasn't able to persuade her using more direct methods.

His hands tingled as he considered those direct methods. As he remembered their combustible passion in the few short hours they'd had together. How could she turn her back on what they'd shared? On him?

He spent the night alone in his vast bed, restless and frustrated.

It was amazing how a single night with Eva had shattered his calm, ordered world. True, that night had marked the end of a four-year sexual drought. But surely if he'd mastered anything it was abstinence?

Yet this morning, despite his lack of sleep, he couldn't sit still, as if his body refused to obey the dictates of his mind and focus on work and unrelenting duty. For the first time ever he found it difficult to fix his thoughts on the range of problems and decisions facing him. He spent most of the time pacing his office, alternately hoping Eva had had as little sleep as he, then remembering the weary smudges beneath her eyes as they'd said goodnight and hoping she'd got some rest.

She needed rest. And looking after. And…him.

Silently cursing his circular thoughts, Paul scraped the back of his neck with his palm and turned away from the window.

'The media summary is in, sir.' His secretary appeared in the doorway. Usually the summary of relevant media reports was in by the time Paul reached his office. This morning he'd arrived so early, he'd had to wait.

'And? How bad is it?' Early stories following the press conference had been generally positive, but you never knew for sure.

'Pretty good, considering.'

'Ah.' Considering the inevitable outliers who'd prefer a sensational story to the truth. Paul nodded and returned to his computer, opening the report.

Most of the stories were sympathetic to Eva. There was an editorial about curbing violence against women. Another story used statistics on the number of assault cases in the country in the last year, lower than for many places, but more than anyone wanted.

Then came two, both originating outside St Ancilla, that ran with the 'profligate party girl' theme, trying to paint the picture of a self-absorbed woman whose public face hid a scandalous wild side. Paul wondered how long they'd be able to continue such reporting when they couldn't dredge up any more incidents to support it.

She'd been a virgin till two nights ago.

The knowledge slammed into him like a fist thudding into his temple.

Which was yet another reason why he needed to tread softly now she'd stipulated no sex. Especially after that assault behind the night club.

Both those factors could explain why he felt not only culpable for this furore, but protective.

No, it was more. He felt *possessive*.

Once again Paul rubbed the back of his neck, trying to relieve taut muscles.

He'd never felt this way about any woman.

It must be taking her virginity that explained it.

And the fact that they'd been tied together for four years, even if only via a formal arrangement.

And the fact that he liked her. Admired her.

Was desperate to have her again.

Was that what this was? Thwarted lust?

No, he'd felt proprietorial about Eva when she'd been in his bed.

He gritted his teeth, pain shooting up from his jaw.

'Can I get you anything, sir? A headache tablet?'

Paul shook his head. 'I'm okay, thanks.' Or he would be when he worked out how to deal with his fiancée. 'Give me ten more minutes then bring in the week's schedule, and the Princess's new assistant.'

'My assistant?' Eva stared at the woman before her. Paul *had* been busy. It was only yesterday they'd given their press conference.

'Yes, ma'am. I thought we might begin by mapping out a schedule for you.'

Eva looked at the young woman, only a few years older than herself, her demeanour serious yet eager. She wanted to warn her that this was only a temporary arrangement. She wouldn't be staying in St Ancilla permanently, so the position of assistant wouldn't be long-term. But, reading her new assistant's enthusiasm, she didn't have the heart. Besides, she and Paul had agreed no one else would know their arrangement was temporary.

She drew a fortifying breath, remembering the scurrilous headlines and the tension in her mother's voice when she'd rung to explain the situation. No, this was the best way forward. It was silly to have second thoughts now.

'Thank you, Helena. That's an excellent idea.'

Helena nodded, passing over a surprisingly large print-out.

'I've colour-coded a range of events. Those in gold are ones King Paul thought you could assist him with.'

Obediently Eva scanned the first page. There was at least one gold-shaded event each day, sometimes more. She stifled a sigh. Impossible to expect to avoid him.

She was torn between wanting to be with him and knowing it was best to keep her distance. Being close to him, like on their dinner date last night, made it too easy to forget their relationship had no future.

'As for the others, they're suggestions only, based on my reading of your work in Tarentia and knowing your interest in art and education.'

Eva looked up, surprised.

Helena shrugged. 'I researched you. I know you studied both at university and about your volunteer work in disadvantaged schools.'

'You *are* thorough.' Back in Tarentia, she got press attention when attending royal or high-profile charity events, but her few hours a week volunteering generally went under the radar.

'It's my job. You'll see I've marked those in green.'

'And the blue?'

'Designed to build positively on yesterday's press conference.'

Eva scanned the list.

Visits to a range of groups—including one that provided positive male role models to local kids, a women's shelter and a program designed to help troubled or violent teenagers through sport and learning.

Eva paused then pointed to an hour blocked out this afternoon. 'This isn't colour-coded. Is it a mistake?'

Helena leaned forward. 'No mistake. The King and the press office had a long list of suggestions for your schedule, but I added a few of my own. They're perhaps not so worthy but I think them important.'

She paused. 'His Majesty mentioned you needed to go shopping. I thought you might like to revisit the designer who created the dress you wore last night.'

The dress Paul had so approved of, and which had appeared in various press articles today. Paul had been right. There might not have been paparazzi photographing them while they ate, for which she was thankful, but they'd managed to get quite a few shots of Paul and Eva arriving at and leaving the restaurant.

Eva nodded. A couple more outfits would be good. She'd packed for a week's visit, not for a month and a half, if not more. It wasn't as if she was on a private holiday, not with this schedule. For some of the time, she'd be acting as Paul's proxy. She had to look the part.

Eva nodded. 'I like her designs, plus it would be good to support a local enterprise.'

'Exactly!' Her new assistant gave her a brilliant smile. 'Good press for you and for the designer. It will certainly boost her business, dressing our Queen-to-be.'

Eva's chest cramped on the words but she knew her expression didn't give away her pain. Queen of St Ancilla was something she'd never be.

Once more she felt doubt open up inside her. Surely this schedule would cement her as a fixture in St Ancilla's royalty? Wouldn't that make her eventual split from Paul more difficult?

But to leave now would undo all the good yesterday's press conference had done and she knew Paul would be immoveable. He'd flat-out refuse to end their betrothal yet.

Helena pointed to other appointments squeezed in the schedule. 'This is an old family-run company that makes shoes. It used to be one of St Ancilla's traditional industries but increasingly it's under threat from cheap imports. But their shoes are of excellent quality and I thought...'

Eva laughed. 'So long as they can make more than hiking boots and lace-up brogues, I'll be happy.' Though now she thought about it, she needed a new pair of hiking boots.

'And this one?'

'A lace-making guild.'

'Let me guess. Another traditional industry here?'

Helena spread her hands. 'Why not kill two birds with one stone? You need some clothes and they need—'

'It's fine, Helena. If I can do my bit for local tradition and businesses, I'm happy to help.'

Which was how Eva found her days filled with a schedule even busier than the one she had in Tarentia. At least in Tarentia she knew the place intimately. Here, in Paul's kingdom, she was a newcomer and had to do much more preparation for every engagement.

Despite the years she'd put into studying Ancillan history, politics, geography and language, she didn't feel nearly as confident in saying or doing the right thing.

She relied on Helena and Paul. Inevitably Paul, for she saw him daily, not only during their joint engagements but every evening over dinner and sometimes at breakfast.

Eva tried to keep her distance, not relax in his company or take it for granted, but it was a battle she'd already lost. Keep her distance? Impossible. This strange situation inspired intimacy, created by their common purpose and the secret about their faux engagement.

Yet it would be over soon enough.

That was what Eva told herself constantly but it had little effect. Each day she looked forward to the time she'd be with him. She responded to his easy smile and ready charm. More than once she found herself basking in his approval as he complimented her on how she'd handled some situation. As for those times when he touched her...a hand at her elbow or the small of her back...it took everything she had not to shiver in response and lean into his hand.

She enjoyed those touches too much.

That was why she didn't object when those occasional touches grew more frequent, and not just in public.

Such as now, three weeks after the fateful night of the ball and her disastrous night-club visit.

As she entered the small dining parlour Paul held out a chair for her at the breakfast table and gave her a smile that made her head swim. She'd no sooner seated herself than he put his hand on her shoulder as he leaned in and placed a letter on the table before her. Instantly delicious heat flowed through her from his touch.

It was a letter from a local group. It referred to her recent visit and followed up her suggestion to seek royal approval for an initiative they'd discussed.

Eva tried to concentrate on the text. Yet she was too aware of Paul behind her, of the warm clasp of his hand and the soft feathering of his breath across her scalp.

It was only when he walked round to take his seat opposite her that she managed to fill her lungs properly.

Every time he touched her, there it was again. The need, almost overwhelming, to turn to him and give up pretending she didn't want him.

Memories of their night together interrupted her sleep. Sometimes, seeing Paul's face in repose, noting tired lines she hadn't registered before, she wondered if he suffered the same way. But he didn't push her to change her mind.

Eva told herself she should be thankful he'd taken her at her word. That he didn't try to pressure her.

Yet a carping voice inside declared it was because he

wasn't that attracted after all. One night had been enough
for him.

How she detested that voice.

'You were a hit.'

Eva looked up, blinking into those mesmerising eyes,
and took a moment to understand what he meant.

'Oh, the letter.' She lifted her shoulders. 'They were very
enthusiastic. Very forward-thinking.'

'It sounds like you were too. Your suggestion was a good
one. I'll have the relevant people look at it today.'

Eva glowed at his words, but made herself look away,
reaching for a jug of fresh juice.

It was good to be appreciated but, she told herself, she
couldn't allow herself to hang on Paul's approval as if it was
the most important thing in her world. Soon she'd be moving on to an exciting new career surrounded by new people.

As soon as she worked out what that would be...

'Actually, if you're receptive to that, I had another idea
I wanted to run past you.'

It was easier to talk about the needs of his people rather
than her own need for him. These weeks sharing a new level
of intimacy had only made her long for more.

Desperately she dragged her mind back to work, explaining the idea she'd had following a discussion with
staff from an inner-city school.

'You want to give them access to the royal hunting
lodge?' He leaned back in his seat, his brow pleating.

'Not the inside. Well...' She paused. 'That's another possibility but for the future.' She hurried on. 'These children
live in a poor neighbourhood. They don't get out of the city,
and here is a gorgeous, forested area close to the capital
where they could—'

'Get lost and need a search-and-rescue team called in?'

Eva surveyed him steadily. This wasn't the response
she'd expected. 'Is it really so dangerous there?'

Paul shrugged but she refused to be distracted into watching his powerful shoulders.

'If they venture up the mountain into the wildlife reserve.'

'But if it's a wildlife reserve, isn't there a boundary fence?'

'Well, yes, there is. A couple of kilometres from the lodge.'

'So a class group could visit the lodge, access the grounds but not go through into the reserve?'

Slowly Paul nodded but he didn't look enthusiastic. 'The place isn't set up for school groups. There aren't amenities for casual visitors.'

Eva sipped her juice then reached for some fresh figs and honey. 'I'm not suggesting letting a bunch of kids run wild and unsupervised in a heritage-listed building. My sources tell me there are amenities that can be unlocked at the back of the lodge—toilets and a basic kitchen that are quite separate to the rest of the building. They're in good condition but don't get used now there's no hunting there.'

'You *have* done your homework.' For once he didn't sound impressed. Eva tried to read his expression but couldn't.

'I thought you'd be pleased to put the place to good use. The smaller children would love it. Plus the older ones doing environmental studies or botany. And when I was talking to one of the art teachers it hit me how terrific the place would be for kids interested in sculpture. The plaster lobsters, for a start, would be fun inspiration.'

Eva waited for him to smile at that one but his mouth remained flat.

'You don't like the idea.'

She put down the honey and sat back, curiously deflated. It wasn't that she'd had an earth-shatteringly unique idea but that it had seemed a perfect use for a beautiful, neglected place.

The feeling of connection and partnership she'd begun to experience around Paul disintegrated under his frown.

'It's a very worthy proposal. I'll think about it. In the meantime—'

'*Why* don't you approve?'

Paul noted that obstinately raised chin and clear, questioning gaze and knew Eva wouldn't give up. It was her tenacious look.

He'd learned to respect it even if she chose the most inconvenient times to stand her ground. Such as these past weeks, sticking to her determination to avoid physical intimacy.

Maybe that was why he felt out of sorts. As if his skin didn't fit any more. After weeks living under the same roof, Paul was more than ever conscious of Eva sleeping a corridor away. Thirty metres and five doors away, to be precise.

More than once he'd prowled the distance in the middle of the night, drawn to her by a longing so fierce, so all-consuming, it drove him crazy.

But, instead of tapping on the door and waiting for her husky invitation, he'd stand there, hands clenching and unclenching, shoulders high and senses on alert for any sign that she was awake and waiting for him. Then he'd turn silently away and trudge back to his room, or more often his study or the gym, since sleep would elude him.

Because he respected her right to say no.

Even though he was going slowly out of his mind with frustration and thwarted longing.

'Paul?'

He blinked, focusing on bright eyes and parted lips. He recalled that moment when he leaned close, touching her shoulder, inhaling her fresh hyacinth scent, revelling in the fact she didn't shy away. But it wasn't nearly enough for a man raw with hunger.

'It's not a matter of approval. It's just—'

'You don't like it.'

The light had gone out of her bright eyes, snuffed out by his inability to share her enthusiasm.

'I'm considering it.'

She arched one eyebrow and waited, making him feel for the first time in years as if he had to explain himself.

Maybe he did. Eva knew a lot about his past but there was much he preferred to keep to himself. Territory he chose not to visit.

'On the face of it, it's an excellent idea.'

'But you're not happy about it. I thought you'd be pleased. The way you spoke about the lodge that night made it sound like you'd be happy to tear it down. I know it wouldn't create an income stream but at least this way someone would get benefit from the place.'

Paul reached for his coffee, sipping it slowly as he considered what, if anything, to tell her.

'You're right,' he said finally. 'Far better that it gets used.'

Eva said nothing, just regarded him across her untouched meal. She looked as if she'd happily sit there all morning if that was what it took.

Paul drained his cup and put it down with a decisive click.

'Look, it's just me being selfish, okay? But I promise the proposal will be considered properly.' In fact, it made so much sense he could just about guarantee the suggestion would become reality soon.

'You're not selfish.'

A huff of laughter escaped him. 'Of course I am. I'm just like anyone else.'

Eva shook her head, the morning light picking out strands of honey and caramel in her hair. 'You spend almost every waking hour working for your people, to help

St Ancilla thrive. Your plan to release me from our engagement was for *my* benefit, and you're even promising to return my dowry, despite the fact it wasn't you who spent it. I've known you for years and have never seen you do a selfish thing yet.'

Paul stared at Eva, taken aback by her intensity as she leaned across the table.

'You make me sound...'

He shook his head. Didn't she realise what he'd done that night at the old lodge was pure selfishness? There'd been no noble holding back. One kiss was all it had taken for his vaunted control to drop, and he'd grabbed for what he wanted.

'I'm no knight in shining armour, Eva. The simple fact is I think of the old lodge as my private place, and now I discover I don't like sharing.'

'I wondered if it might be something like that,' she surprised him by saying. 'You love it there so much?'

Love? The place had been a punishment then later a bolthole.

'My attachment to the place is complicated.'

Eva folded her hands together on the table as if waiting for him to continue.

Paul gave a mental shrug. Why not?

He sat back in his chair. 'My father was...' *Appalling. Irascible. Impossible to please.* 'Difficult. Very difficult. Everything had to be done his way. He tried to mould me into a copy of himself.'

'I'm so glad he didn't succeed.'

Paul felt a little jab of heat through the chest at Eva's words. It was true he'd made it his life's aim *not* to be like King Hugo, but hearing Eva say so, especially when she smiled at him that way...

'My mother ran interference when she could but, from the time I was old enough to realise what sort of man my father really was, we were on a collision course. Nothing I did was good enough. I wasn't hard enough, didn't follow his instructions blindly. As a result, I was punished regularly.'

Eva's expression grew tight with disapproval. 'He beat you?'

What would have happened if Paul's mother had turned such a look on her husband when he'd lost his temper instead of turning meekly away?

He shrugged. 'Yes. But eventually only rarely, because it didn't have the desired effect.' Because Paul had been too proud and too determined to let the old man see how close he was to breaking.

'He tried other methods. One day, when I'd questioned something he said, he had me packed off to the hunting lodge. Told me that if I wanted to be so bloody independent I could have a taste of real independence and see how I fared. I assume he thought I'd give up after a day and ask to come back with my tail between my legs. Or that it would be a salutary, toughening up experience.'

'I don't understand. Why would staying at the lodge be tough?'

Paul felt a grim smile tug at his lips. 'Because I was only nine. I was left there alone in the middle of winter. The electricity was turned off and the water. I was given a couple of days' rations but no matches. The guards posted at the perimeter had orders not to let me out till I said I was ready to apologise.'

Across the table, Eva's jaw dropped open. 'That's… that's…'

'That was my father.' Paul reached out for a pastry and bit into it with relish. Even now he recalled how sharp true hunger pangs were, and how harsh even a Mediterranean winter could be.

'After five days, the captain of the guard was allowed in to see how I was doing.'

'Five days!' She shot to her feet, her hands planted on the table. 'He left a nine-year-old alone there for five days? What sort of parent…?'

She choked down the rest of the sentence, making Paul feel all sorts of a fool for distressing her.

Seconds later he was on her side of the table, taking hold of her hands. Her fingers felt cold as they clutched his.

'Shh. It's okay. I survived.'

'But that's just *criminal*!'

'That was my father. You're not supposed to say it about a parent, but it's a relief he's dead. He can't harm us any more. Plus, we're spared the need to put him on trial for his crimes against the state.'

Still Eva goggled up at him. 'But *five days*! How did you survive?'

'Well, I was skinnier when they took me home than when I went there.'

Instantly Paul regretted his wry words as he saw her horror.

'It wasn't too bad, really, even though my attempts to trap animals to eat were a dismal failure. I had more success with heating, though, so I was warm. I'd seen a documentary showing people lighting fires by rubbing sticks together. It took me a day and a half—' and hands rubbed raw to the point of bleeding '—but I finally managed it. I set water traps outside to collect rainfall so I had enough to drink. It was actually a bit of an adventure, camping out in one of the smaller rooms with a stack of books from the library and a roaring fire.'

Compared with his regimented life at the palace, it had been bliss. Except for the hunger pains, and those times in the middle of the night when his nine-year-old imagination had turned the lodge into a terrifying place.

'He was a monster.' Eva clutched Paul's hands and his fingers curled around hers.

Even Paul's mother, though supposedly worn out with worry about him all those years ago, had welcomed him home by trying to make him promise never to cross his father again. It felt good now, having someone so unequivocally on his side, even after all this time.

But it was more than that. This wasn't just anyone, this was *Eva*. The fact that she cared so much, even about ancient wrongs like that, made him feel something he'd never felt before.

He felt fuller, as if emotions rose so close to the surface they scraped at his skin. Yet he felt stronger too, as if her caring ignited a fire in him he hadn't known about.

'He's gone now.' He wanted to wrap his arms around Eva and pull her close. It seemed the most natural thing in the world. To comfort her, and himself. To be together.

Paul stiffened his spine and fought the impulse, trying to respect the boundaries she'd set. Instead he lifted one of those cool hands to his lips and kissed her knuckles.

'It's not so bad, Eva. After that my father realised how futile it was trying to discipline me that way. Instead he'd simply banish me for a week or so till he could stand seeing me again.'

'Not to the hunting lodge!'

He smiled against her hand. 'It was never mentioned, but after that there was always power and water and plenty of food. I developed a love-hate relationship with the place but, even after all these years, if ever I need time and space I head off to the lodge, which is why there were sheets on the bed and provisions in the kitchen.'

He lowered her hand but kept hold of it. 'From a purely financial point of view, the old place doesn't pay its way. Though in the last couple of years it's been used for staff retreats and planning sessions. Principally, though, it's my bolthole.'

'Then you should have said so upfront. It doesn't *have* to be opened to school groups.'

Paul shook his head. 'Why shouldn't they get some benefit from it? You're right. It's in an amazing setting and it's selfish not to share.'

'I never said you were…'

This time he couldn't resist the lure of that quaint little frown and her pouting lips. He swooped down for a brief kiss, luxuriating in the taste and softness of that lovely mouth before pulling back.

Satisfaction filled him as he saw her dazed eyes and their hint of smoky blue.

In that moment Paul came to a decision. Not with logic or argument but with pure instinct. And nothing had ever felt so right.

Eva was his.

It didn't matter if their betrothal had been arranged as an affair of state, or that the reason they were still officially engaged was to preserve her reputation and scotch any scandal.

Eva was his and he wanted it to stay that way. He wanted her. Wanted her in his bed, but wanted much more besides.

Eva was his and he intended to claim her as his bride.

The thought of her as his wife, not merely his fiancée, brought on that burgeoning emotion, filling up all the empty cracks and fissures he hadn't known *were* empty till these last few weeks, when he'd begun to yearn for more.

On impulse, he raised both her hands to his lips, drawing in the delicate, sweet scent of her skin, watching her eyes widen and her mouth soften.

He was a determined man.

He was determined to keep Eva. All he had to do was find out how.

CHAPTER ELEVEN

A WEEK LATER, Paul invited Eva back to his study after an official reception.

Usually he hosted such events alone. Tonight, with Eva circulating among the foreign delegates and charming them, Paul had felt some of his burden lift. It had been an important event, designed to encourage interest in doing business here in St Ancilla. And, from the discussions he'd had, the signs were encouraging.

As he led her along the corridor it struck him that Eva had been lightening his load for several weeks. She allowed him more time to pursue the discussions he needed to while she acted the perfect hostess.

More, she often gave him a valuable different perspective, noticing things he hadn't. Details that helped him at the negotiating table. But other things too, such as reminding him his work shouldn't be all about securing the nation's finances. More than once she'd brought his focus back to small-scale local issues that made such a difference to his people.

Like school excursions for disadvantaged students. He remembered her delight when she'd heard that the first such outing to the hunting lodge had been a success. And the way her eyes had shone when he'd announced the purchase of a bus to be shared by several city schools for excursions.

After years of public austerity, the finances weren't

quite so tight, and it felt good to direct funds where they'd benefit the people.

'Here we are.' He opened the door and stood aside for Eva to enter.

He caught her spring scent as she moved past him, elegant and desirable in a gown that looked as if it was made of dusky-pink cobwebs, ethereal and enticing. Another dress by a local designer. In a few short weeks Eva was putting St Ancillan fashion on the international map.

Right now, though, Paul was more interested in imagining his hands around that slim waist, or slipping up under the delicate skirt to touch silky skin.

'Paul...?'

'Sorry.' He dragged his gaze to her face, noting a hint of fatigue around her eyes. He ushered her to a seat but she shook her head.

'I'm tired so I won't stay long.'

Disappointment stirred. They had developed a habit of retiring here or to his private sitting room to unwind and discuss the day. Another luxury he'd only just discovered and had no intention of giving up.

'I won't keep you long. Have I been working you too hard?'

Something, some hint of emotion, rippled across Eva's features but was gone so fast he might have imagined it.

Except Paul noticed everything about her now. He was reminded of the early days of their engagement, when she'd hide her emotions behind a polite façade.

His gut squeezed at the idea of Eva retreating from him. He wanted to find out why she was so fatigued and fix it. Except her very posture, perfectly poised and regal, spoke volumes to a man who knew her. He guessed sheer willpower kept her upright after a long evening of formal entertaining.

Quickly he turned to his desk, unlocking a deep drawer

and withdrawing a crimson velvet box that had been brought up from the treasury.

He moved to where she stood, the box unaccountably heavy in his hand. This was a threshold he was about to cross, yet he had no qualms about it. Giving this to Eva made sense in every possible way. But he felt the gravity of the moment. Felt and welcomed it.

'I'd like you to wear this at the ball next week.'

His birthday ball. What better time to share his intentions with Eva? He'd been tempted to tell her tonight but it wasn't the right time. He preferred not to blurt it out when she was longing for her bed. He wanted her full attention. The moment had to be perfect.

Hesitantly she took the box, her forehead crinkling in curiosity. Then she snapped open the lid and any sign of weariness was banished by surprise. Her face lit with the reflection of light bouncing off the gems she held.

'I don't think—'

'Wear it for me, Eva. Please.' Paul couldn't remember ever hanging on a woman's answer quite so urgently.

He reminded himself it was just a tiara. That the important thing would be winning Eva's agreement to stay with him. But within the St Ancillan royal family this piece held great significance. It was proof of his intentions at a time when he still trod warily around Eva's doubts and fears.

He'd taken advantage of her once, making love to her when she'd been vulnerable, and it could be argued she wasn't thinking straight. This, for the sake of his own conscience, was his promise to her, even if she didn't know that yet.

'Are you sure? It's absolutely gorgeous, of course, but—'

'It's the most formal occasion on the royal calendar. If you'd known you'd be here for it, you'd have brought something similar from Tarentia, wouldn't you?'

'Yes, I would have.' Her eyes lifted from the brilliant

stones to his face and Paul felt that for once he'd managed to counter her objections easily.

'You'll look stunning wearing it.' He didn't dare reach out and touch her, knowing the temptation to do more than allow a fleeting caress would be too strong. 'You'd look stunning without it, I know, but it might have been made especially for you. I'd be honoured if you'd wear it. For me, Eva.'

For a second something bright and potent shimmered between them. Later he'd wonder if it was the radiance of light sparking off aquamarines and diamonds, but in this moment Paul knew, *felt*, it was more. A moment's communion between them. An instant of shared emotion.

His heart lifted as Eva closed the box and nodded. 'Thank you, Paul. I will.'

Eva crossed her room on wobbly legs that gave way when she reached the wide bed. Her fingers bit into the crimson velvet of the box as she subsided onto the mattress.

Her thoughts were a whirling mess that matched a stomach unsettled by nerves. All day she'd been on edge, worried but telling herself not to be.

It had been difficult to concentrate on her role as hostess as a voice of doubt kept nagging at her.

Then, just as she'd thought she could escape to the solitude of her suite, Paul had waylaid her. She should have forestalled him, pleaded tiredness straight away, but she'd been either too light-headed to think of it or too weak to resist the temptation of a little time alone with him.

She feared it was the latter. Though she knew it was bad for her, that this need for his company was something she had to wean herself off. The desire to make the most of their last weeks together was too strong.

Slowly she unlatched the lid of the antique box and lifted it. Instantly the room seemed brighter. It was a classically elegant piece, a master jeweller's work from over a century ago.

Fashioned from platinum, it was set with stones of graduating size, the largest at the front angling down to smaller, yet still magnificent emerald-cut stones on either side. The gems were aquamarines, a pure, clear pale blue, set in a delicate frame of looping diamonds that sparkled brilliantly.

Even she, brought up seeing and wearing heirloom gems regularly, had rarely seen a piece so exquisite.

And Paul thinks it could have been made especially for me.

Her heart pounded an out-of-kilter beat and something behind her ribs caught.

He's exaggerating.

But part of her wanted to believe it was true. That he found her attractive. That he believed she shone as brightly as these amazing stones.

Had he known she'd be wearing silver next week? That this would be the perfect match to the gown being designed for her?

No, it was a lucky chance. That was all.

Yet part of her, a tiny superstitious part she didn't know, felt she was *fated* to wear this.

As if!

Reluctantly she closed the lid, cutting off the blinding brilliance, groping for sanity, perspective.

He just wants you to look good at his birthday ball. It's nothing personal.

But it had felt personal. Sounded it.

In her head Eva replayed his voice, deeper than usual and carving a groove of longing through her stupid heart, asking her to wear it *for him*.

The way he'd looked at her.

Even through her stress and tiredness, she'd seen that look and felt herself tremble in anticipation.

Or was she reading too much into a glance and a simple act of kindness? He was lending her a tiara so she'd look the part of his fiancée at a significant event.

One she hadn't originally been invited to because he'd planned to end their engagement.

That severed her wayward imaginings.

Paul was making the best of a difficult situation.

He had no idea how much more difficult her continued presence was making things. Only today, at a visit to an embroiderers' guild, she'd been asked if they might have the honour of working on her wedding dress.

Within the last two weeks she'd fielded similar requests from lace makers and from the designer responsible for to-night's fabulous dress.

Each time she was asked, Eva felt sicker in the stom-ach. Because she was living a lie and now others were in-vesting in it, building their hopes on it. Eagerly awaiting the wedding.

She'd been stunned by the alacrity with which most St Ancillans had welcomed her. There'd been a few who'd looked askance, as if doubting her suitability as a consort for their King. And still there'd been a few sensational ar-ticles about her, works of total fiction. But she didn't let those bother her.

No, what bothered her was the feeling that she was sink-ing deeper and deeper into this mire of make-believe. That with every passing day it would be harder to break free.

Because she wanted to be what everyone believed her to be—Paul's intended bride.

And then there was the other worry. The one that had haunted her since last night when she'd realised she'd been in St Ancilla a whole month.

The possibility, faint but disturbing, that she might be pregnant.

CHAPTER TWELVE

IT WAS LATE and Eva had already danced with a who's who of dignitaries. She'd chatted with ambassadors and made small talk with a host of St Ancillans, some of whom were familiar to her now. There was an air of jubilation and good will, as if this celebration signalled more than Paul's birthday. As if people knew that, after years of austerity, things were looking up.

Eva enjoyed herself, especially the two waltzes with Paul, clasped close in his embrace as if he'd never heard of royal protocol and simply wanted to envelop her. Her heart still hammered too fast after the sheer delight of swirling through the glittering crowd, lost to the joy of being in his arms.

But reality had intervened soon enough. It had been in the supper room, when she'd been confronted with a plate of tiny pancakes topped with smoked salmon and gleaming caviar.

She'd tried to tell herself it was the heat and the press of the crowd, but for a moment she'd felt nausea well. Instantly she'd retreated, excusing herself for the quiet of a withdrawing room, taking slow breaths and dampening her nape and wrists with cold water.

She was fine now. No more nausea. It was probably just nerves.

Except she'd been in St Ancilla five weeks and still hadn't had her period.

Usually that wouldn't bother her. Eva's cycle was notoriously irregular. Which meant she was worrying about nothing.

Except this time there was just a possibility she was pregnant. Condoms weren't a hundred percent effective.

Heat danced in her veins as she remembered Paul straining against her. His hoarse shout of elation as he'd powered into her and she'd been swept up into bliss.

Yes, pregnancy was definitely a possibility.

But not, she told herself, probable. And the more she fretted…who knew? Could stress delay her period?

She needed to take a pregnancy test.

She wasn't able to leave the palace, walk into a pharmacy and ask for a test kit. The world would know within hours.

Instead she'd contacted her best friend and asked her to buy one and send it to her. A courier had arrived with the parcel while Eva had been dressing for the ball. She'd been torn between the need to discover the truth straight away and the knowledge that she'd never maintain the façade of calm she needed at the royal event if she discovered she was pregnant.

Or if she discovered she wasn't. Eva was honest enough to realise part of her would be disappointed at the news she wasn't carrying Paul's child, despite the complications a baby would create.

Tonight, as soon as she returned to her suite, she'd take the test.

Decision made, she stood straighter before the mirror, taking time to smooth a stray lock of hair, fixing it back into the low-set knot behind her head. She smoothed the glittering silver dress with hands that barely trembled. On her head sat the gorgeous tiara Paul had loaned her.

Wearing this dress and jewellery, she looked the part of Paul's bride-to-be. All she had to do was keep her composure a little longer and she could escape to her room.

Eva hadn't counted on the pair of women gossiping at a side entrance to the ballroom.

They stood with their backs to her, yet their voices carried down the otherwise deserted corridor.

'Do you think it's true, that she really was trawling night clubs looking for a one-night stand? That she's the sort who's never satisfied with just one man?'

'It's possible. That photo…' A shrug of plump shoulders. 'On the other hand, you noticed what she's wearing, of course.'

'It's an amazing gown. I'll give her that. She dresses well.'

'Not the dress, the tiara. My sister-in-law used to be a lady-in-waiting to the old Queen. If I remember rightly, that's the tiara she told me about. The one that's never been worn by anyone but the Queen of Ancilla. Now, I ask you, would he give her that to wear if he knew she was some little tart he can't trust to keep her legs together?'

Eva faltered to a stop, stunned. Not by the carelessly vicious gossip but by the news she was apparently wearing something that rightly belonged to the country's Queen.

Could it be true? Why would Paul let her wear it in that case? They were due to end their engagement soon. Such a gesture could only dredge up more speculation about them.

Her heart thundered and her skin prickled all over as she tried to make sense of the gesture. But this wasn't the time or the place. Any minute now, the gossips would turn and see her.

Too late. Her half-formed thought of heading back the way she'd come died as the women both sank into deep curtseys.

There, stepping out of the ballroom in front of them,

was Paul, the scowl on his face as black as his superbly tailored evening clothes.

Eva sucked in a deep breath, stunned by the cold fury on his face. She'd seen him look like that only once before, when discussing the man who'd taken advantage of her behind the night club. Then he'd looked as though he'd wanted to commit murder.

Now she watched his features settle into a mask of glacial calm. He spoke to the women, but so low she didn't catch his words. An instant later they were hurrying away, heads down, as if glad to escape.

As they left his eyes caught hers. Heat stole through her and a jangle of emotions stirred. Eva set her shoulders and moved towards him, head up.

'Eva. I…' He paused as someone spoke to him from inside the ballroom. Then he held out his hand to her. 'Come. It's time for our final dance.'

'Then we need to talk.'

He nodded, holding her eyes. 'We do, indeed. We have something important to discuss.'

The rest of the ball alternately flew and dragged by.

Dancing another waltz in Paul's arms was a brief, glorious respite from doubt and anxiety. Even the fact that he held her closer than ever, his body moving in sync with hers so deftly they might have been one, was a source of joy rather than dismay. But then came the long, ceremonial process of farewelling their guests.

Eva didn't see the two women who'd been talking outside the ballroom. Had they left without saying goodbye, or had Paul ordered them gone?

Whatever the truth, by the time they settled upstairs in Paul's private sitting room Eva was exhausted and nervous. Both of which she refused to show.

When Paul offered her a drink, she asked for sparkling water. A whisky was tempting—she'd appreciate that sudden shot of heat, as she felt unaccountably chilled—but until she knew there was no pregnancy she'd avoid alcohol.

She sat stiff-backed on a sofa, while he sprawled, long-legged on one facing her.

They both began speaking at once then stopped. Paul gestured for her to go first.

'Is it true?' she asked in a voice brittle with suppressed emotion. 'What that woman said about this tiara?'

'You understood that? They were speaking Ancillan. I thought you weren't fluent.'

Eva pursed her lips. 'We've been engaged for four years, Paul. Of course I've been learning your language.' In fact, she'd started many years earlier, even though it was a no-toriously difficult language to learn, because of her infatu-ation with Paul.

If only it were still just infatuation!

For the first time she could recall, he looked flustered. 'I knew you'd had lessons. I've heard you speak a little at official events. But I thought…' His gaze sharpened. 'Did you understand what your attacker said in that back alley?'

Eva sipped her water and inclined her head, suppress-ing a shiver. Occasionally she still heard that voice, those words, in her dreams.

'Eva!' He leaned forward, as if to reach for her, and she sank back, feeling too fragile to let him touch her.

Paul frowned. 'In that case, allow me to apologise on behalf of my fellow Ancillans. I wouldn't have had you hear such things for anything, either that night or tonight. Those harpies—'

'Was it true? About the tiara?'

He swirled amber liquid around his glass.

'The piece is from the family vault. It's been worn by several generations of women in my family.' His sudden smile was like sunshine breaking through a stormy sky.

'It could have been made for you, Eva. I'm so pleased you wore it.'

With difficulty Eva ignored the compliment and concentrated on what he'd said about the tiara. She'd guessed it was a special piece, given its obvious age and quality.

'She said it was only ever worn by the Queen. Is that right?'

Paul hesitated before answering then shrugged. 'Traditionally, yes.'

'And this is generally known?' Her skin frosted as she absorbed the implications of what she'd done, wearing the beautiful thing. 'Does everyone see this as proof we'll marry soon?'

Already she found it increasingly difficult, fending off well-meant queries about when the wedding would be. After their long engagement, it seemed people believed it was imminent. Paul hadn't thought of that when he'd suggested she stay here for six weeks.

His dark eyebrows crammed together as if he didn't like her words. 'Very few people would understand the significance of you wearing it.'

'But some in the court clearly do. They see it as further proof that we're to marry.' Eva paused, throat closing on the word. This act of theirs grew harder each day.

He put down his glass and shot to the edge of his seat, leaning forward and capturing her free hand.

'Does it matter what others think?'

'It does if they expect a wedding in a few months. Hasn't it struck you that we're digging ourselves into an ever deeper hole by continuing this pretend engagement? That we're building up public expectations?'

Something shifted in Paul's expression.

'What if it's not a pretence? What if I said I wanted you to stay and marry me?'

Her restless fingers froze in his grip. 'Sorry?'

'What if I asked you to wear the tiara because I want you to be my Queen?'

'You're not serious?'

But, looking into those dark blue eyes, she saw no hint of humour, much less doubt. Paul looked like a man convinced he knew what he was doing.

A great wave of emotion shuddered through her and she had the simultaneous desire to laugh and burst into tears.

Shock, she realised. She was in shock.

Eva lifted her glass to trembling lips and downed her water in one draught. She gripped the tumbler so hard it felt as though it were soldered to her skin.

'What are you saying, Paul?'

'I'm saying we're good together, Eva.'

'Just because we were sexually compatible.' He'd never know how much it cost her to use the past tense. She still burned for him. Just having him hold her hand incinerated her control and left her longing to be possessed by him.

His mouth quirked up on one side and inevitably there it was. Desire, like hot honey, swirling through her.

'Actually, I wasn't referring to sex. I've been trying very, very hard not to think about that, though I admit I haven't been very successful.'

He paused, watching her face intently as his thumb swiped across her wrist, as if he knew that made her shaky with longing. 'But, yes, you're right. We're extremely compatible physically. I'd even say combustible. I can't stop thinking about us, together.'

Another pause in which Eva would swear she saw a heat haze shimmer in the air between them.

'We share something very special sexually.'

That rough-suede voice was a caress. Eva's nipples peaked as her skin drew taut and everything inside clenched.

'That night was a mistake.'

'It was no mistake, Eva. But let's put that aside for now.'

Easier said than done when she felt as if she was on fire just from his words.

'We're good together. We understand each other. We have similar values and goals. We make a great team—you must see that.'

Eva clamped her lips shut, scared of what she might blurt out.

'These last few weeks have been a revelation. I never realised how much difference it would make to have a partner beside me.' He shook his head. 'Even in such a short time you've made a difference here and you've lessened my load. I actually feel like I don't have to work sixteen hours a day just to keep the place afloat.'

Inside something seemed to unfurl. Like petals of a flower opening.

Eva was glad she'd made a difference. It was what she'd trained for, after all, but mainly she'd wanted to help Paul. She'd found a real sense of achievement in the weeks since she'd been here. Imagine what she'd be able to do with more time.

A hint of a smile hovered at the corners of her mouth. She felt the quiver, felt the rising joy, for just an instant before she suppressed it.

Paul's voice was deep and serious. 'Our arrangement has been working so well. Why not make it permanent?'

His eyes glowed and his expression was almost tender. *Almost.*

Because sexual desire and an appreciation of her work ethic and skills wasn't love. It might make her feel good but it wasn't enough.

Eva had changed since she'd arrived in St Ancilla. Perhaps she saw more clearly how futile it was to hope for more than Paul could give. Perhaps she'd set a higher value on herself and wasn't ready to settle for less than she needed.

Paul saw the benefits of an arranged marriage. The convenience. That was all. He didn't see *her*. Or, if he did, only in so far as she filled his own needs.

He wasn't a selfish man. He didn't know how she felt about him. If he did, she guessed he'd never suggest marriage. But her feelings were already shredded from playing the part of his fiancée up close and personal this last month. Imagine how tough it would be if they married!

'I'm glad to be able to help, Paul.' His name felt heavy on her lips.

She breathed slowly and put her empty glass down on a side table. Then she gently tugged her other hand free of his grip.

A second later she was on her feet.

She had to end this. Now.

And, if you're pregnant, then what?

But she couldn't be, surely? How unlikely was it that there was a baby? He'd taken precautions, hadn't he?

She pressed a hand to her stomach then let it fall, scared he might read the tell-tale gesture.

If there's a baby, then we'll just have to face that complication when the time comes.

For now, all she could do was face her current reality.

That Paul wanted her in a convenient marriage. He'd be a kind, caring husband but he would never love her. While she was still, despite her every effort, head over heels in love with him.

Eva paced towards the window, peering out at moonlight silvering the Mediterranean. It looked so lovely, so perfectly romantic. But this wasn't a romance, it was reality.

'It wouldn't work, Paul. I don't want to marry you.' She kept her eyes fixed on the view, knowing she wouldn't be able to do this if she looked him in the eye.

'In fact, the reason I wanted to talk with you tonight was to tell you I've decided to go home next week.'

'Next week!' His voice came from behind her and she felt the warmth of his breath cascade down her bare neck, sending tiny ripples of delight skittering across her skin. He must be standing close, his head tilted down towards her. For a second she allowed herself to imagine that was regret as well as surprise in his voice. 'But you can't. It's not—'

'It's what's going to happen, Paul. I can't do this any more.'

Eva swung round and was confronted with the sight of his solid jaw clenched tight. She knew Paul, knew how determined he could be. She couldn't afford to give him a chance to win her over because she knew how fragile her defences were against him.

'Please, Paul. No more arguments. We've been over this before. I don't want to marry you, and you don't want to marry an unwilling woman.'

Was it her imagination, or did he flinch?

Eva couldn't stay to find out. Without raising her gaze to his, lest she waver, she hurried past him. Out she went into the cold, empty corridor, her bruised heart lying heavy against her ribs.

He didn't try to stop her.

That hurt most of all.

CHAPTER THIRTEEN

PAUL PACED THE CORRIDOR. The place was in darkness but for pearly moonlight spilling through the windows. The clean-up from the ball had finished and everyone was in bed.

Except him.

Eva's announcement had come out of the blue, her news so shocking it was impossible to relax and switch off. He kept reliving her words and that terrible air of finality as she'd spoken. It hadn't been posturing. She'd meant every word.

Why?

He couldn't understand it. Her attitude made no sense.

Her words had sliced through him, as if she'd taken one of the antique swords from a display case downstairs and run him through with it.

Had he ever known such hurt? It made the time he'd fractured his collarbone on the polo field fade into insignificance. Even discovering the full extent of his father's crimes against the nation and against his half-sister Caro hadn't hurt like this. Because he'd been able to do something to correct those.

But Eva leaving—not just for a couple of months but for ever—there was no remedy for that.

Paul's pain increased, as if that phantom blade cut down through his chest and kept going. He stopped mid-stride, pressing his palm to his belly, trying to force the sensation away.

He hadn't seen this coming. He'd imagined Eva was happy here. She seemed it. Her enthusiasm for the projects she was engaged in and the people she met brightened each day. The only negative was that she was on edge whenever he got close. Then he'd see her shoulders creep up as if she was girding herself for his touch.

But he understood that too—sexual frustration. Because whenever he touched her there were sparks. They'd start at the point of contact and spread right through him. And he'd swear she felt those sparks too. He'd caught Eva's dazed look as he'd wrapped his hand around her waist to waltz, or held her close beside him while they'd entertained guests. Soon, he promised himself, she'd be his again. Because the physical connection between them was impossible to ignore.

He'd assumed she must be as frustrated as he at her 'no sex' rule, yet he'd held back, respecting her need for time and space. Even if...

Paul's thoughts frayed as he noticed something down the corridor. A line of light under Eva's door. It was close to three a.m. and she was still up.

He didn't hesitate. He'd been trained to take charge, to make things happen.

In two beats of his heart he was at her door, head inclined, listening. Was that movement inside?

He raised his hand and tapped on the solid wood. For several seconds he waited, listening, then tapped again. He was reaching for the handle when the door swung open.

Golden lamplight silhouetted her, congealing his thoughts into a hard knot in his gut. Eva's hair was loose on her shoulders and she'd wrapped a robe around herself, cinched tight at her waist.

Paul's breath dried out, like a mistral wind sighing out of his lungs in an arid rush.

She was beautiful.

But she was more than simply beautiful.

He didn't have the words to do her justice. There was just the heavy thrum of his heart beating *mine, mine, mine*.

'It's very late, Paul. I need to...'

Paul inserted a shoulder in the gap between door and jamb and kept moving. The gap widened. For a second they stood toe to toe, so close her heat drenched him, then she moved back and he shut the door behind them.

Eva rubbed her arms as if she were cold, her hands disappearing up the wide sleeves of her robe. It was pale silk, with a delicate pattern of wisteria blossom, making him think, as her long straight hair swung across it, of geishas and oriental luxury.

The notion intensified when she moved, her breasts shifting free against the thin material and he realised she was naked beneath the patterned silk.

He'd been going to say something but now the words eluded him. He swallowed hard as he took her in.

She spoke but for a couple of seconds it was lost in the white noise of his blood pumping hard, roaring in his ears.

Eva folded her arms in an attitude of annoyance, pulling the fabric tight over her breasts, and dimly he realised she was waiting for him to answer whatever she'd said. Paul dragged his gaze back to her up-thrust chin and prim mouth.

'You're angry.'

'I'm tired, Paul. There's no point rehashing our last discussion. I want to go to sleep.'

With a clarity that tasted bitter in his mouth, he noticed she wasn't talking about rehashing the discussion *tonight*. She meant *ever*. She'd had her say and didn't want to open the subject again.

'Yet you're still awake. What's the trouble? Too much on your mind to sleep?'

He glanced over her shoulder and noticed a suitcase open on an antique carved trunk. It was half-full.

Ice shafted through him, chilling his blood.

She was packing?

Didn't she mean to wait till next week, as she'd said?

Urgency gripped him, twisting his gut into knots.

He'd planned to talk to her tomorrow. Convince her to stay. He could be persuasive, and he'd had no doubts he could make Eva change her mind—or at least agree to stay a little longer, which would give him the time he needed to…what?

It was obvious she'd already thought things through. That, all the time he'd imagined her enjoying herself, she'd been counting the days till she left.

And yet there were times, lots of them, when he'd sensed she was anything but distant or uninterested.

'I often don't sleep straight away after an event late in the evening. But I was just about to turn the light off.' Her gaze flickered away from his and he knew she was lying.

To make him go.

Because she didn't want to give him the chance to change her mind?

Because she intended to leave sooner than she'd said?

It seemed only too likely.

She wouldn't listen to him. Wouldn't be persuaded.

But there was one way he might get through to her.

Paul wasn't even conscious of forming the thought when he found his fingers brushing the softness of her cheek, down past her chin to her throat then feathering up to push into the heavy curtain of her hair.

Her breath was a sharp inhale and her eyes widened, catching his. She opened her mouth, probably to stop him, so he raked his fingers purposefully across her scalp, moulding her skull as he lowered his head.

Eva's words never came.

He felt the puff of warm air from her mouth to his, scant centimetres away, but there was no objection.

Her head seemed heavier in his grip, as if she tilted back into his touch, leaving her face turned up towards his. Even then Paul waited, watching, breathing her in, till he saw, like a mist parting over the sea, a hint of blue in the steamy grey of her eyes.

Something stabbed at his chest. Not pain this time. Satisfaction. Anticipation. Relief.

He breathed deeper, inhaling her sweet floral and woman scent, feeling it go straight to his head.

'I want you, Eva. So badly. And I think you want me.' He slid his other hand around her waist, drawing her flush against him before she could conjure words to push him away.

Paul watched those expressive eyes, expecting rejection, waiting for the flash of sudden anger.

It didn't come. Instead there was her scent curling around him, her warm body lush and soft, and those eyes, those incredible eyes, wide with... Yearning? Invitation?

He didn't need more. His mouth touched hers and paused, waiting, till her lips trembled and opened. Slim hands grasped his shoulders, fingers tightening, and he swept her up against him, delving deep into her mouth with a hungry, desperate kiss.

It wasn't suave or practised. This kiss was too full of urgency and a relief that teetered on the brink of fear that any second now she'd push him away.

Teeth rubbed, lips and noses squashed, but it didn't matter. Because the desperation wasn't just his, it was hers too. He felt it in the clutch of her hands and the arch of her body.

'Eva...' he breathed against her mouth, tilting her head

back with his hand so he could pepper her face then her throat with urgent kisses. 'I need you, darling. I can't...'

He couldn't say it. *I can't let you go.*

Instead he showed her with his mouth, his hands, his body pressing against hers, how much he needed her.

Her hands were in his hair, fingers tunnelling across his scalp, dragging his head lower as if she feared he might try to escape.

Paul worked his way back up to her mouth and kissed her hard, tongue tangling with hers, and still he couldn't get enough of her.

He needed more. So much more.

Wrapping both arms around Eva, he hoisted her off the ground, still kissing her. With eyes barely slitted open, he covered the space between door and bed. The back of her legs hit the mattress and they tumbled down.

Eva's robe came unfastened in the manoeuvre and he slipped one hand past woven silk to skin just as soft and luxurious. His fingers spread wide, covering her hip then sliding across her abdomen.

'Paul.' It was a husk of sound. So raw and soft he couldn't tell if it was entreaty or protest. Reluctantly he opened his eyes and lifted his head.

Her gaze captured his, misty blue and approving. Her hands moved down from his shoulders and tugged at his shirt, dragging it open regardless of buttons.

Triumph stirred. And something more profound. His chest welled with it, his arteries fizzed and his mouth curved up into a smile that dragged already taut flesh even tighter.

He cleared his throat, intending to tell her how much she meant to him. But she leaned in and bit him on the side of the neck, right at the most sensitive spot, then suckled there, soothing the pinprick of hurt with a lavish wave of erotic delight.

Paul's heart hammered so fast it seemed to tumble in his chest. Especially when she pushed him a little to one side, enough to tug at his belt.

He'd been intending to take this slow, to seduce her by slow degrees till there was no possibility she'd consider—ever—the idea of leaving him. His intentions disintegrated at the feel of her fumbling at his waist. Instead he reached into his back pocket and withdrew the condom he'd got into the habit of carrying these last weeks—in case the opportunity to use it arrived.

This time, despite Eva's questing hands, he managed to ditch his shoes, socks, underwear and trousers, though his shirt still hung open off his shoulders as he settled between her bare thighs.

The blurring urgency of the last few moments stilled as they lay together, Eva's robe wide open so he could feast his eyes on her bare breasts bobbing high with each shallow breath. But, delightful as the sight was, Paul's attention kept going back to her blue-grey eyes. The warmth and emotion he saw there.

This was more than a carnal coupling. Eva's expression told a story that felt familiar. Surely it matched what he felt?

That moment of wondering, of profound feeling, seemed to last for ever. But Paul was only human and now Eva's hands moved again, her legs sliding further open, so he sank lower between her hips.

'Eva, I—'

'Paul, please...'

Propped above her, he lifted his hand to her face and brushed a strand of hair back. He trailed his fingers down her brow and her cheek, undone by the welling tenderness he felt for this woman.

Who moved first, he didn't know, but that first slight shift shattered the stillness. They came together easily, every tilt of the body, every caress of hands and lips, stoking an incredible intensity of feeling. As if in slow motion, Paul registered each exquisite sensation, even as their rhythm quickened. Till, finally, it was too much. Taking this slowly wasn't possible when every touch felt so good. *They* felt so good together.

Eva's fingers dug into his shoulders and she arched against him in a move that tore the last of his control and left him hovering on the brink.

He heard his name shouted in ecstasy, and then she was bucking against him, dragging him over the precipice with her into piercing, perfect bliss.

A long time later, with Eva dozing at his shoulder, Paul decided he had to move. He needed to dispose of the condom. The difficulty was that his bones felt like overcooked noodles and he wasn't sure he could stand.

Moving slowly, so as not to wake her, he slid from the bed and rose, taking a moment to adjust to the world again. He felt sated, exhausted, and yet his blood fizzed with elation. It felt like a weight had crumbled from his shoulders.

A smile tugged at his mouth as he entered the bathroom.

Eva and he still had to talk, obviously, but at least there'd be no more pretence that she didn't want him. Whatever was holding Eva back, they'd work it out together.

He was washing his hands when he caught sight of a box at the far end of the marble counter.

Paul blinked. He had twenty-twenty vision and didn't need to move closer to read the writing on it. But he did, drawn by a force that knocked any lingering satisfaction from his mind.

A pregnancy-test kit.

Everything inside him stilled, then his heart began to gallop.

Was Eva pregnant?

Was that why she was so determined to leave?

But that would mean…

Paul told himself it couldn't be true.

Yet, surely this was evidence?

She'd tested herself for pregnancy and announced she was leaving, despite the incredible chemistry they shared.

Because she didn't want him to know there was a baby.

The thought of a child, *their* child, brought a strange, tight feeling to his chest. As if he were full of emotions that couldn't be contained and were bound to burst free.

Why would she leave without telling him she was pregnant? She must know he'd support her and the child. In fact, it fed right into his plan for them to marry.

Unless she had no intention of telling him about the baby.

His eyes burned as he stared at the package. His gut squeezed so hard, he felt nauseous.

He felt like he'd swallowed a knot of barbed wire.

It went against everything he thought of her—but was it possible Eva intended to get rid of the child without even letting him know she was pregnant? Did she think so little of him she imagined he wouldn't care about the baby they'd made? That he didn't deserve to be informed?

CHAPTER FOURTEEN

EVA WOKE WHEN Paul got up. Not that she'd been asleep, more dazed and spent. And not wanting to be awake enough to focus on what had just happened.

Now she couldn't avoid it.

Her mind raced like a hunted animal, scurrying here and there, hitting a dead end and running in another direction. But there was no escape. Whichever way she looked, and no matter how wonderful it had been, she'd just made a terrible, terrible mistake.

Hadn't she *known* intimacy with Paul would make it harder to leave? Hadn't she withstood temptation for weeks?

Whatever the future held she'd only get her mind round it when she was away from St Ancilla and Paul. How could she plan a career and a new life living in his shadow?

What they'd just shared had been utterly glorious. She didn't have words to describe it. Yet her weakness for him threatened to undermine logic and her need to escape.

Eva sat up and swung her legs over the side of the bed, fumbling at the edges of her robe and drawing them together. The belt had disappeared. Gingerly she stood on wobbly legs, holding the robe closed with one hand, looking for it.

She wanted to be clothed when Paul came back. Eva knew there was no escaping a discussion now. She had no hope of ejecting him from her room but she had no intention of facing him naked. She already felt too vulnerable with him.

Movement caught her eye and she turned.

Clearly Paul had such no qualms about nudity.

He stood in the bathroom doorway stark naked, watching her, making no move to cover himself.

Why should he? He was magnificent. Even in her misery Eva's heart flipped at the sight of his rangy, muscled body and charismatic features.

'You were going to leave without telling me, weren't you, Eva?' He folded his arms across his chest in a movement that accentuated the power of his upper body. Despite being sated and nervous, a fluttering started up in her abdomen like a thousand butterflies taking flight. As if every feminine hormone was hitting overload.

She shut her eyes for the briefest moment and clutched her robe between her breasts.

This had to stop. She had to resist.

When she looked again, nothing had changed, except this time she noticed the grim lines around his flat mouth and vertical furrows above his pinched eyebrows.

'If you were leaving next week there'd be no need to pack tonight. You're planning to go tomorrow.'

Eva followed his gaze to her open luggage and her heart sank.

Rather than retreat, she hiked her chin up and mirrored his stance, crossing her arms defensively.

'Yes, I'm leaving in the morning.' In just a few hours. Yet thinking of her escape only brought twisting pain. 'But I'd never leave without telling you. I was going to see you first.'

His raised eyebrows spoke of disbelief.

'I was!'

'And were you going to tell me then?'

Eva frowned. He was talking in circles. 'I just said I was going to tell you I planned to go.'

'Because you need to leave urgently?' His voice ground down low, a flat, unsettling note that vibrated discordantly.

'Well... Yes. I need to leave. I can't stay any longer.'

Because each day drew her closer and closer to him.

All of St Ancilla believed the fantasy that they loved each other and if she wasn't careful she'd start believing it too. It had taken her too long to wake up to the fact that particular fantasy was impossible. She couldn't afford to let herself slip back into daydreams.

'But you weren't going to tell me about the baby, were you?' It wasn't a question. It was an accusation. Like a shard of ice slicing the thick air between them.

Eva felt a tremor begin at the back of her skull to run all the way down, past her nape to the base of her spine. Her knees shook and she had to focus on keeping them steady enough to stand.

Belatedly she remembered the pregnancy kit in the bathroom.

Why, oh, why hadn't she packed it?

'Your silence is answer enough.' More ice. Except the glare he sent her wasn't cold, it was flaming hot. 'What was the plan? Return to Tarentia and arrange a quiet abortion with no one the wiser? Without even telling me?'

Eva couldn't help it. Her jaw dropped, her mouth sagging open.

She tried to speak but choked on the words.

While she floundered Paul strode across the room. He stood so close he might have been about to scoop her up for a kiss. But the way he towered over her was more daunting than lover-like.

'Why, Eva? Couldn't you at least trust me with the truth after all we've been to each other?' To her amazement, his voice grew gruff, as if with emotion.

Eva blinked up at him, trying to get a fix on his mood. Anger, yes, but something else too.

'It's not like that.'

'No?' His lip curled in disbelief. 'You mean you intended to tell me about the baby after all?' He shook his head. 'Your actions tell another story, Princess.'

His tone dripped scorn and it galvanised something within her, giving her the strength she needed.

'I'm no liar.'

Except for the one great secret she'd striven so hard and so long to conceal—her love for him.

'Then why not tell me about the baby?' He stared down his supercilious nose at her.

Eva's hands found her hips, digging into slippery silk. Her heart pounded a protest that he should be so ready to judge her.

'There may not even be a baby. I didn't take the pregnancy test.'

For a second longer that scowl lasted, before turning into a frown of puzzlement. He inhaled deeply, his chest rising, decreasing the distance between them.

'I don't understand.'

Nor did she. Not really.

Her shoulders dropped a little as she shook her head.

'It's possible I'm pregnant. But when it came to the point I discovered I didn't want to find out.'

'Eva?' His arms dropped to his sides, and the stern lines folding the corners of his mouth turned into marks of concern rather than scorn. 'If there's a baby, you know I'll be there, don't you? It wouldn't be the end of the world.'

She looked up into his deep-blue eyes and felt the pull between them. If there was a baby, there'd be no escaping this. She'd be tied to Paul always, even if they didn't marry. What hope then of moving on with her life?

Her head spun with the whirling tangle of thoughts. The desire to bear his child versus the need to make a clean break. The ache that made her want to lean against that broad chest and surrender herself to a life with Paul versus the need to build something positive for herself— a life where one day she might be loved as well as loving.

'I know you would,' she said heavily.

'And that's not enough for you?' His tone changed. It almost sounded like hurt vying with pride.

When she didn't answer, he went on. 'I know it's ultimately your decision whether you have a baby, but surely I deserve to know?'

He looked so wounded, Eva wanted to reach up and cup his cheek with her hand. But she didn't dare touch him. She knew where that could lead.

'Of course I'd tell you if I were pregnant.' She sighed, her hands leaving her hips and dropping to her sides, her shoulders slumping as defeat dragged at her. There seemed no way out of this. 'Maybe that's why I didn't want to find out the truth before I left. Because I needed to get away, have time to myself before I confronted the need to tell you.'

Eva heard Paul's sharply indrawn breath and imagined it sounded shaky. But it was probably just the tremors racing through her own body that made it seem so. She couldn't seem to stop them.

'Why, Eva? Why do you need to get away?' Gone was the angry man full of masculine pride. To her eyes, Paul looked as gutted as she felt.

Because I want you to care more than you do.

She bit her lip. There she went again, slipping back into her fantasy world. Except the jarring voice of reality wouldn't be silenced.

As if Paul could ever love you. You're a convenience to him. First for your money, then for sex, and now because he realises you can share his heavy workload.

The biting words stilled her emotional turmoil and gave her the strength to step back, putting space between them.

Time to end this for good. The truth would do that.

Eva was beyond counting the cost to her pride.

She drew a slow, shuddery breath and told him.

'I need to get away from you to save myself.' Even to her own ears that sounded melodramatic as she watched Paul's face pale.

'Save yourself? I'd *never* hurt you, Eva. You must know that.'

She lifted her hand towards him, wanting to smooth away the anguish lining his face, but made her arm drop without making contact.

'I know you wouldn't. Not intentionally. Just hear me out.'

She snagged a fortifying breath, but it didn't help, not when those indigo eyes were watching her with a mixture of disbelief and dismay.

Abruptly Eva turned and made for the window, leaning one hand on the carved surround. A breeze ruffled her hair and drifted across her face. It smelled of salt and cypress pines. She pulled the robe around her and fixed her gaze on the moonlight tinting the dark sea, gathering her courage.

In her peripheral vision she saw Paul move to the other side of the window. She sensed his impatience and his confusion.

'You'd never aim to hurt me, Paul, but you do—every day.'

He stiffened, ramrod-straight, but to his credit didn't interrupt.

'I need to get away,' she repeated, feeling the brand of truth in each word. 'Because I love you.'

Was that an indrawn breath or the distant hiss of the sea?

'Eva, I—'

'Let me finish. Please.' Now she'd started, it seemed almost easy to explain what she'd avoided sharing for so long.

'It's not that I fell for you the night we made love.' It *had* been making love, for her at least. 'This isn't the result of some mad hormonal rush. I just wish it were.'

It would be easier to deal with.

She leaned her head against the window frame, eyes fixed on the distance. Because she didn't want to see Paul's appalled expression.

'I fell in love with you when I was fifteen, with as little thought as any teenager gives to her first crush. But for some reason I never grew out of it. I did try.' Her mouth curved in a brief, phantom smile. 'After a couple of years of long-distance yearning, I dated a few guys, kissed them, even planned to lose my virginity to one of them.'

Beside her Paul moved abruptly, straightening, seeming to grow taller, but Eva kept her eyes on the sea, glistening like molten silver.

'But it never went far. I always pulled away because it didn't feel right. Because I had my heart set on you.' She shook her head. 'You have no idea how thrilled I was when my parents asked if I'd be happy to marry you. It was like a dream come true.' She paused. 'Except, when we came here to celebrate the betrothal you were so wooden and cold. It was obvious even to me that you'd agreed out of duty. You barely even looked at me, much less smiled the way you used to.'

'Is that why you wouldn't let me kiss you?'

She swung round, feeling the hurt and anger well up in her throat despite her determination to stay calm. 'What did you expect? I knew you had a reputation as a bit of a playboy, and that women flocked to you, but you didn't even attempt to talk with me, not properly. You just expected me to kiss you because we'd signed a contract. As if you'd bought me with a signature on a piece of parchment!' That still hurt.

'That's not true! I didn't really know you.' He shook his head. 'My father made it clear you were a dutiful daughter, doing what her family expected. I was trying to do what was expected of me too, but you barely looked at me—'

'Because I was *shy* and petrified you'd discover how I felt. Especially when I discovered how uninterested you were. Everywhere we went there were beautiful women ogling you, vying for your attention, yet you were stuck with me.'

Paul was clearly about to interrupt so she hurried on.

'It doesn't matter. What does matter is that I spent the next four years preparing as best I could to be your wife, doing the degree my parents approved of, but on the side learning Ancillan and everything I could about your country. I was convinced that once we were married and you saw how good a wife I was you'd fall for me.' Her throat closed on the words and she had to swallow a knot of burning emotion.

She waved a dismissive hand. 'But I saw my mistake last month when you rejected me. I realised nothing I ever did would change how you felt. That's when I discovered I didn't want to waste my life with a man who didn't love me. I want to be appreciated, desired, loved for myself.'

'Is that why you went to the night club—looking for someone who desired you?' She couldn't read Paul's tone and his expression gave nothing away.

She shrugged. 'It turns out I'm not into casual hook-ups, which is why I decided to leave so early.'

And then it all went wrong.

Eva drew her robe closer around her. 'The details don't matter. What's important is that I've grown up. I'm no longer the little innocent who turned you into her Prince Charming.'

That was only half a lie. Eva still thought him the most appealing man she'd ever met, but she saw him as he was. Honest and hard working but prone to shoulder too much. Decisive and inclined to take charge. Sexy and gentle and…

'For my own good I need to leave because I don't want to be married to you, Paul. It would be emotional suicide. That's why I don't want to know yet if I'm pregnant. Because I need some space and time before I face that possibility.'

Admitting it should have made Eva feel weak but instead pride rose. She could do this, despite the gnawing grief at the thought of leaving.

'Because you couldn't bear it if we've made a baby together?' His voice ground low and harsh.

'I don't...' Eva floundered, caught between fear of the implications and heady joy at the idea.

'Because you can't bear to be near me.'

'Can't you see, Paul? Every day we're together it eats away at me—this pretence that I'm special to you, that you care.'

'I *do* care.' Sparkling eyes snared hers but she fought their terrible pull.

'Of course you care. You're a decent man. But you don't love me. And that's what I want. A man who loves *me*.'

For a long, long moment he stood, unmoving, looking down at her from his superior height, his expression unreadable.

'That night I tried to kiss you, the night of our betrothal ball, it wasn't what you thought.'

Of all the things he might have said that was the least expected. Why wasn't Paul agreeing that it was time she left? Why rehash the past?

'My father had a word with me after our betrothal.' Paul's mouth quirked up at one side but she read no amusement in that lop-sided smile. 'Too late, he told me I shouldn't assume you *wanted* to marry me. He mentioned you'd been seen with a handsome young count in Tarentia. But that you'd been made to give him up to do your duty and marry me.'

Eva's head jerked up. She knew who he was talking about. She'd gone on a date with the count, had kissed him, and thought about doing much more with him, to cure herself of her infatuation with Paul. But when it came to the crunch she'd shied away.

Paul spread his hands. 'I was a young man with a young man's pride, so perhaps I didn't handle it well, but I had to know how you felt about me.'

'That's why you offered to kiss me?'

He inclined his head. 'When you declined and looked at me with that frozen stare I knew you didn't really want to marry me. I decided then and there to set you free.'

Eva stared, amazed at this new explanation for the excruciating scene she remembered.

'I told my father I was calling off the engagement.' Paul's expression turned grim. 'That's when he informed me he'd already spent the portion of your dowry that was handed over on our engagement. I had no way of paying that back so no way of releasing you.'

Eva stared, realising how well that explained his distance, always polite but never anything more than that.

'Thank you for telling me.' The truth made it better somehow. 'But you didn't love me then and you don't now.' She was proud of the fact her words sounded even, almost crisp. 'So it's better that I leave.'

Warm fingers folded around hers and Eva looked down to see his strong hand cradling hers. The sight made her heartbeat blip and her breath hitch.

'No, I didn't love you, Eva.'

Her breath released in a silent sigh. The truth shouldn't hurt. She'd known it so long she should be used to it. Yet the pain was there, the ever-present ache behind her ribs.

'But I do now.'

'Sorry?' She swung her head up to meet eyes of heart-

stopping blue and an expression that made her insides
dance. He wasn't smiling. If anything, Paul looked grave.

'I love you, Eva.'

She tugged her hand but his grip held. So did that stunning, bright gaze, like lapis lazuli.

'Don't, Paul. You don't have to pretend. I'll tell you if
there's a baby, I promise.'

'This has nothing to do with whether or not you're pregnant.'

Her heart stuttered then took up a chaotic rhythm.

'I love you. That's why I don't want you to go. Because I
want to marry you and spend the rest of our days together.'

Her lips trembled. Eva realised her control was crum-
bling. Any minute now there'd be tears, for this was too
much. She blinked and straightened her crumpled mouth.

'You want someone to share your burdens, that's all.
But believe me, Paul, there'll be women lining up to the
other side of the island once they know you're single again.'

'I don't want any woman but you.'

She opened her mouth but her words died when he
pressed his finger to her lips.

'When you came to St Ancilla this time, I'd resolved to
end the betrothal. But, when it came to it, I was strangely
unsettled. I knew it was the honourable thing to do, but it
didn't sit right and I didn't know why. Later that night, I
discovered why.' He drew a deep breath that expanded his
chest hugely. 'I wanted you, Eva. I'd never known anything
like it—desire so brutally potent it cut through every scru-
ple, every good intention to keep my distance.'

Heat licked Eva's veins. She knew exactly what he
meant. It had been like that for her too. It still was.

Stiffly she shrugged. 'Lust. That's all.'

His head swung from side to side. 'Don't downplay it,
Eva. I've never felt anything so powerful in my life. Well,
except for once.'

She didn't want to hear this. Surely he wasn't going to tell her about some other woman? She cringed.

'It was the same night. When I saw that guy groping you, threatening you.' Paul's mouth twisted. 'I felt a roar of rage so powerful, I couldn't control myself. The idea of him touching you... I couldn't bear it. I'd have acted no matter who you were, but that fury was because he hurt *you*.' He hesitated. 'And because you're mine.'

Eva blinked, thrown off-balance by his words. 'Officially yours, because of the betrothal agreement, but not really yours. Not in ways that matter.'

He was playing with her emotions and she didn't think she could bear it.

'That's what I used to think. But that night it made no difference. I always counted myself a civilised man, Eva, but that night, once I got my hands on him, I didn't want to stop.'

Stunned, she stared up at him, seeing something in Paul's face she'd never seen before.

'I told myself it was the heat of the moment. And later that it was just sex and four years' abstinence that made our night together seem remarkable. But my feelings for you didn't dim. They grew. I watch you with my people and you're wonderful. I look forward to the time we spend together every day. I value your opinions. I admire your courage and determination. I *care* about you, Eva.'

'I know you do, Paul, but that's not love.'

Why wouldn't he just let her *go*? This was torture.

He reached for her other hand, grasping them both tightly, as if willing her to understand.

'I'm trying to sound reasonable, Eva. Because what I feel doesn't seem reasonable at all. My heart thuds faster when you're around. Or even when I think of you. When you smile at me, my heart squeezes so tight, sometimes I can't breathe. I think of you all the time, imagining what you're doing, wondering how I can make you smile, make you stay with me. The thought of you leaving scares me.'

He ground to a halt and to her amazement Eva realised his breath had turned ragged and there was a pulse beating frantically at his temple. As if he was in true distress.

What he described was so familiar. And the look on his face...

'Paul, you—'

'Please, Eva. It's my turn. Let me tell you.'

He waited and, torn between hope and disbelief, she nodded, her heart racing dangerously fast.

Paul squeezed her fingers, his eyes never leaving hers. She shivered from her scalp to her toes, rocked by the profundity of that stare. She'd never seen him look so serious, or so determined.

'I want to share my life with you, Eva—not because you're a perfect princess who'll do me proud, but because I can't imagine not having you by my side.'

He swallowed and her gaze tracked the jerky movement, reading his tension. Eva dragged in a sharp, sustaining breath that burned in her tight lungs.

'I want to have children with you and raise them together. Not as I was raised, but in a loving, warm family.' His searing gaze held hers and she could almost swear she heard sparks sizzle. 'Or, if we can't have children, then we'll make a wonderful aunt and uncle team for our nephews and nieces.'

'Oh, Paul.' Her throat was so clogged, the words were a whisper she doubted he heard.

He was turning her inside out.

'I want to grow old with you, Eva. Though not just yet. There are too many things I want to enjoy with you before we reach old age.' Paul lifted first one hand then the other to his lips, kissing her knuckles, sending flutters of delight through her.

'I can't tell you the exact moment I fell in love with you, darling, but I can tell you I will always love you.'

He sighed, then breathed in deeply while Eva still struggled for breath. What he said, the way he said it, was unlike anything she'd ever imagined. Far better than any fantasy. For this was *real*. So real and raw, it came close to pain.

'Are you going to say something?'

His voice was the same, strong and deep, but she didn't miss the hint of a tremor. Eva felt it too in the powerful hands grasping hers.

She freed one hand, saw him frown as she did so then planted her palm on his wide chest. There it was again— a tremor. His heart beat strongly but unevenly. Its rhythm matched hers, too quick and hard for comfort.

Slowly Eva smiled, the radiance of love given and returned unfurling within her. She watched him see it and his own mouth curved up into a grin so wide, she felt it brand her with its brilliance.

'I say *yes*. Please.'

They had so much to talk about, so much to share. But that would wait. It had to, for suddenly his arms were around her, her hands were grabbing his shoulders and they were kissing with all the passion, longing and triumph of lovers who'd finally, against the odds, found each other. Lovers secure in the knowledge that this was the beginning of their very own happily-ever-after.

EPILOGUE

As THEY WALTZED together at his birthday ball, around them whirled a multitude of guests, some from his wife's homeland of Tarentia, some from further afield—like his half-sister Caro and her husband Jake, who lived mainly in Sydney. Though most guests in the gilded ballroom came from St Ancilla.

It warmed Paul's heart, the way his people had welcomed Eva, and the way she'd responded with true generosity of spirit. On the day of their wedding, nine months ago, there'd been no whisper in his country of disquiet or innuendo about his bride, no raking up of scandalous old gossip.

His people loved her almost as much as he did.

His heart lurched as he looked down at her, slim and smiling in his arms, her off-the-shoulder dress of aquamarine a perfect match for her favourite tiara.

The enormity of his feelings hit him and he hesitated a second longer than optimal on a turn. Instantly bright silvery eyes snared his. His heart gave a mighty thump. They were so attuned, he still found it hard to believe.

'Paul?'

The music ended and he raised Eva's fingers to his lips. He didn't dare kiss her on the lips, as he'd learned that even a crowd of onlookers couldn't stop him wanting more when he tasted her mouth.

She really was the most special woman.

Suddenly it was imperative that he tell her so. Putting her arm in his, he led them through the glamorous crowd, nodding and chatting briefly as they passed, but never stopping.

Caro, vibrant with her red hair, jade-green dress and glorious smile, caught his eye from one side of the room. She waved a beckoning hand to where she stood with Jake and another couple, Eva's brother Leo and a woman he didn't recognise.

Soon, he mouthed to his sister. He had something vital to do before mingling with guests.

'Is anything wrong?' Eva asked under her breath as his pace quickened.

'No, nothing wrong.'

He pressed her hand as they approached wide French doors guarded by a staff member in formal dress. Moments later they were on a private terrace looking out over the royal gardens. From around the corner came the sound of voices where guests took in the views.

The door closed and Paul turned to his wife.

'You're beautiful,' he breathed, his gaze fixed on her shining eyes.

'Thank you.' Her smile grew impish. 'You brush up well yourself, Your Handsomeness. Half the women in there are in love with you, but you're mine, and I'm not letting you go.'

'Excellent.' He lashed his arms around her. 'As for other women, I didn't notice them. I was too busy warning off the men salivating at the sight of you.'

Eva shook her head as if she didn't believe him, but it was true. Love made him possessive. It was a good thing he trusted his wife totally.

'Why are we here?'

His mouth curved in a private smile. 'Because I need to kiss you, my sweet, and tell you how much I love you.'

Eva looped her hands around his neck, a siren smile

curving her lips. 'Wonderful. I was just thinking the same thing. I love you too, Paul, so very much.'

Grinning now, he lowered his head, only to pause when she put her finger to his lips.

'Since we're here to talk about important things...'

'Yes?' Impatience stirred. It had been hours since he'd kissed her.

'I have something to tell you too. A birthday surprise.'

He nodded. Hard to believe it had been a whole year since the extraordinary night he and Eva had confronted their feelings for each other.

'You know I love surprises.' He glanced around them. 'Though perhaps with a little more privacy.'

His wife shook her head with an attempt at prim censure that didn't reach her eyes. Then her expression turned serious. She reached round and grabbed one of his hands. A moment later it rested on her belly. Instantly his fingers splayed wide. He loved touching Eva, even through her dress...

'We're going to have a baby.'

He gaped down at her. 'We are?'

It had turned out that early pregnancy scare was a false alarm. He hadn't minded. He'd been happy to have Eva all to himself, though lately he'd thought she fretted a little whenever her period arrived. 'Are you happy?' he asked.

She nodded but her eyes looked huge as she surveyed him. As if waiting for his response.

'Good,' he growled, feeling a whole host of emotions slam into him. Delight, pride, excitement and not a little fear.

Paul tilted her chin up with a hand that was just a fraction unsteady, all the while holding her gaze.

'I didn't think anything could come near the joy of hearing that you love me. And now you give me this.' He pressed a gentle, almost reverent kiss to her lips. 'I don't know how I can ever give you anything to make you as happy as I am now.'

Her mouth eased into a wide smile as she threaded her fingers through the hair at the back of his skull.

'You don't have to do anything, Paul. Just keep loving me the way you do.'

'Always, my darling.' He pulled her close for a kiss that was as tender as it was passionate, and Paul, King of St Ancilla, knew without doubt that he was the luckiest, happiest man on the planet.

* * * * *

HOW TO UNDO
THE PROUD
BILLIONAIRE

JOSS WOOD

CHAPTER ONE

"YOUR PHONE IS RINGING."

In his expansive corner office on the top floor of their company headquarters, Radd Tempest-Vane pulled his attention off the report in his hand, his eyes bouncing from his brother's face to his smartphone, just released to the market, half-buried by a pile of reports. He pulled it free, cursed when papers fell to the expensive carpeting and turned the phone to show Digby the screen.

"Naledi Radebe." Frustration jumped into Digby's navy blue eyes, so like Radd's own. They had been born eleven months apart and had on occasion been mistaken for twins. All three Tempest-Vane brothers shared the same dark brown hair, deep blue eyes and six-foot-plus height. Radd ignored the suddenly tight grip on his heart. So much time had passed, but sometimes he still thought of Jack in the present tense.

He probably always would.

"Are you going to answer her call?" Digby asked from the sleek leather couch next to Radd's desk, his eyes already back on the screen of the laptop resting on his knees. Every few weeks, depending on their schedules, he and Digby met—either here or at Digby's equally luxurious office at The Vane—to strategize, plan and discuss supersensitive, for-their-eyes-only company information.

"No, I'm busy. All the arrangements for her wedding to Johnathan Wolfe have been finalized and he's happy."

Radd returned his attention to his laptop. He didn't have time to deal with the attention-seeking socialite today. The last time he checked, he and his brother had a massive international empire to run, deals to make, new markets to conquer.

An empire to restore to its former glory, a family name to rehabilitate and a multi-billion-dollar deal to protect.

Beyond the floor-to-ceiling bank of electrochromic glass was an extraordinary view of Table Mountain and the endlessly fascinating Atlantic Ocean seaboard. If he was in the habit of looking out of the window, Radd might've noticed that it was a perfect day to spend on the beach or, at the very least, outside.

But Radd's attention never strayed far from business so, instead of looking at his stunning view, his eyes flicked over to the massive electronic screen on the wall opposite him to look at the changes he'd made on the complicated spreadsheet they were working on. Something looked off with the figures; he'd made a mistake somewhere. Radd gritted his teeth and scraped his hand over his face, trying to wipe away his frustration. He wasn't in the habit of making unforced errors, and wasting time upped his annoyance levels.

His phone jangled and, once again, he let the call go to voice mail.

"It's your fault for agreeing to play wedding planner," Digby commented.

"Naledi thinks that because her father tied the purchase of the mine to her wedding, she can boss me about. Dammit, I'm far too busy to play wedding planner," Radd growled.

"And too rich and too important…" Digby mocked him.

Dig was the only one allowed to tease him, and nobody could cut him down to size quicker than his silver-tongued sibling.

Radd was more acerbic, impatient and abrupt than his brother. A previous lover once called him robotic and, had he cared enough to respond—he hadn't—he might've agreed with her assessment. Feelings were messy, prickly and uncomfortable, and thanks to his narcissistic parents and his brother Jack's death, he'd cultivated an attitude of stoicism, training himself not to react, to get perturbed, upset or excited.

Though, knowing he was a week away from acquiring the mine almost tempted his habitually unemotional heart to flutter.

Initially, it had been Jack's burning ambition to rebuild the Tempest-Vane group of companies; he'd been almost evangelical in his quest to restore respect to the family name. For generations, their ancestors had been on the right side of history and people from all walks of life had known that, despite their immense wealth, the Tempest-Vanes stood for equality, freedom and tolerance.

Then the businesses and assets fell into their father's hands and the Tempest-Vane name became synonymous with excess, dissipation, laziness and entitlement. And all those excesses had been splashed on the front pages of tabloids, locally and internationally.

It was hard enough to be the child of celebrity parents, but it had been hell being the sons of Gil and Zia Tempest-Vane.

Radd leaned back in his chair and closed his eyes, remembering the humiliation he had felt every time a scandal hit the papers. Jack, as the eldest, frequently took them to task, but Gil and Zia ignored his pleas to calm down, to stay out of the news. And then they stopped taking his calls or replying to his emails.

None of the brothers were particularly surprised when their parents' lackadaisical efforts to stay in touch dwindled to infrequent text messages and once-a-year, if they were lucky, visits.

Then Jack died and their parents' behavior—before, during and after the funeral—was the final straw.

Although their escapades still hit the gossip columns with alarming and irritating frequency, years passed with no contact between them. Then, a year and some months ago, Radd received an email from his father, demanding a meeting with his sons. They were coming home, and there was someone they wanted them to meet…

The next news they had of their parents was of their deaths; Gil and Zia's car had left the road in Southern California and crashed into the sea below. Radd still wondered who was so important to his parents that they were prepared to reach out and break the almost twenty-year silence.

He had a vague theory, but no proof to back it up.

Radd sighed, glanced at the spreadsheet and was reminded of what they were doing and why. He'd been sixteen when he realized all the family businesses were gone, along with most of the once-impressive Tempest-Vane fortune. Somehow, his parents had not only managed to strip the company of its most valuable assets, but also spend a good portion of the proceeds of the sales. The rest they had squirreled into untouchable trusts.

And they'd managed to do it on the q.t. To this day, Radd abhorred secrets and surprises.

Now, thanks to a little luck and lots of sweat—he didn't do tears—the ranch and The Vane, the beloved Cape Town icon and the hotel Digby so loved, were back under their ownership.

But the final contract had yet to be signed, and Vincent Radebe, the current owner of the diamond mine they were trying to reacquire, and his demanding daughter stood between them and their end goal. The Sowetan-based businessman hadn't been shy about tacking on some nonbusiness-related demands. His youngest child, and only daughter, was recently engaged and he was determined to give her the wedding of her dreams.

Because the Tempest-Vane brothers owned the most exclusive and sophisticated hotel and wedding venue in Cape Town, Vincent wanted the reception to be held at The Vane. Vincent also demanded Radd accommodate the wedding party at Kagiso Ranch, their six-star, phenomenally exclusive game reserve, for the week leading up to the wedding. All at cost.

Frustratingly, Radd could only find an opening for both venues eight months after his and Vincent's initial discussion, thus delaying the sale. They couldn't launch the extensive PR campaign, and the rebranding of the Tempest-Vane group of companies—reassociating their surname with corporate social responsibility and social justice instead of their parent's wild life, dissoluteness and licentiousness—until they owned the mine.

Radd's low store of patience had run out seven and a half months ago.

His phone rang again, and Radd snatched it up, thoroughly annoyed. "Naledi, what's the problem?"

"Radd, my life is ruined!" Naledi wailed. Radd rolled his eyes as he put his phone on speaker. "Everything is falling apart!"

"Of course her life is tough, she only received twenty-one million on her twenty-first birthday," Digby murmured, loud enough for Radd, but not Naledi, to hear.

Radd knew what Digby was thinking: when they were twenty-one and twenty-two, they'd ceased all contact with their dysfunctional and narcissistic parents and the only cash they had had access to was in a trust fund set up by their grandfather to pay for their education. Luckily, Gray Tempest-Vane vastly overestimated the amount needed to pay for their education and they'd taken every extra cent they had had and invested in a tech company developing a new type of payment system for internet transactions.

One small online retailer had picked up their system, then another and then they had landed Yours!, one of the three biggest online retailers in the world. The offers to buy them out had started rolling in and, five years ago, they had sold the company to a tech giant, and Radd and Digby had become two of the youngest billionaires in the world. Still, certain financial doors remained closed, thanks to their father's legacy of defaulting on loans and being economical with the truth. Vincent Radebe was a case in point, but they'd persisted.

Radd intended to change the collective mindset of the old school captains of commerce and industry.

"What's the problem, Naledi?" Radd demanded, gripping the bridge of his nose between his thumb and forefinger.

"The flowers have arrived at Kagiso Lodge…"

"And?" Radd asked, eyeing the mountain of work he needed to plough through before the end of the weekend. Because life was currently finding it fun to screw with him, Vincent wanted him to host the pre-wedding party so, the first thing on Monday morning, he was flying to Kagiso Lodge.

Just shoot him now.

"The flowers are there, but my florist isn't! She's had the gall to schedule an operation for appendicitis."

"What do you want me to do about it, Naledi?"

"Find me another florist, Radd," Naledi demanded in her breathy, baby-doll voice. Radd wasn't fooled; Naledi was her father's daughter and below her gorgeous surface resided a band of tungsten, a hard layer of give-me-what-I-want-now.

Jesus wept. Radd was worth over a billion dollars and he'd been reduced to asking "How high?" when the Radebes said "Jump." Normally, he was the one who issued orders, who expected to be obeyed, who made demands and expected others to work their asses off to give him what he wanted before he wanted it.

The ill-fitting, uncomfortable shoe was on the other foot, and Radd didn't care for the sensation.

"The staff at the lodge have all taken flower arranging courses, Naledi," Digby interjected in a reasonable tone. He mimed putting a gun to his head and pulling the trigger.

"I will *not* settle for less than the best!"

"Then we'll most definitely find you a florist and we'll make sure they are at the ranch tonight," Digby told her, sounding ridiculously reasonable. Radd sent him a heated *What the hell?* look, and Digby mimed the word *Mine*. Then, in case Radd didn't catch his meaning the first time, he mimed the word again.

Right. Gotcha.

After agreeing to find Naledi a florist, Radd disconnected his call, immediately pulled up another number and impatiently waited for his assistant to answer his call.

As briefly as possible, he told Andrew what he wanted. "Find me a florist, get them to meet me at the office at two-thirty. I'll fly them to Kagiso tonight and return them to Cape Town when they're done. It shouldn't take more than a day."

"Rate?" Andrew asked.

"I don't care, just get me someone good."

Radd disconnected and looked longingly at the state-of-the-art coffee machine on the far side of the room. Normally Andrew provided him with a steady supply of caffeine but, since the offices were empty, as he and Digby were discussing sensitive corporate and financial matters, it was self-serve. And, somehow, despite both of them having above-average IQs and post-graduate degrees in business, neither he nor Digby could make a decent cup of coffee.

Radd tried to ignore the headache building behind his eyes. "Andrew will work on the florist problem."

"I doubt he's going to find a celebrity florist who'll drop everything to fly to Kagiso at a moment's notice."

Radd wasn't so sure. Despite being a relentless pain in his ass, the Radebes were an influential African family, and working for them would add cachet to anyone's resume. Kagiso Ranch was also one of most exclusive safari destinations in the world and, while they tried to fly under the radar, he and Digby were two of the country's richest, and therefore most eligible, bachelors.

Between them and the Radebes, there was serious name recognition.

Digby nodded, rolled his shoulders and pulled his laptop toward him. "Well, there's nothing we can do until then."

Radd looked at his watch, a vintage Rolex Daytona, one of only a few in the world. It had been his grandfather's, then Jack's, and it was his most prized possession. He set a mental alarm. Three hours had to be more than enough time for Andrew to find someone because, really...

How difficult could it be to toss some flowers into a vase?

Brinley Riddell noticed a Porsche Cayenne reversing out of a parking space right in front of the path leading to the beach and swung her nineteen-sixties Beetle Betsy into the spot, ignoring the angry hoots of the driver she'd cut off.

You snooze, you lose.

As she yanked up her handbrake and pulled the key from the ignition, her cell phone buzzed with an incoming message. Seeing her best friend's profile picture on her screen, she swiped her screen to read the message.

What are you doing tonight and tomorrow?

Was that a trick question?

I'm dining with Bradley Cooper tonight and brunching with Oprah at The Vane at nine.

Brinley grinned at her facetious reply. She and Abby, friends since school, shared a small cottage in Bo Kaap, and Abby knew reading was Brin's favorite way to spend a Saturday night.

Abby, the queen of Cape Town's clubbing scene, replied with a short, pithy sentence and a couple of rolling eye emojis.

You've got to get a life, Brin. Good thing I'm here to make that happen.

Brin didn't reply because a) she wanted to get to the beach, and b) they'd had this argument a hundred times before. Brin was very happy to spend the evening alone, while Abby needed people and attention like she needed air to breathe. In that way she was very much like Brin's influencer, socialite sister Kerry, but, thankfully, in every other way that was important, she wasn't.

She wasn't rude or mean or self-absorbed or selfish. Abby liked men but, unlike Brin's half sister, she didn't use or play games with them. Abby wasn't high maintenance.

In a smooth, much-practiced movement, Brin shoved her hand through the open window and grabbed the outside handle to open her door. None of her car doors locked but, by some miracle, her car had yet to land in a chop shop. Maybe it was the bright pink-and-rust color or maybe car thieves had standards, but so far, so good.

Slamming her car door shut, Brinley stepped onto the pavement and pushed her soft, loose curls off her face. It was one of those perfect African days. The summer sun was high in the sky but a soft wind kept the temperature from being unbearable. Standing at the top of the steep set of stairs leading to the beach, she smiled, struck as she always was by the beauty of the white sand and turquoise water. This was one of her favorite beaches and, since moving to Cape Town six months ago, she'd spent many of her free days down here, swimming, reading and, because she could, ogling the hot surfers and the volleyball players.

Looking was always fun, but Brin had a strict "Look, don't engage" policy. When she'd left Johannesburg, she'd promised herself that she'd give herself all the time she needed to find herself, to discover who she was and what she stood for...

She was a very messy work in progress and dating added complications she didn't need. And men weren't, let's be honest here, anywhere as satisfying as coffee, chocolate or bacon.

Brin leaned her butt against the door of her car and tipped her face to the sun, loving the gentle heat on her skin. She pulled in a series of deep breaths, telling herself that there was no need to rush, that she was allowed to stand still, to take a breath and to take the moment.

There were no emails to answer, text messages to look at, a demanding sister/boss to run after, people to please. It had taken all her strength and a great deal of courage to walk away from her dominating mother and sister, and she constantly reminded herself that she no longer answered to anyone and was a free agent...or she was trying to be.

God, leaving them had been the one and only thing she'd ever done for herself and by herself, and had she not, she would've lost herself forever. It had been so damn close...

Brin stared out to sea, trying and failing to remember a time when Kerry's wants, needs and ambitions weren't crucially important. Their family revolved around her half sister, and Brin might have still been in Johannesburg, working as Kerry's very underappreciated personal assistant, had she not caught *her* sister kissing *her* boyfriend.

As long as lived she'd never forget their glib, unremorseful responses.

"Look, let's be honest here. Your sister is smarter, incredibly successful and so much sexier than you. What was I supposed to say when she suggested we hook up...no?"

Well, Malcolm, yes.

Kerry's eyes had held malice as she had twisted the knife of betrayal. *"And, darling, don't you think that you are punching above your weight with Malcolm?"*

Strangely, Kerry's betrayal and her mother's reaction to the situation hurt far more than discovering Malcolm was a cheating jerk. On hearing about their fight, their mom instantly dismissed Brin's feelings and, without hesitation or thought, defended Kerry's actions, reminding her that her half sister was special, that she should be given a pass because she was beautiful and super famous. And really, who could blame Malcolm for choosing Kerry over her?

Everyone did. And always would.

Standing there, feeling slapped by her mother's dismissive words, being told she was overreacting, Brin knew she needed to leave, to run, as hard and as fast as she could.

By the next morning she was in Cape Town and, so far, she'd resisted their constant pleas, demands and manipulations to return home because, deep down, she knew her only role was to make their lives easier.

She'd swapped her garden flat for a tiny second bedroom in Abby's house, the use of Kerry's Benz for wheezy Betsy, and her waitressing job barely covered her bills. But she was free of criticism, of being micromanaged, of standing in her sister's very long shadow. In Cape Town, she could breathe.

She could be Brin.

That was, if she lasted in Cape Town. Brin thought about her depleted bank account and rubbed the back of her neck. She'd picked up a couple of gigs doing floral designs to supplement the money she earned from waitressing, but living in Cape Town was pricey and her expenses far outstripped her income. Her savings were depleted and, if something didn't change soon, she was heading for trouble.

Might-have-to-go-home or ask-my-family-for-a loan trouble. *Bleurgh.*

About to walk down the steps, Brin heard the low rumble of an expensive car and watched as a deep red supercar swung into the parking lot. This was Clifton, one of the wealthiest parts of the country, so seeing seriously expensive cars wasn't a novelty, but this was a James Bond car: glamorous, powerful and just a little, or a lot, dangerous.

And sexy. Brin was surprised to see the beast slide into the just-vacated parking spot next to hers. It was a beautiful machine, but not her style. She'd be terrified to drive it, thinking that the smallest scratch would cost her a few years' salary to fix.

Who needed that sort of pressure? Betsy got her, wheezing and spluttering, where she needed to go.

Brin felt the heat from the pavement burning through her cheap flip-flops, the heat of the sun on her bare shoulders. She couldn't wait to dive into the water; she was in desperate need of some Vitamin Sea.

"Brinley Riddell?"

Brinley slowly turned at the deep, growly voice and saw the driver of the supercar looking at her. He was tall, broad and whip-her-breath-away good-looking. Brin sighed when he rested his thick arms on the car roof, his big biceps pulling the fabric of his shirt against his skin.

Hot, hot, hot. And...kill me now.

Unlike his brother, Radd Tempest-Vane stayed out of the gossip columns, but Brin instantly recognized the city's sexiest and most elusive bachelor billionaire. He was even better looking, if that was at all possible, than the photos she'd see of him in magazines and on-line. His wavy hair was, in real life, a deep, rich brown, his face more angles and planes, and his mouth a great deal grimmer than she remembered. And those eyes, God, his eyes...

Navy blue most would call them. But, to Brinley, they were the color of the inside of a blue pansy or the deep, dark shade of blue delphiniums. They were eyes holding a thousand secrets...

Her knees a little soft, Brin leaned back against Betsy as he approached her, idly wondering what the hell Radd Tempest-Vane, her best friend's boss's boss, was doing here at two-thirty in the afternoon. Since he was dressed in casual chinos and an untucked white button-down shirt with the sleeves rolled up, tanned arms corded with muscle on display, she presumed he wasn't headed for the beach.

His body was staggering, all leashed power and fe-line grace. When their eyes connected, fireworks exploded on her skin and, deep inside, her womb throbbed, wanting or needing some intangible thing—unexplain-able, unfamiliar.

"You are Brinley Riddell?" Radd demanded as he approached her.

He was here because he was looking for her. Brin swallowed and swallowed again. Why?

"Yes, I'm Brin," Brin said, watching as he echoed her stance and leaned his butt against his car, facing her. He pushed his hands into the pockets of his pants, his expression inscrutable.

"My name is Radd Tempest-Vane."

They both knew that she knew who he was, so Brin wasn't sure why he bothered to introduce himself.

"I know." Brin yanked her eyes off him and gestured to his car. "Nice car," she said, wanting to break the silence between them. "What is it?"

"Aston Martin DBS Superleggera," Radd curtly replied, his eyes not leaving her face. She felt pinned to the tarmac, unable to move.

Her stomach whirled and swirled, and all the moisture from her mouth disappeared. She wondered whether his mouth would soften when he kissed her, how his hands would feel on her naked skin. Brinley just knew that Radd was the type of guy who could give her everything she needed sexually and a great deal of what she never knew she wanted.

So this was what sexual chemistry felt like…

If Malcolm was out of your league, sister dear, then Radd Tempest-Vane inhabits a galaxy far, far away. He's dated A-list Hollywood celebrities, international supermodels and, on occasion, a princess or two.

Brin did not appreciate hearing Kerry's voice in her head and she silently cursed. She was not going to build him up into some mythical creature just because he was crazy-rich, famous and lava-hot. It was a sure bet that Radd, like her sister, was another bright spotlight, drawing energy from those around him to shine.

It's just attraction, Brin reminded herself, *a biological urge*. It didn't mean *anything*…she wouldn't let it.

Brin gave herself a mental slap and ordered her body

to return some blood to her head so she could think. When she felt like she could construct a proper sentence, she pushed her sunglasses into her hair and lifted her chin. "You know my name and you aren't dressed for an afternoon on the beach, so I presume you are here, looking for me."

"I am." Radd nodded but didn't elaborate.

Okay, was she going to have to have to pull teeth to get him to explain? "Would you like to tell me why?"

Because, honestly, she had no idea what Africa's sexiest billionaire could want with her. Unlike her sister, she was neither bold nor beautiful. She didn't socialize in the same circles he did; hell, she didn't socialize at all. She was everything he wasn't: run-of-the-mill, down-to-earth, habitually penniless.

Brin saw something flash in his eyes, an emotion she didn't recognize. Confusion? Surprise? If he hadn't been Radd Tempest-Vane, with a reputation for being ruthless, cucumber-cool and hard as a rock, she might've thought he was feeling a little off-balance.

No, she was just projecting her feelings onto him. After all, being tracked down by a billionaire at the beach was something that happened in romance novels, not to ordinary girls living ordinary lives. From what she knew of him, and it wasn't much, this Tempest-Vane brother was tough and determined, a prime example of an alpha male who didn't suffer fools. He had a reputation for going after what he wanted and not stopping until he achieved his goal. He was shrewd, powerful and intimidating.

"My PA has spent most of the morning trying to find me a florist to do some arrangements at my ranch before a wedding party arrives midmorning Monday. He was not successful in his quest to find me a celebrity florist at short notice," Radd said, his tone businesslike.

Brin wasn't surprised. It was the end of spring, and the wet and dismal Cape weather had retreated, leaving warm days and cooler nights. It was a busy time for functions, parties and weddings.

"After being unsuccessful at reaching anyone, my assistant called his assistant for help, and she *suggested you*."

God bless Abby, Brin thought. "You need a floral designer?"

Radd gave her a try-to-keep-up look. Along with gorgeous and ripped, he was arrogant, too.

Fabulous.

But if he was offering work, she'd jump at his offer, any offer. All she needed was an idea of what the client wanted, the flowers—obviously—and supplies. She was good at what she did, she just needed a chance to prove it. And doing work for a Tempest-Vane brother, or for one of his companies, would be a bright, shiny gold star on her résumé.

And, as a bonus, her bank would stop sending her you-are-low-on-funds reminders.

"I can help you," Brin told him, trying to not to sound too eager. "When do you need me to start, where must I be and how much are you going to pay me?"

"Now, at Kagiso Ranch and twenty-five thousand."

Right. Well. Brin placed her hand on Betsy to stabilize herself.

Holy damn, Superman.

CHAPTER TWO

RADD'S FINGERTIPS DUG into his biceps and it took every bit of determination he possessed to keep his tongue behind his teeth.

Because Brinley Riddell was drop-dead stunning.

Radd pulled in a deep breath, then another, trying to ignore his racing heart and the fact his pants were a size smaller across the crotch than they'd been ten minutes before. He looked around, desperately looking for an alternative explanation for his racing heart and why his nerve endings were on fire.

Maybe he was getting sick, but that wasn't likely since he was super fit, took vitamins and was as healthy as a horse. No, it was because this woman had the power to drop him to his knees…and that was crazy. He was clearly losing his mind.

He liked women and women liked him back, but he'd never been the type to allow any female to rob him of his breath, or his ability to speak.

Brinley Riddell, damn her, had come closer than most.

Radd dropped his sunglasses over his eyes and, while she took in his job offer, allowed himself the immense pleasure of looking at her from behind his mirrored shades.

She was the embodiment of a rainbow-nation child,

a variety of races and mixed genes. Her skin was a rich, luscious creamy light brown, her cheekbones were high and sharp, and her mouth was wide, sensuous and made to be kissed. Her hair was a tumble of long, loose, dark curls and, he'd bet his car, soft to the touch.

She was tall for a woman, five eight or five nine, but he still had five or six inches on her. Her tiny denim shorts showed off long and shapely legs, and the wind occasionally lifted her loose vest, allowing him glimpses of spectacular breasts under two orange-colored triangles. Her stomach was as flat as a board, but he'd caught a glimpse of her ass as he'd pulled into the parking area and it was, yeah, stunning.

She was possibly the most attractive woman he'd met in a long, long time. And if he hadn't been in such a bind, he'd walk away right now. It didn't happen often, but when he met a woman who could impact his life, he always, always left.

He liked sex, had it as often as he could—which hadn't been too often lately, thanks to his workload—but he chose his partners carefully. They were always attractive, knew not to talk to the press and, most importantly, they accepted he wasn't interested in anything more than a few hours of mutually shared pleasure.

And, crucially, they didn't make him feel anything beyond the normal drive for sexual fulfillment. After being tainted, teased and tormented by the gossip generated by his parents crazy-ass lifestyle and escapades—up until their death he'd lived his life on a knife-edge waiting for the next story to break or shoe to fall, another scandal to slap him sideways—he'd decided, years ago, to not only live his life out of the limelight, but to do it solo. He could control his words, actions and choices, but not anyone else's.

Also, critically, casual affairs allowed him to remain emotionally numb and, after spending the part of his life coping with his unstable and narcissistic parents and then dealing with Jack's death, he and Numb were comfortable companions.

And, it was proven, relationships brought surprises, and surprises were something he could, without a doubt, live without.

Radd pulled his thoughts back to what was important. He needed to get Brinley to agree to fly to Kagiso with him this afternoon and to make—he'd checked—an arrangement for the lobby, two for the long dining table, one for the veranda and more than a dozen smaller arrangements, one for each of the guest's beds and bathrooms.

"It's a tall order, but the original florist committed to the time frame, so it's doable." Radd finished his explanation, searching Brinley's face for a reaction. When she just stared at him, he rubbed the back of his neck again. "Is it doable?"

Brinley held up her hand, silently asking him to slow down. He'd give her a minute to catch up, but they were running out of time, dammit. They had to be at the airport in forty-five minutes, and it was, even in the Aston, a thirty-minute drive.

Knowing they were short on time, he'd arranged for Abigail to return to the home she shared with Brinley and pack her a bag, then drive to the airport to leave it with his air steward. If Brinley said yes, and he had no intention of letting her say no, they would leave for the airport immediately.

"Well?"

"Twenty-five grand?" Brinley whispered. "And I'll be back in Cape Town tomorrow night?"

"I'll go to thirty if you make up your mind in the next minute," Radd stated, impatient.

Two dimples appeared as her mouth widened into a smile, and he felt like she'd slammed a battering ram into his solar plexus. God, that smile should be registered as a dangerous weapon.

"Deal," Brinley said. "But I need to go home, shower and change, and pack a bag."

"Your friend is packing a bag for you and she will deliver it to the airport. You can shower and change on my plane, but we're leaving now," Radd said, standing up straight. He had her agreement, excellent. Now all he had to do was keep his hands off her for twenty-four, twenty-five hours.

Surely, he could do that?

Brinley didn't move from her position. "Wow, you certainly don't waste time."

"I know what I want and I know how to get it," Radd replied, sounding edgy. *Tough.*

Brinley lifted a stubborn chin and patted her crappy car. "I'm not leaving Betsy here."

He didn't understand why people named their cars—it was stupidly sentimental and frankly ridiculous—but, strangely, the old-fashioned name seemed to suit. It did look like a down-and-out old lady.

"I suggest you use some of those dollars I am paying you to buy a new car. That car is held together by rust and a couple of bolts."

"Don't insult my car, and I am not leaving it here to be stolen. I'm taking it home or I'm not going with you," Brinley stated, stubbornness in those light, unusual-but-exquisite silver green eyes.

Radd looked toward a black SUV parked a few spaces from them and jerked his head. The doors immediately opened and his long-time chauffeur, Marcel, stepped out of the SUV.

"If you give Marcel your keys, they will make sure your car—" he refused to call it Betsy "—makes it home."

Radd thought there was a good chance that it would blow up or fall apart before it hit the motorway, but that wasn't his problem. And if it did, he could easily replace it with something better and safer.

A car that wasn't on its last legs. Or, he glanced down, on its last bald tire.

This woman had a death wish...and the thought made his heart cramp. Was he feeling concerned, a little protective and, if so, why? He'd met her *maybe* fifteen minutes ago.

She was not *his* problem, Radd reminded himself. She'd be out of his life by tomorrow afternoon, and he'd never think about her again.

Radd watched as Brinley reluctantly handed over her keys to Marcel, along with a long list of dos-and-don'ts. Frustrated, he stepped in and cut off her rambling explanation. "Marcel will figure it out. We need to go."

Panic flashed across her face, but then she straightened her shoulders, reached for her beach bag and pulled it through the open window. Radd turned to open the passenger door to his car to reveal a state-of-the-art interior. He liked his car; it was fast, technologically advanced and the best money could buy.

Brinley sighed, placed her bag on the floor and lowered herself into the comfortable leather bucket seat.

Radd kept his eyes on hers and watched as shock, then disbelief, jumped in and out of those incredible eyes. "Wait!"

What now? "Problem?"

"Did I hear you right? That you are paying me in US dollars? That's nearly four hundred thousand rand."

Radd lifted his brows at her shocked expression. "I can pay you twenty-five thousand in rand if you like."

Brinley sat back, folded her arms and shook her head. "You're mad. Who charges that sort of money for a day's work?"

"Apparently celebrity London-based florists," Radd responded, his tone super dry. "Can we agree on the currency so we can get moving? Rand or US dollar?"

Brinley narrowed her eyes at him. "Oh, I'm not an idiot. If you're offering US, that's what I'm taking. And it's thirty, not twenty-five, because I made up my mind in a minute."

She was smart as well as beautiful. Beautiful was easy to dismiss, but brainy? Not so much. "Fine."

Radd closed her door, bid a smiling Marcel goodbye and, gesturing to her car, wished him good luck.

Marcel, with the familiarity of a staff member who'd taught him to ride a bike, then a motorcycle and a car, grinned at him. "I think you're going to need that good luck more than me."

And what, Radd wondered as he dropped into his seat, *the hell did Marcel mean by that*?

The bathroom on Radd's jet was almost as big as the one in her flat back home, but a thousand times more luxurious. Brin washed with the expensive toiletries she found in the cabinet, amused to find the air steward had left a glass of ice-cold Prosecco in the bathroom for her when he had went in to lay out some towels.

Brin, with one of those soft, huge towels wrapped around her frame, stepped into the master bedroom and eyed the massive king-size bed, covered in a blue-

and-white duvet with a bold geometric pattern. Another glass of icy Prosecco stood on a coaster by the credenza, and her suitcase was already on a stool in the corner, ready to be flipped open.

Brin eyed the suitcase as she sipped her drink, yummy bubbles popping on her tongue. It was the bigger of her two suitcases. Why had Abby packed so much for an overnight trip? Shrugging, Brinley opened the lid and looked down at the hastily scrawled note on top of her clothes.

I had no idea what to pack for an overnight trip to one of the most luxurious places in the world, so I packed everything!

Woohoo! B, by next week you're going to have enough money to open Brin's Blooms! Feel free to spoil me.

Seriously, I'm happy for you.
Have fun. Love you!
xxx

Brin sat down on the bed, suddenly overwhelmed. This morning she'd left for an afternoon at the beach, and now she was on a jet, flying northeast, accompanied by the sexiest man she'd ever met.

And, provided she didn't mess up, she'd have more than enough money to open up her own florist shop, to pay the deposit and several months' rent, to buy stock.

Hell, she'd even probably have enough left over to buy a new car. Sorry, Betsy, but locks would be great, and air-conditioning even better.

Could she do this? Brin's fingers clutched the cool cotton of the bedcovers, hanging on for dear life. Oh, the dream of owning her own business was, in theory, lovely. It was easy to dream big when the possibility of success was remote but if nearly a half-million rand hit her bank account, she'd have to act, to put her money where her mouth, or her mind, was.

Brin gulped. Would she succeed with little to no experience? So many small businesses failed within the first year, would hers be any different? And was she cut out to be the boss, to make the decisions? She'd always worked in the background, taking orders rather than giving them, implementing someone else's visions and decisions.

Could she make her own?

But what choice did she have? She'd rather stab herself between her eyebrows with a rusty fork than go home, admitting to her mom and sister that she couldn't cut it.

If she did this, she'd have to *trust* and *believe* in herself.

Take a deep breath, Brinley. All she had to do was arrange some flowers and put up with Mr Arrogant for a day. She'd worked for Kerry, the definition of difficult, for years, so she knew she could deal with a bossy, arrogant, emotionally unavailable man with shadows in his eyes.

Brin sipped her drink, the cool Prosecco sliding down her throat as she considered the man sitting in the lounge area of this flying palace. He was driven and determined and, yes, autocratic, but he intrigued her. Oh, within two minutes of meeting him she knew he was emotionally distant and naturally cynical. But Brin sensed that he was, under his can't-be-rocked exterior, turbulent. She saw it in the way his one index finger tapped a hard bicep, in the changing shades of blue of his eyes, in the way he hauled in air as if to calm himself.

It was as if finding a floral designer was a bother, beneath him, and...well, she supposed it was. He was a billionaire businessman, ruthless and, it was said, intolerant, so why was he the one running around organizing a floral designer for a pre-wedding week at his ranch? That was normally a task that would be delegated to an underling.

Brinley wasn't complaining, she was glad he'd offered her the job, but why was he bothering with what should be a minor detail in his life?

After racking her brain, there was only one reason she could think of that explained why he was involved in the minutiae of this wedding.

He was the groom and this was his low-key, possibly secret wedding. It was the only explanation that made sense.

And, frankly, Radd's impending marriage was a relief. She didn't believe in coloring outside the lines, hers or anyone else's, and his engagement meant she could, she *would*, stop thinking about whether his bottom lip was as soft as it looked, whether he had a six-or eight-pack, and whether he sported hip muscles sexy enough to make a girl weep.

Brin placed her chin on her hands and tried to make sense of her raging attraction to Radd Tempest-Vane. He was gorgeous, ripped, sexy...

Any normal woman with a pulse would be attracted to him. But he belonged to someone else and Brin Riddell didn't poach.

Besides, Brin wasn't looking to become involved with anyone, anywhere. She was just starting to reconnect with herself, to work out who she was away from her dominating sister and mother, and any type of relationship would jeopardize any progress she'd made.

Kerry's light had always shone so much brighter than hers, and competing was impossible. Brin always felt like she stood on the outside of her family circle, knew her longing to be accepted had always been her driving force.

But it was like trying to shove a square peg in a round hole and she'd twisted herself up into complicated knots asking for something they'd never be able to give her, so she had to look to herself for what she needed.

Now, after months of being away from them, she was feeling less anxious, a lot braver—she would never have jumped on an offer like Radd's six months ago!—and a tad more resilient.

Best of all, her heart, battered and bruised, was starting to heal. And she'd never risk it again. Any type of involvement—physical or emotional or a combination of both—with a man like Radd, who was tough, hard and alpha to the tips of his toes, would be the equivalent of asking someone to use her heart as a bowling ball.

Not happening.

Brin rolled her shoulders and twisted her head from side to side. She'd veered off into thinking about her past and that annoyed her, Brin didn't live there anymore. She needed to concentrate on the fact that Radd Tempest-Vane was offering her the opportunity to be completely free of her family. She'd be a fool to allow him to see her attraction or allow it to derail this amazing opportunity.

She just needed to calm down and think rationally, drink some water and rehydrate. Maybe she needed some food.

Her stomach rumbled in agreement and Brin smiled. No, she *definitely* needed some food.

And—she eyed her suitcase—she needed to dress.

Then she would walk back to Radd and ask him what he and his bride wanted her to do with the flowers waiting for her at Kagiso Lodge.

And maybe, if she asked nicely, the lovely steward with the gorgeous brown eyes would bring her something to eat.

Radd looked up at the sound of the door to the master suite opening and watched Brinley walk into the lounge area of the jet, dressed in an ivory-and-pink sleeveless dress printed with huge flowers. Her makeup was light but expertly applied and she'd pulled her hair back into a tail, making her cheekbones look more defined than they already were.

Radd squirmed as the jet lurched and bounced. He gripped the arm of his chair, irritated his captain hadn't warned him about turbulence. Then, he realized Brinley hadn't reacted to the dip and sway of the plane. He glanced out of the window and saw the clear blue sky and reluctantly admitted it was the woman in front of him making his stomach dive. It had nothing to do with the weather, the plane or the pilot.

Radd leaned sideways to take another look out the window, struck by the dry beauty of the Karoo landscape miles below. He'd done this trip a hundred times, more, but he'd never noticed the beautiful, arid landscape was touched by patches of green and purple. His country, Radd admitted, had its problems, but God, it was so beautiful.

He couldn't wait to get to Kagiso, though this trip would be less relaxing than usual thanks to his sexy companion and the wedding party due to descend on Monday.

But at least he had a day and two nights to enjoy Kagiso, the favorite of all his properties. He loved the bush and the animals, but he was honest enough to admit that he also adored Kagiso because there were no memories of his parents associated with the ranch.

No fights, no strange people in wrong beds, no loud music, fights and screaming accusations. The cops had never arrived at Kagiso, no divorces had been demanded or hospital visits required.

Unlike their family home, the two-hundred-year-old farmhouse set among ancient vines, Kagiso was never mentioned in the newspapers or the tabloids.

Digby didn't care so much but he loathed being talked about, hated gossip. The only news coverage he was prepared to tolerate was related to business or his role as co-CEO of Tempest-Vane holdings.

Radd shifted in his chair, uncomfortable. He tried not to think of the past but, occasionally, he did find himself wishing for the moon: that Jack was still alive, that his parents had loved their sons more than they loved money, the attention of the press, and their constant pursuit of pleasure, that his father hadn't plundered, stripped and sold their heritage…

But the past couldn't be changed, so looking back was futile. It was far better to think of nothing at all, it was easier not to remember, to stay numb. And the best way to do that was to concentrate on work.

And that was why he was on a plane flying north, for *work*.

And Brinley was just another person who'd dropped into his life for twenty-four hours. The day after next she'd be a memory, a week from now she'd be forgotten. He had a mine to buy, a PR and rebranding exercise to plan, and a company to expand.

He wouldn't countenance any distractions.

No matter how sexy they were.

Radd, sitting on the far end of the four-seater couch, gestured for Brinley to take the chair to the right of him, thinking it was better to keep the source of temptation at a safe distance. Brinley sat down, crossed her long, lovely legs and Skye, his steward, hurried forward to ask her if she required more Prosecco.

Brinley refused alcohol and asked for sparkling water. Then she gestured to the fruit bowl on the table in front of them. "Do you mind? I missed lunch and I'm starving."

Skye, well trained, immediately responded with an offer to make her anything she wanted. And that wasn't a boast, Radd had once made an offhand comment in Skye's presence about craving sushi and, in no time at all, he had a perfectly plated platter placed in front of him.

Brinley smiled at Skye. "Oh, would you mind? A grilled cheese sandwich would be wonderful but, if it's a hassle, I'll just eat fruit."

Skye looked disappointed at receiving such a prosaic request. "I'm sure we can do better than a toasted sandwich," he replied. "Is there anything you don't eat or are allergic to?"

Brinley shook her head. She grinned at Skye, those sexy, deep dimples flashing and…yep, Radd's stomach launched itself off its sky-high diving board again.

Seriously, this was beyond ludicrous. He could easily imagine Digby rolling on the floor at his dilemma, laughing his ass off.

Because Radd was never knocked off-balance.

By anything.

His parents—and life—had thrown all manner of trials his way and he'd negotiated his way around all of them, most—Jack's death being the exception—without allowing the world to see him breaking a sweat. He'd trained himself not to react, to meet both victory and failure dispassionately, and rarely responded with anything other than impassivity. It helped that he went out of his way to avoid trouble and gossip.

He never gave the press anything to talk about because he couldn't stand to have his private life played out in the public domain.

"No, I'm poor so I can't afford to be fussy," Brinley told Skye, pulling his attention back to the present.

Skye wrinkled his nose, sympathy in his eyes. "I hear you, sister."

Radd snorted. Skye, like all of his staff, was exceptionally well paid. He and Digby were demanding, he wouldn't argue with that, but their staff were well recompensed.

Skye rubbed his hands together. "I'll see what I can conjure up. Radd, is there anything, in particular, you'd like?"

Radd saw Brinley's surprise at Skye's lack of formality. Radd was the boss and everyone knew it, so calling him "sir" didn't mean anything. Besides, Skye was older than him and Radd didn't need, or like, toadying.

He just needed people to do their job, and Skye did his particularly well. "Whatever you make will be fine with me. You can bring me some sparkling water, too."

Skye nodded, told them he'd be back in a few and left the stateroom, leaving them alone. Radd leaned back in his seat and linked his fingers together on his flat stomach, content to watch Brinley's profile as she stared out of the window into the endless blue below.

"How long until we land?" she asked without making eye contact.

Radd checked the time. "Probably about an hour. It'll be dusk when we arrive."

Brinley turned back to face him. She leaned back in her seat and Radd saw the flash of ivory-colored wedge-heeled shoes with ribbons wound around shapely ankles. She was such a contradiction, and he couldn't quite make her out.

Her dress was designer, but the shoes weren't. The bikini she'd had on earlier was expensive, but her flip-flops were the type that could be bought at any flea market. She drove a worn-out car, but her beach bag was Gucci.

She was a paradox. He didn't like being curious. He wished he didn't feel the urge to pepper her with questions and he didn't care for not having the answers.

"Why are you frowning at my shoes?"

Radd jerked his head up to look into her eyes, wishing he could call them silver or green, yet they were neither one shade nor the other. They were a curious, lovely combination of both.

Radd wondered whether they'd darken or lighten or change color in anger or, more interestingly, when she was consumed by desire...

Dammit, Tempest-Vane! Not helpful.

"Uh..." Radd wiped his hand over his face before gesturing to her dress. "Cheap shoes, fancy dress. Expensive bag, crappy car."

Embarrassment skipped through her eyes before she lifted her stubborn, proud chin. "My sister is in the—" Brinley hesitated before continuing "—fashion industry and has a closet bigger than most clothing stores. Up until I moved to Cape Town six months ago, she passed a lot of her clothes on to me."

She was obviously reluctant to talk about her sister and that made him curious. Why did she move to Cape Town? Was he imagining the tinge of annoyance he heard in her voice?

She was his temporary employee, a woman who'd be out of his life tomorrow afternoon. He didn't need to dig into her life, for God's sake. He needed to get this conversation, and his thought patterns, back on track. She was only here to do a job for him.

It suddenly occurred to Radd that, in his haste to acquire a florist, he didn't know if she had any skills. This was not, by any stretch of the imagination, his finest day. "How much experience do you have in flower arranging?" he demanded.

Brin looked at him from under long, thick lashes. "Mmm, not much. I'm more of a buy-flowers-from-the-garage-and-shove-them-into-a-glass-vase type."

Oh, God, he was so screwed.

Brin grinned, leaned forward and patted his knee. "Relax, I'm joking."

His heart restarted with a lurch and a shudder. "Not funny," he growled, surprised she had the cheek to tease him. Few people were that brave.

"I couldn't resist," Brin said, amusement dancing in her eyes. She reached into her bag, pulled out her phone and tapped the screen.

She held the device out to him and told him to swipe left to see her photos. He flipped through, saw wedding bouquets and huge tumbling arrangements, and tried to act like he knew what he was looking at. They looked fine, which was a relief.

"I've done a few weddings, some corporate functions and arrangements for parties. I've always loved flowers and gardening and making stuff grow." Brin told him, and he heard a note of insecurity in her voice. "It used to be a hobby, but I'm good enough to turn it into a career. Or so my clients tell me."

He wasn't in the business of handing out reassurances or support, and he'd never been the cheerleading type—he most definitely wasn't a hand-holder—but the urge to allay her insecurities was strong. Radd gripped the bridge of his nose and applied pressure to push these uncomfortable notions out of his head. Brin was not like anyone he'd ever met and she, for some reason, possessed the power to disarm him.

Why this woman and why now? He needed to stay detached, to be indifferent and emotionally uninvolved. He'd trained himself to be stoic and disengaged, but there was something about Brinley that made him want to step out of his carefully crafted cocoon.

He had to stop, retreat and pull himself together. If he had any sense, he'd pull out his laptop and ignore her for the rest of the flight.

He was paying her to do a job, he wasn't required to entertain her.

Brin leaned forward and pointed to her phone. "So is my work okay?"

Radd handed her phone back and shrugged. "I guess. I don't know anything about what you do." There was no way he'd tell her he liked the unstructured arrangements the best, they looked wild and free and...lush.

Lush? Holy hell, who was this person who'd taken possession of his mind?

Brin looked momentarily disappointed at his reply but she recovered quickly, and he appreciated the fact she didn't pout or sulk. "Can you give me some idea of what flowers I'll have to work with?" Brinley asked, putting her phone back in her bag. "And what you want?"

Was this a trick question? "I think they are blue. And we need them in vases."

Brinley gave him a look that was part amusement and complete frustration. "And that's all you have for me?"

"Pretty much," Radd admitted.

"Excellent," Brinley murmured, sarcasm coating every syllable. Skye placed two glasses filled with ice in front of each of them and cracked open a bottle of water.

"Well, will your fiancée be at the lodge? Maybe she can spare some time to give me an idea of what she wants," Brinley asked.

His...*what?*

Radd heard Skye's snort and sent him a hot glare. Skye's expression turned neutral and he quickly finished pouring their drinks. When he left the room, Radd looked at Brinley. "Why would you think I'm the one getting married?"

"You aren't?"

Radd noticed her dismay and wondered why she looked so damn disappointed on hearing he wasn't about to be hitched and stitched. To clarify, he told her he was very single. Then he wondered why he felt the need to do so, because explaining wasn't something he ever did.

Radd watched as Brinley hunted for a reason for her confusion. "I just thought that, because you are so involved in all of this, you have a personal connection to the event. Men of your...um, men like you, high-flying businessmen, have people to organize stuff like this."

Fair point. But those were men who didn't have a multi-billion-dollar investment riding on this wedding and weren't dealing with a spoiled bride and her doting father.

Radd drank half of the contents of his glass before putting it back on the table. "It's crucial we keep the bride, and her father, happy, and trust me, they make it difficult."

Brinley's grasp on her glass loosened and the tension in her jaw eased. "Oh. Well, who is getting married and why do you need to keep them happy?"

He could tell her; it wasn't common knowledge, but neither was it a secret. "We are in negotiations with Vincent Radebe, he is selling us something we want. A condition of the sale is we provide his daughter Naledi with the best wedding experience possible. And that means pre-wedding festivities at Kagiso Ranch and an out-of-this-world wedding at The Vane next Saturday."

Radd had heard the expression *color drained from her face* before, but he'd never seen it happen until this moment. Brinley's eyes widened and, as her face paled, the freckles on her nose and cheeks stood out in stark relief.

She was going to faint, he just knew it. Radd sprang to his feet and placed his hand against the back of her head, pushing her head gently down to rest between her knees, his fingers covered by soft, fragrant curls.

Maybe she'd had too much sun, too little food, or maybe she was dehydrated. It was possible.

Or maybe, just maybe, the fact she was doing flowers for a celebrity couple was overwhelming. Which was, he admitted, a little disappointing. Brinley didn't seem the swooning type.

She certainly hadn't with him.

CHAPTER THREE

HAVING STUMBLED BACK to the bathroom, Brinley gripped the basin and stared at her pale face in the mirror. Her eyes looked haunted and she'd chewed all her lipstick off. She looked like she felt, shocked but also resentful.

For the last few months, since she'd left Johannesburg and drastically reduced contact with her family, her life had been peaceful. She'd started sleeping well and stressing less, and she'd worked hard to find a new normal. While she wasn't completely happy—how could she be when she was constantly counting pennies?—she was content and that was, for now, enough.

The past six months had been drama free, but this day certainly wasn't. She didn't know where to start to try and make sense of it all...

Firstly, Radd Tempest-Vane wasn't engaged, dammit, and he'd stripped her of the much-needed psychological barrier between them. If he was in love with someone else, she would've had a very good reason to ignore her attraction to him.

But the man had the temerity—the sheer audacity—to be single!

It didn't matter, Brin told herself, *it shouldn't matter*. Her insane physical reaction to him was nothing more than simple biology, an age-old instinct to mate, to procreate. She was young, healthy and yes, she had urges. This was a very normal reaction to a good-looking guy.

There was no need to overreact.

Besides, she had a far bigger problem than her inconvenient attraction to Radd.

Brinley straightened her arms and stared down at the expensive floor, sucking in deep breaths to get her heart to stop racing. There were a million couples at any one time who were in the process of getting married, but she was traveling to Kagiso Ranch to do the flowers for Naledi Radebe, Kerry's archenemy.

Naledi and her sister had once been friends, good friends, but their relationship wasn't strong enough to survive Kerry being chosen instead of Naledi for some advertisement campaign. Then came the allegations of Kerry dating someone Naledi was seeing. At a party, slaps had been exchanged and the pictures in the press hadn't been pretty. Someone pressed assault charges, the other responded with charges of her own, though the criminal charges were eventually dropped and the fight moved to the civil courts.

Then came the social media war that left them both bleeding but, eventually, the vitriol eased and now it was just the occasional caustic tweet throwing shade. Neither had ever made the attempt to mend fences.

Knowing she needed more information, Brin picked up her phone, accessed the onboard Wi-Fi and did a quick search, immediately picking up an article announcing Naledi's engagement to Johnathan Wolfe and, God, yes, he was the same guy Kerry had had a fling with two years ago.

Oh, crap and dammit.

Reasonable or not, Naledi would lose it if she realized her enemy's sister was doing her flowers. It wouldn't matter to Naledi that Brin and Kerry seldom spoke, Brin shared Kerry's blood and that would be enough to make her lose it.

Kerry would probably also call her a traitor, screaming that blood should always stand with blood.

Nobody had ever called either of the two society princesses reasonable.

God, this was disastrous. Brin paced the small area of the bathroom, wondering what she should do. She could tell Radd her nebulous connection to the bride but if she did, he'd turn the plane around and dump her still-broke butt back in Cape Town. He had a massive business deal riding on the outcome of this wedding and he wouldn't risk upsetting the Radebes.

He'd find another florist, and she would be out of thirty thousand US dollars. She needed that money. Really, *really* needed it, and if she spent twenty-four hours at Kagiso and did a decent job, she could create a life that excited her...a little shop, and working as a floral designer, adding pops of color and interest to homes and events, would make her happy. Unlike Kerry, she didn't need a big stage, or lights or action. It wasn't big or bold, but Brin didn't need big or bold, she just needed it to be *hers*.

Brin flicked her thumbnail against her bottom teeth. Radd had told her that she was due to leave the lodge tomorrow afternoon and the wedding party was only flying in on Monday morning. She could do the flowers, get paid enough to set up her own business and leave before Naledi arrived. She'd leave it up to Radd to explain who the florist was. She owed this to herself and, if she didn't take this opportunity, she'd regret it for the rest of her life.

Brinley looked at herself in the mirror, pleased to

see the color had returned to her face and her eyes no longer looked haunted. Progress.

She could pull this off, she *had* to.

Brinley walked back into the salon to see Skye placing a platter between two bone china plates on the dining table. Silver cutlery, crystal glasses and three thousand count linen napkins made her think she was eating in a five-star restaurant.

Brinley stepped forward and saw the platter was, actually, a beautiful seafood salad—and she grinned. Thanks to her skeletal budget, seafood was something she never ate.

"Oh, Skye, it looks fantastic," Brin said, walking up to the table. Skye pulled out her chair and Brin sat down.

Radd walked over to the table and took his seat, pulling the bottle of white wine from the silver ice bucket. "You're looking better," he commented.

"Low blood sugar, I think," Brinley replied, as Skye piled seafood salad onto her plate.

Radd's eyes sharpened. "Are you sure that's all it was?"

Brin didn't like lying, but what choice did she have? She was not giving up her dreams, not when she just needed a scant twenty-four hours to make them come true.

She shrugged as she placed a linen serviette across her lap. "It's been an interesting day."

"Just so you know, Ms. Riddell, I don't like secrets or surprises. In fact, they are my least favorite thing in the world. So, if there's something I should know, tell me now."

Oh, wow, there was the ultra-tough, fantastically shrewd businessman. He was both sexy and a little scary, and Brin was thankful she'd never have to meet him in a boardroom. He'd chew her up and spit her out…

"I haven't eaten all day and am probably a little dehydrated. I'll be fine by the time we land," Brin hedged.

Radd looked skeptical, but Brin just kept her eyes on him, hoping he'd change the subject. It took everything Brin had not to look away, knowing that if she did, he'd see it as a sign of weakness or, worse, for the lie it was. Their stalemate was broken by Skye clearing his throat and they both turned their attention back to him.

"We'll be landing in forty minutes. Bon Appétit."

"Leave your bags," Radd told her. "The staff will take them up to the lodge."

Brinley nodded and followed him to the jet's exit. Even from a few steps away from the door, she could feel the air was different: warm but earthy, primal. As she stood at the top of the stairs and looked over the bush beyond the airstrip, she felt instantly connected to this old-as-time land.

Wide-open skies, fresh air, thick vegetation. It was wild and luscious and so different from the city life she was used to.

Brin noticed the open-top game viewing vehicles parked to the side of the airstrip, two rangers dressed in khaki shorts, dark green shirts and hiking boots next to them. Walking down the steps, Brin stopped, turned and looked back up to Radd, a few steps behind here.

"This is a ridiculous question but where, exactly, are we?"

Radd's stern mouth tipped up at the corners. "We're on the southern edge of the Kalahari Desert."

When they reached the grass strip, Radd took her hand—making bubbles pop on her skin—and tugged her away from the plane, turning her around to look in the opposite direction. Purple-blue, craggy mountains cast shadows over the plains below.

Conscious of her very small hand in his, Brin found her head dipping sideways to rest on his shoulder. She felt him tense, heard his intake of breath and slammed her eyes shut, mortified by her lover-like response. Abruptly, she pulled her hand from his, defiantly folding her arms across her chest.

Note to self: touching Radd makes your brain turn to mush.

Radd started to speak and Brin forced herself to concentrate.

"We're in what we call the green Kalahari," Radd explained. "The reserve is home to Kalahari black-maned lions, black desert rhino, Hartmann's mountain zebra, cheetah, gemsbok, roan antelope, the pangolin and many, many more animals. The guests, and the money they pay, fund our conservation efforts. The land and animals are our priority."

Brinley heard the tiny crack in his voice suggesting emotion and saw the passion in his eyes. In this brief moment, Radd wasn't the hard-ass billionaire businessman, but an ardent man advocating for something he believed in. Brin understood, at a fundamental level, how important Kagiso was to him.

Radd's cologne mixed with the smell of foliage, dust and wild Africa, and the combination made Brin's head swim. The fading rays of the sun touched his dark hair and turned his ink pot eyes to a shade of black. All Brin wanted to do was stand in this spot and taste Africa in his mouth and on his skin, feel his arms gathering her into his body.

Radd lifted his hand and he brushed his thumb over her bottom lip, then across her cheekbone. What was he doing? Where was this coming from? She thought she'd seen attraction and desire in his eyes but, because his expression remained implacable and because he was so out of her league, she wasn't sure.

Was she his type? Could he, possibly, be as attracted to her as she was to him?

Radd lowered his head and Brin thought, hoped, he might kiss her, but a millisecond later, he jerked his head back and stepped away from her.

"We are not going there, Brinley."

She took a quick, awkward step backward. Yes, of course, she knew that! Hadn't she been telling herself exactly that? Brinley stared into the distance, annoyed with herself. Why was the concept of Radd Tempest-Vane being strictly, completely, Area 51-off-limits not sinking in? She was reasonably intelligent, it wasn't a difficult concept to grasp.

Radd lightly touched her back and led her over to the first of the game viewing vehicles. One of the rangers immediately sprang into action, opening the front passenger door for her. When he put out a hand to help her into the vehicle, Radd spoke to him in an African language, his voice, as always, commanding.

The game ranger stepped back, replied and nodded.

"You speak… What language do they speak here?" Brin asked as she lifted her skirt to climb into the deep green vehicle. She placed her hand in his and allowed him to steady her as she stepped onto the running board. She settled in her seat as Radd walked around the vehicle and climbed into the driver's seat.

"Tswana," Radd rested his forearms on the wheel and stared at the thick bush on the other side of the airstrip. "*Kagiso* means peace in Tswana. I spent a lot of time here with my paternal grandfather as a kid, pretty much every school holiday. I'm told I could speak the language before I could speak English."

Wow. "That's amazing. I wish I spoke an African language."

Radd turned the ignition and the engine caught. "Why don't you? It's pretty obvious you have some African blood."

"My mother is biracial, and my biological father is white. My grandfather was Sotho, but we only ever spoke English at home," Brinley replied, not meeting his eyes. "My mother's side of the family left their culture behind a long time ago."

"That's sad."

He had no idea.

"Why are you driving and not your staff?" Brin asked, wanting to change the subject.

Radd changed gears as he navigated a sharp, upward turn to the left. He took his time answering and, for a moment, Brin didn't think he would. Eventually, he sighed and shrugged. "As a rule, I like to drive myself. And I've been driving these roads since I was ten years old. I love it here."

Brin frowned, not understanding. "More than you love your magnificent flat in Camps Bay or your vineyard in Stellenbosch?"

"Have you been researching me, Miss Riddell?" he asked in a silky voice.

"You wish." Brin snorted. "I know about your properties because your rooftop garden at your flat and the garden at your vineyard were both featured in a gardening magazine I subscribe to."

"Oh, right. I remember my landscaper asking me for permission to take the magazine photographer to both properties."

Brin thought Radd would be hard-pressed to describe either property, and was starting to suspect that Radd had tunnel vision and didn't see or care for much outside of work. If she had gardens like his, she'd never leave them.

Radd's hand tightened on the wheel and he opened his mouth to tell Brin those other properties were just assets he owned, but that he considered Kagiso his home, a place of freedom and peace.

His memories of this land were only happy ones…

The smell of grandfather's pipe, camping underneath the stars or in caves containing rock art done by the San people, running wild with Jack and Digby and the children of the staff working the ranch. Swimming in the concrete water reservoir on hot days, falling asleep to the sound of jackals barking at night. The three brothers making plans for the rest of their lives, plans that didn't include their parents…

Radd shook off his thoughts and when he turned his head to look at Brin, he saw the hulking shadow moving slowly in the distance. He braked, stopped and touched Brin's shoulder, pointing to a space between the trees.

"There's a black rhino at eleven o'clock. Highly endangered, completely awe-inspiring," Radd whispered.

Brin's hand landed on his thigh and Radd sucked in a deep breath as her fingertips burned through the fabric of his pants into his skin. Desire roared through him, as turbulent and as fierce as an African thunderstorm. He stared at her exquisite profile, reluctantly admitting he'd wanted her from the first moment he saw her standing near her worn-out Beetle earlier.

He. Wanted. Her.

More than he ever expected, more than he could believe. But this was just—*this had to be!*—a normal reaction of a man to a sexy woman; it didn't mean anything beyond a need to work off excess sexual energy.

He hadn't had sex for a while and he was past due. Right, when he used his brain, his attraction to Brinley was simple and easily explained.

The rhino moved deeper into the bush and Brinley sighed, a sweet, soft sound. His blood plummeted south as he wondered whether she sounded like that when she fell apart in a man's arms. Specifically, *his* arms.

Then she turned to look at him, her mouth now just a couple of inches from his own. In the sinking light, her eyes were the color of a mermaid's, now a silver-aqua shade and fully able to rip his breath away. Through her light makeup, he could see the hints of her freckles, and he wanted to pull her dress off her body and discover where else those sweet dots appeared. Her eyes locked on his and, in them, he saw awareness, desire and yearning: everything he was feeling.

He wanted to taste her, no, he needed to taste her. Just once so he could stop obsessing about whether her mouth was as sweet as he imagined.

Radd touched his lips to hers, aiming to keep his kiss light, chaste if he could. But a few seconds after their lips connected, she opened her lips and he couldn't resist, he had to go on in. His tongue pushed past her teeth to slide against hers and she arched her back in that feminine, age-old silent way of asking for more.

But instead of waiting for him to give her what she wanted, Brin, surprising the hell out of him and without breaking contact with his mouth, turned in her seat. Moving gracefully, she lifted her skirt and straddled him, bent knees on either side of his thighs. She reached for his shirt and bunched the fabric in her hands as she deepened the kiss, asking, no, demanding, more.

Thoughts of resistance flew out of his brain. His hands found the bottom of her dress and he pulled it up so his hands could stroke the back of her smooth thighs, roam over her gorgeous backside covered in cool cotton. He explored the valley of her lower back, the curve of her slim hip, her luscious butt. Pulling away from her mouth, he kissed his way up her jaw, down her neck, but Brin moved her hand from his chest back to his face, tipping his head so she could feast on his mouth again.

And feast she did. So much passion rested under her surfer-girl exterior and he wanted more, he wanted all of her. He wanted her tongue in his mouth, but also wanted it on his neck. He wanted her hands on his chest, in his pants. He wanted to explore all her valleys and dips, the knobs of her spine, the ball of her shoulder, discover the color of her nipples, taste the sweetness between her legs.

He didn't think he'd ever wanted anyone as much, or as fast, as he wanted Brinley Riddell. And for the first time in, well, forever, his reaction terrified him. Women never knocked him sideways, he refused to give them that much power. That Brin could was...

Bizarre. Unsettling.

And yes, completely unacceptable.

The low rumble of a vehicle pierced the night sounds of the bush and Radd quickly reacted. In one smooth movement, he lifted Brinley off his lap and deposited her back in her seat and. a few seconds later, he cranked the engine and pulled away as the lights of the other vehicle appeared behind him.

Brin whipped around to look at the second vehicle before slumping back in her seat. "Wow. Close call."

"I'm their boss and the owner. If they caught us naked, they'd turn a blind eye," Radd replied, his tone brusque.

Brin didn't reply, but Radd felt her eyes on his profile and wondered if her heart, like his, was about to jump out of her chest, whether she wanted him to stop the vehicle and resume where they left off.

He very much did.

Radd stared at the dirt ahead, easily navigating around a chameleon in the middle of the road. Out of the corner of his eye, he could see her chest rising and falling quickly, the small tremor in her fingers resting on her slim thigh.

Yeah, she was equally affected.

The chemistry between them could not be denied; it was a living, breathing entity. Could it be bigger and bolder than what he normally experienced because he'd gone without sex for too long? Radd did some mental arithmetic and realized the last time he'd gotten laid was four, and a bit, months ago… No wonder he felt like a pressure cooker about to blow.

But honesty compelled him to reluctantly admit that, while he felt frustrated by his lack of bed-based activity, it wasn't the longest period he'd gone without sex and he'd never felt this off-balance before. Forty percent might be sexual frustration, the rest was his unexpected and unwelcome need to kiss Brinley from tip to toe, to discover her secrets, to hear what noises she made when she came, whether she was as tight and warm and fabulous as he imagined her to be.

Brinley was sexy and smart but, under her natural passion, he could tell that she was inexperienced, a little unsure. While he preferred women who were more skilled, who could keep up with him in the bedroom, he rather liked the idea of teaching Brin a little of what he knew…

Radd slapped his hand against the back of his neck and welcomed the slight sting in his hand. She was his employee, she'd be out of his life tomorrow night, and he wasn't the type to seduce innocents. And, despite being in her late twenties, if she wasn't innocent, then she was definitely inexperienced.

And, no matter how sweet her kisses or how deep her passion ran, he wasn't anyone's teacher. Except for being Digby's brother, he wasn't anyone's anything.

Besides, he'd watched the crap show that was his parents' marriage and had front row seats to how love made people irrational, how it made them lose control. Every relationship, good, bad and dysfunctional, required work and involvement and emotion, and he didn't have the time or inclination. He kept his relationships at surface level. If you didn't allow anyone behind the armor, no one could do any damage. If one didn't engage, actions and words couldn't be misconstrued.

It was a simple concept that served him well. And Brinley Riddell—free-spirited, gorgeous, inexperienced and intriguing—would not be the first to find his chinks.

And to ensure that didn't happen—it wouldn't, but Radd never took chances—he'd keep his distance. He'd drop her off at the lodge and retreat to his private villa at the end of the property. He had his laptop and enough work to keep him occupied and, if the gods were smiling on him, Brinley would complete her flower arranging in record time and he could whip her back to Cape Town, pay her and put her out of his mind.

That was the plan, because the other plan fighting for his attention—to keep her, naked, in his bed for the next twenty-four hours—was not only a nonstarter, but stupid.

He was reserved, implacable, emotionally detached and occasionally difficult, but stupid he was not.

CHAPTER FOUR

SHE'D KISSED RADD TEMPEST-VANE, the man who held her future in his admittedly exceptionally skilled hands.

Idiot. Idiot. Idiot.

Brin licked her lips, thinking she could still taste him—fresh, gorgeous, comprehensively, powerfully male—on her lips, on her tongue. She hadn't had much time to explore his body, but she knew his thighs were strong, his stomach ridged with muscle, his chest wide. His hands were big, broad and capable, and his arms powerful.

One touch of his lips to hers and she'd turned into a wild woman, devoid of sense and thought. Oh, she'd like to be able to say that she would've retreated had he pushed for more, but she didn't know if that was the truth.

His hands on her legs and butt had felt so amazing and, had she been able to form the words or pull her mouth from his, she'd would've begged him to touch her breasts, to slide a big hand between her thighs.

She wanted him. More than she'd ever wanted anyone or anything before.

She was *so* screwed.

One kiss, a mild grope and it was like she hadn't spent most of the past half day telling herself why hooking up with Radd was a comprehensively bad, bad, *terrible* idea. Maybe she should just record a voice note and push play every time she forgot the hundred reasons why she shouldn't kiss/touch/sleep with Radd Tempest-Vane.

Shall we list them again? For the hundredth and sixtieth time?

She was in the process of finding her authentic self, working on her insecurities, her dark thoughts. She did not need to complicate the process with unwanted attraction.

And it *was* unwanted, because Radd was who and what she didn't need. Having just rid herself of two bossy people, she did not want another super confident, autocratic, overbearing person in her life.

No matter how gorgeous, sexy, hot and rich he was....

And man, he was stupidly rich.

Brin sighed. While she'd been exposed to her sister's rich-ish existence, it was nothing compared to Radd's billionaire lifestyle, and she didn't know how to operate in such a rarified world. Few, she imagined, would. Nor did she want to, money wasn't what drove her. Being accepted, feeling like she belonged, did. Radd's universe—rich, opulent and excessive—wasn't what she was looking for.

It wasn't where she belonged. It would gobble her up and spit her, and her battered and bruised heart, out. It was a scenario she'd prefer to avoid, thank you very much.

Oh, and she was kind of...sort of...keeping a secret from him. But, since it wouldn't impact their deal, she could live not telling him about Kerry's and Naledi's stupid feud.

Hands off him, Brinley Riddell, no matter how much you want to touch. Just do your job, get paid and slide out of his life. Brin glanced at her watch, squinting at the dial in the ultra-low light. *You have to be here for another twenty or so hours, surely you can control your heart and your mind and your hands for that long?*

And her mouth! For someone who'd always had a problem talking back, her mouth was working at supersonic speed. What was up with that?

Brin caught the glimpse of lights between the trees and, as Radd steered the vehicle up a steep hill, the lights became brighter and bolder. He turned to the left and there, on the edge of a cliff, sat an impressive building that looked like part of the landscape. Brin looked beyond the building to the plain, stretching out for many miles below. Her breath caught and, taking in the exceptional view, all thoughts of seeing Radd naked faded away.

Radd stopped the car and they took in the vista as the blood-red sun dipped below the horizon. She could see animals moving slowly across the plain but, because they were too far away, couldn't identify the creatures.

This was Africa: wild, vast and incomprehensively beautiful.

Far too soon, Radd accelerated away and parked the vehicle closer to the entrance of the lodge. He half turned in his seat to face her. "My manager, Mari, will meet you inside and, after getting you settled into your room, she'll show you what you have to do and where you can work. The lodge is empty at the moment, you will be the only guest tonight. The chef has prepared supper for you and Mari will be on hand to bring you anything you require—food, snacks, tools, wire, whatever you need."

"Oh, um… I thought you'd be staying here, too," Brin said. Not sure whether to be pleased or disappointed, Brin nibbled the inside of her cheek. Being alone would give her some time to shore up her defenses, to get her head on straight.

But being alone would mean not being with Radd. Her body very much wanted to be near Radd, stupid thing.

"There are guest rooms within the lodge and a handful of suites. My personal suite, we call them villas, is at the far end of the property." Radd ran his hands through his hair in an impatient gesture. "Let's clear the air, Brin."

Brin wrinkled her nose. *Ack*, a conversation starting with those words rarely went well.

Radd rested his forearms on the steering wheel and stared past the hood of the vehicle to the dark shadows beyond. Brin followed his gaze and saw him looking at an expansive deck. Brin saw dark water and realized the entertainment area ended in a large infinity pool, its water seeming to tumble off the side of the cliff.

Oh, wow, she couldn't wait to see Kagiso Lodge in daylight. It would, she was sure, live up to all her expectations.

"For some strange, inexplicable reason, you seem to be forgetting you are here to work, Miss Riddell. I am paying you an extraordinary amount of money to arrange flowers. You are here to do a job."

Brin's eyes slammed into his and the deep navy, almost black, eyes were harder than she'd ever seen them. His lips were now thin slashes in his face and a deep frown pulled her attention to his hard-as-granite eyes.

He was acting as if she were the only one who'd enjoyed their kiss, like she'd thrown herself at him, like she was at fault. *Seriously?*

"Are you reminding yourself or me?" Brin demanded, once again surprised at her fast response and lack of deference. She really didn't recognize this mouthy person!

Radd just stared at her, his expression inscrutable. She'd known him for just a few hours, but she didn't like him hiding behind that enigmatic expression.

Don't rock the boat, Brin, just swallow the hot words in your throat. Just exit the vehicle and walk away.

But that was what she always did, and this time she wanted a reaction. She refused to slink into the shadows, happy to accept the blame for something that wasn't her fault. Maybe she'd grown a spine since leaving Johannesburg.

"Might I remind you that you kissed me, that your hands were on my butt, your fingers slid under the band of my panties? I was not alone in the madness. I know why I am here, *Mr. Tempest-Vane*. I haven't forgotten, not for a minute. But don't you dare pretend, oh-so-suddenly, that the attraction is all on my side."

Radd released an irritated sigh, his broad shoulders lifting and falling. "Fine, our kiss got out of hand, I'll admit you are right, I *am* attracted to you. But I'm damned if I'm going to do anything about it." Radd muttered. "You're not my type, you're too..."

Oh, this should be good. "I'm too... What?"

She heard the whoosh of his breath, what might have been a hot curse followed by the word "dangerous." He thought she was dangerous? That couldn't be right. What threat could she pose to Radd Tempest-Vane?

"Go on in, Brinley," Radd said. "Mari is inside, she'll sort you out."

He sounded exhausted, like he was all out of patience with her and the situation. Brinley, no longer prepared to hang around when she wasn't wanted, picked her bag up off the floor and reached for the handle of the door.

"I'll see you in the morning," Brin told him, determined to hold on to her manners. One of them should.

Holding her bag strap, Brin walked up the steps leading into what she presumed was the lobby of the hotel. There was no reception desk, just two expensive, stone-colored modern couches facing each other and, above them, two massive abstract paintings reflecting the colors of the rapidly fading sunset.

Turning left, Brin walked into an open plan lounge and instantly realized why all the travel magazines rated this one of the most luxurious lodges in the world. The furniture was obviously expensive but looked incredibly comfortable, deep cushions and gleaming wooden side tables and footstools in greens and golds and browns, all the colors of the African bush.

She could get lost in the decor, but her eyes were immediately drawn to the huge floor-to-ceiling sliding doors that were pushed open to reveal the deep deck and the sparkling infinity pool. As the sun faded, stars popped through the deepening darkness, first one, then another, then a handful.

The air smelled verdant and rich and primal, and Brin placed her hand on her heart, conscious, yet again, of that strange feeling of connection.

Despite never visiting this part of the country before, her soul recognized this place...

"Miss Riddell?"

Brin, not wanting to pull her eyes off the night sky, reluctantly turned around and watched a slim woman cross the deck to her, her elegant hand outstretched. This Iman lookalike had to be Mari, Radd's manager.

God, she was gorgeous.

"Welcome to Kagiso."

"Thank you, it's beautiful," Brin replied.

Mari lifted her eyebrows. "Radd didn't accompany you in?"

Brin shrugged. "He went on to his villa."

"As I'm sure you want to do, as well," Mari smoothly replied.

"I'm really happy to stay here and look at the stars," Brin confessed.

Mari sent her a small smile. "Well, in your villa, you can soak in an outdoor bath and look at the stars."

Oh, God, that sounded…blissful. Indulgent, luxurious.

"And I can send your dinner to your room, along with any beverage you desire."

It was Brin's turn to raise her eyebrows. *Anything* was a big word. "Anything at all?"

Mari nodded. "Pretty much."

Wow. Okay, then. Brin looked up at the diamond-on-velvet sky again before following Mari's long-legged stride inside the lodge. She crossed the slate floor, running her hand along the top of a butter-soft leather couch, her eyes taking in the world-class sculptures on the floor and stunning art on the wall.

Good job, Radd. This is amazing.

Mari opened a side door and led her down a stone pathway, past a cozy library and what looked to be a beautifully appointed office. "Yours?" Brin asked her.

Mari laughed. "I wish! No, that is the office the guests use for the important calls, video conferences and emails they can't afford to miss. That's the only room where there is Wi-Fi, otherwise we encourage our guests to disconnect to reconnect."

She'd avoid the office, Brin thought, smiling, liking the idea of being unreachable.

"And this is our multipurpose room, we can hold mini-conferences here or cocktail parties or discos." Mari stopped by a door at the end of the main building and pushed open the door. She flicked on a light and moved back to allow Brin to enter the room.

"Why would anyone want to be here when they could be on the deck?" Brin asked but didn't wait for a reply, her attention caught by the various shades of blue flowers standing in buckets on the long stainless-steel table.

There were delphiniums, blue hydrangeas, cream roses and lilies, blue grape hyacinths, blue roses and delicate orchids and freesias. Brin dropped her bag to the floor and hurried to the table, dipping her head to smell the freesias, running her finger over the delicate petals of a creamy, blue-tinted rose. Her eyes danced over her supplies, huge glass vases and earthenware pots, tape, shears and wire, delicate ribbon and buckets of glossy green fillers. A list of arrangements sat on the desk and Brin quickly perused it, making adjustments here, leaving or adding flowers there.

Looking at the stars from a bubble bath could wait, because she'd just stepped into her own version of heaven. And it was filled with flowers.

It was just past five the next morning when Radd walked into the dining room and headed straight for the coffee machine in the corner. He jammed his cup under the spout. At the sound of footsteps, he turned and smiled when he saw one of his oldest friends crossing the room to where he stood.

"You're up early," Mari said after they exchanged a hug. "Did you sleep well?"

That would be a no. He'd tossed and turned for hours, unable to push the memory of how Brinley tasted from his thoughts. He'd kissed a lot of women, slept with about as many, but he'd never lost sleep before. He didn't like it.

He seemed to be saying that a lot around Brin.

Speaking of Brinley, he wondered where she was. The door to her villa had been open when he'd passed by and her bed had been made. He'd called out but received no reply.

"Did you arrange for one of the rangers to take Brin on a game drive?" Radd asked as Mari fixed herself a cup of coffee.

"No, I wouldn't have done that without your permission," Mari answered him, a tiny frown marring her smooth forehead.

Then where the hell was she? "She's not in her room, have you seen her this morning?"

Radd felt his stomach lurch and cold water ran through his veins. God, he hoped she hadn't gone for a walk. The resort wasn't fenced and the animals—wild, free and dangerous—could, and had, stroll through the grounds. Just last week they'd had a leopard lying in the branches of the acacia outside villa four.

He'd been so desperate to lay his hands, and his mouth, on her that he hadn't given her the safety speech. Goddammit, how could he be so stupid?

Mari placed a hand on his arm. "I'm sure she's fine, Radd. Let's just stay calm, okay?"

Right. He never panicked, so why was his throat tight and his lungs heaving? Pulling in a few deep breaths, he shook his head to clear it, and forced away thoughts of Brinley being mauled by a hyena or bitten by a Cape cobra.

Overreacting much, Tempest-Vane?

"Why don't you check the conference room?" Mari

suggested. "Maybe she decided to get up early to get the arrangements done."

Now, why hadn't he thought of that first? Oh, maybe because he'd had no sleep, was sexually frustrated and generally pissed off that a woman he'd met yesterday— yesterday, for God's sake!—had managed to rock his world.

He couldn't wait for later, to be able to bundle her onto his plane and send her back to Cape Town and out of his life. He didn't like feeling this off-kilter, so out of control.

Control wasn't just important, it was *everything*.

Holding his coffee cup, Radd walked out of the dining room and down the stone path leading to the conference room. He opened the door to the light-filled room, his eyes widening at the enormous bouquets sitting on the steel table in the middle of the room. They were a riot of white, cream, blues and greens, lush and wild. Somehow, despite the flowers being imported and exotic, she'd managed to invoke the feel of the bush in the arrangements. He was reminded of the colors of new spring growth, the African sky in summer, the way the sun hit the land at the beginning of the day.

The buckets on the floor were mostly empty, save for a couple of stalks of greenery.

Her work was done, and done exceptionally well, but where the hell was Brin?

Walking farther into the room, Radd's booted foot kicked something soft, and he looked down to see a leather tote bag lying on the floor. Radd looked around. Seeing the high-backed couch at the other end of the room, he strode over to it and his heart finally settled into an even rhythm. Brin was curled up on the plump cushions, her hands tucked under her head, dark curls resting on her cheek. Since she wore the same clothes as yesterday, it was obvious she'd never made it to her room last night.

He gently picked up one curl, then another, and pulled them off her cheek. Her makeup had worn off and he could see the spray of freckles on her straight nose, a tiny scar in the middle of her forehead. Her eyelashes, long and thick, touched her cheek and highlighted the blue stripes under her eyes. How late had she worked?

Radd gripped the back of the couch and stared down at her, fighting the wave of lust threatening to consume him. He could handle desire, he wasn't a kid and could walk away, but the wave of protectiveness surprised him. He wasn't sure what to do with it.

Why was he feeling this way? Why was he feeling anything at all? He wasn't used to paying this much attention to his feelings, to even *having* feelings. He'd trained himself not to react, to push emotion away.

He needed to go back to feeling nothing.

And he would, because Brinley wasn't, in any way, his type. He dated—okay, slept with—sophisticated women, tough women, women who knew the score.

He dated cool blondes and raven-haired pixies, African queens and fiery redheads. Looks weren't important, but their emotional independence was.

So why the hell had he kissed Brin last night? Why had he spent hours last night imagining what her slim, firm and glorious naked body would feel like pressed up against his—damn good, of that he had no doubt. Why, goddammit, was he standing here staring down at her?

There was only one explanation: he was losing his damned mind. He should only have one priority, and that was making sure that Naledi's wedding went off without a hitch and getting Vincent to sign the final deed of sale. Restoring the mine to the Tempest-Vane group of companies was all that was important.

The acquisition of the mine, and their announcement that they would be increasing capacity and employing thousands of workers, would be front-page news. That news would lead to an interest in their PR and rebranding exercise.

They would garner attention, but it would be the *right* sort of attention.

The hope was that the PR campaign and the rebranding exercise would, finally, dilute the interest in his parents fast-paced and over-the-top lives, and their still recent deaths. More than a few journalists had, over the years, blown up minor incidents in his and Digby's lives, trying to show that he and his brother were like Gil and Zia. Digby's escapades—fast cars, boats and bikes and his one-date love life— garnered attention but nothing he did was ever, thank God, salacious. Or smarmy.

Scandal sold papers, but Radd was determined to show the world they were apples that had fallen very, very far from the family tree.

Along with a couple of personal interviews he intended to give to trusted journalists, the world would see that he and Digby were serious, responsible and restrained. That the Tempest-Vanes could be trusted again.

Damn you, Gil and Zia.

Radd rubbed his jaw and hauled in a deep breath, seeking calm. Thinking about his parents reminded him of his need to remain numb. Feelings, he'd decided a long time ago, were counterproductive. Love was a mirage, a myth and a lie.

Besides, Brinley wasn't his type.

He was repeating himself. Again. He obviously needed more sleep and so, he presumed, did she.

Responding to his squeeze of her shoulder, Brin slowly opened her eyes and Radd was briefly reminded of that photo of the Afghan Mona Lisa, the girl with the light green eyes in her dark face. Brin's skin tone was much lighter, but her eye color was as intense, splashes of light in her face.

Gorgeous.

"What time is it?" Brin asked, her voice sexy with sleep.

"Just after six," Radd replied as she swung her long legs off the couch. She stretched and the hem of her T-shirt rose an inch, maybe two, revealing a strip of smooth skin. He wanted to put his mouth on that strip, nudging the shirt up with his nose to find her breast, her nipple.

Or go lower...

Radd cursed and tipped his head back to look at the high ceiling. It was going to be a long, long day, but by this afternoon she'd be on his plane. Then he'd be able to forget her and her irritating effect on him.

Yet the thought of her leaving left a bitter taste in his mouth. That had to be because Brin's company was preferable to Naledi's and her father's, to that of the guests he had yet to meet.

Brin stood up and bent down to touch her toes, wrapping her arms behind her knees and pushing her pert bottom in the air. Oh, hell, she was bendy...

Not what he needed to know.

"Did you sleep here last night?"

Yeah, he understood he was being rude, but rude was better than taking her in his arms, lowering her to the couch and doing several things to her he was pretty sure this couch, or this room, had never seen. Or maybe, knowing his guests, it had.

"I finished around two," Brin said, unfurling her long body and standing up straight. She placed her hand over her mouth to cover her yawn. She looked past him to the bouquets of flowers on the table. "What do you think?"

There was that note of insecurity in her tone again, the silent wish to be reassured. Normally he would ignore it, but Brin had done a great job and what would it hurt to tell her so? "They look amazing," he truthfully answered.

Brin's eyes locked on his as a hopeful smile touched her lips. "Really? Honestly?"

"I never say things I don't mean."

Brin walked over to the table, pulled out a cream rose only to jam it back into the same spot. "I'm not happy with the balance of this one."

Radd put his hand over hers and pulled it away from the arrangement. Goosebumps raised the hair on his arms and blood flowed south, tenting his pants. And all because he was holding her hand. Could he be any more ridiculous? Radd dropped her hand and, to keep from reaching for her and showing her how much he appreciated her efforts in a more basic, biblical way, he shoved his hands into the pockets of his jeans.

Brin stepped away from the table and turned her back on the flowers. "Full disclosure, I didn't follow the exact instructions of the original florist. She wanted more structured arrangements, but I think these work a lot better, especially now that I've seen the interior of Kagiso Lodge. It's beautiful, luxurious, but it's not rigid, or fussy. So, I followed my instincts."

And they were spot-on. Speaking of instincts, his instincts were yelling that they'd be great in bed together...

Tempest-Vane! For God's sake.

"But Naledi might not appreciate her original designs being changed. Maybe I should change them back, tone them done."

No damn way! "For every flower you move, I'll deduct ten grand off your payment." Radd told her, his tone suggesting that she not argue. "You've already lost ten thousand because you moved that one flower."

Brin looked at him, askance before realizing he was teasing. "Okay, okay." She lifted her hands and took a step back.

Brin wrinkled her pretty nose. "I need coffee. And a shower." She sent him an uncertain look. "If you're happy with what I've done, you can tell your pilot to come and collect me."

That would be the best option. She could be gone by noon, and he could spend the rest of the day alone in his favorite place, something he never got to experience anymore. He could simply soak in the essence of Africa and recharge his soul.

That's what he should do, but Radd didn't reach for his phone. Instead, he opted to buy a little time. "Coffee is in the dining room."

Brin followed him to the door, sending him a shy smile when he stood aside to let her walk through the door before him. She seemed surprised by his manners and a little grateful. It was a nice change from the women who either didn't notice or chided him for being gentlemanly, saying that women were perfectly able to open doors for themselves. Of course they were, what the hell did that have anything to do with showing a little bit of courtesy?

Women, would he ever understand them?

Then again, because he was resolved to live his life solo, he would never need to.

Brin looked back into the room, and he gripped her elbow before she could walk back and fiddle with her flowers. "They are fine, Brinley."

Brin looked startled. "How did you know what I was thinking?"

"You have the most expressive eyes in the world," Radd replied, his tone terse. "Come on. Coffee—we could both do with a cup."

Or an intravenous injection containing pure caffeine. And a reality check.

CHAPTER FIVE

BRIN, SITTING IN the passenger seat of a short-wheelbase Land Rover, held her hair back off her face and turned in her seat to look at Radd. Dressed in a red T-shirt, the hem of its sleeves tight around his biceps; old, faded jeans; battered boots; and a Kagiso Lodge cap on his head, he looked the antithesis to the urbane, ruthless businessman with the fearsome reputation she'd met in Cape Town. Light stubble covered his jaw and his broad hands held the steering wheel with complete ease as he whipped the Land Rover down a side road, driving them deeper into the game reserve.

It was obvious that he knew where he was going and how to get there. With each mile they traveled, she sensed his tension ebbing. He loved it here, Brin realized. He'd never admit it, but she sensed this was his happy place.

She didn't have a happy place, not yet. Maybe her shop, if and when she finally opened it, would become the one place where she was totally at ease, utterly in control.

Brin leaned back in her seat, enjoying the early morning sun on her face. She was exhausted, but thrilled with her work last night. On entering the conference room, she'd just wanted to inspect the flowers, map out a plan of action for this morning and see what she was up against. But then she'd picked up a bunch of blue orchids and she'd felt compelled to make a start. One bouquet led to another and soon she was losing time, lost in the moment, immersed in her creativity. Not much could make her forget who and where she was but her craft did...

As did Radd.

When he'd kissed her last night, she'd forgotten why she was at Kagiso, that they were in an open-top vehicle in the middle of the African bush, that she and Radd inhabited completely different worlds. In his arms, she didn't feel like Kerry's little sister, someone who was broke, insecure and still trying to find herself.

In Radd's arms, she felt like the best version of herself.

Brin sighed and rubbed her moist hands on her jeans. He shouldn't be taking up this much mental space. In a couple of hours she would be back in Cape Town and, in two or three more, back in her cottage in Bo Kaap. By tomorrow, or Tuesday, depending on how quickly Radd's funds moved through the banking channels, her money would be in her possession, and she would be free.

Free of the worry of having to go back to Johannesburg with her tail between her legs. Free of the fear of returning to her job as Kerry's assistant—the woman had gone through three already in six months. Free of worrying that she'd eventually fade away, that she'd always be remembered, if she was remembered at all, as being Kerry Riddell's half sister.

But when she returned later, it would be to a Cape Town they both lived in, but where they would no longer connect.

And that was the way it should be.

Because, realistically, there was no chance of her and Radd interacting in an ongoing and meaningful way. Aside from the fact that he was a billionaire and she was broke—okay, she wouldn't be broke for long—they were very different people. He was completely assured and very at ease with himself and his place in the world.

The fact that he constantly dated different woman told her he was commitment-phobic, so she'd never be anything more than a few nights of fun.

But, more than that, Radd was the type of guy she should avoid. He was strong-willed and assertive, a man of very definite opinions. He was also domineering and hard-assed, and she was pretty sure he was the "my-way-or-the-highway" type.

She'd spent the last ten years under the thumb of two very dominating and demanding women, and she wasn't willing to put herself into a situation where she lost her voice, lost herself, again. She was just starting to bloom, slowly understanding who she was and what she stood for. Hooking up with Radd—tough, demanding and dictatorial—would erode all her progress. No, finding herself, restoring her self-belief and confidence, was more important than dropping into a torrid affair with a man who'd discard her when he tired of her.

And he would because, according to the tabloid press, he tired of everyone. When it came to woman, Radd had the attention span of a fruit fly.

So no falling in lust with Radd Tempest-Vane, Riddell. It would be a bad, bad, terrible move.

Falling in love would be the height of stupidity, and she refused to be that girl, the one who "couldn't help herself."

Brin sighed, wondering why she was getting so worked up about something that wouldn't happen. She would be leaving in a couple of hours and soon this would all be a strange memory.

Radd changed gears as he approached a steep hill, idly pointing out a warthog snuffling in the grass next to the road. Brin grinned at the pig, thinking that it was both ugly, cute and very dirty. It looked up at them, snorted and belted into the bush, its tail pointed toward the sky.

They crested the hill and the bush thinned out, revealing a swathe of open savanna. To the left of the road, the grass had been mowed within and around a small, fenced-off area. Brin leaned forward and saw a couple of gravestones beyond the iron fence.

Brin looked at Radd and saw that, while he'd slowed the car to almost a crawl, he was looking straight ahead, as if he were pretending not to notice the graveyard. She placed her hand on his bare, muscled forearm and ignored the heat shimmying up her fingers, along her arm.

"Who is buried there, Radd?"

Radd didn't meet her eyes. "I spoke to one of the rangers this morning, and he said that he saw a pride of young male lions out here yesterday, somewhere just over that ridge. Let's go see if we can spot them," Radd said, a muscle jumping in his clenched jaw.

She loved to see a pride of lions but, strangely, hearing the history of the small graveyard seemed more important.

"I'd rather look at the graveyard," Brin told him. "Stop the car, Radd."

Radd released an aggravated hiss, but he hit the brakes, causing Brin to lurch forward. She braced her hand on the dashboard and lifted her eyebrows at him. "Was that necessary?"

"It's just a graveyard filled with people you don't know!"

Wow, if the temperature of his words had dropped any further, his voice box would've iced over. Brin knew he was trying to intimidate her and that he expected her to cower in her seat and tell him to drive on. The impulse was there, but Radd didn't frighten her. He should, but he didn't. Weird, but true.

It was clear the graveyard was personal and private, so if he didn't want her to look, she'd honor his request.

"Can I take a look around, pay my respects, or would you prefer that I didn't?" Brin asked, keeping her tone nonconfrontational.

Radd whipped his cap off his head, ran his hand through his hair and jammed it back down. He leaned across her and opened her door, so Brin hopped out of the Land Rover and started to walk in the direction of the graveyard. Radd, snapping her name, stopped her progress. "Brin, wait."

Brin watched as she reached behind his seat and pulled out a rifle. He exited the vehicle and slung the weapon over his shoulder. Brin's eyes widened as he walked around to join her, his eyes scanning the bush around him. "Is the rifle really necessary?"

"This is wild land, Brinley, filled with wild animals. Guests are never supposed to leave the vehicle, ever, and if they do, they are on a walking tour, guarded by our armed rangers."

Brin nodded to his weapon. "And do you know how to use that?"

Radd rolled his eyes. "If I didn't, I wouldn't be carrying it."

Designer tailored suits and Hermes ties, Aston Martins and private jets. Battered boots, a cap and a rifle.

Who was this man and how many more sides did he have to him? God, he was intriguing.

But, intriguing or not, she was leaving his life in a few hours and that was a good thing. She had work to do, a future to create, and Radd was not only a massive distraction, but also completely wrong for her.

Radd pushed open the small gate leading into the cemetery and gestured Brin to step through. The grass inside the fence was neatly cut and the headstones were free of dust and debris. It was fairly obvious that the area was well looked after.

Brin stopped at the first headstone and stared down at the faded words, unable to make out dates or names. This grave was older than all the others. Brin asked Radd whose it was and when he didn't answer, she turned around, frowning when she saw him standing at the gate, his back to her, his hand rubbing the back of his neck.

Could Radd, normally so implacable and composed, be feeling disconcerted and maybe a little sad? Or maybe even a lot sad.

Moving on, Brin stared down at a bright, newer headstone, reading the words. The date of his birth and death followed the name, Jack Tempest-Vane, and the words *His absence is a silent grief, his life a beautiful memory*. Brin tipped her head to the side, did a mental calculation and quickly realized Jack had to be Radd's brother, and that he'd died when Radd was in his late teens or early twenties.

Brin put her hand on her heart and gently touched his tombstone before moving deeper into the small cemetery, smiling at the cruder gravestones marking the resting place of beloved pets. Then she frowned when she saw one black, flat, unadorned marker glinting in the sun. Brin wandered over to the far corner of the plot.

Gil and Zia Tempest-Vane.

Radd's parents.

They were buried in the family plot but just, tucked away out of sight. Brin dropped to her haunches and brushed twigs off the face of the marker. Black marble, white writing. Just their names and dates of their births and deaths—less than two years ago—were etched into the stone.

Brin placed her hand over her heart as a wave of sadness passed over her. Radd and Digby would've chosen their final resting spot and their choice was a statement in itself. A part of us, but also…

Not.

"Brin, let's *go*."

Brin had a hundred questions for Radd, but his hard face and *Don't ask* expression had the words dying on her lips. Closing the gate behind her, she followed Radd down the path back to the Land Rover and quietly thanked him when he opened the passenger door for her.

After slamming her door shut, Radd stowed the rifle behind the seat and walked to his side of the car. Instead of starting the vehicle, he rummaged behind the seat again and pulled out a thermos. Unscrewing the top, he poured coffee into the thermos' mug, took a sip and handed the mug to Brin.

"Sorry, but we'll have to share."

"This isn't five-star service, Tempest-Vane," Brin teased him, wanting to push his tension away.

"If you were on a proper game drive with one of our rangers, you'd be having breakfast at the edge of a water hole, sitting at a table. You'd have a mimosa in your hand and a croissant on your plate while the chef whipped up a crab, lobster, asparagus and truffle omelet."

Brin took back the cup and looked at him over its rim. "I'm sorry you lost your brother and your parents."

Radd's jaw hardened and his hand gripped the steering wheel, the knuckles white. He stared past her, his expression grim. A minute passed, then another. Brin tightened her grip on the mug and looked back at the graveyard, accepting that Radd wasn't prepared to discuss his family. And why would he? She was his temporary employee, someone he'd hired to do a job for him, someone he'd shared a kiss with.

A melt-your-socks-off kiss, but still. It meant nothing to him, and it should mean nothing to her. She was trying not to let it.

Whether she was succeeding was up for debate.

"I'm presuming you know something about my parents…"

Brin darted a look at him, unsure how to reply. Sure, she did, who didn't? She'd read about their escapades in the newspapers and celebrity magazines, admiring the way they thumbed their nose at the world.

But she was also old enough to realize her entertainment was Radd's embarrassment. "It must have been hard."

Brin caught the flash of pain that jumped in and out of Radd's eyes. "Hard? Yeah. It was *hard*."

And wasn't that the understatement of the year? Radd jerked his thumb at the graveyard. "We had a funeral in Paarl, at the family home, but their ashes are over there. It's a tradition for family members to be buried here, but we were pissed at them, still are, I guess. When they died, we weren't talking."

"For how long?"

"The best part of twenty years."

Brin's mouth fell open. "*Wow.*"

Radd shrugged. "To be fair, it wasn't such a big deal, they weren't around much. And, God, they were a constant source of humiliation."

Brin wanted to hug him, to pull him into her arms, but she knew he wouldn't appreciate any displays of sympathy. Look, she wasn't completely crazy about her own family, but she couldn't imagine never seeing them again. "You didn't speak to them *once* in all that time?"

One of Radd's powerful shoulders lifted in a shrug. "My father left a message for me two days before the accident, saying they were coming home, that there was someone they wanted us to meet."

Brin's curiosity bubbled. "Who was it?"

"God knows. Knowing my parents, it could be their dealer or a sister-wife for my mother. My parents were as mad as a box of frogs," Radd replied, taking the mug of coffee.

"Did you ever look into their papers, check their phone messages, read their emails?" Brin demanded. "Do you have his computer, his diary, his phone? What did you keep?"

Radd's lips twitched at the corners. "Slow down, Nancy Drew. We boxed all his personal effects, the boxes are stored in an attic at Le Bussy, the family home. Look, it was a throwaway comment from a person not renowned for truthfulness. It was probably some stripper he'd met who'd caught his eye."

Brin wrinkled her nose. "Did he ever introduce you to strippers before?

Radd's smile broadened a fraction. "No contact for twenty years, remember? Have some more coffee..." Brin took the cup back, sipped.

"You have an active imagination," Radd continued.

"I'm convinced my father was just blowing smoke, he was really good at doing that."

"But…"

That muscle in his jaw jumped again, his expression hardened and the strong hand on the wheel tightened. Then, Radd glanced at her and his fabulous blue eyes were a deep, dark, intense blue. And filled with pain. And guilt. And a little anger.

She'd pushed too far and he was closing down.

"I'm asking you never to repeat what I just told you, Brinley," Radd stated, his voice colder than a dip in the Bering Sea.

"You have my word." Brin passed the coffee mug to him and watched as he took a long sip, briefly closing his eyes. Handing her the mug again, he pulled his sunglasses from off his T-shirt and slipped them over his face, likely more to shield his eyes than to block out the glare of the sun.

"Shall we go look for those lions?" Brin asked, changing the subject, and relief flashed across his face.

"Absolu—" Radd's reply was interrupted by the jarring, strident tones of his phone ringing, and he lifted his buttock to pull his phone out of the back pocket of his jeans.

"Those things don't belong in the bush," Brin muttered, annoyed by the interruption.

Radd sent her his sexy half-smile, half-smirk. The one that always warmed her. "I couldn't agree more. But, unfortunately, I'm not on holiday and they are a necessary evil." Radd lifted the device to his ear and briefly lifted his hand to point toward a large tree, and a massive antelope standing in the tree's shade.

"Male kudu…hey, Dig."

Brin and the kudu exchanged interested glances as

the vehicle slowed down to a crawl. She could hear Digby's voice and, though his words were indistinguishable, judging by the horrified expression on Radd's face, he was the bearer of bad news. And, by the way, Radd looked at her, it involved her. Oh, crap, could Radd have found out her tenuous connection to Naledi? And did it matter? The flowers were done, and she was leaving; Naledi would never find out.

It wasn't, shouldn't be, an issue.

"Okay, well, thanks for letting me know. I'll call you in the morning to make further arrangements."

Radd disconnected the call and gently banged the expensive device against the steering wheel as the vehicle rolled to a stop.

"Problem?" Brin asked.

"Yeah. The pilot called Digby this morning, he picked up a problem when he was flying back yesterday. The technicians are working on it, but the plane won't be able to pick you up today and the repairs will take a few days, maybe more."

Brin felt cold, then hot, then cold again. Oh, crap, no.

"The Radebe's have agreed to use their own jet, which will leave Johannesburg, collect them in Cape Town, offload them here and return to Johannesburg." Radd placed his forearm on the steering wheel and faced her, her expression troubled. "So, what the hell do I do with you?"

Color drained from Brin's face and Radd noticed her trembling hand. Whipping the coffee cup from her grasp, he tossed the liquid onto the veld grass and screwed the cup back onto the thermos, watching a dozen emotions jump in and out of her eyes.

A few minutes back, when they were talking about

his parents—a topic he never discussed, not even with Digby—he'd felt like he was sitting on a hot griddle, but it was obvious he'd swapped places with Brin. Later, he'd try and work out why he'd revealed so much to Brin and why he felt comfortable opening up to her, but right now, he needed to focus on this latest hitch in his plans.

Brin bit her bottom lip. The plane's delay was an inconvenience, but it didn't warrant her deer-in-the-headlights expression. "Do you have somewhere to be tomorrow?"

"No, I mean, yes! Yes, I have to go back to Cape Town!" Brin quickly replied, her eyes sliding away as her cheeks turned a pretty shade of pink. Damn, she was a really bad liar.

"A job? A doctor's appointment? Lunch? A date?" He narrowed his eyes, inexplicably annoyed at the idea of her seeing someone else.

"Yes, a doctor's appointment and a date."

Lies number two and three.

Radd tapped his index finger on the knob of the gear lever. "I told you that I don't like lies."

"You told me you don't like secrets and surprises," Brin pointed out.

She was splitting hairs, because lies and secrets led to surprises. "So, why are you lying about needing to be somewhere tomorrow?"

"I can't stay here, Radd. I just can't," Brin replied, still not able to meet his eyes.

"It's a luxurious resort, not a jail cell, Brinley," Radd retorted. "What's the problem with you staying and leaving with me on Friday?"

Brin stared down at her intertwined hands, her lower lip between her teeth. "I need to get back to Cape Town, Radd. You promised I'd be back today. Can I hire a jet or, more realistically, another—smaller—plane?"

Damn, she really didn't want to stay. Radd felt the stabbing pain in his chest and frowned. Could he be feeling hurt? And if he was, what the hell was wrong with him?

"Sure, but it's expensive. And I haven't done your transfer yet and that amount of cash will take a couple of days to clear." He named a figure that had her eyes widening. "Do you have that sort of cash lying around?"

Brin shook her head. "No."

He didn't think so.

"I could hire a car…"

What the hell? Why was she so determined to get away, to leave him? And wasn't he feeling like a complete idiot for talking to her about his parents, for opening up?

So stupid.

"Brinley, what is the problem? You obviously don't have any commitments back in Cape Town. You're staying in a luxurious villa at one of the world's best safari operations. We have world-class chefs, an extensive wine list and a spa. Consider the extra few days a holiday, a bonus for doing such a fabulous job on the flowers."

Brin pushed her curls back, pleasure at his compliment in her light, bright eyes. "You really like the flowers, don't you?"

"I told you I did, didn't I?" Radd snapped, confused by her lack of confidence. Why couldn't she see how good she was and why did she seem to need assurance? This woman was a constant contradiction; he couldn't figure her out.

And if she stayed, he'd have a couple more days to do that.

And more opportunities to get her into bed.

Because really, that's what he wanted. He wanted to

explore her long, slim body with its subtle curves, feel the weight of her breasts in his hand, pull her nipple into his mouth. Explore all those soft, secret, wonderful, feminine places he adored...

While they were both stuck in Kagiso they could indulge in a no commitment, no promises affair... Short on drama, but long on pleasure.

But Radd knew he couldn't push her, that if he did, she'd find a way to haul her very pretty ass back to Cape Town.

"Tell me about your guests?"

It was a strange question and not one he'd expected. But, because it was a little step in the right direction, he quickly answered her. "Naledi Radebe, obviously, and her parents, Vincent and June Radebe." He racked his brain, trying to remember who else would be attending the pre-wedding week. He mentioned a couple of names, and Brin didn't react.

"You didn't mention the groom," Brin pointed out.

"Apparently he's on a film set and the movie only wraps up on Wednesday night. He and the best man will fly in on Thursday night. It's a sore point and the bride is not happy."

Brin's shoulders dropped an inch. "And do you expect me to spend a lot of time with them?"

God, *no*. "Hell, *I* don't expect to spend a lot of time with them," he replied. "I might have to join them one night for dinner, maybe for a drink occasionally, but this is a family holiday. They don't want me there all the time. And I, most definitely, do not want to spend a lot of time with them."

"Not your type of people?" Brin asked.

Few were. He far preferred to be on his own, or with

Digby. "It's a business relationship, and I like to keep clear boundaries."

Those boundaries were important, in business and in his personal life. *Can you try and remember that, Tempest-Vane, and stop talking to her about your family?* Radd looked at his watch. "So, are you staying or going, Brinley?"

Brin twisted her lips, obviously deep in thought. "I'll stay, if I can keep a low profile. And I don't want you telling the bride, or any of the wedding party, that I did the flowers. Tell them that you hired a designer from Cape Town and that she's already left."

"Why on earth would I do that?" Radd demanded. The bouquets were stunning, why wouldn't she want to take the credit for them? "Look, the Radebes might not be my cup of tea, but they are influential and if they know that you did the flowers, they might use you again."

Brin shook her head. "Don't tell them, Radd. Please?"

If this was her attitude toward potential business, then she would never make it. But that, Radd reminded himself, wasn't his problem. Brin would be out of his life soon, a lovely memory. If he ever thought about her at all.

He only wanted her in his life for the next few days. And, judging by his past encounters with the fairer sex, five days of her constant company was about three days too many. He got claustrophobic and irritated when he was in someone's company for too long; Brin wouldn't be any different. And, let's be honest here—because he always was—if they didn't end up sleeping together, it was going to be a goddamn long week.

Because, *people.*

As much as he wished things could be different, that

he had a normal approach to relationships, the truth was that he was the product of two of the most dysfunctional people in the world. His parents not only had a wide-open marriage, but they'd had no loyalty to each other or to the rest of their family. Their pleasures and gratification—sexual, financial and emotional—always came first.

But weirdly, despite the numerous affairs on both sides, his parents had been insanely jealous. He recalled vicious fights, the throwing of crystal and china, of shoes and handbags, his mother screaming and his father's mocking responses. He recalled rooms being trashed and walls punched and, in the morning, when it all was over, he remembered lines of coke on tables.

He had no idea what a good marriage looked like; his parents were his only reference.

So much about relationships rattled him. He was terrified he'd not only lose control and his temper, but also his dignity, so he avoided anyone who made his heart accelerate, his breath catch. If he liked a woman a little too much, he dropped her quickly, walking away without a second glance.

Because what if he took a chance on love and it backfired? What if his partner ran to the press after a fight? What if she had an affair and the press found out? What if she…

Radd shuddered. God, no! He'd lived through that scrutiny as a child and teenager and he would not, ever, go through that again. The only way to guarantee that was not to get involved with anyone, ever.

But none of his mental ramblings had anything to do with Brin's flowers. And it was her choice whether to take the credit or not.

"Fine," Radd told her.

"And I can keep a low profile when your other guests arrive?" Brin asked, and something in her expression made him pause. Why was she so determined not to interact, to keep her distance? Naledi was a social butterfly and her face was instantly recognizable, but Brin had no interest in making her acquaintance. It was unusual, and Radd didn't trust unusual.

"Is there something you're not telling me?"

Brin shrugged and rubbed her fingertips over her brow, her hand effectively hiding her eyes from him. "It's been a long and confusing day and it's not even seven yet. I'm really tired."

"Yet I still don't know whether you are staying or going."

Brin scrubbed her face with her hands before slumping in her seat. "I'm not going to lie, I don't have the money to pay deposits to hire a plane or a car. So you..." she drilled a finger into his chest "...need to pay me."

"And I will when I get the chance," Radd replied.

Brin hauled in a huge breath. "Provided I don't have to join or interact with the wedding party, and if I can stay in the background, then I'll stay."

Radd worked hard to keep his expression inscrutable, to stop himself from doing an air pump. "Good." No, it was damned excellent.

Brin gestured to the bush beyond their car. "Do you think we can go back? I'm really tired and would love a nap." She sent him a mischievous grin that tightened his pants and ignited flames in his stomach. "And, seeing that I'm now your guest, I'd like that crab, lobster and truffle omelet."

Radd grinned and accelerated away. When she forgot to be insecure, Ms. Riddell could be quite bossy. He rather liked it.

CHAPTER SIX

LATER THAT EVENING, Brin walked from the dining area of the main lodge onto its expansive deck and plopped down on one of the wide two-person loungers, kicking off her shoes to swing her bare feet up onto the cushion. Leaning back, she tipped her head up, sighing at the swish of stars making up the Milky Way.

"I can't get enough of this sky."

"It's pretty impressive," Radd agreed. Brin pulled her eyes away from the sky to watch him gracefully walk across the deck, holding a bottle of red wine and two glasses. Stopping next to her lounger, he dashed wine into the glasses while kicking off his flip-flops. He'd pulled on a light, hooded sweatshirt to counter the slight chill in the air but still wore the cargo shorts he'd changed into after their game drive earlier that morning.

"Shift over," Radd told her and dropped down into the space she created. His shoulder pressed into hers, his thigh lay alongside hers, and Brin felt like he'd plugged her into an electric substation. He was so big, so solid, so very masculine...

Untamed and a little intimidating, like the land he so loved.

Radd handed her a glass of red wine and Brin placed it on the floor next to her, in easy reach. He placed his arm behind his head, sighed and look upwards, and Brin could almost feel the tension leaving his body.

Radd relaxing had happened in increments all day, a sigh here, a roll of the shoulders there. Kagiso was good for him, Brin decided. No, Kagiso was great for him.

"It's not often I'm here on my own, and I forget how much I love it when it's empty," Radd said, his soft words echoing her thoughts.

"Except that you are not alone, I'm here," Brin pointed out.

"But you're surprisingly restful company, Brinley Riddell." Radd turned his head to look at her and his small smile made her stomach flip over. And over again. "You don't feel the need to fill silences with chatter, you're happy to be quiet. That's pretty unusual. Why is that?"

Brin lifted her wineglass and took a sip. "Probably because I have a sister who dominates every conversation and a mother who encourages her."

"And your dad?"

"Stepdad," Brin corrected him. "He's sweet but quiet. He's been in my life since I was a three, but we've never really bonded, I guess."

Brin felt his eyes on her face but didn't look at him, choosing instead to track a satellite moving across the sky. "Why not?"

"Because my mom fell pregnant with my sister and, from that moment on, it became all about her," Brin admitted. "I was never in any doubt about who their favorite child was."

Radd didn't respond and Brin appreciated his silence, there was nothing worse than trite sympathy. Not that she believed Radd could, or would, be trite but...still.

"If it makes you feel any better, my parents didn't have favorites. They disliked us all equally."

Brin rolled onto her side, resting her head in her hand. The amazing sky couldn't compete with this fascinating man. "Why do you think they had kids if they were so uninterested in being parents?"

A cynical smile touched Radd's mouth. "That might be because my great-grandfather, my father's grandfather, set up a trust fund in the fifties, when the Tempest-Vanes were seriously rolling in cash—"

"As opposed to how poor you are now," Brin interjected, her tongue literally in her cheek.

Radd's chuckle at her quip warmed her. "Brat. But I'm talking about family money, not what Dig and I made since my parents lost everything." Radd lifted his wineglass, took a sip and placed it back on the floor. "Anyway, my father was the only T-V descendant—Great-Grandfather's other son died in his teens and his daughter didn't marry or have kids—so it was up to my father to restock the family tree. Great-Grandfather told my father that he'd give him two million for every male child they produced."

Brin wasn't sure how to respond to that blatant, old-fashioned misogyny and finally settled on: "Nice of you lot to cooperate and be male."

Radd's chuckle danced over her skin. "The first and only thing we did right," he said, and his lack of emotion saddened Brin.

She risked putting her hand on his chest, somewhere in the region of his heart. "Scale of one to ten…how bad was it?"

Radd's chest lifted and fell in a jerky movement, and then his hand clasped hers, pushing her flat palm against his chest. "Honestly, about a five. I mean, we weren't beaten or neglected, we had everything we needed. We went to an expensive boarding school and we were happy there. We spent a lot of time here at Kagiso. As long as we were together, we were okay. And Jack was five years older, so he stood between the parents and us."

Brin shifted down and placed her head against Radd's shoulder, happy to hold his hand in the moonlight. "And then he died. How?"

"Brain aneurysm," Radd replied. "It was a shock."

Now that was the understatement of the year, because Brin could see the devastation in his eyes. "I'm sure it was. And around the same time, you divorced your parents."

"Divorce... That's a good way to put it," Radd mused. His hand tightened and Brin winced, but didn't pull away. Whatever he was thinking about was painful, and she knew the wound was still raw.

"Did you sell their art and car collections?"

Radd shook his head. "Everything they owned, including their property and cash, and two massive life insurance policies, was put into a trust. Neither of us is a trustee or a beneficiary."

Brin frowned. "Who is?"

"That's the question. We don't know, we can't find out and frankly, we don't much care."

She thought he did, a little. But something in his voice had her cocking her head, questioning. "Why do I think you know more about that than you are saying?"

Brin smiled at his shock. "How the hell do you know that?" he demanded.

She shrugged. "Just a guess. Can you tell me?"

Radd hesitated. "I have no proof, but I suspect the person he wanted us to meet and the beneficiary of that trust is the same person."

"Could be," Brin agreed. "But it would be hell to prove."

"Yep."

"Look, I know your parents were…unconventional, but can you tell me what caused you to divorce them? Can you trust me with that information or is it too personal?"

"Jesus, Brin, that's a hell of a question."

The night wrapped them in its soft embrace and Brin couldn't help dropping a kiss on his shoulder, hoping, in a small way, to give him an anchor while horrible memories battered him from every side. Because she did not doubt that, whatever it was that caused that final break, it had to be truly horrible.

Radd eventually started to speak, and Brin held her breath. "Digby and I were used to being teased about their antics, about their rock-and-roll lifestyle. We learned to either ignore it, roll with it or mock it. It helped that we were popular at school and good sportsmen. But, God, the stories never stopped. It felt like every week something about them hit the headlines…"

It hadn't been that bad but, to their kids, it must have seemed like it.

"We genuinely believed that the press just reported on the stories but, at Jack's funeral, we realized Gil and Zia had an unholy pact with the tabloids, and they were the source of most of the exposés. They loved the attention."

Brin winced.

"Jack died and photographs of his funeral—Digby and I insisted that it was to be a small, very intimate and very private affair—were leaked to the paparazzi, and we lost it. We were livid. We quickly worked out that our parents were the only people who could've given the photos to the press and when we confronted them, they confirmed it."

Brin blinked away her tears and wished she could dig his parents up and, well, *punch* them. She wasn't a violent person, but she'd happily step into the ring with Radd's parents. She couldn't believe they thought it was okay to profit off their oldest son's death…

"After that, we didn't have any contact with them," Radd concluded on a small shrug.

Brin buried her face against the ball of his shoulder, her body shaking with anger. Her mother wouldn't win any prizes in the "best mommy" competition but, compared to Radd's parents, she was a saint. Her heart ached for the two boys who raised themselves.

Brin felt Radd pull away from her and, when his hand cupped her cheek, she opened her eyes to find his face inches from hers, his expression concerned. His thumb swiped her cheekbone and his breath caressed her cheek. "Are you okay?"

Brin shook her head. "No, I'm so damn angry I want to clout something!" Brin retorted.

"Why are you… *Oh.* You're angry for me?"

Why did he sound so bemused, like that wasn't possible? Brin sat up, pushed her hair and slapped her arms over her chest. "No, I'm not angry, I'm livid. What was wrong with them? How dare they do that? Are you freaking *kidding* me? That is insane and horrible and—"

Radd shoved a glass of wine into her hand. "Sip." Brin took a large gulp and sighed when the soft, complex liquid slid down her throat.

"And, while I appreciate your reaction, it all happened a long time ago," he added.

"Still…"

Brin sucked in a deep breath and, knowing that she needed to lighten the atmosphere, that they were wading into deep, dark emotional waters—a place she couldn't afford to visit and if she did, couldn't stay long—she dredged up a teasing smile. "You're thirty-six. Damn, you're old."

Radd's eyes narrowed at her, but she caught the flash of relief, in his eyes. They'd gone too deep, too fast, and he wanted to swim back to shore. "Who are you calling old, wretch?"

"You."

"You do know that there is a pool about six feet from us and I can drop you in it?" Radd threatened.

"You wouldn't dare…"

Brin squealed when, in one fluid movement, he stood up and lifted her up against his chest, without, she had to admit, any strain at all. Radd walked her over to the pool and swung her away from his body.

"Radd, no!" Brin really didn't want to go for a swim in that still, cold water. She released a wild laugh and tightened her grip around his neck. "My hair takes forever to dry, it's too cold and I'm sorry I called you old!"

Radd's fingers dug into her ribs and she squirmed as he tickled her. "How sorry are you?" he demanded, a huge smile making him look ten years younger.

"Very." Brin's eyes connected with his and his arms tightened, pulling her tighter to his chest. *He is so warm*, Brin thought, *so strong*. Brin saw his eyes leave hers to look at her mouth and, when their eyes reconnected, she saw that desire, hot and heavy, had replaced his amusement.

"You are so damn beautiful," he rasped.

Brin knew that he was going to kiss her and that she was going to let him. How could she resist? And why should she? A sexy man held her in his arms, the night was stunning and they were alone…

"Children, it's good to see you playing nicely but, Radd, I need to talk to you."

Okay, so not alone.

Brin slid down Radd's body and, when her feet touched the ground, she turned to see Mari standing at the entrance to the lodge, looking stressed. Radd took a step away from her, ran his hand over his jaw and nodded. But Brin heard his low, under-the-breath curse at Mari's timing.

Yep, it sucked.

Radd walked over to the lounger, picked up the bottle of wine and the glasses, and placed them on the closest wrought iron table. "Come on over, Mari. And bring a glass for some wine."

When Mari turned away, he handed Brin her glass and she shuddered when his fingers brushed hers. She lifted her glass in a toast, her hand trembling. "Thanks for not dropping me in the pool, old man."

Radd's hand shot out, gripped the back of her neck to pull her closer and his mouth, hot, hard and insistent, swiped over hers. A second, maybe two later, he lifted his head and his eyes glittered with frustration, lust and a healthy dose of humor. "Oh, I still can. And before the week is out, I probably will."

Brin had the feeling that he wasn't only talking about an unscheduled dip.

Brin watched as Radd flipped on the outside lights and the atmosphere on the veranda changed from sensual to sensible. Slipping on her flip-flops, Brin started to excuse herself but, before she could, Radd waved her to a chair.

Radd leaned against the railing behind Brin, his wineglass resting against his bicep. "What's the problem, Mari?"

Mari crossed her elegant legs, hauled in a deep breath and tried to smile. "Apparently your guests will be here for breakfast, not afternoon tea."

Radd frowned. "Okay, that's not a huge problem, is it?"

Mari's deep brown eyes reflected her frustration. "No, that's easily handled."

Radd moved to take a seat next to Brin, and Radd placed his hand on her arm. "Ready for dinner?"

As if she could think of food when he was touching her. Sparks ran up and down her arm and warmth settled in her stomach and between her legs. Really, her reaction to him was instantaneous and inconvenient.

"I still need a little more of your time, Radd. Sorry, Brin."

"Do you want me to leave?" Brin asked.

Mari smiled at her. "That's not necessary."

Radd stroked her arm before lifting his hand off her skin. He placed his forearms on the table, his focus shifting to Mari. Mari started to run through the coming week, the guests and their preferences. Brin was impressed by their no-notes discussion, both owner and manager had all the facts at their fingertips.

Brin admired Mari's ability to answer Radd's rapid questions, but she was very impressed by Radd's insightful and detailed questions.

He deep dived into the operation, and Brin's eyes bounced from Mari's delicate features to Radd's masculine face, frequently losing track of what they were discussing.

She'd expected Radd to only have a surface-based

knowledge of Kagiso. He was, after all, the not-here-that-often owner, and he had many fingers in many business pies. But Radd could, at a moment's notice, drop into Mari's position and run the lodge with precision and assurance.

Radd caught her stare and a small frown creased his eyebrows. "Why are you looking at me like that?"

Brin lifted one shoulder, a little embarrassed to be caught out. "Um, I'm just impressed at how much you know about the day-to-day running of the lodge."

"It is my lodge," Radd pointed out.

"I know but I thought, because you own so many other businesses, that you'd oversee the place and leave the details to your management team," Brin said.

Mari laughed, her eyes dancing. "Radd is a control freak, Brin. Actually, I'm surprised that he didn't spend the night looking over your shoulder, telling you where to put each individual flower in your arrangements."

"I'm not that bad," Radd protested.

"Yeah, you are," Marri told him, patting his hand affectionately. She smiled at Brin. "Even as a kid, he was incredibly bossy. The only person Radd ever listened to was Jack."

Brin placed her chin in the palm of her hand, watching the interaction between the two. That they knew each other well wasn't in dispute, and Brin was both glad and sad—weird to be both at the same time—that her instincts about Radd's controlling personality were spot-on. Glad because who didn't want to be right, and sad because, well, if there was a man she could see herself becoming entangled with then Radd Tempest-Vane was right at the top of that list.

Attraction played a huge part, but she also liked the man, which was unexpected. Then again, she occasionally liked her mom and sister, too. But they were, in their entirety, bad for her. Radd would be, as well.

While she enjoyed their conversation earlier, loved seeing a glimpse of the real man behind the ruthless veneer he wore, she wasn't under any illusions it *meant* anything. Radd wasn't looking for anything permanent, neither was she.

But, while resisting Rich Radd, the implacable billionaire, was easy, she was crazy attracted to the flawed, sexy, sweet man she'd glimpsed earlier. Resisting that Radd was going to be as hard as hell.

But that wasn't who Radd was all the time; Real Radd was hard, tough and uncompromising. Real Radd would overwhelm and dilute her...

"Oh, and they've added an extra person to the party," Mari added.

Radd's frown pulled Brin's attention back to the conversation. "What?"

Mari rolled her expressive eyes. "One of the bridesmaids changed her plans and Mrs. Radebe is demanding we accommodate her."

Radd pinched the bridge of his nose and muttered a harsh curse. "These people are going to drive me insane."

Brin caught the flash of uncertainty that flashed across Mari's face. "An additional guest is going to require an additional room. With Brinley in a villa, we're short of beds."

Right, the universe was trying to send Brin a message. She needed to go back to Cape Town, needed to leave Kagiso and remove herself from Radd's orbit. It would've been lovely to spend the balance of the week enjoying the six-star resort, but if Mari needed the space for paying guests, she'd have to vacate. Radd would have to find a way to return her to the city now.

And again, she felt both glad and sad.

Radd stared at her, his eyes boring into hers. In those inky eyes, she saw a variety of emotions, most of which she couldn't identify. He seemed to be weighing his options, turning over possibilities, looking for pros and cons.

"There's Digby's villa."

Radd shook his head. "No, Mari, out of the question. When we established the lodge, Dig and I agreed that we'd never hire our personal residences to guests. That's his personal space and it's not happening." Radd turned to Brin. "Digby's villa is next to mine." A barely there, almost satisfied smile touched the corners of Radd's lips, and Brin frowned, wondering what he was up to. "Brin can move into my villa."

Uh, *really*? "And where will you sleep?" she demanded. Radd's smile deepened and his eyes heated. Brin, seeing the answer in his eyes—*with you, obviously*—quickly shook her head. "That's not a good idea."

Before Radd could reply, Mari pushed her chair back and quietly excused herself. Brin, not wanting to break eye contact with Radd, didn't acknowledge her leaving and neither, Brin noticed, did her boss.

"I'm not sleeping with you, Radd," Brin told him, annoyed that her voice sounded a little shaky. And not very assertive.

Radd nodded. "Okay."

Brin didn't trust his immediate agreement. "Look, I'm adult enough to realize that we are hectically attracted to each other, but I'm not the type to fall into bed with hot billionaires."

"Okay."

"Stop saying that!" Brin snapped.

Radd leaned back in his chair, stretched out his legs and linked his hands on his flat stomach, looking supremely relaxed. "What do you think is going to happen if you move into my villa, Brin?"

"We're two unattached, single people who are attracted to each other," Brin replied, annoyed. "What the hell do you think is going to happen? Do you think we'll spend all our time playing tiddlywinks? We'll end up having sex."

"Do you want to have sex with me?"

How could he sound so relaxed, like they were discussing the weather? "I'm not answering that question."

"So, that's a yes, then."

"It's not a yes!" Brin snapped.

"Then it's a no?"

Brin refused to look at him, wanting to lie but unable to. So she kept quiet, hoping for a hole to open up and suck her into another vortex, a different paradigm. She waited, but nothing happened and she eventually, what seemed like years later, looked at Radd.

He still looked relaxed and worse, amused.

"You are so damn annoying." Brin pushed her curls back off her face and cupped her hand behind her neck, feeling out of her depth and a little emotional. God, at times like these she wished she were more like Kerry, sophisticated and cool, able to give as good as she got.

People like Radd and her sister could run rings around her without moving at all.

The amusement faded from Radd's eyes and his expression turned serious. "You're seriously upset about this."

Well, yes. She didn't like feeling as though she was the ditsy hen and he the sly fox.

Radd sat up straight, leaned forward and placed his hand on her knee. "Look at me, Brinley." Radd waited for her to meet his eyes before speaking again. "I don't want you to leave Kagiso, not yet. And yes, we need your room and a solution is for you to move in with me. But that's all I'm asking you to do."

"But—" Brin waved a hand between them "—you know."

"Do I want to sleep with you? Hell, yes. Does your moving into my place guarantee that's going to happen? Hell, no." Radd tapped his finger on her knee when her eyes slid away. "Keep looking at me, Brinley. You're in control here, you're calling the shots. Would I like to see, taste and have you? Sure, I would. You're a gorgeous woman and making love to you would be a privilege. But that's your decision, always. If you're not interested or not ready, I get it, and I'll either sleep on the couch or in the hammock on the veranda."

"You will?"

Radd looked annoyed at her questioning his motives. "I'm hard-assed and demanding. I'm abrupt and reticent, but I don't force, coerce or bully women into sleeping with me." Radd ran his fingers through his hair. "But if you don't feel comfortable, if you don't trust me enough, then I'll make a call and hire a plane to get you home by nightfall."

If he'd tried to persuade her, if he'd brushed off her concerns or dismissed them out of hand, then Brin would've taken him up on his offer to get her home, but because he did neither, because she instinctively trusted his integrity, she glanced down and stroked her finger over the raised veins in his broad, masculine hand.

"You must think I am desperately naive and old-fashioned," Brin quietly commented.

Radd took a moment to answer her. "I think you are refreshing and out of the ordinary. I don't often invite people to share my personal space, Brinley. Neither do I talk about my past, but I like talking to you. I like you. And if all I can get is your company, then I'll take it."

Was he being sarcastic? Was he just saying that to get his own way? To manipulate her into doing what he wanted her to do?

Brin looked into his eyes, steady and strong, and the honesty reflected in those inky blue depths reassured her. She allowed her suspicions to drain away. She believed him but, more than that, she trusted him. Trusted him to keep his word, to not push her, to respect her boundaries.

Boundaries that were, let's be honest, not that solid, barriers that could easily be decimated.

"You'll sleep on the couch or in the hammock?"

"I will." Then Radd smiled and her heart flipped over. "Unless you invite me to share *my* bed."

Radd stood up abruptly and held out his hand for her to take. "I'll get Chef to deliver our dinner, and your luggage, to my villa. We can eat on the deck, it overlooks a watering hole."

He was too self-confident by half, a little presumptuous and a lot arrogant, but that didn't stop Brin from sliding her hand into his and allowing him to lead her out of the dining room.

The next morning, Radd looked around his private villa, thinking that this open-plan space had always been his refuge, the one place he felt utterly at home.

He'd personally designed the spacious two-roomed, open-plan villa and some of his most treasured pieces of furniture had ended up here. In the corner sat his grand-

father's desk, above it on the wall were family photographs from the original farmhouse, demolished shortly
after the new owners took possession of the property.

The enormous bed came from Le Bussy, the wine
farm in Paarl, brought over by the first Tempest-Vane
to arrive on the subcontinent.

There were antique fishing rods on another wall, all
used by generations of Tempest-Vanes, and the four-
seater sofa and its two matching wingback chairs,
restuffed and recovered, were all old but supremely
comfortable. Beyond the bedroom was a massive bathroom, complete with a slipper bath and his and hers ba-
sins. Floor-to-ceiling doors opened up onto an outdoor
shower and Radd loved nothing more than to stand beneath the hard spray, looking up into the branches of
an ancient shepherd tree shielding the villa from the
harsh African sun. There was something incredibly
sexy and primal about showering outside, especially at
night when the stars hung so low he felt he could pluck
them from the sky and hold them in his hand.

He could easily imagine standing in that space with
a naked Brin, licking droplets of water off her breasts,
her flat stomach, running his hands down her long legs,
tipping her head back to suckle on her elegant neck...

God, he couldn't think about her like that, naked,
while she lay on his bed, gently sleeping.

Radd tipped his face up to the sun, enjoying the still
pleasant heat, and whipped off his T-shirt, enjoying the
prickles of sunshine on his shoulders and back.

God, he loved Kagiso.

This was the place where he recharged his batteries,
where he could spend hours looking over his land or at
the water hole, completely content to while away the

hours on his own, watching the light change and the animals wandering into his line of sight.

Kagiso, particularly this villa—with its wide veranda, comfortable seating, a telescope and a plunge pool—was the place he ran to when life became a little too real, a bit harsh, the demands of business overwhelming.

Here, on his own, he could breathe, he could relax, he could simply be.

This space was his bolt hole and, to an extent, sacred. It wasn't a space he shared, not even with Digby, as close as they were.

Radd stood at the railing of the veranda and turned his back on the water hole to look into the room, past the lounge area to the massive bed, draped in mosquito netting against a stone wall. Brin lay on her side, her hands under her cheek, deep in sleep.

God, she was beautiful. Fresh, lovely, unusual. And she was in his space, in this place that he regarded at his little piece of paradise.

Radd watched her sleep for another minute or two before forcing himself to pull his eyes off her delicate profile, to stop himself from tracing the curve of her lips, the arch of her cheekbones, from counting the number of freckles on her nose and cheeks.

She was unlike anyone he'd ever met before, feminine and strong, yet curiously vulnerable and more than a little sweet.

He wasn't normally attracted to sweet woman, to vulnerable innocents. He didn't have the time and energy to dance around them, to watch his words, to reign in his forthright observations or to measure his words. Yet, despite her softness, he didn't feel the need to censure himself around Brinley, she'd proved that she could handle him at his most irritable and demanding.

He admired her pride, the fact that she was not intimidated by his wealth, success or power. He enjoyed her sly sense of humor and was constantly surprised that she seemed to get him. She was unlike any woman he'd encountered before.

And last night he'd opened up to her, told her things about his past and family he'd never discussed with anyone but Digby. And he was *not* okay with that.

What the hell had he been thinking?

Nobody but the two brothers knew that Gil and Zia left all their worldly assets to a trust, that they'd sold photographs from Jack's funeral to the press. And, because he'd been seduced by a sweet-smelling woman and a warm, star-filled night, there was always a chance that tomorrow, or the day after, or next week, or next month, these nuggets of information could land in the gossip columns, as another episode in the Tempest-Vane saga.

Radd felt the cold fringes of panic claw up his throat and his fingers curled around the railing, slowly turning white. He didn't think Brin would go to the press, didn't think she was the type, but he should not have taken the chance. What the hell had he been thinking?

Dammit. He should've got her to sign a nondisclosure agreement...

Yeah, fantastic plan, Tempest-Vane. She'd take that well. Not.

Radd tipped his head up to the sky, wishing he wasn't so distrustful, so god-awful cynical. But his employing her, and his attraction to her, had happened so damn fast he was still trying to catch up.

The only thing he could do, what he would do, was to keep his mouth shut from this point onwards.

Radd rested his arms on the railing of the balcony and stared down at the water below him, uncomfortable with his mental ramblings, his deep dive into his psyche. He had to reign this emotion in, go back into his cool cocoon where little touched him. He was here, at Kagiso, to get Vincent Radebe to sign the final papers that would give them ownership of the mine and, when that was done, they'd launch the PR and rebranding campaign.

He had to stick to things he could control and Brinley Riddell, with her light eyes and soft curls, was not on that list.

He'd best remember that.

CHAPTER SEVEN

Brin, sitting at the dining table on the deck of Radd's villa, her bare feet up on the railing and a coffee cup in her hand, turned at the sound of the door opening. Her heart picked up speed, as it always did when it was in the same room as Radd, and she whipped around to see him walking into the villa, tossing his hat onto the king-size bed.

Today he was dressed in the bottle green polo shirt all the game rangers wore, khaki shorts and boots, and he looked as wild and as tough as the land stretched below them.

Radd caught her eyes, smiled and her stomach joined her heart's around-her-body race. "Morning."

"Hi, how was your game drive? See anything interesting?"

Radd took the seat opposite her, leaned across the table and snagged a piece of her jam smeared croissant. He chewed, swallowed and took the coffee cup from her hand and drained the contents before handing her empty cup back.

She lifted her eyebrows at him.

"Relax, fresh coffee, croissants and fruit are on its way," Radd told her, bending down to unlace his boots. "The drive through the park was awesome, you should've come with us."

"There wasn't space," Brin reminded him. The wedding party filled every seat in the vehicle, and Naledi and her friends weren't the type of people she'd get up before dawn to spend time with. She couldn't complain though, Radd had taken her for a drive on both Monday and last night, Tuesday, leaving his game rangers to look after the guests.

"I like it when we're on our own," Brin quietly admitted.

"Me, too," Radd softly replied.

Brin turned her head to look at him and her breath caught in her throat at the desire blazing in his eyes. His hair was ruffled, his jaw thick with stubble and as sexy as sin. Brin felt a tremble roll through her and she couldn't help licking her lips, wishing his was covering hers, his tongue in her mouth, his hand pushing her thighs apart.

Oh, God, she wanted him, here in the sunlight at just past eight in the morning…

And, judging by his clenched fist resting on the table and the flush on his cheekbones, he wanted her, too. Brin looked from him to the daybed where Radd slept, hanging from chains in the corner of the veranda. It was big enough for an orgy—hammock, her ass—and she wondered if she was brave enough to say something, anything, to get him to join her on that wide surface.

Are you ready for that, Brin Riddell? Ready for a hot affair that would end the day after next, when they returned to Cape Town? She didn't know, she wasn't sure…

Brin pulled her eyes off him and searched for something to say to break the tension. "Did you see anything interesting?" she asked.

Radd ate another piece of her croissant before attacking his other boot. "A leopard, a pangolin, a herd of elephants."

Nice. "I've never seen a pangolin."

"They are pretty rare," Radd said, sitting up and, copying her, put his bare feet up on the railing. "They are the most traded animals in the world and are highly, highly endangered. I tried to explain that to the bride and her maids, but they weren't that interested. They spent most of the drive talking about the hen party and getting slammed in Ibiza."

Brin wrinkled her nose. Torture.

Radd rolled his eyes. "One of them even asked me who did the landscaping at Kagiso?"

"At the lodge?"

Radd shook his head and nodded to the savanna. "Out there."

Brin laughed and shook her head. "Dear God, far too much money and not enough sense."

"Then they had the bright idea of doing a group shot on the edge of the dam. It took me ten minutes to persuade them that the dam was home to a ten-foot crocodile known as Big Daddy."

"Is that true?" Brin asked.

"No, but there is a resident pod of hippos in the dam who don't like being disturbed."

"And hippos kill a lot of people in Africa," Brin replied.

Radd sent her an admiring glance, his dark eyes warm. "You've been reading up."

Brin shrugged, knowing that her cheeks were probably pink from his praise. "I love it here, I'm fascinated. Though it would be amazing to be here without…"

Brin stop speaking, not wanting to say anything negative about his guests. Radd finished her sentence for her. "Without the wedding party? Not your type of people?"

Not at all. "I'm sure they are very nice when you get to know them," Brin diplomatically replied.

"But you wouldn't bet your life on it," Radd told her, laughing. "Honey, your lips say one thing, but your eyes tell the truth. They aren't windows to your soul, they are six-foot-high billboards. And, even if I couldn't read your eyes, your total avoidance of the wedding party would be a damn big clue that you don't like them. Why, is it because they are rich?"

"I'm not that shallow," Brin replied, not happy that he could read her so well.

"No, you're not. Neither are you a snob or quick to judge, so I'm curious as to why you have made up your mind about Naledi and company so quickly. In fact, even before they arrived…"

Brin heard the knock on the door and thanked God and all his angels and archangels for the distraction. Someone above was looking after her because Radd's questions were coming a little too close for comfort. Radd stood up and walked into the villa, and Brin released a relieved sigh. She heard his low murmur of thanks and he soon returned holding a tray, which he placed on the table between them. A full carafe of coffee, a huge bowl of fruit salad, fresh croissants and fig jam. But, instead of resuming his seat, Radd pulled off his shirt and Brin sucked in her breath at his broad chest, lightly covered with hair, his ridged stomach, the hint of hip muscles sliding beneath the band of his shorts.

He stood with his back to her, looking past the water hole to the savanna beyond, and Brin looked her fill, taking in the way the early morning sunlight bounced off his dark hair. She longed to run her hands over his broad shoulders, kiss the bumps of his spine and discover whether his butt was really as firm as it looked. She wanted to take a bite out of his thick biceps, feel if the hair on his legs was as crisp as she imagined.

He'd been a perfect gentleman and, honestly, she was over it. She wanted to enjoy that amazing outdoor shower, share that slipper bath, drop into that plunge pool naked...with him.

She wanted his mouth on hers, his hands skating over her body, her thighs parting...

As if he could hear her thoughts, Radd turned and his eyes slammed into hers. His hands, gripping the railing behind him, turned white and, as a band of heat warmed her from the inside out, she felt her nipples contract.

Radd's eyes dropped to her chest and before her eyes, she saw him swell, his erection tenting the fabric of his cotton shorts.

He wanted her.

She wanted him.

But Radd didn't move. His eyes just burned and a muscle in his cheek danced. "If I kiss you, there's no going back, Brinley," Radd growled the words, his low tone saturated with emotion.

Brin swallowed and nodded.

"Say the words, Brinley. Know what you are asking."

Brinley gathered her courage and forced her brain to form the words, to verbalize what she wanted. He was right, there was no going back from this.

"I want you, I'd like...you know." Brin floundered, heat flooding her face. But she wouldn't look away, she refused to feel embarrassed about wanting Radd. She was an adult, unattached, and so was he. They were allowed to do this.

Radd momentarily lifted his hands to cup her face in his hands. "God, you are beautiful."

Brin stared into his eyes as she waited for him to kiss her, enjoying this moment of delayed gratification.

Radd seemed equally happy to draw out the moment, leaning over her but not yet touching her. He simply stared at her and, when the moment became too intense, gratification too difficult to ignore, Brin lifted her hand to touch his jaw, heavy with stubble. Her thumb drifted over his bottom lip.

"Kiss me, Radd."

Was that her voice, sultry and sexy? It had to be, because Radd's lips curved into a smile and he lowered his head, whispering his response.

"Gladly."

His kiss, long-awaited, was heat and heaven, both decadent and divine. Radd kept his hands on her cheeks, the only contact they had apart from their mouths, knowing that this was enough, right now. In a few minutes, they'd want more but for now, this sweet and sexy exchange was both reassuring and ridiculously raunchy.

At the same time Radd's tongue slipped past her teeth to slide against hers, he easily pulled her to her feet and against his chest. His erection pushed into her stomach and one hand rested on her bottom, acquainting himself with her shape. His other hand skimmed up her side and came to rest on her breast, his thumb sliding across her tight nipple.

Her thoughts hazy, her mind and body focused on what he was doing to her—his lips on her nipple through the material of her vest had her whimpering with delight—and the way her hands skimmed over his body. It took Brin a few moments to realize that the banging she could hear was not her heart but an insistent rap on the door to the villa.

Pulling back, she pulled a strand of her hair from Radd's stubble and cocked her head.

"Come back here," Radd growled, his hand encircling her neck to pull her mouth back to his.

Brin sank back into his kiss, but another hard rap on the door fractured the moment. Radd cursed but his eyes didn't leave hers. "Ignore it," he told her.

"Radd!"

Yep, that was Naledi's voice and she didn't sound happy. Brin stared at Radd and watched as irritation and frustration jumped into his eyes. "What the hell does she want now?"

Another rap, harder this time, told them that she wasn't going away.

"I swear to God I'm going to kill her. And then I will fire the staff member who escorted her down here."

Brin winced at his hard, cold tone and stepped away from him, immediately feeling cold and exposed, and more than a little vulnerable. The moment had been so perfect, would they ever be able to re-create it? Would she ever be this brave again? She wasn't sure.

Radd saw something on her face, because his expression softened and he bent down to skim his lips across hers. "Don't retreat, Brin. Let me just deal with this and I'll be back, okay?"

Radd waited, his deep blue eyes nearly black with need, looking for reassurance that she wouldn't change her mind, that they'd be able to pick up where they left off. She wanted to tell him that they would, but she wasn't sure; Brin didn't know if she could be brave twice.

And Radd knew it.

"One step forward, ten back," Radd muttered, his frustration evident in his snappy sentence.

Another rap on the door resulted in Radd snapping out a harsh "Relax, for God's sake, I'm coming!"

Brin watched as he picked up his shirt and dragged it over his head, his eyes blazing with annoyance and his thinned lips reflecting his displeasure. Brin was glad that she wasn't on the other side of the door, she didn't want to be on the receiving end of his anger.

Brin heard the outside door open and, although she couldn't see the door, and their unwelcome visitors couldn't see into the room, she could still hear the exchange.

"Naledi." Radd's greeting was polite, but anyone with a brain in their head would recognize the annoyance in his voice. "How can I help you?"

"I need an extra room, the bridesmaids sharing the Serengeti have had an argument and need some space, and I understand that you have another villa that is available," Naledi replied. "I need them separated."

"Mari, I assume that you explained to Ms. Radebe that wouldn't be possible?" Radd asked.

"I did."

Brin smiled at Mari's tart response and hoped that the Radebes would leave the staff an enormous tip when they left on Friday. If they didn't, and Brin wasn't convinced they would, she hoped Radd rewarded them for not killing their demanding guests.

"Her job is to cater to our every whim and I do not understand why I am standing here and nothing is happening. She's not a very good manager, and I think you should fire her."

Brin's eyes widened. Okay, there was no way that Radd would stand for that type of talk. Not only was

Mari exceptional at her job, but she and Radd had been friends since they were kids. He'd jump to her defense, any minute now.

Brin waited, and then waited some more. When Radd didn't defend Mari, her heart dropped to her toes. She knew how it felt to be falsely accused, to be blamed for something that wasn't her fault. She'd endured Kerry's unreasonable anger on too many occasions to count and she'd prayed, wished, her mom would stand up for her, just once.

But that never happened.

Even Kerry's making out with her boyfriend had been swept under the rug, dismissed. Her wants, needs or feelings meant nothing. Like Naledi, keeping Kerry happy was all that was important, no matter who it hurt.

Brin mentally begged Radd to stand up to the witch!

"I'm sorry you think that, Naledi."

What? That was it? Come on, Radd, do better!

"The food is mediocre, the service second rate and I'm really not happy with the flowers."

What? Radd told her she'd loved the flowers when she'd arrived! And how dare she criticize Mari's staff when they'd been run off their feet with ridiculous requests. And the food was divine!

"I'm afraid it's not possible for anyone move into the spare villa, Naledi, it's privately owned and isn't part of the lodge," Radd said.

"Well, call the owner and get permission!" Naledi retorted. "Come on, chop, chop!"

Brin felt her temper catch alight. Man, she sounded just like Kerry. What, did these socialites and influencers all go to bitch school?

"It wasn't a suggestion, Radd, I need an extra room. And you, Mari—is that your name?—get your act together. And tell your staff to do the same. I do not want to have another conversation about your lack of attentiveness again."

Radd would say something now, of course he would. He wouldn't let her revolting attitude go unchallenged. When neither Radd nor Mari defended each other or themselves, Brin decided she'd heard enough.

Stomping across the room, she stepped into the narrow hallway and took in the scene before her. Radd stood statue-still, his face a cold, hard mask and Mari's eyes held the fine sheen of tears.

Naledi, dressed in a pair of skin-tight shorts and a tiny top, looked like she was enjoying herself immensely. *It is dangerous,* Brin thought, *but someone has to say something.* Then, *This isn't your fight, retreat now and keep the peace.*

She wanted to, and Brin felt herself take a step back, the tension making her throat close. How many times had she been in Mari's position, desperate for someone to be the voice of reason? To stand up for her, to stand up for what was right?

It would be easy to walk away, she'd done it a hundred, five hundred, times before. Walking away was what she did. And did well.

So walk away then…

She wanted to, she did, but her feet refused to obey her brain's command. *You're not really going to insert yourself into this fight, are you, Brin? It's not your problem and you don't handle confrontation well. You can't, at the best of times, stick up for yourself, remember?*

But she could try, just this once, stick up for Mari and her staff and restore a little balance.

"Good morning, Naledi." She, at least, could aim for a modicum of politeness.

Naledi gave her an up-and-down, not-worth-my-notice look. The last of Brin's hesitation fled and her only thought was…*oh, game on*.

"Did you dump an extra dose of bitch tonic in your coffee this morning, Miss Radebe?" Brin asked her, making sure her voice was loaded with disdain.

"Excuse me?" Naledi spluttered.

"You are acting like a spoiled child," Brin told her, keeping her tone low. She knew, from dealing with her sister, that cutting sentences quietly stated had far more of an effect than loud accusations.

"Brinley, stay out of this," Radd told her, his voice as hard as granite.

Not a chance. Not now that she'd begun, anyway. She ignored Radd's order and held Naledi's dark, dismissive eyes. "Mari and her staff are wonderful and incredibly talented, and you know it. They deserve an apology and, better yet, to be treated like human beings and not your personal slaves. Furthermore…"

"Brinley, enough!"

"Too late, Radd. If you won't stick up for them then I will!" Brin told him, furious at his lack of support for his people. "I know how Mari and her people feel, it's deeply frustrating trying to please people who refuse to be pleased."

Brin's temper was slow to erupt but unstoppable when it did, and she was fast losing control of it. The combination of having her morning of passion interrupted—would that ever happen again?—her disappointment in Radd for not sticking up for his people, and feeling like she'd rolled back six months and was dealing with her sister again was a volatile combination.

Hauling in some air, she sent Naledi a scathing look. "God, if your fans could see you now. You're acting like an entitled, spoiled, complete witch. And here's a fun fact, the world does not revolve around you."

Brin, shaking with anger, jammed her index finger into Radd's bicep. "Seriously, if you cave and open up that private residence, I swear I will never talk to you again."

"Are you going to let her talk to me like that?" Naledi screamed at Radd. "Who does she think she is?"

Brin caught Mari's eye and she lifted her chin in a quick movement that neither Radd nor Naledi caught. But Brin understood her silent message: *Thanks for the support but enough. Now, retreat.*

It was a good plan. Because if she stayed she might be tempted to scratch Naledi's eyes out.

"Let's all calm down, shall we?" Radd said, his voice perfectly cool and even. "Mari, escort Miss Radebe back to her room. Can you send a bottle of champagne, our best vintage, and have the staff squeeze some fresh orange juice for mimosas? And maybe a basket of croissants? I'll catch up in a few minutes."

"Of course," Mari replied.

Brin felt Radd's hands on her waist and she yelped as he easily lifted her and walked her backward into his villa. He kicked the door closed with his foot and backed her up against the wall. Brin looked up into his furious face and dismissed her fear. Radd would not hurt her, physically.

Emotionally, he could rip her apart.

"How dare you interfere in a situation that has nothing to do with you? You have no idea what you are risking!" Radd demanded, his voice coated in anger and disdain. "This is *my* property, *my* business, *my* guests, *my* staff. You are…"

She waited for the "nothing," the "you're not important," but the phrases never left his lips. Instead they hung between them, loud and tangible.

Radd's hands dropped from her shoulders and he shook his head, frustration rolling off his body in waves. "Don't confuse my attraction to you with me giving you permission to meddle in my life, Brinley Riddell. Because that will never, ever happen. Understood?"

Radd waited for her nod before dropping his hands and leaving her, slumped against the wall.

Radd wasn't a fool, he'd seen the disdain in Brin's eyes hours earlier when he didn't defend Mari or his staff. But worse than that was seeing her respect for him fade.

Radd, walking back along the wooden path toward his villa, jammed his hands into the pockets of his shorts, convinced that his head was about to split apart.

Five days ago, if someone had dared to interfere with his business, his decisions or his life, he would've, without hesitation, told them off and immediately broken off their liaison. Thanks to having a reputation of being cold as ice and unemotional, nobody, ever, questioned him. Few people had the strength or the guts, but Brin had simply waded into a battle that wasn't hers to wage.

He was both frustrated and proud of her.

Radd rubbed his hands over his face, irked. Before she dropped into his life, his emotions were tamped down, buttoned-up, kept corralled and constrained. Brin, somehow and strangely, held the key to unlock a myriad of unwanted and unneeded emotions.

But she didn't know, and he couldn't explain, that he was caught between doing what was *right*—yes, he should've defended his staff—and what was *needed*, which was keeping the Radebes happy until the sale agreement for the mine was finalized.

Was the mine and the PR campaign worth it? In a few months, it would be the second anniversary of his parents' deaths. Yeah, sure, some upper-echelon businessmen were still pissed at his father, at deals that went south, money that was lost. But, Jesus, that happened more than twenty years ago...

Did his actions still reflect on him and Digby? Was buying the mine, being manipulated by Vincent, hosting this damn week and the wedding worth all the crap and stress he was dealing with?

For the first time in, well, forever, Radd wasn't sure whether it was. And, God this hurt to admit, was their stupidly expensive PR and marketing campaign just a way to boost his ego, an expensive way to show the world that you *could* get oranges from apple trees?

Would anyone, apart from him and Digby, and the workers at the mine, even care whether there was a new school, better working conditions, an increase in salaries?

Shouldn't that be the norm, not the exception?

Radd rubbed his hands over his face, feeling utterly exhausted. And he still had to deal with Brin, who probably thought he was a weak fool. But she had no idea how much control he'd needed not to tell the spoiled socialite exactly what he thought of her and her asinine demands. That was why he had remained quiet, he'd been trying to control his own temper. Brin hadn't held back and, while he did wish she hadn't jumped into the fray, he couldn't help but admire her for doing so.

Brinley, Radd was starting to believe, was a good person to have in your corner. But he knew that he'd lost that chance...

God, what a mess.

Radd walked into his villa and nodded to the housekeeper, who was smoothing down the cover of his enormous bed.

"Hey, Greta."

"Mr. Radd." Greta smiled at him as she carefully placed a pillow in the center of the bed. "I'll just gather the dirty towels and get out of your way."

"No hurry," Radd told her, moving into the living area. Walking over to the always-open doors leading to his deck, he gripped the top of the frame and looked toward the plunge pool. Brin stood in the clear water, her slim back to him, looking through the rails of the balcony to the water hole below.

A couple of buffalo cows stood at the water's edge and Radd scanned behind them, instantly picking out the rest of the herd standing in the dense bush. In the far distance, a giraffe and her calf ambled across an open patch of savanna. Not knowing how to break the tension between them—he knew that she was aware of his presence—he looked up at the sky, which was that perfect shade of African blue, so thick and heavy he could shove his hand through it.

Radd tried to break the heavy silence. "Let's clear the air, Brinley."

Brin didn't pull her eyes off the water hole. Right, the silent treatment.

Excellent.

Radd dropped his arms, pulled his phone out of his pocket and placed it on the nearest table. Kicking off his flip-flops, he whipped off his shirt and walked over to the plunge pool, dropping into the heated water behind her.

Damn, the water felt good. The best thing—apart from feeling Brin in his arms—that had happened to him this morning. Pushing his wet hair off his face,

Radd joined Brin at the side of the pool, his arms brushing hers, and she immediately pulled away and put six inches between them.

Yeah, getting back in her good graces wasn't going to be easy.

Radd sighed, wondering why it felt so imperative for him to do so. She'd just walked into his life and in a few days she would be out of it, so why did he care so much about what she thought of him? He didn't give a damn about how people viewed him, well, except for Digby and a handful of old, good friends. Women, let's face it, were easy.

But Brin wasn't. Easy, that is, nor was she run-of-the-mill.

She had a backbone he hadn't expected, a fierce temper when roused by injustice. And complete disdain for anyone who used their position and power to intimidate.

He liked that. Hell, he liked her. More than he'd like anyone for a long, long time. And that was very bad news indeed. She had the power, damn her, to be the catalyst for him to change. He didn't want to change, he liked his life the way it was.

"I sent lunch but was told that you didn't eat either," Radd commented.

"I'm sorry to have wasted the food, but I wasn't hungry."

Hell, he didn't care about two plates of food; he wanted to know what was going on in her head. Brin reached for her sunglasses and slid them onto her face, covering her beautiful eyes. Like her conservative, full-piece swimsuit, her lack of eye contact was another barrier to regaining the easy, laidback companionship they'd shared before.

And it had been easy; he enjoyed having her in his

space and appreciated the fact that she didn't need to be entertained. In the time they spent together alone, he felt completely comfortable reading a report or working while she read or dozed. And when they did talk, their conversation flowed. She had a self-deprecating sense of humor he enjoyed, and he found himself laughing at her wry observations. Her love for Kagiso was obvious, and she seemed eager to hear about his life on this farm as a child and tales of his wild Tempest-Vane ancestors, most of whom were eccentric. A few were certifiably nuts.

They'd been comfortable, relaxed and, dare he say it, happy.

Until the ugly scene this morning.

Radd opened his mouth to try to breach the distance between them, but Brin whipping her glasses off her face and tossing them onto the deck had his mouth snapping closed. When her eyes slammed into his, he saw her anger and, wait, was that embarrassment?

"I'm am very sorry I interfered this morning. You're right, it had nothing to do with me and I shouldn't have said anything. I'm sorry if I put you in an uncomfortable position." Brin hauled in a breath and managed, just, to meet his eyes. "I didn't like the way Naledi spoke to Mari and I was upset that you didn't stand up for Mari, for your staff. But you were right, it had absolutely nothing to do with me."

Radd could tell, despite being a man and generally clueless, that she was still properly, deeply upset. He rubbed his stubble-covered jaw, trying to make sense of her extreme reaction. Yes, she and Mari seemed to like each other, but they weren't best friends, so why was she so intent on defending her and his staff?

Making a concerted effort to keep his voice low and

nonaccusatory—he was trying to understand, not start another fight—he asked for more of an explanation.

Brin hesitated before throwing her hands in the air. "You are part of their social group, a member of their elite club! You're as powerful as them, certainly as rich! You should protect and defend those weaker than you, the people you employ!" Brin hauled herself out of the pool in a fluid movement, all long legs and feminine grace.

And damn, she was even more beautiful when she was furious. Radd couldn't resist looking at her firm, high breasts. In the pool, against his shorts, parts of him were rising, too.

Not that she'd appreciate his response…

Brin's eyes dropped down and widened when she saw his evident need for her. She threw up her hands and scowled at him. "Really?"

He shrugged. "I'm a guy, you're wearing next to nothing, and I can't help thinking about what we were doing when we were interrupted earlier."

Brin stomped over to a lounger, snatched up her towel and wrapped it around her torso, hiding her curvy body. Damn.

Radd blew air into his cheeks and pulled himself out of the pool. He walked across the deck to where she stood, water running off him and darkening the planks of the light wooden floor.

"I wasn't meaning to make light of your anger, but you're an incredibly sexy woman, a woman I want."

"That ship has sailed."

"I gathered that." Radd folded his arms across his chest and looked for words to regain some lost ground, preferably without having to explain why keeping the Radebes happy was so very important to him. She knew the basics, the surface stuff, but he couldn't find the words to explain the PR campaign, rebranding their name, putting his parent's ugly legacy to rest. Rebuilding a legacy they could be proud of...

"I need to keep the Radebes happy. Can we leave it at that?"

"At the risk of alienating your staff, losing their respect? My respect?" Brin's words were as hard and cold as an Arctic wind. "Oh, but wait, our opinions don't matter, because we're not as rich or as powerful or as successful as you."

"I didn't say that!" Radd snapped back, stung.

"But it was what you meant!"

"The hell it was!"

A tide of red crept up Brin's neck and he could see the light of battle in her eyes. Radd knew that he was in for another tongue lashing. He wasn't wrong. And that was okay, he far preferred angry Brin to the subservient creature who'd apologized earlier.

"I know your type. Hell, I worked for people like you, Radd! I was blamed and castigated for things I didn't do, things that weren't my fault and over which I had no control! People like you, like my...like Naledi are entitled and demanding and disrespectful, and why the hell am I arguing with you about this?" Brin pushed her fingers into her hair, pushing away the long, wet curls. "This is ridiculous! Just get me out of here! Take me back to Cape Town!"

Oh, hell no. "Running away, Brin?"

"Just removing myself from your company," Brin replied, turning around and walking into the room. Radd watched her go and, when she stopped suddenly, he looked past her to see Mari standing by the doorway, looking uncomfortable.

"Sorry, I knocked."

His villa was like Grand Central Station today. If another person arrived uninvited, he just might lose it. Radd pulled in a deep breath, then another and tried to hold on to his temper.

"What is it?"

Mari sent him a *Don't mess with me* look. Another female who was mad at him. Wonderful. "I had Simon bring a vehicle over and Chef has packed a basket of food for your dinner and breakfast."

Mari turned her attention to Brin, sending her a sweet smile. "Thank you for sticking up for us, Brin, but it wasn't necessary. We've had worse guests than the Radebe party and we know how to handle them. Mostly it's best if you just let them rant and vent and then do what you intended to do all along. Radd knows this, as do I."

Brin rolled her eyes at Mari's calm statement.

Mari turned her attention back to Radd. "I think you and Brin need a break, and it would be sensible to put some distance between Brin and Naledi right now. She's still demanding an apology from you, Brin."

Radd's "that's not going to happen" coincided with Brin's "I'd rather die."

Mari rubbed her forehead with the tips of her fingers before refocusing her attention back on the pair of them. She was acting as if they were both high-maintenance toddlers. "Guys, that wasn't a suggestion. And I think we could all do with a break."

"I think Cape Town is far enough away," Brin said, her expression stubborn.

"Let's not get carried away, honey," Mari said on a small smile. She turned to Radd. "Take Brin to The Treehouse, Radd. Leave now, while the Radebes are having their afternoon siesta. Your vehicle is parked by the staff quarters and you can avoid the lodge altogether."

Radd nodded, thinking that Mari's suggestion held a lot of merit. Maybe if he and Brin were alone, truly alone, they could recapture some of their earlier ease. And, even if they didn't, they'd give Naledi time to calm the hell down.

And it had been a while since he'd been to The Treehouse.

Pulling a towel out of the pile on the shelf near the door, he swiped the cloth over his chest and rubbed his hair. Mari sent him a *Get this done* look and he gave her a small nod, hoping he could get Brin to agree.

How to do that?

He thought it best to stick to the facts and hopefully, whet her curiosity. "The Treehouse is a secure, completely private and lavish platform above massive boulders. Behind the structure is woodlands, and it's my favorite place for watching the sun rise and set."

Brin's eyes narrowed. "How many beds?"

He couldn't lie. "One. But it's a huge bed and the same rules apply there as here. You've got to ask..."

"Yeah, that didn't work out so well this morning."

"It would've worked out fine if we hadn't been interrupted," Radd muttered, still feeling resentful. He now had to work ten times harder to get back to that place they had been, and Radd wasn't sure if they would get there.

The thought depressed him. And the fact that he could feel depressed, depressed him more.

God, he was losing it.

Radd, irritated with himself and with Brin for not making this situation easier, found his patience slipping. "I'm going to The Treehouse. Come if you want to. If you don't, fine."

Brin took her time making up her mind and Radd forced himself not to display his impatience. This slip of a girl didn't need to know how much she rattled him. And how much he hoped she said yes.

"Does this place have a shower?"

"Solar-powered."

Radd sent Mari a *Help me* look, and she rolled her eyes before speaking. "If the lodge is a six-star establishment, then The Treehouse is a notch above. It's a pretty special place, Brin, and you'll regret not seeing it. It will be worth putting up with his company, I promise you."

Thanks, Mari, Radd thought, narrowing his eyes at his old friend.

"Fine," Brin muttered, stomping inside.

Mari smiled at him. "Prepared to do some groveling, Tempest-Vane?"

The hell he was! He was alpha to his core, groveling wasn't part of his vocabulary. God, he wasn't even good at apologizing! Mari's eyebrows rose higher at his silence and he finally gave in, his shoulders slumping. "I might have to do a little damage control," he reluctantly admitted.

Mari patted his shoulder. "Try not to hurt yourself trying something new, my friend."

Ha-ha, Radd thought, glaring at her departing back.

CHAPTER EIGHT

WHAT WAS SHE doing in this vehicle? Why hadn't she stayed in Radd's villa and given them both some time apart and space to cool down?

Brinley pushed her sunglasses up into her hair and shook her head at her behavior. While she didn't believe she had been completely in the wrong to defend Mari, she shouldn't have jumped feet first into Radd's business. And Mari, smart and independent, didn't seem the type to need defending. But Naledi just pushed every button Brinley had...

And what had she been thinking, allowing her fight with Radd to reignite after she finally had found the courage to apologize? And what was she doing here? Was she just a glutton for punishment?

But the heart of the matter was that, despite the fact she was still irritated with Radd, she didn't want to miss out on one moment she could be with him. She would leave his life the day after tomorrow and, annoyingly, wherever he was, was where she wanted to be.

He was arrogant and irritating and implacable and annoying and sexy and...

Brin shook her head and noticed that Radd was finally, after an hour of driving in silence, slowing down. He braked and switched off the ignition.

"We're here."

All she could see was rocks. Confused, Brinley exited the vehicle at the base of a massive set of boulders towering above her. Pulling her overnight bag over her shoulder, she followed Radd as he stepped onto a walkway made of anchored wooden planks climbing in a zigzag pattern up the rocks. Radd easily carried a huge picnic basket and his own small rucksack. A two-way radio was tucked into the back pocket of his cargo shorts and he had a rifle slung over his shoulder.

Brin turned the corner and looked across the walkway spanning two boulders, and her mouth dropped open. To the left was a rolling carpet of open savanna, dotted by the occasional tree. To the right were more boulders, some of which had tree roots clinging to their mottled surface. Stopping, she pushed her fist into her sternum and looked at the structure in front of her, sophisticated and simple.

At its core, The Treehouse was a wooden deck, encircled with a wire-and-wood railing, thirty feet off the ground. A reed roof covered half of the area and beneath it was an enormous bed dressed in white linen, piled high with pillows and surrounded by a heavy mosquito net, sumptuous and sexy and sensual.

A small table sat in one corner of the deck overlooking the rolling savanna. In the other corner sat a pile of thick, huge cushions, suitable for a sultan's tent. Numerous old-fashioned lamps were placed at strategic intervals along the outside of the deck, providing light when night fell.

Man, it was romantic. All that was missing was an icy bottle of champagne in a silver bucket and blood-red rose petals.

Brin followed Radd across the walkway onto the

main deck and watched as he set the picnic basket down next to the small table. He tossed his rucksack in the general direction of the bed and gripped the railing, shoving his sunglasses onto the top of his head. He scanned the bushveld, and Brin saw the tension ease in his shoulders and the hard line of his jaw soften.

He loved every inch of Kagiso, but this place obviously held a special place in his heart.

Brin dropped her bag onto the bench seat at the end of the bed and, slipping out of her shoes, walked barefoot across the smooth planks to peek behind the screen that formed the headboard of the bed. Her breath hitched again with delight; she'd expected rustic and basic, yet the bathroom was anything but. Instead of a shower, an antique cast-iron slipper bath took pride of place in the center of the space and his and hers sinks covered a reed wall. Pulling open a door made from reeds, she smiled at the private toilet, one of her biggest worries about sleeping in the bush alleviated.

Brin left the bathroom area and walked back toward Radd. By now it was late afternoon and, with the setting sun, the temperature had dropped, too. Rubbing her arms, she sank to sit cross-legged on one of the huge cushions, her eyes bouncing over the incredible landscape.

An eland bull drifted across the savanna and a warthog scampered past him. With the sun setting, the light turned ethereal and magical, a time for fairies and pixies, pure enchantment.

Pity she and Radd weren't currently talking.

She'd expected him to tear strips off her for being rude to Naledi. She kept waiting for the hammer to fall, for him to say something about her behavior, to castigate her for injecting herself into a situation that had nothing to do with her. But hours had passed and he'd said nothing and, maybe, he didn't intend to.

Why? Was he trying to lull her into a false sense of complacency? When she relaxed, would he rant and rave? It was a favorite tactic of Kerry's, which she'd learned at their mom's knee.

"Will you please just tell me that I was out of line earlier so that we can move on?" Brin demanded, frustrated.

Radd handed her a small frown. "But you weren't wrong, I was," Radd said, balancing on his haunches as he inspected the picnic basket. He rested his arm on his thigh as he looked at her. "You were right earlier, Naledi was being a class-A bitch. But I can't afford to piss her, or her father, off. But, you'll be happy to know, I did apologize to Mari, and promised her and the staff a massive bonus when the Radebe party leaves."

Brin's eyes widened at his admission. Really? Wow. For the first time, her angry outburst hadn't been met with derision or payback, sarcasm or delayed mental punishment.

Annoyance crossed Radd's face, but Brin sensed it wasn't directed at her. "Vincent Radebe now owns what used to be a Tempest-Vane mine, one of the most productive diamond mines in the world," Radd said as he stood up, two crystal glasses and a bottle of red wine in his hand. "Over the past ten years, Digby and I have made it a mission to purchase back all the companies that our father inherited and then discarded, including The Vane, Kagiso and other properties and businesses."

"Did you have to buy back the family home and vineyard?" Brin asked, curious.

Radd shook his head. "That was in a separate trust,

and my parents couldn't sell it. It's handed down through the generations from oldest son to oldest son."

"Wow, your ancestors didn't much value girls, did they?"

"Sadly, no."

Brin hadn't expected him to talk and definitely hadn't expected him to open up. Not wanting to stem the flow of words, she wrapped her arms around her bent knees and waited for more. When he didn't speak, she rolled her finger in the air. "You were talking about Vincent…"

"Yeah. Vincent's a canny operator. He quickly sussed out how much we want the mine and made us jump through hoops to get it. He also made us pay over the odds and jerked us around because he lost a pile of money on a deal my father screwed up.

"The mine is productive, well run and profitable, and he wanted to exact a little revenge on Gil through us. We had to work so damn hard to get him to consider selling." Radd dropped down to sit on the cushion opposite her, his navy eyes frustrated. He glanced from her to the picnic basket and waved his glass in its direction. "If you are hungry, there's hummus and red pepper dip and crackers. We're having a cold lobster, crab and prawn salad and crusty bread for dinner, followed by handmade Belgian chocolates."

It sounded delicious, but she was hungry for conversation, for an explanation.

Radd sipped his wine before setting it down next to his cushion and draping his forearms over his bended knees. She could barely remember the well-dressed man in the designer clothes she'd met on that beachfront in Camps Bay, the one driving a super expensive car and looking like a modern-day hero billionaire. This Radd, dressed in an expensive but lightweight cotton shirt and expensive cargo shorts, looked far more disreputable and, in a strange way, more human.

More approachable.

"Vincent tied the purchase of the mine to certain favors he knew I could grant him," Radd explained. "Naledi is his only daughter and she has him firmly wrapped around her little finger. She wanted the biggest, shiniest, brightest, most noteworthy wedding in the country and that meant having it at The Vane. Her wedding at The Vane and a week at Kagiso for the wedding party were sweeteners I had to throw in before Vincent would start negotiations to sell the mine."

Ah, now his pandering to those impossible people made sense. Brin swallowed some more wine before resting the foot of her glass on her knee. "So, when this is over, you'll own the mine?"

Radd nodded. He looked down at his feet, then past her shoulder and then back to his feet. Brin tipped her head to the side, wondering why he was avoiding her gaze.

"There's something else you're not telling me. I mean, you don't have to but…"

He took a long time to answer and, for a minute, Brin didn't think he would. "When we have the mine, we are going to launch a massive PR campaign and rebranding exercise to, hopefully, rehabilitate the family name."

"Because of your parents?"

Radd nodded. "Their reputation is like a bad smell that won't go away." He stared down at the wine in his glass, his expression thoughtful. "Dig and I have worked so damn hard and there are things we want to do, projects we want to explore, but we can't do *everything* alone. And certain business people won't touch us because there's a belief that we are as dishonest as our father, as out of control as both our parents."

"And you think a PR campaign will change that?" Brin asked.

"Maybe not. But it's worth a shot. I also intend on giving some personal interviews explaining our rationale, highlighting our commitment to good governance and community involvement. Make it clear that we are tough negotiators but fair, and that we say what we mean and mean what we say."

Brin couldn't imagine what living with his parents had been like, but it was obvious it had damaged Radd to an extent. She wasn't sure his expensive campaign would change anything, though. She'd begged her sister and mother to change, but nothing she said could sway them. "Sometimes people believe what they believe and always will, Radd. Some minds will never be changed."

"But I still feel the need to try. I need to do it for Jack, for my grandfather, the grandfathers that came before him. They were good men."

"That's a lot of pressure from dead people," Brin pointed out.

"What do you mean?"

Brin shrugged. "I think that if you had to have a conversation with Jack and your grandfather, with all the grandfathers, I'm pretty sure they'd tell you to stop thinking so much and be happy. To stop worrying so much about what people think about you and start living life, on your terms."

Radd looked like she'd slapped him, and Brin cursed her tongue. She waved her words away. "But hell, what do I know? I ran away from a bossy sister and an impossible-to-please mother."

They'd both been hurt by family, sliced and diced by the people who were supposed to love them the most.

"Families can be…" Brin tested the words on her tongue… *Infuriating*? *Annoying*? *Hurtful*? *Soul-destroying*? She settled for "…complicated."

Radd's mouth briefly curled at her understatement. "Tell me about yours. You've given me a little information, but you know far more about me than I do about you."

Brin jerked and hoped he didn't notice. And what could she say, what should she say about her equally messed-up situation? "What do you want to know?" she hedged, desperately racking her mind for a way to distract him.

"Whatever you want to tell me," Radd commented, stretching out his legs and leaning back on his hands. "What do your parents do? Your sister?"

"As I mentioned, my mother raised me as a single mom, then she met and married my stepfather, who is an accountant, and they had another child, my younger sister. I've never met my real dad. My mom helps my sister run her business." There, that was subtle, but still vague.

"In?" Radd persisted.

Ah, damn his curiosity. "Public relations."

Well, being a celebrity, an influencer and sometimes an actor could be called PR, couldn't it?

"You're even more reticent than I am," Radd complained, tipping his head back as Brin climbed to her feet.

Maybe so, but she couldn't tell him that her sister was Naledi's archrival, that if her presence was discovered here, she'd put his plans in jeopardy. No, he most definitely did not need to know that... He'd told her he didn't like secrets, and she was keeping a whopper to herself.

Radd rolled to his feet and came to stand beside her at the railing. Brin could feel his heat, and his sex and sunshine scent made her feel weak at the knees.

"When you went off at me earlier, it sounded like you've had experience being treated badly. Have you?"

Brin chose her words carefully. She wanted to tell him, she *did*, but she didn't want to risk him being angry with her and spoiling the evening. She would tell him, she should, but not now. "My previous boss was difficult. And entitled. Honestly, I was, *am*, surprised I said anything. Normally I keep quiet and accept that status quo."

"Really? What's different about me?"

Because you make me feel like I am standing in a safe zone, a solid barrier between me and the world. Because I feel you might be the one person who gets me. But, while we might be walking this section of the road together, soon our paths will diverge.

"I guess it's because you're not going to be a permanent part of my life."

Brin thought she saw a flicker of hurt in Radd's eyes at her off-the-cuff comment but immediately dismissed the errant thought. Radd didn't feel enough for her to feel hurt. But there was still a part of her that wanted to reassure him, to tell him that, strangely, she felt comfortable expressing her anger and her disappointment to him. She earlier suspected, but now knew, that Radd would never use her feelings or opinions as a weapon, to dismiss or to diminish her.

He might not agree with her but, around him, Brin never felt less than unimportant.

"So what's your big goal, your life quest?" Radd quietly asked her, loosely holding his glass in his big hand.

Brin hesitated, not wanting to spin more threads that would bind her and Radd together, making it more difficult for her to leave. "I just want to be financially secure and to have my own space to stand in, a spot of sunshine that's mine alone."

"And will you get that once I pay you?"

Brin nodded. "In time. In a few months, I'll own my flower-and-coffee shop and, hopefully, in a few years, I'll be able to buy a house, put a little away for a rainy day."

"Hopefully by then you'll also have buried that death trap you call a car," Radd muttered.

Brin smiled at the note of frustration in his voice. He obviously loved cars and Betsy's lack of well, style, class and running ability offended him. But he didn't understand that upgrading her car would mean taking a loan from her sister or mother, and that would be like walking straight back into the spider's web.

It had taken her far too long to disentangle herself to take that risk.

"I just want to be self-sufficient and independent, Radd." Brin quietly stated. "I don't want to have to answer to anyone ever again. I've spent the last couple of months finding myself."

Radd looked pensive. "I've never really understood that expression. I mean, God, you're not a winning Lotto ticket in a coat pocket."

"But I've felt so lost, like I'm a reflection of Ker... of my mother and sister."

"I think whoever you are, the person you *really* are, is there, deep in you. It's just buried beneath all the crap society feeds us, the messages we received as kids, and what the media tells us we should be. Could finding yourself actually mean returning to yourself, to being the 'you' you were before life and people got their hands on you?"

His words slapped her in her soul, in that place deep down inside that no one ever ventured. Man, he got her, understood her on a deep, dark intrinsic level. Despite not knowing everything about the mixed, complicated relationship between her, her sister and her mother, he managed to nail the proverbial nail on the head.

He understood her in a way she needed to be understood. From the moment she met him, she trusted him... She'd jumped into a plane with him, trusted him to pay her the money she was owed, moved into his villa with him.

Had things turned out differently, she would've trusted him with her body. And she might still do that.

Honesty made her admit she was a probably a hair's breadth from falling in love with him—this man who operated in the same world she'd fought so hard to leave—but trust was far harder to find than love.

And, oh, God, Brin hoped he trusted her, too. Because she thought that maybe he did, just a little, she placed her hand on his arm and waited until he looked up and into her eyes. "That's incredibly profound and I appreciate it more than you know. And because you said that, maybe I can say this...?"

"What?" Radd asked when she hesitated, his expression curious.

"Maybe the PR campaign is necessary, from a business point of view," she shrugged. "Obviously I don't know your business, but I do know that you are nothing like your parents and the people who deal with you are fools if they can't see it. It doesn't matter how people see you, Radd, it's how you see yourself. The only way to stop your parents influencing your life is to stop caring, to accept that they made their own choices and that those choices had nothing to do with you."

Radd stared down at his hands, and Brin didn't push him for a response because their conversation was getting so deep, so intense. *But,* Brin thought as she looked up at the stars, *this is the night, and the place for conversations like these.* She wasn't a fool to think that this was the start of something bright and shiny and new, but she did know that they'd impacted each other, that they'd reshaped each other's thinking.

And that, in itself, was incredibly powerful.

After a delicious dinner, and a conversation filled with laughter, Brin sighed. It was almost a perfect evening, but she wanted more. She wanted a night she'd always remember in crystal clear detail, a wonderful memory to give her comfort when she returned to Cape Town and a Radd-free life.

Because a couple of days did not a relationship make.

But it was one thing to make the mental shift to decide to have sex, but *asking* for one night, a step out of time, was something completely different.

Seriously, Brin thought as she stared at Radd's gorgeous profile in the romantic light of the oil lamps, *why can't he read my mind*? It would be so much easier.

But that was his point, wasn't it? He wanted her to make the first move, to take the initiative because then she could never accuse him of pressuring her. But the fear of rejection, something she'd battled with her entire life, kept the words locked firmly between her teeth. Brin tipped her head back to look at the stars, crystals hanging in a pure black sky. It was so quiet, yet, at

the same time, it wasn't. She was used to the sound of
vehicles, the hum of their noisy fridge, barking dogs,
wind in the tree outside her window. The noise of the
bushveld was unlike anything she'd experienced, a di-
chotomy of silence and noise, both at the same time.

It was the sound of the earth and its creatures sighing, sleeping, dreaming. Even if nothing happened between her and Radd tonight—and she hoped to find the
courage soon to ensure it would—it was almost enough
just to sit under the low-hanging sky and listen to the
sounds of the African night.

She heard the rumble, a displacement of air and, because she happened to be looking at Radd at the time,
she saw his attention sharpen, his body tensing.

Brin leaned forward and, needing a connection,
placed her hand on his knee. "What? Is everything
okay?"

A small smile touched Radd's face and he held up
his index finger in a silent request for her to wait. Brin
looked around anxiously.

"Shh, relax. Just listen." Radd slid his fingers between hers, gently squeezing. Brin immediately relaxed;
he'd protect her, she was safe.

Scooting closer to him, Brin placed her temple on the
ball of his shoulder, her thigh aligning with his. Releasing her hand, Radd placed his arm around her back, his
hand curving over her hip. His touch felt right and it felt
real. If she lifted her head, her mouth would meet his...

A deep sound rumbled through the air, sounding as
if it were pulled from the center of the earth and raising the hair on Brin's arms and the back of her neck.
It smacked her soul, the deep roar settling in the pockets of her heart and lungs, and twisting her stomach
inside out.

"That's a big boy," Radd murmured, his voice lazy.

"Lion?" Brin asked, though she knew it couldn't be anything else.

"Mmm…"

How could he sound so relaxed, like he'd just heard the hooting of an owl or the backfiring of a car? "And he's how close?" Brin demanded, her voice a little shaky.

"A couple of kilometers, at least." Brin felt rather than heard Radd's amusement. "And might I remind you that we are thirty feet in the air, and lions can't jump that high?"

He was laughing at her, but his amusement wasn't disparaging or patronizing; it was gentle. And kind.

"Feel free to climb into my lap if you feel scared."

It was an offer she couldn't refuse, a chance she had to take. "Okay."

She felt the muscles in his arms and thigh contract, heard his swift intake of breath. Brin wasn't sure how many minutes, or seconds or years, passed, but then Radd's hand touched her jaw, turning and tipping her face up. His eyes were the color of the sky, his scent as earthy and primal as the African night.

"I'm going to ask this once… Are you sure?"

"Very."

And she was. She wanted *one* night, a perfect night. A night with no expectations but only pleasure, hours of hot hands and wet mouths and for them to pretend that they owned the night.

Radd half turned, and Brin felt his hands on her waist, easily lifting her so that she straddled his thighs. She knew that he was trying to be gentle, but gentle didn't suit this environment or what she wanted. She wanted primal, sensual, hot.

Radd's arms tightened around her bottom and lower back. His eyes dropped to her mouth and his fingers tattooed their way up her spine to clasp the back of her head, to pull it down. Without a word, his mouth slanted over hers and his tongue slid past his teeth. A hot ribbon of lust rippled from her mouth to her breasts, to that secret, dark place at the entrance of her womb. Radd pushed his hand up and under her clothes to learn the shape and feel of her breast. Brin whimpered, twisting Radd's linen shirt in her hand. Nothing mattered but his mouth and his hand and the stone-hard length of him pressed between her thighs.

It wasn't supposed to be this wild, this hot, this quickly. She wasn't experienced, true, but this felt bigger, deeper, darker. Brin lifted her fingers to his jaw and nipped, her tongue making tiny forays into his mouth. She felt Radd's hand slide under her top to unhook her bra and then, as his thumbs slid across her nipples, all hell broke loose.

And Brin welcomed the storm.

Their lips collided and Brin, strangely and uncharacteristically, found herself fighting for dominance of the kiss. Radd yanked her lightweight jersey over her head and, without hesitation, grabbed the hem of her button-down shirt and ripped the fabric apart, scattering buttons in every direction and baring her breasts to his mouth. Time stood still and the earth stopped moving as she bore down on his hard erection, desperate to have him inside her, around her.

Radd lifted his head from her chest and his eyes glittered in the moonlight. "You are so incredibly beautiful."

For the first time in her life she felt beautiful, gorgeous, sensual, a goddess being adored by her mate.

Unable to speak past the lump in her throat, she pulled his shirt up his chest and over his head, throwing it to the floor.

Brin, needing him and, unable to wait, hopped off Radd and shucked her jeans and panties. Barely giving Radd time to shed his own clothes, she climbed back on him, whimpering when her wet core met his heat and hardness.

Sighing, she tucked her face into his neck and inhaled, desperate to use every sense to experience the essence of making love to him, knowing that she'd need to commit this to memory because it was just one time.

The *only* time.

Brin felt the banked tension in his hand as he gripped her thighs, the urgency in his tongue as he looked for, and found, her mouth. She felt him quiver and knew that, with the slightest provocation, he'd spill himself. Needing more, needing everything, she bore down and clenched her internal muscles.

"Brin, we need a condom. I have some in my toiletry bag."

It took a while for his words to make sense, even longer for her to respond. "I'm on the pill and if you are clean…"

"Physical a couple of months ago. No one since," Radd muttered.

"Well, then…"

Radd touched her, expertly and intimately, and Brin released a cry that was part pleasure, all desire. His fingers lifted her up and up and, when she begged him to come inside her, he entered her in a smooth slide. Brin felt a sob build in her throat; he felt so right, the missing piece of her puzzle.

Riding a hot wave of pure sensation, and wanting to

be an active participant in this tsunami-like ride, Brin grabbed his shoulders, swiping her breasts against his chest and seeking his mouth. Brin heard the deep moan in his throat and whimpered as he lifted his hips, burying himself even deeper inside her.

Higher, faster, harder, deeper. Their world receded, and the only question of importance was who was going to come first. Brin whimpered, and Radd shouted as their worlds collided and then exploded. Brin heard his harsh breath in her ear, his hot lips on the cord of her throat. She couldn't tell where he started or she ended, as close as two people could be.

She could stay like this forever, hearts beating in unison, her hands on his back, his holding her hips. She wanted more of this, more of anything he could give her: time, affection, attention.

Love. Love most of all.

Oh, God, no. No, no, no, no, no.

She'd done exactly what she promised herself she wouldn't...

She was so close to falling in love with Radd Tempest-Vane. One more step, a quick slide and she would be there. Brin bit her lip, wondering if she was not confusing great sex with love, an amazing orgasm with affection. She wished she was, because if this was only sex, then walking away would be so much easier. But leaving Radd, carrying on with her life was going to be...well, hard. Different. A little flat and devoid of color.

But she couldn't tell him her feelings, wouldn't let him in on how she felt. Radd insisted on her making the first move to have sex, but Brin wanted him to be the first to breach the subject of feelings and love.

Because while she knew that she was there, or almost there, or something, she had no idea what Radd was thinking or feeling.

And, as she'd learned, people couldn't be forced to give you what you needed, to love you the way you wanted them to....

In the distance, a hyena's mocking laugh pierced the night.

CHAPTER NINE

SEX ISN'T NORMALLY that good, Radd thought as he pulled his vehicle to a stop at the stairs leading up to Kagiso's main reception area. It was a biological function, they were hardwired as humans to want to procreate and to have fun while they did it.

It wasn't supposed to make your soul jump, your heart settle and your stomach tie itself into a complicated knot.

Radd looked at Brin sitting in the passenger seat next to him. Although she was dressed simply, blue jeans and a white T-shirt, her face free of makeup, and her hair pulled back into a sexy tail, she could rival any supermodel. And he should know, since he'd dated a few...

He couldn't wait to take her back to bed.

But sex, great sex, bed-rocking, moon-howling sex, was all they could ever have. He didn't believe in love, commitment or happily-ever-afters; they were a myth, a fairy tale. He wasn't interested in being anyone's husband or significant other.

But if there ever was a woman who could change his mind, Brin would be that person. She was refreshing and without artifice, unimpressed with his wealth, success or looks. She looked past all of that and saw him, saw the man beneath the Tempest-Vane surface. When he was feeling mushy—*vulnerable* was a word he refused to use—he could imagine laying all his fears, and dreams, at her feet, knowing that she wouldn't trample on either.

But that was impossible; he wouldn't see her again after he delivered her to her house tomorrow. He'd kiss her goodbye and walk away and return to the real world. In time, he'd start thinking of her as just another passing ship in the night.

But the thought of never seeing her again sent his stomach plunging to his toes, quickly followed by waves of anger and frustration. He shouldn't be thinking like this, shouldn't be allowing his thoughts to drift in that direction.

And God, he couldn't help wondering if any of their deep conversations would be repeated, if what he shared would end up in the public domain. He didn't think they would, but that familiar dread, so adept at twisting his innards in knots, settled down and made itself comfortable. He knew better than to let his mouth run, if he'd kept his thoughts to himself he wouldn't have anything to worry about.

Damn Brin for burrowing under his skin, worming her way into his heart and wiggling into his soul. Brin, damn her, yanked feelings—good, bad and ugly—to the surface and made him not only confront them but also face who he was, to question what he was doing with his life.

As Radd pulled up to the lodge, his phone dinged with an incoming message. He picked the device up off the flat dashboard and swiped his finger across the screen. It was a message from Digby.

Heads up: Shanna was tanning topless on my balcony and some paparazzi scumbag caught some very mild action from me. I was, mostly, dressed. Photos published online today.

Radd read the message again, trying to make sense of the words. Shanna was Digby's on-off girlfriend and an aspiring actress. And the balcony he was referring to had to be his suite at The Vane and was supposed to be access-controlled and exceptionally private.

Radd felt his blood pressure rise.

How the hell did that happen?

Not sure but suspect Shanna had something to do with setting it up.

Holy Christ.

Don't overreact, for God sake, Radd. It's not that big a deal and it comes with the territory. Oh, and Shanna and I are over, obviously.

He should bloody well hope so. Radd gripped the bridge of his nose between his thumb and forefinger and tried to push the anger away. Radd fought his instinct to fly home, demand a retraction and thump the photographer. But his younger brother was thirty-five and fully capable of fighting his own battles.

They had a right to privacy and the lack thereof shouldn't come "with the territory," it certainly wouldn't with his. This was a great reminder of why he shouldn't make personal connections.

"Good morning, John. How are you?"

Radd looked up to see his concierge, who was about to open Brin's passenger door.

John, elderly and dignified, gave her a regal nod, but Radd saw the hint of pleasure in his eyes at her question. "I'm very well, thank you, Miss Brin. How did you enjoy The Treehouse?"

Brin's under-her-eyelashes look, directed at him, was a little audacious and a lot naughty. "It was lovely, thank you. Some bits were better than others. The food was divine. And the setting magical."

Radd ignored her flirtatious innuendo and impatiently waited for her to join him at the bottom of the stairs. Feeling irritated and off-balance, he placed his hand on her lower back to usher her up the steps leading into the reception area. He steered her toward the deck, away from where they could hear the voices of the Radebe party.

Radd saw the question in her eyes, knew that she'd picked up on his change of mood. He felt his Adam's apple bob, tasted emotion in the back of his throat. He desperately wanted to gather her to him, bury her face in his neck and hold on tight. He wanted to make plans with her for the rest of his life, starting with not letting her go when they touched down in Cape Town tomorrow afternoon.

But because that was impossible, because he didn't trust anybody, couldn't believe in love and commitment—he refused to, love led to hurt and loss, and why would he do that to himself?—he pushed that thought away. Digby's text messages were a fantastic reminder that this was a moment out of time, not the beginning of something real, something lasting. That he could only control *his* words and actions.

It was way past time to backpedal. And to do it hard and fast.

"Are we on the same page, Brinley?" he demanded.

Brin frowned, obviously confused. "I don't understand."

"We had sex last night—" he couldn't call it making love; that was too intimate "—but nothing has changed between us. This can't go anywhere."

Brin blanched at his harsh tone, the softness in her eyes fading. Then, needing to put some distance between her and the verbal blow he'd dealt her, she stepped away from him. Hurt jumped into her eyes but he couldn't let her feelings distract him.

They were on a runaway train and he had to hit the brakes, to stop this madness in its tracks.

"Excuse me?"

Radd raked his hands through his hair. "You, us, nothing is going to happen when we get back home. I hope you know that."

Brin took another step back as pain settled on her face and in her eyes. He noticed a faint tremble to her chin and her suddenly pale face. Too hard and too bold, Radd cursed himself, fighting the urge to apologize. No, he was being cruel to be kind, she had to know that whatever was bubbling between them would expire in less than twenty-four hours.

Then she straightened her shoulders, pushed steel into her spine and her eyes met his. Brin's unexpected and withering glare made him feel two feet tall. But before she could respond, Naledi called his name. For once, it was a welcome interruption.

"Your tribe awaits, my lord."

Radd didn't appreciate Brin's sarcasm.

"Radd! Look who arrived while you were away!"

Radd turned and saw Naledi, wearing an eye-poppingly brief bikini and nothing else, standing a few feet from him, her arms around the waist of her fiancé

Johnathan Wolf. It took all of Radd's willpower to pull
a welcoming smile onto his face, to hold out his hand
for the groom to shake. Radd then turned to Brin and
placed a hand on her back, silently urging her stiff body
forward.

"Johnathan, meet Brinley Riddell."

"Oh, Brin and I know each other," Johnathan cheer-
fully replied. "But I didn't realize you were acquainted
with Radd, Brinley."

Radd turned to look at Brin, watching as the last of
her color faded from her face.

Oh, God...what now?

"And how do you know Brinley, Jon?" Naledi demanded in that hard-as-hell voice that made Radd, uncharacteristically, want to run for cover.

"She's Kerry Riddell's sister, darling."

Judging by Naledi's harsh scream and Brin's white-
as-a-ghost face, her being Kerry's sister was, in Naledi's world, the equivalent of a plague of locusts or a
runaway groom.

This... Radd gripped the bridge of his nose and
squeezed.

This was why he hated secrets and surprises. And
personal connections. And why he kept his distance
from people.

A few hours ago she'd been lying in Radd's strong arms,
completely at ease in her nakedness, exploring what it
meant to give and receive pleasure. They'd made love
over and over—three times? Four?—and with each pass
she'd grown bolder, more confident in her power as a
woman, tapping into that age-old power to make a man
burn and squirm.

Radd had taken her to new sexual heights, far beyond what she'd experienced and even more than she'd imagined. In between their bouts of lovemaking, they'd talked, swapping stories about their childhoods, their favorite places, foods and movies.

Despite knowing that Radd wasn't interested in a relationship, his this-is-only-sex reminder—so blunt!—had thrown her. Had she been hoping, wondering, dreaming for more?

Maybe. Just very little. Well, no more.

Besides, she had a bigger problem to deal with right now.

Once or twice she'd thought about telling Radd about Kerry, about her feud with Naledi, but the time had never quite seemed right and she'd known it would shift the dynamic between them and, frankly, she hadn't wanted what they had to end. Not just yet. She'd thought there would be time, at the lodge or back in Cape Town—or never—for the full truth.

It seemed that time was now.

Brin closed her eyes and wondered why Johnathan, not the brightest spark in an electrical storm, remembered her—the younger sister of a woman he'd slept with—when they'd so very briefly met all those years ago.

Brin opened her mouth to say hello, but Naledi's loud screech made her take a step back. And then another.

"She's Kerry's sister? Are you freakin' kidding me?"

"Actually, she's her half sister," Johnathan replied. "She's Kerry's personal assistant."

"I *was* her assistant," Brin corrected him, only to realize that nobody was listening to her. Brin looked past Naledi's furious face to see that the rest of the wedding party had moved closer, curiosity on their faces.

"What is she doing here? Did she take photos? She's

only here to ruin my wedding!" Naledi's yell was accompanied by the stamping of her feet.

Brin turned her attention to Radd. His expression, as always, was impassive, but his eyes reflected worried confusion, like he was trying to find his balance in a suddenly rough sea.

Brin expected him to try and placate Naledi, to do or say anything to calm the drama queen down because, sure, keeping Naledi calm was imperative. But she never, not in her craziest dreams, expected his next question.

And it rocked her off her feet. "What have you done to upset Naledi?" Radd demanded, his question whipping her skin.

Of course, it follows that this would be my fault, Brin thought, when her shock receded. She was the easiest person to blame: it didn't matter that he'd needed a florist at the last minute, that she'd begged him to take her back to Cape Town, that she'd done everything she could to avoid the Radebes.

Blame had to be assigned, and she was a convenient target. It was unfair but it wasn't, knowing the world he operated in, an uncommon practice.

"She's Kerry's sister, probably sent here to infiltrate my celebrations, to take photographs of me in wretched and compromising situations. Or when I'm looking awful," Naledi shouted.

Oh, seriously? Get over yourself!

"She came here to do the flowers, Naledi. She's a florist," Radd said, sounding annoyed.

"She did my flowers? Are you freaking kidding me? She's a nobody! I knew I hated them, didn't I tell you that I hated them?" Naledi demanded, looking around at her entourage. A couple of the bridesmaids nodded, as did her father. Her mother averted her head and said nothing.

Brin looked at Radd, waiting for him to defend her work. He'd told her numerous times that Naledi loved the flowers and would like to use her again. She held her breath, waiting for him to say something, anything.

When Radd remained quiet, Brin felt like he'd yanked her heart out of her chest and shoved it into a blast chiller. *Come on, Radd, say something... Did our fight yesterday morning teach you nothing? Did you hear me when I told you about being in the line of fire for things I had no control over? Did anything resonate with you?*

Obviously not, because Radd, damn him, remained quiet. But Naledi did not. "I demand you search her phone! I want to see if she has any unauthorized photographs of me, and if she does I will sue her for invading my privacy."

Good luck with that, Brin thought. She didn't have any money anyway. As far as she knew, Radd still hadn't paid her and, judging by his cold, hard, icy fury, he might not.

I abhor secrets and surprises...

"Naledi wants her phone inspected," Vincent stated, stepping forward and placing his hand on his daughter's shoulder.

But this was where Radd would draw the line, he knew she would never do anything to jeopardize his deal. He knew—he had to!—that she'd never do anything so underhand, that she didn't care enough about Naledi or her wedding to ruin it. He'd say no, because he knew her and he'd stand up for her.

Naledi's fist rested on her curvy hips. "I have an exclusive deal with a magazine and if a single image hits the internet before they get the package of photos, I will lose the deal and a huge paycheck."

Brin ignored her, keeping her eyes on Radd's face. *C'mon, Radd, any time now.*

His eyes, as cold as a dark, Arctic night, met hers. Brin held her breath and when he lifted his hand, she thought, for one brief, beautiful moment, that he was offering his protection, a silent but powerful gesture to show she had his support. She started to put her hand in his and gasped when he jerked his back, quick enough to avoid a snake bite.

"Can I see your phone, Ms. Riddell?"

His words took some time to sink in and when they did, Brinley stared at him, feeling hot and cold and utterly alone. She'd grown up as the outsider, constantly looking in, but she'd never felt so abandoned. A cold, wet, sharp wind sliced through her. "You want to see my phone? Why?"

Don't do this, Radd, please.

Radd just stared at her, his hand up, waiting. "This awful scene will be over a lot quicker if you comply."

Brin felt the scrape of a sob in her throat, the burn of tears. Yep, last night meant nothing. She, and her feelings, meant even less. Tossing her head, she gathered her emotions and forced them down, refusing to let Radd or any of the wedding party see her cry. Pulling her phone out of the back pocket of her jeans, she slapped it into his palm. Sucking in some much-needed air, she forced herself to look at Naledi, at Johnathan, Mr. Radebe and finally back at Radd.

Her heart was breaking, but her pride was still intact. Thank God something was.

"Go for it. But you won't find any photos of Naledi or anyone else on the device, because I don't care." She forced herself to meet Naledi's eyes, flat and dark. "I don't care how many Instagram followers you have, about your wedding or your dress or your family. I don't have any social media accounts but, sure, feel free to check."

Radd's fingers closed around her phone and when Naledi reached to take it from him, he jerked it out of her reach. "I'm the only one who looks at this phone," he growled.

Much too little and far too late, Tempest-Vane.

Brin didn't care; he could inspect her phone, so could everyone there. It didn't matter anymore. "Feel free to keep the device," Brin told Radd, her voice brittle. "I'm going to the room to pack up my stuff. I expect to be on a flight out of here shortly or, by God, I will walk."

"Can I explain?"

Out of the corner of her eye, Brin saw Radd drop down into the seat opposite her, his big frame blocking out the soft leather as he fastened his seat belt. Brin briefly met his eyes before looking out of the plane's window. Far below Radd's fancy jet, the city of Cape Town lay nestled between the mountains and the sea.

He's taken his time to approach me, Brin thought; his jet was making its descent and within minutes they would be on the ground. Brin did not doubt Radd had timed it this way to minimize their confrontation. That was fine with her, there wasn't much to say.

She loved him, he didn't love or trust her. Simple, really.

She couldn't wait to get back to her cottage, to what was familiar. Abby's unwavering friendship, her soft bed, being able to cry into her own pillow.

But, at some point, she had to put her feelings and

tumultuous emotions aside and start to think. In fact, moving her attention to her future was easier than nursing her battered and bruised heart.

She didn't want to leave Cape Town—she loved it—but how could she stay in the same city Radd did? And how could she take his now-tainted wad of cash? If she did, and established her flower shop, every time she walked inside she'd be reminded of Radd and this crazy, confusing time where she fell in love with, and had her heart broken by, him.

She'd done a job, fulfilled her end of the business arrangement and she deserved that cash, her sensible, business brain argued. What's the option here? To stay poor and to struggle?

Or to go back to Johannesburg with her tail tucked between her legs?

Her pride wanted her to make the grand gesture, to tell him to go to hell and take his money with him, but if she did that, she'd be in a worse position than she was before. Going back to work for Kerry was the second of two very bad choices…

If only you didn't have to go and fall in love with the man, Riddell, how stupid are you? He was unemotional, driven, rude and single-minded and falling for him was properly idiotic. Really, she needed someone to save her from herself.

"I told the Radebes that there were no photos on your phone."

Of course there weren't. And she so didn't care.

Radd placed his ankle on his opposite knee. Brin allowed her eyes to wander over him: he still sported heavy, sexy stubble, but he'd changed into a pair of dark brown chinos and pulled on an aqua-colored linen, button-down shirt. His cuffs were rolled back and he wore a different watch from the high tech, too-many-buttons-to-count one he'd been wearing earlier. This watch was simple, timeless, gorgeous.

He was back to being the beautifully dressed billionaire while she was still dressed in the same clothes she'd been wearing when she left The Treehouse. Brin felt underdressed and a little gauche. Damn him for making her feel less than, for making her feel like she did when she was the tiny, unimportant moon circling Kerry's glowing planet.

"You're really angry."

Well, duh. Sure, she was furious with him, but she also felt hurt, sad and so very tired of being on the outside looking in. She'd lived on the edge of her family's circle all her life and she just wanted her own spot to shine, somewhere where she was celebrated and loved. Someone to take her side, someone to stand in her corner.

Radd, as he'd demonstrated earlier, wasn't that person. She'd never find the peace she craved with him, within the world he inhabited.

"Rich people and celebrities expect privacy, Brinley," Radd quietly stated.

"I worked for my sister as her assistant for a long time, so that's not something you need to tell me," Brin told him, ice in her voice. "I managed a lot of her PR and I understand how the game is played. I don't like the rules, but I understand them. Apart from the fact that I'm not remotely interested in Naledi and her wedding, I would never invade her privacy like that. I thought you understood that much about me."

"How could I when you didn't tell me the truth about who you are and who your sister is!" Radd raked his hand through his hair. "I asked if there was anything I should know, anything that could ruin this week."

"I was under no obligation to disclose that information to you, or anyone else, Radd. And you're using it as an excuse to push me away."

Radd's eyes narrowed at her accusation. "What?"

Brin felt the shudder of the jet's wheels touching the runway, the change in the sound of the engines as the plane slowed. "And if that doesn't work, you're going to throw in how important it is that you acquire a signed signature for the purchase of the mine, and I've put that in jeopardy. You are not your name or your company!" Brin said, feeling like she'd gone ten rounds with a champion boxer.

"You don't understand what it was like living with parents like mine!" Radd whipped back. "They dragged our name through the mud. They sold every asset my grandfather and great-grandfathers acquired, and Digby and I had to work our fingers to the bone to reclaim what was lost!"

"Everyone has a past, Radd. I grew up in the shadow of my sister. Nothing I ever did, or said, could match the brilliance and the beauty that is Kerry. But I keep reminding myself that my past is exactly that, my past, and shouldn't be allowed to color or inform my decisions. Besides, I have no interest in being with a man who puts money and business first, someone who can't stand up for, or defend, me."

Radd leaned forward and that impassive, inscrutable expression and his blank eyes told her she was dealing with Cape Town Radd, not Kagiso Radd. The Radd he was in the city was hard and unyielding, dogmatic and determined. She'd lost the man she loved, he'd been devoured by this hard-eyed man sitting across from her.

Brin lifted her phone off her thigh and swiped her thumb across the screen. Pulling in a deep breath, she gathered her courage and turned the screen to him. His eyes widened at the picture he saw on her screen.

"We became friends, Radd, and then we became lovers and our connection scares the pants off you. From the moment you rolled out of bed at The Treehouse, I could feel you retreating, your mind going a hundred miles a minute, trying to find a way to put some distance between us. And then I found this picture of Digby and his girlfriend online—"

"How?"

Brin shrugged. "I saw the photo on your phone."

"Snooping, too?" Radd muttered, frowning.

"Our seats weren't that far apart." Brin handed him an I'll-fry-you-where-you-sit glare. "And you're being petty." Brin dropped her hand and continued to speak. "But it did make all the pieces fall into place."

"Good for you."

Brin ignored his sarcastic interruption. "This photograph of Digby's girlfriend reminded you that you can't trust people, that you mustn't let anyone get too close to you. That scene with Naledi confirmed it. You *wanted* an excuse to push me away, Radd. You were desperate for one, because you are too scared to love, too scared to take a chance, too scared to go there, probably because your parents, the people who are supposed to love you the most, didn't and constantly disappointed you."

Radd released a choking sound, but Brin didn't give him the chance to speak. "And boy, you quickly found those reasons you were looking for. Do you really believe a PR campaign and a rehabilitation of your name process is going to bring you the peace you require? It's not. Because until you believe you are more than your name, until you embrace who you are, fully and without reservation, and give yourself credit for the man you've become—hard-working, intelligent, trustworthy—it's all just smoke and mirrors. You're not trying to convince the world, Radd, you're trying to convince yourself."

Brin saw the color drain from Radd's face, knew that he wanted to argue, but she held up her hand, silently asking him to be quiet.

"I kept telling myself that I'm not from your world, that I don't fit in there, but the truth is, you don't fit into *my* world, Radd. And it's got nothing to do with money and power and celebrity and…stuff. I need the people in my world to have my back, as I would have theirs. I need trust and comfort and support, someone who is prepared to build me up, not tear me down. Someone who will let me love them and love me back."

Brin placed her fist over her mouth, silently cursing the tears running down her face. "I deserve to have someone love me like that, Radd, I do. I'm sorry it couldn't be you, but there it is."

The plane rolled to a stop and Brin saw Skye standing in the doorway of the lounge. She dredged up a smile for him, unclipped her seatbelt and stood up. She looked down at Radd, who was staring at his hands, his expression, as usual, implacable.

"Don't bother about getting me home, Radd. I contacted Abby and she's collecting me. It's been…" Brin hesitated. Lovely? Exciting? Soul-touching? Devastating? They all applied so she settled on "…interesting."

"Goodbye, Radd."

Brin forced herself to walk away and kept her eyes on the open door and the steps she had to walk down. She was furiously angry with him, hurt and disappointed that he wasn't brave enough to love her, but his faults and actions didn't dilute her love for him. He was the puzzle piece she'd been looking for all her life to complete her, the part of her soul she was missing. He was her shelter in the storm, her soft place to fall.

Radd, the man and not the image, was whom she wanted to be with, the face she woke up to every morning, the body she cuddled up against at night. The person she wanted to laugh with, love with, make babies with.

But she couldn't do any of that on her own; it took two to have a once-in-a-lifetime love affair. He didn't know it but Radd, scared and a little lost, held her heart in his hands.

Hot tears ran as Brin realized that, from this moment on, she'd have to learn to live without both.

CHAPTER TEN

"You don't fit into my world..."

"I need the people in my world to have my back."

"Someone who will let me love them and love me back."

"Goddammit, Radd, sit still!"

Seated in the back row, Radd ignored his brother's hiss and watched Naledi flash a practiced smile at the professional cameraman as Johnathan slid his ring onto her finger and murmured "I do."

Shouldn't she be looking at her groom, immersed in the moment of tying herself to another person, reveling in their love and good fortune? Shouldn't she be paying more attention to Johnathan than she did to the camera?

"Six months," Digby murmured.

Radd turned his head to look at his brother. "What?"

"I give them six months before they start talking divorce. They'll be single in, mmm, maybe nine." Digby shrugged at his surprised look. "I've seen so many brides stroll through the doors of The Vane, but I've never seen one so into herself as Naledi Radebe. There's only space in that relationship for one person and she's it."

"Brin said something similar." God, even murmuring her name hurt. Why? She was never going to be part of his life. No one was.

And if that was true then why did he spend the last thirty-six hours talking himself out of going to her, calling her? Radd rubbed his chest somewhere in the region of his heart and wondered if it would ever stop aching.

Maybe he was having a heart attack or something. Or maybe he was just missing Brin.

"I need trust and comfort and support..."

He wasn't capable of giving her what she needed.

"Did you see the letter we received from our parent's lawyer?" Digby asked out of the side of his mouth. "The beneficiary of their trust wants to meet us, on certain conditions."

Right now, he really didn't care. And he wasn't even remotely curious who Gil and Zia had left their money to. How to heal the crater-sized hole Brin had left in his life was taking up all his mental energy.

"Brin is Kerry Riddell's sister," Radd whispered the words in Digby's ear.

"Did you hear what I said? About meeting whomever they left their assets to?"

"Mmm. Brin told me I'm living in the past and that the PR campaign is just a way to convince myself I am better than them."

Digby released an under-his-breath curse and closed his eyes. Then he pushed his way to his feet and, when Radd looked up at him, jerked his head. Radd got the message and slowly climbed to his feet, thankful they were in the back of many, many rows and could slip away without disturbing the wedding.

The brothers walked in silence to the open-air bar set up on the magnificent veranda a good distance from the wedding gazebo. Digby walked behind the counter and reached for a bottle of whiskey and two glasses. After pouring a healthy amount into both glasses, he handed

Radd his tumbler before speaking again. "Your florist is Kerry's sister? BS."

"Do you know Kerry Riddell?" Radd asked, after taking a healthy belt of his drink. He welcomed the burn, and then the warmth, hitting his stomach. It was the first time he'd felt anything but ice cold since Brin left him on the plane.

"Yeah, we've met. She's a piece of work."

Needing to talk, a surprising development in itself, Radd rolled the tumbler between the palms of his hands. "I only found out Brin's connection to her when Johnathan told Naledi she was Kerry's sister at Kagiso. Naledi did not take the news well."

"Bet she lost her rag and accused Brin of trying to spoil her wedding."

Radd placed his glass on the bar and started pacing the area in front of Digby. Six steps, turn. Ten steps, turn again. "Good guess."

Digby grinned. "Not that good, because Mari told me. She also told me that you are into Brin."

Radd snorted, stopped and took another sip of his whisky. "We had a brief fling and it's over." He started to pace again. "It was…inconsequential."

Radd looked up at the clear sky, watching for a stray lightning bolt to punish him for that enormous lie.

"Sure it was," Digby mocked him. "That's why you barely reacted when I told you about the heir to the trust, why you brushed that news off to focus on a florist. Face it, Radd, she is your person."

Radd stopped abruptly, whirled around and scowled at his brother. "Are you looking to get thumped? You know how I feel about settling down, about marrying!"

"I do," Digby replied, obviously amused.

"Then why would you make such an asinine comment?" Radd demanded, resuming his pacing.

"You're shouting. And you are pacing."

Radd threw his hands up in frustration at Digby's observation. There was no one around, no guests to be disturbed, so what was his problem?

Digby chuckled at his question, and Radd's hands curled into tight fists. *No hitting your younger brother, even if he deserves it.* "What the hell is so damn funny?"

"You! Look at you, all pissed off and pacing. I haven't seen you this worked up in…well, forever. You are the most impassive, nonreactive person I know, yet here you are, all tied up in a knot over a woman."

Radd wanted to argue but couldn't because, from the first moment he'd met her, Brin had the ability to shove her hand into his soul and pull all his dormant emotions to the surface. Radd scrubbed his hands over his face, his anger fading. He sent Digby a rueful look. "She drives me nuts."

"And that's a very good thing," Digby replied.

"Not from my perspective," Radd grumbled.

Digby smiled, picked up his drink and swirled it around before speaking again. "Since Jack's death, you have tended to be a little…"

"A little what?" Radd prompted him when Digby hesitated.

"Robotic." Digby shrugged. "Look, when Jack died, we had to grow up, and we did, fast. We had to deal with the parents, the gossip around them and the loss of our legacy. In our drive to regain what was lost, we also, to an extent, lost ourselves."

"Explain," Radd commanded, his throat dry. This conversation wouldn't be easy, but it was long overdue.

The path they were on, which had seemed so clear a week or so ago, was now shrouded in fog.

"We both changed after Jack died, in fundamental ways. We worshipped Jack, he was our hero, our anchor point. And the parent's betrayal knocked us sideways, and them returning to their hedonistic lifestyle so soon after his death was another blow."

"Maybe that was the way they coped with his death," Radd suggested, shocked by this new insight.

"Maybe. Or maybe you are giving them too much credit," Digby said, his eyes stormy. "Anyway, as I was saying, Jack's death changed everything. You became an adult overnight and I became a rebel. God, it was a miracle I managed to finish school without being kicked out."

Only because he'd gone to the headmaster and begged him to let Digby stay in school. But Radd didn't tell Dig that, he didn't need to know.

"I acted out, looking for a way to ease the pain, but you internalized everything and cultivated this nothing-can-hurt-me persona." Digby jammed his hands into the pockets of his suit pants, his eyes sober. "I, mostly, grew out of my rebellious stage, but you kept your hard-as-nails facade. I'm not going to lie, it worries me. That's why I am so damn happy that you've found someone to make you feel."

Brin did. Make him feel, that is. He still didn't like it.

But he couldn't deny it. Around Brin, he felt both relaxed and energized, calm and excited. He felt normal...

"Brin seems to think that I'm using the PR campaign to make me feel better about myself," Radd admitted. Digby was the only person he could discuss this with, he'd walked this path with him. And until he figured out whether she was right or wrong, or a mixture of both, he was paralyzed.

He wanted to move on. How and where to, he had no idea, but he wasn't the type to stand still and do nothing.

Digby stared at a point past Radd's shoulder, and Radd knew he was looking at the superb view of Table Mountain. Digby's opinion on Brin's accusation was important, and he was very willing to wait.

Dig's eyes eventually met his. "She's right, Radd, you and I both know it. I don't blame us for trying to restore the company to what it was, it gave two very messed-up kids a goal, a direction we so badly needed. But I'm not, as I've mentioned, a fan of the PR campaign, I feel we'd be beating a dead horse. People will think what they think and we know the truth. And maybe we should move forward without thinking about how the world perceives us."

Digby didn't, and never had, cared what people thought about him. He marched to the beat of his own drum and people could either like it or lump it.

Radd felt like the world was shifting below his feet. Everything that seemed so stable a week ago was now shaky, everything he firmly believed in felt less substantial.

All because a silver-eyed siren flipped his life upside down and inside out.

"Noted." Radd made himself ask the question. "Should we still go ahead with acquiring the mine?"

"Absolutely." Digby nodded. "You survived the pre-wedding week at Kagiso and by now the bride and groom should be hitched and stitched, so why not? Get Vincent to sign the sale agreement and let's get it done. Once the mine is in our hands, we can decide on the PR campaign and where we want to take the company without any pressure from the past. Though I think you should be working out how to get Brin back in your life. It's obvious that you are head-over-ass in love with her."

No, he wasn't! Radd sent Digby a hot look and noticed Dig's eyebrows rising, as if daring him to disagree. He wanted to… He should.

He liked Brin, and adored her body. Sex with her was magical and he loved spending time with her, but that didn't mean he loved her…

Digby flashed him an evil grin. "If you aren't in love with her, then I might track her down and ask her out."

A red mist formed behind Radd's eyes and it took all his willpower not to put his hands around Digby's throat and squeeze. Brin was his.

"Do it and die."

Digby's expression turned mocking, then amused. "Just get over yourself and admit it already, brother."

Aargh!

Okay, yes, maybe he was in love with her. But who fell in love in under a week? Could he trust his feelings, as new and strange as they were? Radd, with considerable effort, pushed aside his fears and, after taking a deep breath, examined his feelings for Brin.

She made him feel whole, complete, the best version of himself. He loved her dirty laugh, her sexy smile, the sway of her hips and the way she crinkled her nose when she was deep in thought.

Nothing else, not the mine, not the business, not even Digby, mattered as much as she did; he was now second in his own life. Brin was all that was important.

He couldn't live his life, didn't want to, without her. *Melodramatic much, Tempest-Vane?* It was hard to admit, but having Brin in his life would enrich it exponentially, far more than the money in his bank accounts had ever been able to do.

She was all that mattered, all that was important.

"Ah, and the penny has dropped," Digby commented, his tone smug.

Radd managed a small smile. Then he winced. "It's all very well me having a come-to-Jesus moment, but that doesn't mean that she'll have me."

"Nope, she'd be mad to take you on. I'm a far better bet," Digby teased.

Radd's "screw you" held no heat. Digby laughed and then his expression turned guarded. Radd turned to see who'd caught his attention and saw Vincent Radebe strolling across the vibrant, immaculate lawn toward them. That meant that the wedding was over.

Radd remembered that the wedding party was supposed to gather by the whimsical fountain for photographs and wondered why Vincent had left the wedding party. Naledi would not be pleased.

The guests wouldn't be far behind him so if Radd wanted to slip away—he couldn't wait to track Brin down—he needed to leave soon. Vincent held up his hand in a "wait, please" gesture and Radd frowned, not bothering to hide his impatience.

"I'm having second thoughts about selling the mine," Vincent said, folding his arms across his chest.

Now why didn't that surprise him? Radd waited for the wave of anger, the crashing waves of disappointment. Neither arrived. Interesting…

Before he could respond, Digby, looking cool, urbane but very, very determined, met Vincent's gaze. "That's your prerogative, of course. Now, if you'd be so kind as to accompany me to the accounts office, I will need your credit card to pay for this wedding at our usual rate. " He turned to Radd. "Shall I add the cost of the wedding party's stay at Kagiso, as well?"

If he was backpedaling on their agreement then they'd make him pay. Nobody pushed the Tempest-Vane brothers around. Not anymore and not ever again.

"Absolutely. Vincent's guests enjoyed the full package at Kagiso."

Vincent's deep brown skin paled. "Uh…"

"Thank you for allowing us to host one of the most iconic, and expensive weddings of the past ten years at The Vane," Digby said, still using that smooth voice. "We are honored and grateful. I'm afraid the bill might sting, but that's the price for lifelong memories."

Radd almost snorted. Naledi and Johnathan wouldn't last the year, never mind a lifetime. "How much are we looking at?" Vincent asked, sounding a little choked up.

"More than a million," Digby suavely replied. "Maybe a million and a half."

"And that's including the stay at Kagiso?"

Radd shook his head. "No, that's just the cost of the wedding. Your cost to stay at Kagiso will probably be another million."

Vincent swore and he rubbed his hand over his bald head. *Yeah, you tight-fisted, bastard*, Radd thought, *we don't play.*

Radd was over playing games with him, was tired of being the puppet dancing as Vincent pulled the strings. It wasn't who he was; he didn't like it and it was time to end this farce. He was tired of paying for his parent's mistakes.

"Look Vincent, we all know you want to sell the mine, it's no secret that you are focusing on telecommunications. You've held on to the mine, probably because it is so damn profitable. We've made you a solid offer and we threw in hosting this wedding, and your stay at Kagiso, at cost. You want to sell the mine, but you're hoping you can squeeze some more cash out of us. It's been fun making Gil's sons dance, you've enjoyed a little payback."

He saw the flash of agreement in the older man's eyes.

"It's not going to work," Radd informed him. "The game stops, here. *Today.*"

"But everyone knows that the mine is the missing piece of the Tempest-Vane empire." Vincent threw his argument back in his face.

Radd caught Digby's eye and his brother nodded, handing him his full support. They could live without the mine, and they would. Brin was right, this was about *stuff*, other people's perceptions and, at the end of the day, not *that* important. The world wouldn't stop turning if the mine wasn't added to the group and, since he knew he wasn't like his father—or his mother—did the rehabilitation of their name matter?

If he took a wife, she might care, but Brin was the only person he could imagine in that role. And she *definitely* didn't care.

God, he loved her. Radd hauled in a deep breath and realized that the boulder that usually lived on his chest was gone. So this was what freedom felt like. He rather liked it.

"It's a business, Vincent, not a lifesaving organ transplant. Sell us the mine, as per our original agreement, or don't. Either way, we'll be fine," Radd told him. He nodded to the wave of guests heading their way, led by the harassed-looking wedding planner.

"You need to join your family, Vincent," Radd told him.

Vincent glanced at the wedding planner and sighed. "Don't you want to know what I've decided?"

"I don't care," he told Vincent, knowing it was the truth. "Frankly, I've got something bigger to worry about."

Digby jerked his head toward the building. "Go get her, Radd."

"Thanks, Dig."

"And if she says no, I'll pick up where you left off. I'm younger, more charming and more handsome than you."

Funny, Radd thought as he strode into the hotel. Not.

Abby held her hand as they walked up the steps leading from the beach to the parking lot, and Brin appreciated her support.

So much has happened between the last time I saw these steps last Saturday and now, Brin thought. She'd flown across the country, visited the most amazing game reserve, met Mari, fought with Naledi and, worst of all, handed her heart over to Radd.

Who didn't want it.

"Brin!" Abby snapped her fingers in front of her face. She'd been doing that a lot since Brin had arrived back home yesterday afternoon. She'd been a wreck, and Abby had taken her in her arms, pulled her into their house and let her cry. Then she poured them huge glasses of wine and pulled every excruciating detail out of Brin.

And today, on finding Brin still in bed at noon, she'd pushed her into the shower and then bundled her into her car, telling her that an afternoon in the sun, swimming in the sea, would make her feel so much better.

Brin was still waiting for that to happen.

She still felt utterly exhausted. She'd hardly slept last night—her brain insisted on reliving every interaction with Radd over and over again, always ending with the vision of Radd's hard face on their trip home, and his scathing words *"This can't go anywhere."*

The crack in her heart widened.

"I sent you a number for my cousin, he's a real estate agent and he's trying to find a florist shop owner who might sell. He's also looking for vacant shops for you to consider."

"I don't think I can take Radd's money, Abby," Brin quietly stated.

How could she explain that it all meant nothing without Radd? That if she was feeling like this, like the shell of the person she once was, she had no interest in establishing a business, and that she might as well go back to Johannesburg and work for Kerry. Her hell-on-wheels sister couldn't make her feel any worse than she currently did.

"I know that this is difficult but you have to think with your head, not your heart," Abby replied, squeezing her hand. "Give it a few weeks before you make any radical decisions about returning his money. You're hurt and upset and you don't want to make a huge decision when you are feeling emotional."

It was a solid piece of advice, but Brin knew she wouldn't take it. As soon as the money hit her account—it was still looking as empty as ever—she'd ask Abby for his bank account number; she was his employee after all. If Abby didn't know it or couldn't get it, she would contact Radd.

Going back to Johannesburg wouldn't be *that* bad—it was, after all, what she knew. She'd have a good salary, a decent car to drive, financial security. And after having her heart broken by Radd—her fault for thinking that she could capture his attention and his love—

her sister's and mother's snubs, criticism and demands wouldn't have the power to wound her.

They would be like the gentle flick of a whip compared to being eviscerated by a blunt teaspoon.

Stupid girl for allowing this to happen, for not guarding your heart. For falling into the arms of a man who she knew was so very far out of her league. *Never again,* Brin vowed.

She was done with men and love.

Permanently.

"Brin…"

Brin lifted her head to look at her friend as she stepped onto the pavement at the top of the steps. She knew that Abby meant well, but she just wanted a little peace, some time to nurse her broken heart, her bruised spirit. She needed time to recover, to mourn what could've been.

"Can you just leave me be, Abs? I'm tired and sad—" Abby's hand shot out and her fingernails dug into the bare skin on her arm. Abby was looking to her right, and Brin followed her gaze.

Radd.

Brin drank him in, all six-foot-something of him, dressed in a lightweight grey suit, his tie pulled down from his collar, leaning against the hood of his fancy car. He'd been to Naledi's wedding, Brin dimly remembered, but he must've left shortly after the ceremony was done. Why wasn't he at the reception and, more importantly, why was he here?

Radd straightened, sliding his hands into the pockets of his suit pants. Aviator sunglasses covered his eyes and he looked as he always did, implacable and remote.

Nothing has changed, Brin thought. So, instead of walking over to him, she turned and walked in the direction of Abby's car. She heard Abby behind her, hurrying to keep up with her long-legged stride.

"Talk to him, Brin!" Abby pleaded.

"There's nothing to say," Brin replied, tugging on the handle to the passenger door. "I'm begging you, Abby, take me home."

"I'll just follow you there," Radd said from behind her. "We need to talk, Brin."

Brin spun around, anger temporarily drowning her sadness. "I think we covered all the bases yesterday, Mr. Tempest-Vane."

Radd winced. "Yesterday I was being a bloody idiot. Today, hopefully, I'm less of one."

"Doubtful," Brin snapped.

"Come home with me, Brin. Let's try and sort this out!"

"There's nothing to sort out," Brin told him, her voice rising.

"Now, that's a lie," Radd replied. "We have a lot to discuss and you know it." Radd turned his attention to Abby and gave her a small smile. "Go on home, Abby, I'll drive Brin to wherever she wants to go later."

Brin narrowed her eyes at Abby. "Don't you dare leave me, Abigail."

Abby shrugged. "He's my boss, Brin. And he'll fire me if I don't do as he says." She raised her eyebrows at Radd. "Won't you?"

"Damn straight." Radd soberly answered.

Did they think she was stupid? Radd wouldn't fire Abby for such a trivial reason, and they both knew it. No, she was being maneuvered into having a conversation with Radd and she didn't like it. Frustrated with both of them, she threw up her hands and pulled out her phone.

"Fine, I'll call for a taxi or an Uber."

Radd moved quickly, and she caught a hint of his cologne as her phone was yanked from her hand. Radd tucked it into the inside pocket of his jacket and folded his arms.

"You and I are going to talk," Radd told her before shoving his sunglasses into the inside pocket of his jacket. "Go, Abby."

Brin heard Abby's car door opening, followed by her engine starting, but she couldn't pull her eyes off Radd's. With dark stripes under his red eyes, he looked like he'd had even less sleep than her. His olive complexion was pale in the late afternoon light.

But his eyes, God, his eyes…

She could see a hundred emotions in those inky eyes: fear, regret, pain. It was as if he'd stripped every layer of protection away and allowed her to step into his mind and it was, like hers, in turmoil.

Radd gestured to an empty bench that faced the sea. "I have some things I need to say and, afterwards, if nothing resonates with you, I'll take you home, no questions asked."

Brin looked around and saw Abby's car exiting the parking lot. What choice did she have? Abby was gone and, since Radd had her phone, she was out of options.

"How did you know I was here?" Brin demanded as they walked over to the bench.

"I texted Abby, she told me."

What a traitor! Her best friend had known she was about to be ambushed and she'd said nothing. They would, Brin decided, be having words later. Whose side was she on?

Radd waited until she was seated before sitting down next to her. He shed his jacket and placed it on top of her beach bag sitting on the bench between them. Rolling up the cuffs of his sleeves, he stared out to sea.

"The sea looks so inviting. Was the water warm?"

Brin rolled her eyes. He wanted to talk about the temperature of the sea? Really? "Is the water ever warm in Cape Town?" she asked, sounding acerbic.

"I can't remember when last I spent any time on a beach."

"That happens when you spend all your time at work," Brin snapped, folding her arms across her chest. She couldn't do this, it was too hard. She couldn't sit here and pretend everything was fine when she loved him so much. It was like having a blowtorch blistering her body, one painful inch at a time.

"I paid you your money this morning. It should be in your account soon," Radd told her.

"I don't want it."

Radd released an impatient snort. "Brin, we made a deal. You worked through the night to fulfill your end of the bargain. Mine was to pay you and that's done."

"I don't *want* your money," Brin replied, sounding stubborn.

"I don't care. Our business arrangement is over," Radd replied.

Yeah, she got that message loud and clear. Why had he come all this way to tell her he'd paid her? He could've texted her or sent her an email.

God, she was exhausted and her brain felt like it was on the point of exploding.

"Please take me home, Radd," Brin begged, not caring if he heard the hint of tears in her voice.

Radd pushed his hands through his hair before turning to face her. He lifted his hand, and his thumb swiped away the one tear she hadn't managed to blink away. "Please don't cry, Brin."

"Then stop making me cry and leave me alone!" Brin cried, placing her face in her hands.

"I can't, sweetheart," Radd's reply sounded tortured, but the hand he placed on her back was strangely re-assuring. "I can't walk away from you, I don't *want* to walk away."

Brin dropped her hands, but she wasn't brave enough to look at him, so she looked at the dune grass growing in the beach sand a couple of feet away from their shoes. "That's not what you said yesterday."

"Yesterday wasn't one of my better days." Radd re-leased a heavy sigh. His hand moved up her back to the back of her neck, which he gently held. "Won't you sit up and look at me, Brin?"

Brin reluctantly straightened, and it took quite a bit of courage to meet his eyes. This was the stripped-down version of Radd, and all his feelings were reflected in his eyes. And he was feeling quite a lot, which was odd for her implacable, once-in-a-lifetime lover.

"I treated you badly yesterday, Brinley, and for that, I beg your forgiveness," Radd quietly stated. "I should've, yet again, stood up for what was right instead of what was convenient, and I disappointed and hurt you."

He had and he did. She couldn't argue with that.

"I should've told Naledi to get lost when she de-manded to see your phone, I should never have invaded your privacy like that. I should've trusted you."

Brin nodded, not quite ready to let him off the hook. "Yes, you should have."

When Radd didn't say anything for the next few minutes, Brin stood up, her heart smothered by disappointment. What had she expected? For him to tell her he loved her? Silly, silly girl.

"Now that you've got that off your chest, will you take me home? Or better yet, allow me to call for a taxi. Or a lift."

Radd took her hand and tugged her back down, his hand sending sparks over her skin, up her arm. She was still as attracted to him as ever, damn it. Why was life torturing her like this?

"I'm not done," Radd told her.

"Well, get done," Brin retorted. She couldn't take much more.

He turned to look at her, and Brin's lungs contracted at the look on his face. It was part insecurity, part hope, all fear. "I've never told someone I loved them before, so I'm bound to botch this up. Give me a sec, okay?"

What? Wait! Did he just say something about love or were her ears playing tricks on her? It was highly possible. Brin laid her hand on her chest. "What did you say?"

Radd sat up, his eyes connecting with hers. "I wanted to say this with finesse, with some sort of eloquence, but nothing, despite practicing all the way here, is coming out right. So...sod it."

He clasped her face in his hands before swiping his mouth across hers. "I'm a fool and an idiot, but I'm the fool and idiot who loves you to distraction. Oh, God, you're crying again."

Brin allowed a little laugh to escape and waved her hands in front of her face before gripping Radd's strong wrists with her shaking hands. "Can you say that again?"

Radd kissed her nose, her cheekbones and then her temple. "I love you, Brinley. So much."

Her tears started to fall in earnest. "But, yesterday, you told me you didn't see me in your future."

Radd sighed, his breath warm against her temple. "I was scared and confused and being a jerk. I thought that the mine and my work were all that was important and I wanted to keep the status quo. Loving you is new, scary territory, a place where I have no control, and I don't like giving up control."

"So what changed between then and now?" Brin asked, leaning back so she could see his face.

Radd dropped his hands from her face but placed one hand on her bare thigh, as if he needed to anchor himself to her. He looked away briefly before facing her again. "I had a conversation with Digby. He said that I was acting like a cat on a hot tin roof and wanted to know why I wasn't being my calm, distant self.

"Since I met you, I've felt more than ever before, certainly more since Jack died. The world seems a little brighter, a lot more colorful." Radd winced, looking embarrassed. "God, that sounds too cheesy for words. As I said, this is all coming out wrong."

Brin shook her head, her heart slowly defrosting. "No, every word is perfect. Carry on."

"You want more?" Radd pulled a face at her.

"No, I want everything," Brin softly told him. "Don't hold back, Radd. I've never had anyone tell me they love me before, so feel free to go overboard."

Radd's thumb stroked her cheekbone. "Oh, sweetheart, I intend to make you feel ridiculously loved every day for the rest of your life. You, not the mine, not my work, not my brother, are now my priority, and making sure you are happy is my biggest goal. I want you to have the money, not only because that was the deal, but also because I want you to have your dream. You are so talented, and I want you to open your florist-and-coffee shop."

Brin's nose wrinkled, her expression doubtful. "You'd support me in that?"

"Sure. You're far too bright and talented to sit at home, waiting for me to finish work. No, chase your dreams, Brin and I'll support you as you do that." Radd's thumb traced the soft skin of her bottom lip. "I am so sorry I made you feel unimportant when you are everything that's important to me."

Brin bit her lip, looking up at him through her lashes. "Really?"

"Yes, *really*."

Brin stared at him, trying to compute his words, struggling to make sense of the bright, sparkly, glitter-tinged feelings coursing through her. Radd loved her.

Radd. Loved. Her.

Holy cupcakes. With sprinkles on them.

"Will you please say something?" Radd growled.

Brin saw the impatience in his eyes and decided to tease him, just a little. "What do you want me to say?"

"Well, an 'I love you' would be nice. And a 'Yes, I'll marry you, as soon as you like,' would be better."

He wants to marry me? Whoa! Really? Brin felt her heart leave her chest and take flight. *Well, okay then.*

"You haven't asked me to marry you," Brin pointed out, just managing to hold back her huge grin and her bubbling laughter.

"I will, as soon as you tell me that you love me too," Radd replied, sounding a little cross.

"Who falls in love in a week?" Brin mused. "It's crazy."

"I do, and I hope you have too or else I'm going to feel like an even bigger fool," Radd muttered. Brin heard the note of anxiety in his voice and knew that it wasn't fair to push him any further. Because, like her, he'd lived without love for a long time and didn't deserve to wait any longer.

"Of course I love you, Radd," Brin quietly told him, her eyes begging him to believe her. "So much."

Radd rested her forehead on hers and closed his eyes. "Thank God."

"And I am sorry about not telling you about my connection to Naledi," Brin said, resting her fingertips on his jaw, rough with stubble. "I didn't want to go back to my family with my tail between my legs. I'm sorry if being related to Kerry caused you any problems with Vincent. I don't want you to lose the mine because of something so silly."

Radd sat back but he kept her hand in his. "Vincent will either sell us the mine or he won't. Either way, I can live with it."

"But it's the company you need to restore the Tempest-Vane holdings to what they once were."

Radd shrugged. "While it would be nice, Digby and I agreed that it's not something we'll lose sleep over. In a few weeks, my brother and I will meet and we'll decide on what we want to do, without reference to the past and our parents."

Brin rested her forehead on the ball of his shoulder. "Are you sure?"

Radd's hand stroked her hair. "Very. It's time for a new chapter, Brinley. Will you help me write it?"

Brin nodded and squeezed his hand. "I will. Ask me again."

Radd tipped his head to the side, his expression puzzled. But it took just a few seconds for her words to register. And then her once hard-eyed, implacable man dropped to one knee in front of her, the late afternoon sun glinting off his dark hair.

"Brinley Riddell, will you marry me?"

Brin nodded once, then grinned. "On one condition."

Radd groaned theatrically and gently banged his head against her kneecap. "You're going to keep me on my toes, aren't you?"

Brin's laughter gurgled and bubbled as she ran her hands through his hair. "I want to get married at Kagiso and spend part of our honeymoon at The Treehouse."

"I'm sure that can be arranged. I happen to know the owner. Is that a yes?"

Brin nodded, her eyes shimmering with emotion. "Yes, that's a yes."

"I'm going to kiss the hell out of you in a second, but I should tell you that I have a condition, too," Radd murmured.

She was so happy she'd agree to anything. Brin grinned at him. "What's your condition?"

"That I buy you a new car. I refuse to allow you to drive that rust bucket anywhere," Radd told her, frowning. "It's not safe, Brin. I can't bear the thought of you not being safe."

"I was going to buy a car out of the money you paid me," Brin told him. There were different ways to say I love you and this was one of them.

"Let me do it," Radd said, looking serious.

Brin lifted a finger and pushed it into his chest. "I'll agree to something sensible and reasonable. I do not need fancy. Or expensive."

Radd bracketed her face with his hands. "Are we doing this? Getting married?" he asked, sounding a little bemused.

Brin laughed. "We are."

"Thank God. I can't wait to make you mine," Radd muttered before surging to his feet and yanking her up and into his arms. His mouth covered hers and Brin sank into his embrace, knowing that he would hold her, that she'd found her person.

She was, finally, home and standing in a bright, golden spotlight all of her own.

* * * * *

MILLS & BOON

Coming next month

THE GREEK'S CONVENIENT CINDERELLA
Lynne Graham

'Mr Alexandris,' Tansy pronounced rather stiffly.

'Come and sit down,' he invited lazily. 'Tea or coffee?'

'Coffee please,' Tansy said, following him round a sectional room divider into a rather more intimate space furnished with sumptuous sofas and sinking down into the comfortable depths of one, her tense spine rigorously protesting that amount of relaxation.

She was fighting to get a grip on her composure again but nothing about Jude Alexandris in the flesh matched the formal online images she had viewed. He wasn't wearing a sharply cut business suit, he was wearing faded, ripped and worn jeans that outlined long powerful thighs, narrow hips and accentuated the prowling natural grace of his every movement. An equally casual dark grey cotton top complemented the jeans. One sleeve was partially pushed up to reveal a strong brown forearm and a small tattoo that appeared to be printed letters of some sort. His garb reminded her that although he might be older than her he was still only in his late twenties and that unlike her, he had felt no need to dress to impress.

Her pride stung at the knowledge that she was little more than a commodity on Alexandris's terms. Either he would choose her, or he wouldn't. She had put herself on the market to be bought though, she thought with sudden self-loathing. How could she blame Jude Alexandris for her stepfather's use of virtual blackmail to get her agreement? Everything she was doing was for Posy, she reminded herself squarely and the end would justify the means...*wouldn't it?*

'So...' Tansy remarked in a stilted tone because she was determined not to sit there acting like the powerless person she knew herself to be in his presence. 'You require a fake wife...'

Jude shifted a broad shoulder in a very slight shrug. 'Only we would know it was fake. It would have to seem real to everyone else from the start to the very end,' he advanced calmly. 'Everything between us would have to remain confidential.'

'I'm not a gossip, Mr Alexandris.' In fact Tansy almost laughed at the idea of even having anyone close enough to confide in because she had left her friends behind at university and certainly none of them had seemed to understand her decision to make herself responsible for her baby sister rather than returning to the freedom of student life.

'I trust no one,' Jude countered without apology. 'You would be legally required to sign a non-disclosure agreement before I married you.'

'Understood. My stepfather explained that to me,' Tansy acknowledged, her attention reluctantly drawn to his careless sprawl on the sofa opposite, the long muscular line of a masculine thigh straining against well washed denim. Her head tipped back, her colour rising as she made herself look at his face instead, encountering glittering dark eyes that made the breath hitch in her throat.

'I find you attractive too,' Jude Alexandris murmured as though she had spoken.

'I don't know what you're talking about,' Tansy protested, the faint pink in her cheeks heating exponentially as her tummy flipped while she wondered if she truly could be read that easily by a man.

'For this to work, we would need that physical attraction. Nobody is likely to be fooled by two strangers pretending what they don't feel, least of all my family, some of whom are shrewd judges of character.'

Tansy had paled. 'Why would we need attraction? I assumed this was to be a marriage on paper, nothing more.'

'Then you assumed wrong,' Jude told her without skipping a beat.

Continue reading
THE GREEK'S CONVENIENT CINDERELLA
Lynne Graham

Available next month
www.millsandboon.co.uk

COMING SOON!

We really hope you enjoyed reading this book.
If you're looking for more romance, be sure to
head to the shops when new books are
available on

Thursday 21st
January

To see which titles are coming soon, please visit
millsandboon.co.uk/nextmonth

LET'S TALK
Romance

For exclusive extracts, competitions
and special offers, find us online:

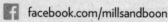

WANT EVEN MORE
ROMANCE?
SUBSCRIBE AND SAVE TODAY!

'Mills & Boon books, the perfect way to escape for an hour or so.'

MISS W. DYER

'Excellent service, promptly delivered and very good subscription choices.'

MISS A. PEARSON

'You get fantastic special offers and the chance to get books before they hit the shops.'

MRS V. HALL

Visit millsandboon.co.uk/Subscribe
and save on brand new books.

MILLS & BOON

THE HEART OF ROMANCE

A ROMANCE FOR EVERY KIND OF READER

MODERN
Prepare to be swept off your feet by sophisticated, sexy and seductive heroes, in some of the world's most glamourous and romantic locations, where power and passion collide.
8 stories per month.

HISTORICAL
Escape with historical heroes from time gone by. Whether your passion is for wicked Regency Rakes, muscled Vikings or rugged Highlanders, awaken the romance of the past.
6 stories per month.

MEDICAL
Set your pulse racing with dedicated, delectable doctors in the high-pressure world of medicine, where emotions run high and passion, comfort and love are the best medicine.
6 stories per month.

True Love
Celebrate true love with tender stories of heartfelt romance, from the rush of falling in love to the joy a new baby can bring, and a focus on the emotional heart of a relationship.
8 stories per month.

Desire
Indulge in secrets and scandal, intense drama and plenty of sizzling hot action with powerful and passionate heroes who have it all: wealth, status, good looks…everything but the right woman.
6 stories per month.

HEROES
Experience all the excitement of a gripping thriller, with an intense romance at its heart. Resourceful, true-to-life women and strong, fearless men face danger and desire - a killer combination!
8 stories per month.

DARE
Sensual love stories featuring smart, sassy heroines you'd want as a best friend, and compelling intense heroes who are worthy of them.
4 stories per month.

To see which titles are coming soon, please visit

millsandboon.co.uk/nextmonth

JOIN US ON SOCIAL MEDIA!

Stay up to date with our latest releases, author
news and gossip, special offers and discounts, and
all the behind-the-scenes action
from Mills & Boon...

 millsandboon

 millsandboonuk

 millsandboon

It might just be true love...

MILLS & BOON

HEROES

At Your Service

Experience all the excitement of a gripping thriller, with an intense romance at its heart. Resourceful, true-to-life women and strong, fearless men face danger and desire - a killer combination!